"All clues point to fun in this queer, grown-up Encyclopedia Brown style zany mystery. And, much like Encyclopedia Brown, you're gonna have to pay *very close attention* to the details if you're going to keep up with Charlotte Illes (who, of course, isn't a detective)."
—Olivia Blacke, author of *Killer Content*

"For anyone who ever wondered how Nancy Drew or Encyclopedia Brown are doing now that they're all grown up, former kid detective Charlotte Illes is here to tell you: Not Great. An immensely fun, voice-y read with a twisty mystery that is very relevant to today, I can't wait to see what Charlotte (and Lucy and especially Gabe) get up to next!"
—Mia P. Manansala, author of the Agatha, Anthony, and Macavity Award-winning *Arsenic and Adobo*

"There's a particular joy in reading a book and wishing you could be friends with the characters—*Charlotte Illes is Not a Detective* kept me guessing and left me with a warm and happy glow."
—Mary Robinette Kowal, author of the Hugo, Nebula, and Locus Award-winning *The Calculating Stars*

"Podcaster Siegel's charming comic debut, which is based on a popular TikTok series created by the author, is terrific fun . . . Not since Lisa Lutz's *The Spellman Files* has there been such a delightful literary marriage of endearingly quirky characters and deliciously dry wit. Fans of Francine Prose's *The Maid* or Meg Cabot's Heather Wells mysteries will equally embrace the arrival of Charlotte and her cohorts on the detecting scene."
—*Library Journal* STARRED REVIEW

"Siegel's debut novel is full of heart, strong platonic and familial love, humor, queerness, and wit, and to top it off, it's a killer mystery. Fans of the TikTok series that inspired the book will love the fleshed-out story and characters, and the author's voice shines through the pages. A fun read through and through."
—*Booklist*

"Charlotte Illes may not be a detective, or a teacher, but she is an absolute delight. I loved following this diverse group of warm and zany characters through an entertaining caper set at a school that I would have liked to attend for myself. Chicken soup for this Encyclopedia Brown-nourished, mystery-loving soul."
–Kemper Donovan, author of *The Busy Body*

Also by Katie Siegel

Charlotte Illes Is Not a Detective

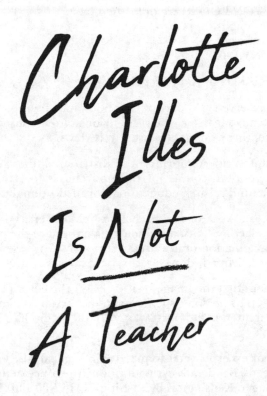

Charlotte Illes Is Not A Teacher

KATIE SIEGEL

KENSINGTON
PUBLISHING CORP.

www.kensingtonbooks.com

For all the teachers: you deserve the world.
At the very least, you deserve more than a dedication in my silly book.
But you've got it, it's yours.
Thank you.

Contents

I can't make mystery solving my whole life again. But I guess I'm always going to be a detective. So . . . I'm going to have to find an in-between.

—Charlotte Illes, *Charlotte Illes Is Not a Detective*

Ten Years Later

WEEKS! Ten WEEKS later.
Sorry, ten *weeks* later.

Chapter 1

Lucy's Not Crocheting (Worrisome)

"The prosecution may cross-examine."

Standing, the prosecuting attorney picked up a notepad and a sheaf of papers. She made her way to the witness stand, smiling gently at the man sitting there. Jurors Number Four and Number Five liked it when she smiled. Either that, or they were thinking about how soon they would get to leave. Honestly, they could have been thinking about anything.

The prosecuting attorney was in her late twenties, Indian American, with curly black hair pulled into a thick braid that fell down her back. Her kind smile was enough to distract most people from the determined gleam in her eyes and the confident set of her shoulders.

She placed a piece of paper in front of the witness, tapping it with a finger.

"Mr. Davies, these photos, marked D-7 and D-8—"

The judge peered over the edge of his bench. "Are these in evidence?"

"Yes, Your Honor."

The judge sat back in his seat.

Returning to the witness, the attorney smiled gently again. "Mr. Davies, do you recognize the location in these photos?"

Mr. Davies examined the photos. "It's a bus stop."

"Is this you sitting at the bus stop?" the attorney questioned.

The witness hesitated for an almost imperceptible moment. "Yes, that's me."

"Do you remember what you were doing at this bus stop?"

Mr. Davies cracked a grin. "Probably waiting for the bus."

Low chuckles ran through the jury as the defense attorney dropped his chin to hide a smile. The judge gave a half shrug to himself, as if to say, "He's not wrong."

The prosecuting attorney smiled, acquiescing. Her smile tightened as she briefly faced the gallery before addressing the witness again.

"Of course. Do you know where you would've been taking the bus *to*, that day?"

"Objection." The defense attorney stood. "Your Honor, the photographs aren't dated. Mr. Davies can't be expected to—"

"I can rephrase," the prosecuting attorney said. "Mr. Davies, is this your regular bus stop?"

"Yes."

"It's not the closest bus stop to your current residence; were you aware of that?"

Mr. Davies shrugged. "I'm a creature of habit. It's the stop I'd use at the old house, before Carly kicked me out." He nodded at the woman sitting at the prosecution's table, her shoulders tensing when he said her name.

The attorney referenced her pad of paper. "You regularly take the bus to visit your mother at her nursing home, is that correct? Multiple times a week?"

"Yes."

"I see you're holding a bouquet of flowers in these photos." The attorney walked up to the witness stand to point at one of the photos. "Were these for your mother?"

"Yes," Mr. Davies said with practiced swiftness. He smiled. "Mom loves peonies."

Okay, Juror Number Four *definitely* liked that.

"That's very sweet," the attorney said, her voice like honey-soaked steel. "And just to confirm, this is the bus stop at the corner of Holmstead Street and Green Street?"

"Yes."

"We can see that, because the drugstore is right behind you in the photo."

"Your Honor," the defense attorney said, not even bothering to stand this time, "I think we've established that this is Mr. Davies's regular bus stop."

"Are you going anywhere with this, Counselor?" the judge asked.

"Yes, Your Honor." The attorney removed another piece of paper from underneath her notepad. "This is a list of all the buses and their routes, marked D-6, which is already in evidence."

She put the paper down in front of the witness. "Mr. Davies, according to these routes, do you see that the only bus that goes anywhere near your mother's nursing home no longer stops at the corner of Holmstead Street and Green Street?"

The courtroom was silent as the witness stared at the piece of paper.

"I . . ." he finally said, glancing over at his attorney before looking back down at the paper, "I . . . is that right?"

"It is," the prosecuting attorney said. "According to this notice, the route changed soon after you moved out of your wife's house. But you've previously stated that you regularly visit your mother at her nursing home, correct?"

"Y . . . yes."

The attorney smiled sympathetically at the witness. "Do you see on this paper that this bus *does* service the stop near your current residence?"

"Yes," Mr. Davies said, reaching for the life preserver he thought he was being offered. "Yes, *that's* the bus stop I use to visit my mother."

The defense attorney tensed as the judge's brows raised with curiosity.

"Then, Mr. Davies," the prosecuting attorney said, angling towards the jury, "what were you doing with those flowers at *this* bus stop?"

"I . . . I . . ."

The prosecuting attorney finished her questioning soon after, relinquishing the floor to the defense, who made his way to the witness stand.

"Mr. Davies," the attorney said, "do you know who took these photos?"

The witness hesitated.

"There's a name . . ." the attorney prompted, pointing at the paper.

Mr. Davies squinted at the print below the photos in front of him. "'Charlotte Illes,'" he read.

"Do you know Charlotte Illes?"

"No."

"Were you aware she was taking your photo?"

"Not at the time."

"Do you know who she is?"

Mr. Davies gave a half shrug. "I think she's a detective."

The defense attorney pointed at the photos again. "These photos are a bit blurry." He flashed a quick grin at the jury. "Any blurrier and I doubt they could've been admitted into evidence. Can you read the name of the store behind you in this photo?"

The prosecuting attorney stood. "Your Honor, the witness already confirmed that he recognizes the bus stop in the photos. Ms. Illes's abilities as an investigator and a photographer aren't on trial here."

"The witness has already confirmed the location of the bus

stop, Counselor," the judge said sternly. "Do you have anything else other than this line of questioning?"

The defense attorney hesitated, then squared his shoulders. "No, Your Honor. No further questions."

"Dick," muttered a low voice from the back of the gallery.

The defense attorney gestured towards the voice while chuckling tiredly. "Your Honor—"

"Ms. Illes," the judge said in the direction of the voice, "I won't warn you again. One more word, and you'll be escorted out."

Charlotte Illes held up her hands to indicate apology, slumping down into her seat as the proceedings continued. She hadn't meant to say that out loud. Well, she had, but she hadn't meant for anyone to hear. After saying, "Ew," a little too loudly after Carly Davies described her husband calling her crazy for accusing him of cheating, Charlotte was determined to be on her best behavior. Mainly because she knew Mita wouldn't be very happy if she got kicked out of the courtroom, and she was a little scared of Mita.

The judge adjourned for the day soon after. Charlotte lingered in the hallway, resting against the wall as she watched the prosecuting attorney speak to her client a few yards away. Susmita Ramachandran was wearing a dark blue sheath dress with a matching blazer, a black shoulder bag dangling from one hand as she put a reassuring hand on Carly Davies's arm before waving goodbye to the other woman. Her perfectly sculpted eyebrows raised sternly as her gaze landed on Charlotte.

Uh-oh.

"Sorry," Charlotte said sheepishly, watching Carly Davies leave. "About the 'dick' thing."

Charlotte Illes was once known as Lottie Illes, a precocious child sleuth who was regularly employed by kids and adults alike to solve their mysteries. As she grew older, she felt the need to grow out of detective work to see if she could find other things to be passionate about. Recently, she'd finally come to terms with there not being anything she enjoyed as much as sleuthing, and that maybe she didn't have to fully leave it in her past.

After coming out of retirement from her kid detective days, Charlotte hadn't expected her mother and her brother Landon to immediately reach out to everyone they knew, telling them that Charlotte Illes was back in the detective business. In retrospect, she should have seen it coming, but had no idea how far they'd gone until she received the contact information for about a dozen miscellaneous acquaintances requesting her services.

While she had no interest in taking on "The Case of The Girl I Briefly Made Eye Contact With at the Bar Last Week" or "The Case of What My Son Does In My Basement All Day (Is Charlotte Single?)," she did respond to a request from Mita, Landon's friend from high school, to help with finding proof of infidelity for a divorce case. It had everything to do with getting her mom and brother to pump the brakes on finding her a mystery to solve, and absolutely nothing to do with the tiny little baby crush she'd had on Mita in high school.

Charlotte had spent two full days following Harry Davies around town before taking photos of him at the bus stop. Unfortunately, she was so busy trying to increase the exposure like her friend Gabe had taught her that she completely forgot to get on the bus so she could continue tailing him.

Fortunately, after thoroughly berating herself for a solid five minutes, she thought to check the bus routes. This allowed her to return to Mita with good news, instead of having to change her name and never show her face in Frencham again.

Mita pulled her bag over one shoulder. "It wasn't the most professional behavior," she said, her lips pursed in a suppressed smile as Charlotte walked over to her. "But it's going pretty well for us, thanks to your bus route knowledge, so I'll let this one slide."

"I didn't just know the bus routes off the top of my head," Charlotte said modestly. "I looked them up."

She knew she should've stopped there, but against her will, words continued to leave her mouth. "Not that it'd be weird to memorize the bus routes. I'm sure a lot of people do it if they regularly take the bus, but I did have to do a little research. So, yeah. Don't give me too much credit!"

Mita was staring at her, bemused.

"Just a little . . . peek into my process," Charlotte finished weakly.

Not exactly sticking the landing, but it'll do.

"Well, however you did it, it was extremely helpful. Thank you." They began walking down the hall. "You didn't have to come in today."

"I know." Charlotte shrugged. "I've always just solved the mysteries and let other people deal with whatever comes after. Thought it'd be good for me to see the 'after' for once."

"Thoughts?"

"I could never be a lawyer."

Mita chuckled. "It's a lot."

Charlotte sped up to pull open the door at the end of the hall. "You were great, though."

"Eh, I was fine. Thanks." Mita breezed past her into the main waiting room of the courthouse. "I shouldn't have asked what he was doing at the bus stop. I *should've* asked where he was going."

"No, no, it was good," Charlotte said, half jogging to catch up with her again. She had put on her nicest sneakers for court, but Mita was still outpacing her in heels. "It put him at ease. And I couldn't see his attorney's face, but it probably put him at ease, too. They didn't see the bus routes thing coming at all."

"You're probably right." Mita smiled at the guard as they passed the security checkpoint and exited the building. "I just don't like making mistakes like that."

"Call it a strategy, not a mistake," Charlotte suggested as they stopped outside. She squinted in the midafternoon sun. "That's what I do when I play board games with Landon. He believes it every time."

Mita fished a pair of sunglasses out of her bag and put them on. "Are you sure I can't pay you for your help?"

Charlotte hesitated. Sure, it would've been nice if she was getting paid for the work that she—somewhat reluctantly—enjoyed. But while she had recently allowed herself back into detective work—investigative consulting—she was determined not to let it consume her entire identity like it had when she was a child. And getting paid for it felt like a dangerous step in the direction of making it her entire identity.

So, she shook her head. "It's just a hobby; I'm not trying to monetize it. Besides, I'm starting my new job next week. Soon I'll be swimming in it."

"'Swimming in it'?" Mita said teasingly.

Charlotte gave her a "you're right" face. "Wading in it. Dipping a toe in it."

Mita smiled. "Well, thanks again. Let me know if you ever need me as a reference—I'll give a glowing review."

"Just please don't give me more than two stars on Rate My Detective," Charlotte said with feigned gravity. "I'm trying to keep my score at a solid three-point-five so I don't get overwhelmed with emails."

Mita laughed. "Alright. See you around."

Charlotte waved as Mita departed down the sidewalk. It wasn't until she'd disappeared around the corner that Charlotte realized she was still waving.

An almost-perfect interaction, she thought, dropping her hand as she pulled out her phone. Recent texts from her friend Gabe appeared on her screen.

Gabe: 911 emergency
Gabe: pls come asap

Charlotte typed out a response:

Charlotte: I made Mita laugh
Charlotte: you owe me cash
Charlotte: five dollars
Gabe: HELLO???
Gabe: NINE ONE ONE

Having been friends with Gabe for upwards of ten years, Charlotte knew "911 emergency" could mean anything from "someone is in the hospital" to "a celebrity I like tweeted something mildly problematic." Feeling victorious after her interaction with Mita, she headed for her car to drive to the shared apartment of her two best friends.

Q

Charlotte barely got one knock in before the door flew open. Gabe stood on the other side, his brown eyes wide behind round, wire glasses.

"I had a dream last night that I was playing the Emcee in *Cabaret* in high school but couldn't remember any of my lines, and then I realized the audience was actually an amusement park, and then I got really sad because for some reason I thought I'd be too short to ride any of the rides, even though we all know I'm five-foot-ten on a good day."

He stared at Charlotte intently. "What do you think that means?"

"Why are you wearing your glasses?" Charlotte replied.

Gabe self-consciously adjusted the frames. "My new job doesn't give me vision insurance, so I'm conserving my contacts. Do they look okay?"

"Yeah, they look great."

Gabe was twenty-five, Filipino American, with warm brown skin and dark brown hair that was pushed out of the way as he adjusted his glasses again. He was wearing a burgundy crewneck sweatshirt with the sleeves rolled up, and dark jeans cuffed at the ankles.

He crossed his arms. "What do you think my dream meant?"

"Did you eat anything right before bed?"

"Cheese Danish."

"I think it meant you had a cheese Danish right before bed. Also, we need to go over the definition of '911 emergency.'"

Gabe stepped back to let her enter the apartment.

"That's not why I texted," he said, closing the door behind her. "Lucy's been on her baking stage for two weeks now, and she keeps making me try everything. I feel like I'm on *Bake Off.*" He shut the door and followed Charlotte into the kitchen. "Seriously. I ate one of her snickerdoodles and almost shook her hand."

Charlotte stopped, staring at the several plastic containers of baked goods that sat on the counter. "Did she make dinner rolls?" she asked, pointing at one of them.

"It's *pandesal*," Gabe said, peering over her shoulder. "Filipino bread roll. She wanted my mom's recipe, but my mom never followed a written recipe in her life, so I just copied one I found online. But she didn't bake anything when she got home from school today."

"Well, that's good, right?" Charlotte glanced in the direction of Lucy's room, lowering her voice. "That means she's on the last stage."

Lucy had broken up with her boyfriend Jake a few months before, ending the long-term relationship after realizing she'd been unhappy in it for a while. Having been friends since kindergarten, Charlotte was well-acquainted with Lucy's post-breakup behaviors. While these behaviors had evolved over the years (Lucy no longer found the need to write letters to the Jonas Brothers in hopes that one of them would be her rebound), Charlotte and Gabe had a pretty clear list of the six stages of Lucy Ortega coping with a breakup.

The Six Stages of Lucy Ortega Coping with a Breakup
by Charlotte Illes (peer reviewed by Gabe Reyes)

1. Listening to music in semidarkness
2. Long, daily bubble baths
3. Watching *Anastasia* (1997) on repeat
4. Researching trips but never actually following through with them
5. Excessive baking
6. Excessive crocheting

"That's the thing," Gabe said, dropping his voice to a hushed whisper. "*She's not crocheting.*"

Charlotte furrowed her brows. "Are you sure?"

"I checked on her earlier. That's why I texted you. She's just lying on her bed, listening to my breakup playlist."

"Stage *One?*" That wasn't good. Charlotte couldn't remember a time when Lucy had regressed to an earlier stage, much less all the way back to the first one. Then again, Jake had been her longest relationship, and even though Lucy had been the one to break it off, the loss had still taken its toll on her. Gabe had reported seven total watches of *Anastasia*, a new record, before Lucy moved on to looking up plane tickets to Rome.

"And the worst part," Gabe continued, "is that I can't hear what songs she's playing, because she's listening with earbuds. My playlist is a spectrum. Is she angry-sad? Nostalgic-sad? Horny-sad?" He grabbed Charlotte's shoulders, shaking her. "I have no idea what her current emotional state is!"

Charlotte grabbed his wrists to stop the shaking. "I'll handle it." She turned on her heel and made her way to Lucy's room, Gabe following close behind.

She knocked gently on the bedroom door. "Hey. It's me."

"Come in," Lucy called from inside.

Charlotte and Gabe peeked into the room. The curtains

were closed, with one small lamp on the bedside table bathing the room in a dim yellow glow.

Lucy was lying on her bed with her open laptop on her stomach. She was twenty-five, Latina (Argentinian on her mom's side, Puerto Rican on her dad's), white, with hazel eyes and straight brown hair, which was currently hidden by the hood of a light pink sweatshirt.

"I didn't know you were coming over." She removed an earbud, pointing past them in the direction of the kitchen. "I baked some stuff; please eat it."

"I *saw*," Charlotte said, trying to hide her concern with enthusiasm as she and Gabe entered the room. She sat on the end of the bed, trying to act casual. "What're you up to?"

"I'm just reading about these Alaska cruises," Lucy said as Gabe threw himself onto the bed. "I was thinking we could go over winter break."

"You hate being cold," Charlotte pointed out.

Gabe mouthed, *Stage Four?* to Charlotte. Lucy was combining stages. This was uncharted territory.

"Yeah, you're right." The glow from the laptop flashed across Lucy's face as she switched to another tab in her browser. "Italy it is."

Gabe put the loose earbud in his ear as Charlotte cleared her throat.

"Hey, I was thinking," Charlotte said. "Why don't we go out tonight?"

"What?" Gabe asked, incredulous.

Charlotte shot him a glare, then realized, as he quickly removed the earbud like it had shocked him, that he hadn't even been listening to her.

Lucy wrinkled her nose. "I don't know," she said. "I was thinking I might take a bath tonight. Maybe watch *Anastasia*." She perked up, as if suddenly remembering something. "Hey, what're those triangle cookies that your mom makes?"

Charlotte narrowed her eyes at the sudden shift to the topic of Evelyn Hartman's baking. "*Hamantaschen?*"

"Yeah! Do you need those anytime soon?"

"Well, Purim is in March, so . . . not for five more months."

Lucy made a disappointed *tsk* sound. "I've been running out of things to bake. Thought that might be nice to try."

"You're still baking?" Charlotte asked tentatively. "Don't you think it's time to move on to something else, like . . . crocheting?"

"Oh," Lucy said knowingly. "My stages of coping." She closed her laptop and put it on the bed next to her as she sat up. "You know, I feel like I've grown out of all that. Now I just do whatever I feel like doing, for as long as I need."

"And you really think you need to watch *Anastasia* for the eighth time this month?" Gabe asked.

Lucy's glare didn't have quite the intensity of Charlotte's, but nevertheless, Gabe raised his hands in surrender. "It's a great film," he said weakly. "Love that little bat guy."

"Well," Charlotte said, "if you feel like you've grown out of your coping mechanisms, maybe it's time to make new ones."

"Maybe," Lucy admitted. She pulled her knees to her chest. "But I don't know if I'm ready to *go out.*"

"You don't have to talk to anyone," Charlotte offered. "We'll just go hang."

"I'll be your boyfriend if a guy won't leave you alone," Gabe added, rolling off the bed and jumping to his feet as he pointed at his imaginary opponent. "I'll be like, 'Hey, that's *my* woman. Back off, bro.'"

Charlotte shared an amused look with Lucy. "Please. I need to hear him talk like that to a real human person."

Gabe looked insulted. "That kind of guy only respects other guys who act super possessive!" He crossed his arms with a huff. "I don't need to explain my character work to you."

Lucy hesitated, then smiled. "Okay, I'll go." She shooed them away. "Now go eat some cookies."

Charlotte turned to leave, holding out a fist close to her chest. Gabe bumped it, and they both headed out of the room.

"That wasn't subtle!" Lucy called after them.

"What was she listening to?" Charlotte asked quietly once they'd returned to the kitchen. "If she's horny-sad, just lie to me."

"It's worse than I thought," Gabe replied grimly, popping open a container of cookies. "It wasn't even my playlist."

Chapter 2

Charlotte Illes Has Trust Issues

April 12th, 2010
From: Sara Thompson
To: Evelyn Hartman
Subject: Lottie's science fair project proposal

Dear Ms. Hartman,

I hope this email finds you well. I just wanted to make you aware of a small disagreement Lottie and I had in class today. The students submitted their proposals for their science fair projects, and your daughter proposed a project in which she would closely observe the behaviors of her classmates, record her findings, and then test her knowledge by putting her classmates through a series of tests and predicting how each child would perform.

While I commended her on her creativity, I told her that I couldn't sign off on her recording information about her classmates or putting them through tests. She informed me that since she had already collected the information, she felt that she might as well run the tests. I had to put my foot down, and she seemed frustrated.

I'm allowing the students to work in pairs if they wish, so I believe she's now joining Lucy Ortega on her project about observing plants' reactions to different types of music. Again, just wanted to let you know in case Lottie mentioned it at home.

All the best,
Sara Thompson

Present Day

The Blob was a Frencham establishment whose reputation varied greatly, depending on the age of the person you asked about it.

Those under the age of twenty-one spent years talking about the day they could walk under the bar's multicolored neon sign into the enticing unknown. Many tried to gain entry with false identification, which always quickly joined the display of fake IDs on the wall just inside the door.

Young people would gather outside on the eve of a friend's twenty-first birthday, counting down the final seconds to midnight and cheering as the birthday person proudly displayed their ID to the bouncer. Even people who went away for college would travel home to Frencham for their twenty-first, just so they could have their first (in some cases, first *legal*) bar experience at The Blob.

Those between the ages of twenty-one and twenty-three would describe the bar as "Fine," "Okay," "There." It was a decent enough place to go the night before Thanksgiving if you needed to get out of the house, as long as you didn't mind running into half of your high school graduating class.

After twenty-three, the disappointment of teenage expectations not being met eventually faded, and The Blob became a pretty nice place to spend the evening. Sure, it didn't have a mechanical bull or topless waitstaff (a favorite tall tale of Nate Horowitz, who spent half of sophomore year *insisting* that his brother managed to sneak him in), but it had twenty-five-dollar margarita pitchers and played listenable music.

The Blob also wasn't actually named The Blob. It had a name that someone could definitely figure out if they cared enough to find out. Most locals just called it "The Bar." But, because of its abstract neon sign that vaguely resembled an amoeba, Charlotte, Lucy, and Gabe had dubbed it, "The Blob."

"Okay, what about him?" Gabe suggested, peering over his shoulder. "He seems like he probably respects women."

They were sitting in a booth along one side of the room. A large mirror hung on the wall, running the length of the row of booths, and Charlotte glanced up at it to see the man to whom Gabe was referring walk past them towards the bathroom.

"Once again," Lucy said, "I—look me in the eye."

She waited until Gabe reluctantly abandoned scouting the bar for potential suitors for Lucy.

"I. Am not here. To meet anyone."

Gabe huffed. "I'm not saying you have to talk to any of them," he said. "I'm just trying to help you dip your toe back into the dating pool. Get reacclimated. De-Jake your taste in men."

Charlotte kicked him under the table.

"Sorry, forget I said Jake." Another kick. "Shit. Sorry. Ow."

As Gabe rubbed his shin, Charlotte studied Lucy's face for her reaction to hearing her ex's name.

"I'm fine," Lucy said in response to Charlotte staring wordlessly at her. "You can say his name. I can hear his name. I mean," she continued, sounding like she needed to convince herself more than her friends, "*I* broke up with *him!*"

"You did," Charlotte said encouragingly.

"Yeah!" Gabe banged his fist on the table so hard their glasses rattled. "You're strong. Say it back."

"I'm strong," Lucy repeated.

"You're independent."

"I'm independent."

"You're"—Gabe's gaze wandered off—"gonna tell me how you'd rate that guy sitting under the TV on a scale of one to ten."

"No." Lucy's attention moved to Charlotte. "Are you excited for next week?"

Charlotte pretended to rack her brain. "Next week . . . next week . . ."

"Starting substitute teaching!" Lucy elaborated, before catching the expression on Charlotte's face. "Oh." She scrunched up her nose. "You knew what I meant."

Charlotte shrugged, taking a sip of her drink. "I don't know if *excited* is the word I'd use. It's . . . definitely happening."

She had really needed a job after getting laid off a few months prior, especially since she refused to charge for her "investigative consulting." Substitute teaching wasn't Charlotte's first choice of a job, but because she had no idea what *would* be her first choice of a job, she had gone with subbing. The decision had been largely influenced by Charlotte's growing disdain for internet job boards, paired with Lucy repeatedly sending her the application anytime Charlotte complained about needing a job.

At the end of the day, she was looking forward to having an income again. As someone who still lived at home with her mom, she didn't love the stereotypes she was playing into by continuing to be unemployed. However, as someone who had become accustomed to sleeping through most of the morning, and who hadn't said more than five words to a child in at least a year, she was a bit apprehensive.

But as Lucy's shoulders slumped, Charlotte's apprehension shifted to guilt. Lucy had helped her go through all the steps of getting this job—background check, fingerprinting, applying for credentials, filling out a job application. She even had Charlotte do multiple mock interviews with her before the actual interview, which ended up being extremely less intense than any of the scenarios or questions her friend had thrown her way.

On top of all of that, teaching was Lucy's calling. She loved it. So Charlotte decided to reel back on the "begrudgingly doing this job only because we live in a capitalist society" act.

"I'm interested to see what Frencham Middle is like now," she offered, referring to their old middle school where Lucy taught as a language arts teacher. "I haven't been back there in, like, twelve years."

Lucy perked up. "It honestly hasn't changed much," she said. "New paint in some places. SMART boards instead of those rickety projectors. Slightly healthier cafeteria food." She drummed on the table with excitement. "This is gonna be so fun!"

"Sooo fun," Gabe echoed dully, drooping into himself, his chin hitting his chest. "You guys get to spend all day together while I sit at home and create Instagram graphics that say things like, 'Don't ever let them dim your shine,' and, 'You are the you-est you you'll ever be.'"

Gabe had recently quit his social media manager job at a mattress company, in pursuit of a job he was more passionate about. However, after failing to find a single job posting that sparked something in him, he realized that his passion for content creation only existed when he was creating for himself. So he gave up on waiting for a spark and accepted a job at a company that, as far as any of them could tell, specialized in inspirational quotes.

"I am again asking if you're positive this is a real company and not just a front for money laundering," Charlotte said. Across the table, Lucy was visibly struggling to work her way through the phrase, "You are the you-est you you'll ever be."

"I think that money laundering would require an obvious and frequent exchange of money," Gabe replied.

Lucy stared into the middle distance. "It should be, 'You are the you-est you *there'll* ever be,'" she murmured to herself. "*That* makes sense."

"Feel like it'd be hard to hide illegal dealings behind an Instagram story of 'Five Positive Affirmations You Should Try Today,'" Gabe continued. "So I'm gonna say no, not money laundering."

Lucy gave up on her parsing and rejoined the conversation. "We're just worried it might be something"—she paused, searching for the right word—"disreputable."

"Solid SAT word." Gabe pulled his feet up onto the bench of the booth and rested his forearms on his knees. "As long as that paycheck keeps hitting, and no one tells me to bury any bodies, I'm not gonna ask any questions."

"If you're good, we're good," Lucy said, shrugging.

"Anyway, back to sulking about how you guys are gonna hang out all the time without me." Gabe hid his face in his arms.

"Aren't you coming in next week to talk to Lucy's class?" Charlotte asked.

Gabe's head popped back up. "Oh, yeah!" he said cheerfully.

Lucy rubbed her hands together, her mouth curling into a scheming smile. "It's gonna be great," she said. "One of the science teachers had an astronaut do a video call a couple weeks ago, and the kids couldn't stop talking about it. But you know who kids love more than astronauts?" She pointed at Gabe with both hands, grinning.

". . . queer nerds?" Charlotte deadpanned.

Lucy dropped her hands as Gabe cackled. "No! Social media influencers!"

"Ohhh. Right." When Gabe wasn't running the accounts for a company of indeterminable purpose, he was cultivating his own sizable social media following.

"I'm going to create a small army of future influencers," Gabe said, mimicking Lucy's hand rub. "And we can all hang out at school!"

"We're not going to be hanging out," Charlotte said. "We'll be *working*."

"That reminds me," Gabe said, ignoring her as he dug into his pocket. "I got this brand sponsorship I need your help with."

"Is it another facial cleanser?" Lucy's expression was wary. "The last one turned our sink green."

Gabe slapped a pack of gum on the table. "Splitz Gum! Designed to be shared with a friend." He pulled out a long stick of gum from the pack and unwrapped it. "See? It's, like, perforated in the middle so you can split it in half and share."

Charlotte narrowed her eyes. "I feel like most sticks of gum are already pretty easy to split in half."

"Right, so, that's definitely not the kind of commentary Splitz Gum is looking for from the content I'm making for them." Gabe took out his phone and opened the camera. "Luce, when I say *go*, break off the other half."

More than happy to help, Lucy followed Gabe's directions as he recorded a short video of her taking half the stick of gum.

"Beautiful, no notes." Gabe began typing furiously, murmuring to himself. "Splitting some Splitz Gum with my bestie . . . use code GABE at checkout . . . hashtag ad . . ."

"Is it any good?" Charlotte asked Lucy, who'd popped the gum into her mouth.

Lucy chewed for a moment. "Um . . ."

Charlotte handed her a napkin to spit the gum into.

"Aaaaand posted." Gabe returned his phone to his pocket as Lucy relieved herself of the gum. "Just gotta do seven more of those over the next two weeks."

"And you're gonna recruit your *other* friends for the rest of these posts, right?" Charlotte asked. "Because I'm not chewing that."

"It's not that bad," Gabe said. "What if you just put it close to your mouth?"

"No."

"What if you held it far away from your mouth?"

"No."

"What if Lucy held the gum, and you're blurry in the background?"

". . . maybe."

Lucy's gaze had wandered past them. "I think that's"—she raised a hand and waved—"Kim!"

Charlotte twisted around in her seat to see a woman wave back. She looked to be in her late twenties, white, with a light tan and short brown hair that fell across her forehead in big curls. A mustard-yellow cross-body purse hung from her shoulder, and she wore a dark blue sweater and jeans.

"That's Kim, my coworker," Lucy said to them as the woman approached.

Kim smiled at Lucy as she reached the table. "Hey! Haven't seen you in, like, six hours." She gave a little wave to the other two. "Hi, I'm Kim. You're Gabe and Charlotte, right?"

Surprise crossed Lucy's face. "How did you know that?"

"You have multiple photos of them on your desk and talk about them all the time," Kim said good-naturedly. She raised an eyebrow at Charlotte. "I'm always hearing the kids talk about their next 'Lottie Illes' reward."

"Their *what*?" Charlotte and Gabe said in unison, the former with confusion and the latter with gleeful anticipation.

"Early on in the year I told one of my classes about The Case of the Aquarium Ghost," Lucy explained sheepishly, referencing a mystery that Charlotte had solved when she was twelve. "The kids loved it, and they kept asking me for more stories, so I started using it as a reward system. Like, if everyone gets their essays in on time, they get a story." She winced slightly. "Are you mad?"

Charlotte thought about that for a moment. As someone who was actively working on removing herself from her younger self's shadow, she didn't *love* that Lucy was introducing a new generation to Lottie Illes. On the other hand, Lucy had been a part of those mysteries as much as Charlotte, and had every right to talk about them.

Besides, from what Charlotte had heard about the struggles of trying to get a bunch of seventh graders to hand in their homework on time, she didn't want to deprive Lucy of any successful strategies for making that happen.

"No, it's fine," Charlotte said, shaking her head. "That's pretty cool."

Lucy's face broke into a relieved smile. "They're going to be so excited to meet you in person." She gestured for Kim to join them at the table. "Charlotte's starting as a sub next week."

"Oh, amazing!" Kim slid onto the bench next to Lucy. "Are you planning on becoming a full-time teacher eventually?"

Charlotte made a noise that was some hybrid of "Ahhhhh" and "Ummmm."

"She's just in it for the money," Lucy explained.

"Ah." Kim gave Charlotte a wry look. "You needed a job for money, so you chose . . . *teaching*?"

"Kim's the other seventh grade language arts teacher on my team," Lucy said quickly, clearly wanting to change the subject before Charlotte got any ideas about getting a different job. "There are seventh-grade lang teachers on other teams, but she and I have the same group of students. She does reading, I do writing."

"Ah," Gabe said knowingly. "You're the one who already had the coveted reading position locked up."

Lucy rolled her eyes. "Stop. It's fine."

"She loves books," Charlotte explained to Kim.

"Oh, I know," Kim said, grinning. "Her classroom library is bigger than mine, which is embarrassing for me. It's cool, though. We kind of mix up our curriculums."

Lucy's face lit up. "We've been working on showing the students how their writing lessons are reflected in the books they're reading, instead of just teaching reading and writing as two completely separate entities."

"The kids love it," Kim said. "This is my fourth year teaching in Frencham, and I've never seen them so engaged with the material." She hesitated, her smile fading. "Though it seems like some people aren't as happy with my teaching."

"You mean those older teachers?" Lucy asked.

"No. Um . . ." Kim's shoulders slumped. "I was holding off on telling you. I thought it might just go away. But I got another one today—"

"Another what?" Lucy pressed.

"Another letter," Kim said. "I've been getting these anonymous letters."

"Anonymous letters?" Charlotte echoed doubtfully, looking suspiciously at Lucy.

Lucy looked back and forth between Charlotte and Kim. "No. I don't know anything about this!"

"What?" Kim asked, confused.

"It wouldn't be the first time Lucy's been part of a scheme involving anonymous letters to get Charlotte to solve a mystery," Gabe explained. "Now Charlotte has trust issues anytime anonymous letters are involved. Actually, I think she just has trust issues, period."

"This isn't like that," Lucy protested.

Charlotte waved her hands. "Okay, I believe you," she said, partially because she did believe Lucy, and partially because she wanted to prove that she didn't have trust issues. "Sorry. Please continue."

Kim folded her hands on the table. "For the past couple of weeks I've been getting these letters in my mailbox at school. They're all worded differently, but the recurring theme is essentially telling me to leave the school."

"Did they use a purple pen?" Charlotte questioned, earning herself a glare from Lucy. Okay, maybe she did have some trust issues.

Kim's brow furrowed. "No, black. Is that important?"

"Why didn't you tell me about this?" Lucy asked gently.

"I don't know." Kim rubbed her thumb on her other hand in a self-soothing movement. "At first I thought it was just a kid being a little . . . P.O.S."

"Piece of shit," Gabe translated quietly for Charlotte.

"I know what P.O.S. means!"

"I didn't want to worry you for nothing," Kim continued. "But now I'm concerned about my job. I've never seen a middle schooler stay *this* committed to a bit."

Lucy put a hand on her arm. "Plus, all the kids love you! I can't think of a single one who'd do that."

"Why are you worried about your job?" Charlotte asked.

"What if it's a parent?" Kim replied, her brows scrunching with worry. "All it takes is one parent to set off the others. I'm not tenured yet, so everything I do is held under a microscope." She raised her eyebrows. "Literally. Two weeks ago, Mr. Baginski requested a lock of my hair to use for his microscope lesson. I didn't want to say no, because I'd get chalked up as 'difficult to work with.'" She made air quotes with her fingers.

Lucy hummed with understanding.

"If this becomes something bigger, it could be so easy for the school to just fire me to make the problem go away," Kim continued. "Or, when it's time for them to decide if they want to give me tenure next year, it could really hurt my chances."

"Can you think of a reason why a parent would be upset with you?" Charlotte asked.

Kim paused, possibly to see if she could think of something, or possibly to decide whether she wanted to share something she'd already thought of.

"No," she finally said. Charlotte studied her face, but couldn't determine the reason for the pause.

"Teachers can't afford any missteps before they're tenured," Lucy explained to Gabe and Charlotte. "We can't participate in union strikes, we're the lowest priority for admin—"

"We can't be bitchy when Tina says something passive-aggressive about our door decorations," Kim added, raising her eyebrows at Lucy.

"If I have to explain one more meme to that woman . . ." Lucy trailed off.

Charlotte resisted the urge to tease by finishing that sentence with what would actually happen: that Lucy would explain it as kindly and patiently as she likely did all the previous times.

"So you're really worried about how these letters could affect you," Charlotte said instead.

"Well, it's not just that," Kim said uncomfortably. She glanced over at the other occupants of the bar, then back at them. "My aunt's also been getting threats."

"Is she a teacher, too?"

"No, she's a life coach. But she's also on the Board of Education, which is what the threats are about." Kim pursed her lips. "She's currently running for reelection, and she's been getting these texts telling her to drop out of the race. No name attached, all from the same untraceable number."

"Sounds like someone wants both of you out," Gabe said. His eyes lit up. "Does your family have any enemies? A blood feud that started with two principals whose hatred of each other lasted for generations?"

Kim gave him a small smile. "Not that I know of."

Charlotte knew it was coming. She had felt it coming as soon as she got the very first whiff of a mystery. *Maybe if I stare at the table and don't make any sudden movements, Lucy will forget that I'm here.*

She risked a glance and saw Lucy staring at her. *Dammit. One day that'll work.*

But it was Gabe who spoke first.

"Charlotte's just gotten back into detective work," he said, cheerfully unaware of his friend's fruitless endeavor to turn invisible. "Maybe she could look into it."

"Investigative consulting," Charlotte corrected. "And"—she

hesitated, choosing her words carefully—"I don't know if there's enough need for concern. I mean, have any of these messages escalated in how threatening they are?"

Kim shook her head. "No. I've been getting more of them lately, but they're all pretty much the same."

"In that case, I don't think you have anything to worry about." Charlotte tried to pump confidence into her voice. She wasn't exactly lying. As far as threatening letters went, this situation sounded fairly mild. And she had learned from her younger years of detective work that sometimes mysteries would simply solve themselves, or become a nonissue. Her gut was telling her that this was one of those mysteries. Or maybe that she *hoped* this was one of those mysteries? She hadn't had dinner yet, so her gut was making a lot of noises unrelated to the current conversation.

"You're right." Kim shook her head as Lucy began to protest. "No, she's right. I've been letting them get in my head, but they're just letters. And Aunt Jen is already determined to ignore the texts she's been getting. I'm not going to let some anonymous asshole freak me out."

She glanced over her shoulder. "I saw my friends walk in a minute ago. I should go join them."

They exchanged *so nice to meet you*s as Kim slid off the bench, bade them farewell, and crossed the bar to where her friends were sitting.

"She's cute," Gabe said as Kim walked away. "Why don't you—shit, never mind. I forgot you were straight for a second."

"Thank you," Lucy deadpanned. She raised her eyebrows at Charlotte.

"Are you gonna yell at me?" Charlotte winced. "Can I finish my drink first?"

"She needs your help," Lucy said.

It wasn't that Charlotte didn't want to help Kim. She did truly believe that the letters might just go away if ignored. But she'd also *just* finished a case. Picking up a new one so soon felt dangerously close to Lottie Illes behavior.

Charlotte's brain whirred through excuses to find one that Lucy would respect.

"I have a lot on my plate right now," she said. "I'm already helping Mita with her case—"

"You said she told you it was basically done," Lucy reminded her.

Note to self: stop telling Lucy things.

"Yeah," Charlotte conceded, "but I want to keep myself available in case she needs me."

Gabe bumped her with his shoulder. "Or in case she *needs* you," he said, his tone dripping with innuendo.

Charlotte scowled. "That's not what I *meant*. Also, never gonna happen."

"Why not? She's queer."

"How do you know that?" Lucy asked.

"I'm subscribed to a New Jersey LGBTQ+ newsletter with an announcements section for anytime someone comes out," Gabe explained. "Charlotte doesn't pay for the subscription. I get a discount because I'm bi *and* trans."

Lucy's eyes narrowed with doubt. "Really?"

"No. But I swear to god I saw her post on IG about it." Gabe pulled out his phone.

"Can we not do this?" Charlotte begged as he opened Instagram and typed in Mita's username. "It's just an old crush. It really doesn't matter if she's straight or—"

"She posted for Pride Month," Gabe interrupted.

"What? Let me see." Charlotte peered at the screen as Lucy leaned over the table to see the screen. "No, I saw that post. She's at a parade with friends, and the caption's just the pride flag emoji. She could be there as an ally."

Gabe *tsk*d at her. "Allow me to turn the tables and give *you* a lesson in detective work. This is my domain, babe." He tapped on the comments, placing the phone on the table.

"So much important information about a post can be found

in the comments," he said, taking on the tone of someone giving a TED Talk. "For example: if someone posts a birthday selfie and their super-online significant other doesn't comment within the first twenty minutes of posting, what does that mean?"

Gabe looked back and forth between them, waiting for an answer. Receiving nothing but blank stares, he finished, "They're on the rocks. Possibly already broken up."

"Doesn't sound very reliable to me," Charlotte said doubtfully.

"Is *this* reliable enough for you?" Gabe pointed at one of the comments. "'My favorite le dollar bean,'" he read. "'Heart eyes emoji.'"

Charlotte blinked. "I don't get it."

"This is how I feel when I have to explain my door decorations to Tina," Lucy said to Gabe as he dropped his head on Charlotte's shoulder, groaning.

"I can't work under these conditions." Gabe lifted his head. "Just trust me. She's a lesbian."

Charlotte shrugged, shaking her head to try to get rid of the excitement that had started fizzling in her brain against her will. After numerous dates with people who were primarily interested in hearing about her time as a kid detective, Charlotte had decided to put dating on the back burner. At least until she felt like her current life was interesting enough to hold a candle to her Lottie Illes era.

Mita wouldn't ask about any of that stuff, though. She already knew all about it. However, Charlotte had become perfectly comfortable with Mita being nothing more than an unattainable crush and wasn't going to let Gabe get her hopes up now.

"Okay, so she's a lesbian," she said, crossing her arms. "I'm still not gonna ask her out. Can we go back to trying to set Lucy up against her will?"

"Noooo," Lucy begged as Gabe's head whipped around to

survey the bar again. "I'm canceling all attempts to set anyone up tonight. Let's just hang out."

Gabe turned back to the table. "No one asked if *I* wanted to be set up," he complained.

"Do you wanna be set up?" Charlotte asked flatly.

"Definitely not by you, but thanks for checking," he replied sweetly, patting her hand.

The next week, the night before her first day of subbing, Charlotte went to bed hours earlier than she was accustomed to. Unfortunately, she had forgotten-slash-ignored Lucy's suggestion to incrementally adjust her regular sleep schedule to make waking up for school easier. After trying to will herself to sleep for four hours, she woke up with a start at 5:30 a.m. when her alarm went off.

Charlotte allowed herself one long whine of frustration into her pillow before pulling herself out of bed. Her body moved as if she were a marionette operated by a puppeteer with a hand cramp as she made her way to her dresser.

Lucy had approved several items of clothing for Charlotte to wear to school: some button-downs, cardigans, and a couple pairs of black jeans (blue jeans could be worn on certain Fridays if you paid five dollars, Charlotte had been told). She grabbed the first Lucy-approved items she saw through sleep-weighted eyelashes: a brown sweater over a white, collared button-down and black jeans.

"Wow," her mom said as she trudged into the kitchen. "Didn't sleep well?"

Evelyn Hartman was in her early fifties, white, and Jewish. Gray streaked the dark brown, almost black hair she'd passed down to both of her children, and she was looking amusedly at Charlotte with their shared brown eyes.

Evelyn's regular sleep schedule was late to bed, early to rise (although her daughter wasn't usually awake to see her this early in the morning). Charlotte wasn't sure how her mother functioned on so little sleep, but Evelyn seemed as wide-awake as she did at any other point of the day.

Growling in response, Charlotte made a beeline for the coffeemaker.

"I'll take that as a no," her mom responded.

Taking a big gulp of coffee, Charlotte carried her mug upstairs as she waited for the caffeine to work its magic. Her phone was making noise, and for a moment she thought maybe she had accidentally hit snooze on her alarm instead of shutting it off. Then she realized that Lucy was video calling her.

Taking another big swallow of coffee, Charlotte answered. "What?"

"Just wanted to make sure you were awake." Lucy's expression grew concerned. "Are you sick?"

"Thanks." Charlotte brought the phone close to her face. "This is 5:30 a.m. Charlotte. You can see why I don't take her anywhere."

"You look great. Um, drink some coffee."

Charlotte held up her mug, almost sending its contents splashing over the side. "On it."

"Okay, see you at school. Don't go back to sleep!"

The call disconnected, and Charlotte rubbed her eyes with the back of her hand. She wasn't sure if the caffeine was already starting to hit, or if just drinking the coffee was having a placebo effect, but either way she was having a slightly easier time keeping her eyes open.

Migrating to the bathroom, Charlotte splashed some water on her face and ran damp fingers through her short, wavy hair. She avoided the mirror, knowing the view wouldn't be pretty, and instead put her back to it as she brushed her teeth.

Her therapist had recently suggested she take some moments throughout her day to check in on her emotions, so as she scrubbed at her molars, Charlotte took stock of how she was feeling:

Charlotte Illes Feelings Check-In
—Tired
—Exhausted
—Sleep-deprived

Those were all basically the same feeling.

—Grumpy

That was a new one. For this specific check-in, not in general. Charlotte was well-acquainted with "grumpy."

—Nervous

First day of a new job; of course she was nervous. Anyone would be. Totally natural.

Charlotte realized she had stopped brushing and was just standing there with a mouthful of toothpaste. She turned around and spit into the sink, making a mental note not to multitask during future emotional check-ins.

"Landon and Olivia are coming over for Shabbat dinner on Friday," Evelyn said as Charlotte returned to the kitchen. "Will you be here?"

"Yeah." Since her mother was not particularly religious, they only had special dinners for Shabbat when her brother was home, as a family event. Ever since Landon and his girlfriend, Olivia, moved down from North Jersey to an apartment thirty minutes from Frencham, their family dinners had become more frequent.

"You can invite Lucy and Gabe if you want," her mom offered as Charlotte turned on the sink to rinse out her mug.

"Lucy has . . . something." Charlotte willed her brain to re-member what specifically Lucy had on Friday evening. "Foot-ball game. At the high school. Eva's cheering." Eva was Lucy's younger sister. "I'll ask Gabe."

"Okay, well, tell Lucy she'll be missed."

Charlotte shook her head as she dried her hands on a towel. "I will not, because she'll bake you a full challah if she finds out, and we're trying to get her past the baking stage."

"Watch out for the bear!" Evelyn called as her daughter headed for the front door.

Charlotte retraced her steps back to the kitchen, not sure she had heard her mother correctly. "Is that a new way of saying goodbye I haven't heard about, or is there an actual bear?"

"I thought you would've heard about it already." Evelyn waved her phone at her daughter. "I got a township alert that there was a bear sighting near the woods by Ruby's house."

"Who's Ruby?"

"You remember Ruby. You went to preschool together."

Her mother looked at her expectantly and got a blank stare in return. "She had a birthday party at her house and you got a ladybug painted on your face."

"I don't remember that."

"Really?"

"I was *four*."

Evelyn waved a hand dismissively. "The bear's across town, nowhere near the school. Just letting you know."

"I will definitely keep an eye out," Charlotte said, turning to go. "I'm not trying to get killed."

"It probably wouldn't kill you," her mom said reassuringly.

"No, if I missed my first day of school because of a bear attack, *Lucy* would kill me."

Exiting the house, Charlotte journeyed out into the predawn darkness, picking up a few stray candy wrappers dropped by trick-or-treaters the night before. She tossed her bag onto the passenger seat of her car, sitting in silence as she stared out at the streetlamp-lit street.

I could probably make just as much money doing detective work, she thought. *More, even, if I could get some rich clients. Rich people get their shit stolen all the time. I could be a detective on retainer for a rich older woman who regularly has mysteries to solve. I'll live in a guest house on her estate and just hang out until she needs me to find the priceless earrings that went missing after a gala she hosted at her home. I was invited to the gala, but I stayed in the guest house and watched TV. There's actually a movie theater in the guesthouse—*

Charlotte's phone, which she had dropped into the cupholder, lit up with Lucy's contact photo again.

"What?"

"Just wanted to make sure you left the house."

"I'm coming, I'm coming . . ."

Charlotte hung up the phone and started the car.

🔍

Pulling her staff ID lanyard over her head, Charlotte stared up at the front of Frencham Middle School. It hadn't changed much since she'd been a student there. The biggest upgrade was the green electronic sign installed along the front sidewalk, advertising teacher conference dates and congratulating the football team on their recent win in yellow text that lazily scrolled across the board.

Feeling like she was invading someone else's territory, Charlotte entered the school.

The main office brought back memories of waiting to meet with the vice principal in a very uncomfortable chair, either to request permission to snoop through someone's locker, or to explain why she had been caught snooping through someone's locker after she'd been denied permission to do so.

The same wall of mailboxes sat along one side of the office. There was no more candy bowl on the front desk, which caused a twinge in Charlotte's chest as she signed in. Mrs. Benowitz had passed away during Charlotte's senior year of high school. The secretary always got a kick out of Lottie's shenanigans, often assisting in cases by feeding her information (and candy).

"ID?" the secretary requested after Charlotte introduced herself as a new substitute teacher. The woman didn't seem like she'd be one to slip an eleven-year-old a classroom key to aid her in a missing iPod Shuffle investigation.

Charlotte bent over the desk to present her ID without removing the lanyard from her neck. When she realized the other woman wasn't going to meet her halfway, she leaned in more, the desk digging into her stomach.

The secretary glanced at the ID. "Char . . . Charoltte?"

"Charlotte. Illes." Charlotte grunted as she tried to adjust to a more comfortable position. "It's a typo. I can show you my license—"

"No, it's fine." The secretary faced her computer as Charlotte stepped back, her internal organs groaning with relief.

As she accepted her room key and attendance sheet, she heard the door to the front office open, followed by a stern, "Charlotte Illes."

Charlotte instinctually dropped the room key onto the desk, before remembering that she had every right to be holding it. She looked over to see a woman who had *never* gotten a kick out of Lottie's shenanigans.

Mrs. Parnell was the aforementioned vice principal who had been in charge of handling the discipline of Lottie Illes. She was in her early sixties, white, with pink blush generously applied over pale cheeks. Her gray hair was cut in a severe bob, and red cat-eye glasses dangled from her neck on a gold chain.

In her hand was the same travel mug she would carry around when Charlotte was a student: bright blue with a cartoon smiley face on one side, which almost always presented a fun dichotomy with the expression on its holder's face.

Charlotte quickly picked up the key. "Hi, Mrs. Parnell," she said, trying her best not to seem suspicious despite not having anything to be suspicious about. "You . . . look great."

"Hm." The vice principal took a sip of her coffee, carefully assessing Charlotte as if attempting to discover what ulterior motive Charlotte could have for being there.

Unable to find anything to verbally comment on, she said, "I heard you'd be joining us."

"And were thrilled by the news?" Charlotte cracked a tentative smile.

Another "hm" from Mrs. Parnell. "I found all your little hiding spots."

Charlotte choked back a laugh. Lottie had scattered about a dozen "detective kits" in various locations around the school, containing all the child sleuth necessities: mini flashlight, screwdriver, magnifying glass—the works. On her last day of eighth grade, she had decided to leave the kits in their spots, just in case (also because she had forgotten where some of them were).

"Emptied them all out," Mrs. Parnell added proudly.

"You found them *all*?" Charlotte asked.

"Sure did."

Charlotte narrowed her eyes. "Even the one behind the vending machine in the cafeteria?"

Mrs. Parnell hesitated, then nodded. "That's right."

Charlotte made an impressed face. "Well, you definitely found them all." She waved her key and attendance sheet. "I have to get to my class. Nice catching up with you!"

She slipped past the vice principal and out of the office, holding back a grin, because:

1. Mrs. Parnell definitely hadn't found all of the kits.
2. Lottie never put a kit behind the vending machine in the cafeteria.

Charlotte had barely made it two steps out of the main office when Lucy came running down the hall. She was wearing black and white tapered plaid pants with a rust orange mock turtleneck sweater. Her long brown hair was pulled back into a French braid, and her rainbow-patterned staff ID lanyard swung wildly from her neck as she came to a stop in front of Charlotte.

"Hi," she said breathlessly. "Good morning. Love this sweater on you. There's a problem. Kim's room. Come on."

"Wha—"

But Lucy was already hurrying back down the hall.

Pocketing her room key, Charlotte followed.

Chapter 3

A Gift for You! Blackmail!

April 24th, 2012

I wish I knew how to whistle, Lottie thought as she wandered to the back of the art classroom. People always seemed to get away with acting casual when they knew how to whistle. That's how it usually worked on TV, anyway.

Lottie tried whistling casually as she waited for a classmate to finish washing her paintbrushes. The other girl turned around, giving Lottie a strange look.

"Why're you breathing like that?" the girl demanded.

Lottie stopped trying to whistle. "Why are *you* breathing like that?"

"I'm not breathing like that. *You* were breathing like that."

"I don't even remember how this whole thing started," Lottie said. "Are you almost done?"

The girl rolled her eyes as she turned back to the sink, washing the last of the paint off of her brushes before walking away.

Lottie stepped forward, glancing around to see if anyone was watching. The art teacher was busy with a student, and everyone else was focused on their renderings of a bowl of fruit that sat on a stool at the front of the room. Lottie herself had opted for a croquis-style drawing (though calling it that was probably giving her too much credit—she had really just been trying to finish the assignment as soon as possible).

Confirming the coast was clear, Lottie crouched down and opened the cabinet underneath the sink. Reaching inside, she felt around until her wandering hand came into contact with a plastic sandwich bag.

She swiftly extracted the bag and shut the cabinet doors, holding one of eleven (twelve? She'd lost count) detective kits she had hidden around the school.

The Official Lottie Illes Detective Kit
Created by Lottie Illes
Mini flashlight
Screwdriver
Magnifying glass
Handkerchief (for handling delicate clues)
Tissues (for blowing nose)
Pencil
Pencil sharpener
Notepad
Bobby pins
Rubber bands
Small photo of Zac Efron cut out of a magazine
(exclusive to the computer class detective kit)

Kit in hand, she hurried to the closet at the back of the art classroom, removing a key from her pocket as she did so.

Checking one more time to make sure no one was watching, Lottie unlocked the closet and quietly slipped inside, closing the door behind her. Unable to see in the sudden darkness, she opened the bag and fumbled around for a moment before pulling out a small plastic flashlight. Handling it carefully (these cheaply made flashlights were built for children's party favors, not hardcore sleuthing, and were always falling apart), Lottie carefully switched it on and pointed the beam at a low shelf in the closet.

On the shelf sat an assortment of students' ceramic creations, each piece sitting on an index card identifying its young artist. And one of those creations was going to lead Lottie to the culprit of her case.

"Okay," she whispered to herself, "who's making these clay flowers?"

She sucked in a breath as the dim beam of the flashlight landed on a ceramic rose sitting on the far end of the shelf. Now all she had to do was read the name on the index card—

Out in the classroom, the PA beeped. Muffled by the closet door, she heard:

"Lottie Illes, please come down to the main office. Lottie Illes to the main office."

Uh-oh.

She heard her teacher calling her name as she scrambled to switch the flashlight off, the round plastic disc that protected the bulb popping off in the process. Making a frustrated mental note that she needed to invest in better detective supplies, Lottie dumped the flashlight pieces into the bag and stepped back into the classroom, hoping that she wouldn't be seen exiting.

Luck was not on her side as she was met with the stern gaze of her art teacher.

"How'd it go?" Mrs. Benowitz asked as Lottie entered the main office a few minutes later. The secretary was in her mid-seventies; a white woman with a cloud of gray hair and bright blue eyes. A pair of gold, rectangular-rimmed glasses hung from her neck on a multicolored beaded chain.

"I got *interrupted*," Lottie said pointedly as she plopped down into one of the chairs along the wall. She slumped into the chair. "And then I got caught. But Ms. E believed me when I told her that the closet was unlocked. Can I keep the key a little longer? I was so close."

"As long as it'll help you solve your case," Mrs. Benowitz said, smiling. "But you know the rule—you didn't get it from me."

Lottie nodded in agreement. "Why'd I get called down?"

"You'll have to ask Mrs. Parnell."

"I didn't even *do* anything," Lottie whined.

Mrs. Benowitz raised an eyebrow, amused.

"I mean," Lottie clarified, "I didn't do anything she could've found out about."

She straightened as Mrs. Parnell's office door swung open. The vice principal stepped out, silently jerking her head towards the open doorway to summon Lottie inside.

"I hope this won't take too long," Lottie said as she settled into a chair across from Mrs. Parnell's desk. "I was working on a drawing in art class, and I'd really like to get back to it."

The vice principal didn't seem like she believed a word of that. Sitting down and folding her hands on her desk, she said, "You were on the roof of the school yesterday afternoon."

Lottie screwed up her face. "What? No I wasn't," she said. Well, lied. Technically, she was lying. Because she *had* been on the roof of the school the previous afternoon. It was the best location for watching students get on the buses as they left for the day, and she'd been trying to see if she could catch anyone carrying a ceramic flower.

"One of the bus drivers said they saw someone lying on the roof," Mrs. Parnell said. "And you and I both know you're the only student at this school who somehow manages to get into places you're not supposed to be."

Lottie was oddly flattered by this statement.

"I'll have to call your mother," Mrs. Parnell continued.

"Hang on," Lottie protested. "Did the bus driver say it was *me* up there? Because it doesn't sound like there's any proof. It could've been anyone."

Mrs. Parnell gave her A Look. "Lottie."

"Mrs. Parnell," Lottie replied in the same tone.

The two stared at each other for a long moment. Finally, the vice principal sat back in her chair. "Return to class. And stay off of the roof."

"I didn't even know we had a roof," Lottie said, her shoulders loosening with relief as she got to her feet.

"Out."

Lottie hurried out of the office, closing the door behind her. She mimed wiping sweat off of her forehead before waving goodbye to Mrs. Benowitz and returning to art class.

She had a closet to break into, and a case to solve.

Present Day

The inside of the school, from what Charlotte could see during the walk to Kim's classroom, had not changed much more than its exterior. It was interesting how something she would otherwise struggle to recall an image of in her head could be so familiar now that she was back. Those were the same white floor tiles. The same fluorescent ceiling lights. The same green lockers that were so easy to break into.

They walked past a water fountain, and Charlotte remembered finding a math-test cheat sheet taped underneath it. A few steps later, they passed the classroom where she had spied out the window at the parking lot to catch the kids who were keying teachers' cars. Around the corner was the girls' locker room, where she'd eavesdropped on . . . well, frankly, countless conversations.

Lottie Illes had left her fingerprints on every inch of this school (not literally—she'd actually been very paranoid about never leaving fingerprints).

Lost in thought, Charlotte almost ran into Lucy as she stopped outside of a classroom. Bright, multicolored letters spelled out "Ms. Romano" across the door, accompanied by paper cutouts of book covers and various book characters and symbols.

Lucy knocked gently on the door before pushing it open and poking her head inside.

"It's me," she called into the room. "I brought Charlotte. Can we come in?"

Charlotte heard a murmured reply from inside. Lucy pushed the door open wider, and they both entered.

The interior of the room matched the door. Multiple bookshelves hugged the walls, above which colorful posters promulgated the benefits of reading. A large "Books We've Read" chart displayed lines of stickers next to students' names. Multicolored pom-poms hung from the ceiling over the rows of desks. At the back of the room was a reading corner, consisting of a big purple rug with multiple bean bag chairs scattered across it.

Kim sat behind her desk at the front of the room, watched over by an anachronistic poster of a cartoon William Shakespeare presenting the classroom rules with a laser pointer. She was staring at her computer, chin in her hand, eyes rimmed with red as she clicked her mouse. A small box of tissues sat in the middle of her desk, next to an opened envelope and a folded piece of paper. Both were out of place on an otherwise very organized desk.

"Feeling any better?" Lucy asked gently as they approached.

Kim turned away from her computer. "Not really. But I stopped crying, so I guess that's a step in the right direction." She noticed the time on her computer. "Ugh. The kids will be here soon."

"Can I show Charlotte the letter?" Lucy held a hand out.

Kim picked up the folded piece of paper and passed it to her. She faced her computer again as Lucy gave the paper to Charlotte, who unfolded it and read the letter to herself:

Leave the school. If you don't give your notice soon, I will tell parents about your college job.

The letter was typed. Charlotte checked the back of it for any other writing, but found nothing.

"This is the envelope it came in?" she asked, pointing at the desk.

"Yeah." Kim turned away from her computer again. "I don't know why I'm trying to lesson plan right now," she said wearily to Lucy as Charlotte picked up the envelope and examined it. "I can't concentrate on anything."

She peeled a blue, star-shaped sticky note off a stack that sat next to her computer. "I'm just going to write some bullet points and call it a day."

The front of the envelope displayed Kim's name above the school's address in sloppy handwriting, clearly disguised. The stamp in the corner featured an illustrated elephant holding a wrapped present in its trunk, as if to say, "A gift for you! Blackmail!" Unsurprisingly, there was no return address.

Finding nothing else of note on the envelope, Charlotte returned it to the desk. "So, in college, you were a"—her brain skimmed through jobs a college student might have that wouldn't be looked kindly upon by parents—"weed dealer?"

Kim shook her head, her mouth quirking up into a tiny smile. "Not a weed dealer. I danced at a strip club during junior and senior year."

"Ah."

"I'm not, like, embarrassed by it," Kim continued. "Dancing helped me pay off my student loans, with money still left over." She snorted. "It also taught me a lot about listening and being patient, which helps me more as a teacher than half the stuff I was taught in grad school. Anyway, it's not a secret, but . . ."

She waved a hand in the air, as if gesturing at the looming threat of parents finding out, complaining to the school, and getting Kim fired.

"*Can* you get fired for that?" Charlotte asked Lucy. "I'd think there'd be some anti-discriminatory rule or something."

Lucy pursed her lips. "Like we said last week, it's a lot easier to be let go for very little reason when you're untenured." She looked at Kim. "If that happened, you *could* sue."

Kim buried her face into her hands. "That's just . . . so much. I really don't want to have to go through that."

Lucy hummed sympathetically, taking hold of Charlotte's arm. "We'll be right back." Pulling Charlotte out of the room, Lucy called over her shoulder, "Try to get your planning done."

As soon as the door to Kim's classroom shut, Charlotte said, "I'll do it."

Lucy's eyebrows shot up. "You'll do what?"

Charlotte steeled herself. "I'll take the case."

"*Wow.*" Lucy's jaw dropped. "I thought I was going to have to talk you into it."

"I know." Charlotte rested her shoulder against a locker. "And I knew you'd eventually wear me down, so I figured we might as well just skip that part to save time."

Lucy grinned, pulling her into a hug. "Thank you, thank you, thank you."

As Charlotte waited out the embrace, she spotted the doors to the music room at the end of the hall, through which she'd once chased a kid who'd been dubbed "The Silly Bandz Bandit."

Above all else, she did want to try to help Kim, now that the threats had escalated. But she also liked the idea of solving a mystery on Lottie Illes's turf. Feeling a surge of competitiveness as she was released from the hug, she said, "Alright. Let's solve a mystery."

Ignoring Lucy's baffled expression at her sudden enthusiasm and borderline cockiness, Charlotte walked back into Kim's room.

🔍

After telling Kim she'd look into the letters and being handed every piece of threatening mail that had been received (six in total), Charlotte almost forgot that she was supposed to be watching students for the rest of the school day.

When the bell rang, signifying the start of homeroom, she stood in front of the teacher's desk, her confidence replaced by apprehensiveness.

"Okay," she said, referencing the sheet of paper in her hands, "I just have to take attendance . . ."

Charlotte trailed off as the loud chatter of two dozen pre-teens continued.

Oy. She resisted the urge to just give up, despite knowing it'd be the easiest way to relieve the stress that was creeping into her shoulders.

"HEY," she yelled.

The volume lowered as heads turned towards her.

"I just have to figure out who's not here, and then you can go back to talking." God, she sounded old.

"Nia isn't here," someone called out from the back of the classroom.

"Okay . . ." Charlotte skimmed her list of names to mark Nia as absent. "Anyone else?"

She received several confirmations that no one else was absent. After a quick head count to confirm, she said, "Great, easy. I'm done here."

The chatter resumed as Charlotte walked around the desk and fell into the teacher's chair. Maybe this wouldn't be so bad.

The doorknob rattled, and Charlotte looked over to see a girl peek into the room, her expression wary.

"Are you a sub?" the girl asked.

"Yup. Are you Nia?"

"I'm late," the girl said. "Mrs. D tells me to go to the office when I'm late."

Charlotte scowled. She'd been sent to the main office plenty of times for being late to homeroom (preschool sleuthing often uncovered the juiciest leads).

"You're fine," she said, gesturing for the girl to enter the room.

Hesitantly, Nia pushed open the door and walked in. She was eleven or twelve (it was a sixth grade homeroom), Black, with cool brown skin and dark brown hair pulled up into two puffs on top of her head. She wore light pink glasses, and had on a dark purple backpack with straps securely over both shoulders.

Nia hurried to an empty desk next to the wall as the PA beeped and morning announcements began. Charlotte pulled out her phone.

> **Charlotte: this teacher stuff is so easy**
> **Lucy: I hate you**
> **Charlotte: kidding**
> **Charlotte: I am killing it though**
> **Charlotte: I need to talk to Kim more about potential suspects**
> **Lucy: Hang on, I'll text her**

"Hey, maybe don't stand on the chair," Charlotte called out to one kid as she waited for Lucy to get back to her. The kid rolled his eyes, but sat back down.

> **Lucy: She wants to know if we can meet her at her place after school. She's going to have her aunt come over to show the messages she's been getting too**
> **Lucy: We have conferences from 1-3, so after that**
> **Charlotte: is there not school during that time??**
> **Lucy: Early closing**
> **Lucy: The rest of the week is early closings for parent/teacher conferences**
> **Charlotte: WHAT**
> **Charlotte: no one told me that**
> **Lucy: Someone definitely told you that**

Charlotte had a vague memory of someone telling her that.

> **Charlotte: okay that works for me**
> **Lucy: You should loop in your junior detective so he doesn't feel left out**
> **Charlotte: good idea**

Charlotte shot off a text to Gabe as the bell rang for the end of homeroom. As the kids noisily filed out of the room, she read through her schedule for the day. First period: hall duty.

Teachers on hall duty, in Charlotte's experience, had been her number-one obstacle for getting any sleuthing done during school hours. Lottie had quickly learned how far a bathroom pass could get her, as well as certain routes throughout the school that would get her the least face time with teachers stationed in the hallways.

Charlotte locked the classroom and headed for the chair placed at the end of the hall. As she reached the corner, a woman rounded it, almost crashing into Charlotte.

"Oh, dear!" the woman cried, grabbing Charlotte by the shoulders to steady both of them. "Sorry about that!"

"No problem," Charlotte said, taking a step back. The woman looked to be in her fifties, Latina, with a light brown complexion and dark brown hair pulled back into a high ponytail.

"I always tell the kids to watch where they're going, and here I am, plowing people down." The woman glanced at Charlotte's ID. "Are you a new substitute?"

Charlotte realized she recognized this woman. She hadn't had her as a teacher, but she was pretty sure she'd taught eighth grade language arts when Charlotte was a student.

"Yeah. I'm, uh, Charlotte?" She wasn't sure what the etiquette was for introducing herself to other teachers. She *had* decided to tell the students to call her Ms. I, solely to avoid anyone from Lucy's class recognizing her name and requesting Lottie Illes stories.

"Oh!" The woman's eyes went wide. "Yes, Miss Illes, of course!"

Oops. Should've gone with the last name.

"Miss Ortega told me you would be substituting here," the woman continued. "I'm her mentor, Mrs. Hernández."

Oh, right. Because it was Lucy's first year teaching at this school, she'd been assigned a teacher as her mentor. For first-time teachers, as it had been explained to Charlotte, mentors had regular meetings with their mentees and helped them work towards getting their state certification. Since this wasn't Lucy's first year teaching, her mentorship with Mrs. Hernández was more informal.

"Nice to meet you," Charlotte said. "I remember you taught here when I was a student."

"I remember you, too," Mrs. Hernández said, smiling. "You were always the talk of the school."

Charlotte felt her face flush. "Ah, well. Yeah." She tried to think of something more intelligent to add. "Thanks" wasn't the right response. "Talk of the school," while not inherently negative, wasn't exactly a compliment.

The other woman continued talking before the silence got too long.

"I know Miss Ortega was also a student here," she continued. "You both had Miss Todd for eighth grade writing?"

"Yeah, we did." Charlotte didn't remember much about Miss Todd, but she knew she'd liked her. She'd often encouraged Lottie to try writing mysteries for her creative writing assignments. Lottie never did (she preferred writing villain redemption arc stories and *White Collar* fan fiction), but she'd always appreciated Miss Todd trying to tap into her interests.

"Well," Mrs. Hernández said, leaning in conspiratorially, "that makes sense, seeing how Miss Ortega teaches. Miss Todd was always a bit untraditional."

Charlotte fought to keep her expression pleasant. "What do you mean?"

"Oh . . ." Mrs. Hernández waved a hand, indicating that she thought the topic was too silly to talk about, as if she hadn't been the one to bring it up. "Some of the teachers are bothered by how she and Miss Romano run their classes."

She paused again, and Charlotte resisted rolling her eyes. "Bothered by what?"

"Well," the older woman continued, clearly happy Charlotte

asked, "for one, she doesn't teach out of the textbook." She paused once again, waiting for a big reaction to this news.

Charlotte stared blankly back at her.

"And," Mrs. Hernández continued, still working to get the reaction she wanted, "she and Miss Romano are constantly mixing up their lessons."

Charlotte remembered what Lucy and Kim had said at the bar about combining their curriculums. Her inclination was to defend Lucy, but she really didn't want to stay in this conversation any longer than she needed to, and doubted anything she could say would sway Mrs. Hernández from her opinions.

"Interesting," she said instead. "Well, I have to go to hall duty—"

"I've spoken to her about how that's not the best way to teach her class," Mrs. Hernández added, either not hearing Charlotte or pretending not to so she could continue talking, "and she always thanks me for the advice, and then keeps doing it the wrong way!"

She flicked her hands in the air as if shooing away the negative emotions that were surrounding her. "It's all just very silly, but I'm hoping soon she learns the right way to do things. Maybe you can talk some sense into her."

Charlotte fought back a snort of laughter. When it came to her friendship with Lucy, one of them *was* usually attempting to talk sense into the other, but it definitely wasn't in that order.

"Oh, I . . . I didn't go to school for teaching," she said weakly. "I don't really know anything about any of this."

"Just suggest teaching out of the textbook to her," Mrs. Hernández said, patting Charlotte on the arm as she walked past. "And feel free to come to me if you need anything!"

"Thanks," Charlotte said, narrowing her eyes at the woman's departing back. Shaking her head, she walked over to the chair and began her hall duty.

"I can't believe she said that."

Charlotte and Lucy were sitting in the latter's classroom, eating their lunches. A small group of students sat at a table at the back of the classroom. "The usual lunchtime crew," Lucy had called them.

Swallowing a bite of her turkey sandwich, Charlotte said, "And she was talking about it like there were 'other' teachers who had a problem with it, but it was clearly just her problem."

"Oh, no, it's other teachers, too," Lucy said, her fork hovering over her food. She hadn't taken a single bite of her chicken and rice the whole time Charlotte was talking. "When Kim first told us about the letters, and people being unhappy with her, I thought she was talking about them. What I can't believe is that she complained about it to *you*, and told you to *talk sense into me*?"

"I thought you liked your mentor," Charlotte said, gently nudging Lucy's hand towards the food to bring her attention back to it. They only had forty minutes to eat, which was much more time than she usually took to eat lunch, but still somehow felt restrictive.

Lucy stabbed at a piece of chicken. "I do," she admitted. "I mean, she's a huge improvement from Bill."

Bill had been Lucy's mentor at her first teaching job, who'd done a little mentoring and a lot of having Lucy grade papers for him.

"Bill sucked," Charlotte said bluntly.

"Right. So, yeah, the bar was low." Lucy's shoulders slumped. "But, I don't know. I was excited to have a Latina mentor. I thought I'd be able to relate to her better than I did with Bill, and that she might understand my experience better. I was hoping she'd be excited about my ideas for doing things differently. But no, she hates me."

"She doesn't hate you," Charlotte said. "She just . . . wants you to be different."

"*Thanks.*" Lucy took another bite of chicken, chewing

thoughtfully. She pointed her fork at Charlotte. "Did you notice how she called me Miss Ortega?"

"Oh, yeah. Am I supposed to do that, too?"

Lucy shook her head. "I mean, in front of the kids, yeah. But she only does it when she's talking about the younger teachers, like me and Kim. I tried to call her Ramona once, just to test the waters, but she just kept calling me Miss Ortega, so I got self-conscious and went back to calling her Mrs. Hernández."

Charlotte furrowed her brow. "Weird."

Lucy sat back in her chair, her face troubled. Charlotte started to wish she hadn't told her what Mrs. Hernández had said. Of the two of them, Lucy always tended to care more about getting people to like her and took it hard when they didn't.

"Do you guys know each other?" one of the kids called from the back of the room. Charlotte recognized the student from one of her earlier classes, along with a couple others. One of them was Nia from homeroom, sitting in the middle of the group, reading a book.

"Yes!" Lucy shook off her gloom. They had already spoken about Charlotte not wanting the kids to know who she was for as long as possible. "This is my friend, Ms. I. She's a substitute."

Nia looked up from her book, noticing Charlotte for the first time. "She didn't send me to the office when I was late. Hi, miss."

Charlotte gave her a little wave, but the girl had already returned to her book.

"Did you guys go to school together?" another kid asked. He was white, with messy blond hair that fell over his forehead. His tan, freckled arms were crossed over a T-shirt displaying a character that Charlotte could only assume was from an anime.

"We did," Lucy said. "We've known each other for a long time."

Nia looked up from her book again, her eyes narrowing slightly behind her pink frames.

"Miss, are you gay?" the first kid said to Charlotte. She was

Black, with a dark complexion and brown curls that fell to her shoulders and bounced as she spoke.

"Uhhh . . ." Charlotte glanced at Lucy, not sure how she was supposed to answer that.

"Isabel," Lucy scolded, pronouncing the "I" with a long *e* sound, "we talked about this."

"Not everyone is comfortable being open about their identity," another kid said solemnly. She was white, with pale skin and long, wavy copper hair. Charlotte had clocked a trans flag and she/her pronoun buttons on her backpack when she first walked into the classroom.

"Sorr-*y*," Isabel huffed. "I just thought she was giving off fruity vibes."

Charlotte examined what she was wearing. "Is it the sweater/collar combo?" she asked Lucy.

Her friend shrugged, and Charlotte turned back to the group. "Um, yeah. I'm queer. Bi."

Isabel nodded sagely. "I knew it. So am I."

"Me, too," said the fifth and final kid of the group. He was South Asian, with short, curly brown hair and medium brown skin.

"I thought Ms. Ortega was fruity, but she said she's not," Isabel continued.

"You think everyone's fruity," the anime shirt kid pointed out.

Isabel rolled her eyes. "Whatever."

Charlotte felt slightly stunned as the kids resumed their chatter amongst themselves. "Nice of you to give all the openly queer kids a safe space for lunch."

Lucy laughed. "Oh, these aren't all the queer kids. They're just the kids who don't like eating in the cafeteria. I think over a fourth of my students are openly queer."

"Oh," Charlotte said, now fully taken aback. A warm feeling spread through her chest, and she smiled, before a pang of something sharper dampened the feeling.

Lucy continued talking before Charlotte could pinpoint the feeling that interrupted the perfectly nice moment she'd been having.

"That's Neil on the far left," Lucy said, indicating the kid in the anime shirt. "Good kid, *great* artist, struggles with his schoolwork. His parents are very hands-on, which I think stresses him out.

"Kat's next to him," she continued. "She's trans, has been out since, like, fourth grade, I think. Super smart. Isabel, you already know. I'd say she'll probably be president someday, but it's more likely she'll just change the whole system." Lucy looked over at Charlotte. "I've never been more sure of something in my life: if anyone can single-handedly get rid of the electoral college, it's Isabel Caballero.

"Arjun. I don't think he's out to his parents, and he's not as open as most of the other kids, but he's very sweet. I'm actually surprised he volunteered that he's bisexual."

Lucy leaned in closer. "Okay, and Nia. She and Isabel are cousins, and she is your *biggest* fan."

"What."

Lucy gave Charlotte a cheesy smile in response to her apprehension. "She loves all things detectives and mysteries. After I told the first Lottie Illes story, she started requesting a new one almost every class. She wrote Lottie Illes fan fiction for a creative writing assignment last week."

Nia was peering at them over the top of her book. Realizing they were looking back at her, she quickly ducked back down behind the book.

"I think she figured out who I am," Charlotte whispered.

Lucy winced. "I'm not surprised, honestly. Sorry about that."

"No, it's fine." Charlotte sighed dramatically. "It's tough being a former semi-famous kid detective, but someone has to do it."

Lucy kicked her chair, snickering. She glanced over at her computer screen as a new email appeared in her inbox.

"These people need to stop hitting Reply All on school-wide emails," she complained, opening the message. "They've been coming in all morning. Actually, you'll love this."

Lucy angled to the side to let Charlotte see her computer screen. "Mr. Weissman keeps a bobblehead of Albert Einstein by the door of his classroom, but it went missing today after second period. He wants to know if anyone's seen it."

"Kid stole it," Charlotte murmured, reading the replies. One teacher had replied saying she saw a bunch of kids playing with it in her class, but didn't see who left with it. No one else had seen it.

Lucy gave her a sideways look. "You can do better than *that*."

Charlotte grinned, sitting back. "I can only handle one case at a time," she said. "Plus, this is a little below my pay grade."

"You can't have a pay grade if you don't let anyone pay you," Lucy said pointedly, closing her email. She raised her voice. "Have any of you seen Mr. Weissman's bobblehead?"

"In the little window by his door," Isabel called back.

"Not anymore. It's missing."

Nia's head jerked up. "Was it stolen?"

Lucy shrugged playfully. "Maybe."

Isabel stood up. "You guys. We should find it."

"How?" Arjun's eyebrows pinched together. "We don't know who took it."

"That's the whole point of solving a mystery!" Isabel looked down at her cousin. "Right?"

"We'd have to examine the scene of the crime," Nia said slowly, as if checking off boxes. "Search for clues, interview witnesses—"

"I can draw the bobblehead to show people what it looks like," Neil offered. He flipped to a new page in his notebook and began sketching.

"What about the security cameras?" Kat suggested. "Maybe we can see who left the classroom with it."

"They don't give students access to security footage," Charlotte said, causing the kids to fall silent. "And the room's impossible to sneak into."

The group stared at her.

"How do you know that?" Kat asked.

Nia said something under her breath that didn't reach the front of the room, her eyes wide with excitement.

"What?" Isabel said to her cousin. "What do you know?"

Nia looked at Charlotte. "Are you Lottie Illes?" she asked eagerly, her enthusiasm spilling out.

Isabel gasped. "Oh my god. You are. You totally are."

The kids broke into excited chatter, talking over one another as they ran to the front of the room and swarmed Lucy's desk.

"Hey, HEY!" Lucy waved an arm over her head, drawing their attention away from an overwhelmed Charlotte. "This is top secret. Ms. I doesn't want anyone knowing who she is. I know you guys will respect that."

"Are you undercover for a case?" Nia whispered from the back of the group. Neil stepped to the side so she could see Charlotte.

Shaking her head, Charlotte said, "No, not for a case. It's sort of just a general . . . undercoverness."

"She probably has a lot of enemies," Kat explained to the others. "That's why no one can know who she is. Right?"

The kids looked at Charlotte, who in turn looked at Lucy. She wasn't sure how to explain the stress of constantly being compared to your younger self to a group of kids who had only been alive for a little over a decade.

Lucy had gotten lost in her own thoughts. "You *do* have a lot of enemies," she said, her expression growing cloudy with concern. "Maybe you *should* be undercover more often."

Charlotte cleared her throat, jerking her head at the kids (specifically Arjun, whose eyes had gone wide with fear).

"But there's nothing to worry about!" Lucy said, recovering her teacher voice. A bright smile replaced her worried expression. "What's important is that we keep this between us."

"So can you help us find the bobblehead?" Isabel asked Charlotte. "You're a teacher. You could look at the cameras."

Charlotte shook her head. "Security footage is never any good during passing times. The halls are so full it's impossible to notice small details."

Nia raised her hand.

"Yes, Nia," Lucy said gently.

"How did you ever see the security footage?" the girl asked, dropping her hand. "You said they don't show it to students, and that the room's impossible to sneak into."

Charlotte smiled. "Sometimes the school's secretary let me take a peek. But I'm telling you, your best bet is finding out from other students who's seen it." She looked at Lucy. "Who was the teacher who saw it in her class?"

"Mrs. Chen."

Isabel faced the other kids. "Okay. I'll go interrogate Mrs. Chen. Arjun and Neil, you guys go take pictures of the scene of the crime."

"My phone camera's broken," Arjun said.

"My dad took away my phone last week 'cuz I'm failing math," Neil added. "He gave me this weird old phone for emergencies. It doesn't even have texting."

"Imagine," Lucy said drily, exchanging a look with Charlotte.

"Ughhhhh." Isabel held her fingertips to her forehead like the weight of the world was on her shoulders. "Fine. Nia, go with them. You're good at noticing little stuff, anyway. Maybe you'll find a clue."

Nia's eyes brightened as she nodded enthusiastically.

"I'll go see if I can convince Mrs. Parnell to let me see the security footage," Kat said.

Charlotte snorted. "Good luck with that. Parnell doesn't let students get within ten feet of the teachers' lounge, much less let them look at the cameras."

"Didn't you break the rules all the time when you went here?" Kat asked Charlotte.

"I mean . . ." Charlotte fumbled for words. "I . . . some."

"Mrs. Parnell hates rule-breakers." Kat smiled, flipping her hair over one shoulder. "But she *loves* me."

The kids returned to the back of the room as they continued planning. "I didn't know Parnell had the capacity to like students," Charlotte said to Lucy.

"Be nice."

"She didn't even like *you*, and everyone liked you."

"She didn't like me because I was friends with you," Lucy said. "Which, might I remind you, was very difficult for me, because I desperately needed everyone to like me."

"What do you mean 'needed'?"

Lucy kicked Charlotte's chair, scrunching up her nose.

"Ms. I?" Nia had returned to the desk.

"What's up?"

"Can we have . . ." Her eyes darted over to Lucy, as if asking for permission. "I mean, do you still have your detective kits? Ms. Ortega told us about them."

"*Do* you still have any?" Lucy asked Charlotte. "I know you left a bunch here."

Charlotte pushed her chair back and stood, thinking. "Parnell just told me this morning that she found a bunch of them."

"And held on to them for safekeeping?" Lucy asked drily.

"Yeah, as if." Charlotte's mind sped through the school, trying to remember her different hiding spots. *Locker room kit: probably gone. Under the bleachers at the pool: definitely gone. Mr. Klein's desk, Miss Alston's closet, behind the loose ceiling tile in the girls' bathroom: gone, gone, gone. The bass—*

Charlotte straightened. "Is there still a giant bass in the music storage room?" she asked Nia.

"Yeah."

Charlotte turned to Lucy. "Can I go . . ." She stopped. "Why am I asking you? I'm an adult. I'm going to the music room; be right back."

"Can I come?" Nia pleaded.

They both looked at Lucy, who glanced at the clock.

"Be quick about it," she said. "Lunch is over soon."

Two minutes later, Charlotte and Nia were crouched in the walk-in closet off of the music room that served as storage for the students' instruments.

"Since the bass is so big, no one ever took it home," Charlotte said, unzipping the soft, black case for the giant instrument. "I knew this would always be here if I needed it. Can you hold this up?"

Nia lifted one end of the double bass, watching curiously as Charlotte felt around underneath.

"It should be . . ." Charlotte's fingers touched the flap of an inside pocket, and a moment later she pulled out a small sandwich bag. "Here it is! Suck it, Parnell." She froze. "Don't tell Lucy I said that. Shit. Don't tell Ms. Ortega I called her Lucy. Or that I said shit. Twice."

Nia giggled as Charlotte helped her lower the bass. Then she examined the bag critically. "I thought it'd be cooler."

Charlotte pulled out the small purple flashlight. To her surprise, it still worked. "Yeah, well. It was 2009, and I was eleven. My access to high-tech gear was limited. But, hey"—she returned the flashlight and pulled out a small screwdriver, raising her eyebrows at Nia—"this is pretty cool, right?"

"Do you really want me to answer that?" Nia said seriously.

Charlotte dropped the screwdriver back into the bag, scowling. "Let's get you back to class."

"Hang on." Nia pulled the top of the case back over the instrument and zipped it up. "We need to leave it like we found it, so no one will know we were here."

Charlotte's impressed expression shifted to concerned as the bell rang. "Uh-oh."

Nia grabbed the sandwich bag from her, and they ran back to Lucy's classroom.

🔍

"I feel like I should have a badge," Gabe said as they traveled up the front walk to Kim's townhouse. "'Gabe Reyes. He/him. Junior detective. Filipino. Bisexual. Single and looking.' Okay, that might be too much for a badge. Just my name and pronouns and 'junior detective.'"

"Why would you have a badge?" Charlotte asked as Lucy rang the doorbell. "*I* don't even have a badge." She stared at a sign stuck into the front lawn that read VOTE FALCONE FOR SCHOOL BOARD in blue block letters.

"I'll get you a badge, too. 'Charlotte Illes. She/her. Senior detective. Bisexual. Jewish and . . . vague European descent. Closed off to love.'"

"Can you two behave?" Lucy pleaded as Gabe dodged a punch to the arm.

The door opened.

"Hi guys, thanks for coming." Kim was wearing an apron, her curly hair pulled back in a bandana. "Sorry, I'm a mess; I'm making brownies for the bake sale at conferences tomorrow night. Aunt Jen is already here. She's . . ."

She hesitated, waving for them to enter. "Well, she'll explain it. Come on in."

Chapter 4

A Vague "Or Else"

Kim led the trio into the small living room. A well-worn couch sat along one wall, facing a small TV perched on a scratched-up wooden stand. To its left sat a faded gray armchair, with a small glass coffee table between the two. Covering the far wall was a tall oak bookshelf, with several small framed photos scattered amongst the books.

"I don't know where she went . . ." Kim said as the three sat on the couch. "Aunt Jen?"

"Be right there," called a voice from the other room.

"Can I get you guys anything?" Kim asked. "Water, iced tea . . . ?"

As they politely declined her offer, a woman entered the room from what Charlotte assumed was the kitchen. The woman: late forties, white, with warm fair skin and straight brown hair sharply cropped just above the shoulders. Her dark brown eyes critically assessed the new arrivals in a way that made Charlotte want to straighten the collar of her shirt.

"Had to take a call from a client," she said, wedging her phone into the front pocket of her jeans. "He was panicking about a job interview; had to talk him out of canceling. Hi, I'm Jennifer Falcone."

Lucy stood to shake her hand, with Charlotte and Gabe following suit. Charlotte tried not to visibly wince at the woman's strong grip.

After introductions were made, they settled back onto the couch as Jennifer took a seat in the armchair. Kim disappeared into the kitchen for a moment, returning with a high-backed chair that she placed across from the couch.

As Kim sat, Charlotte addressed Jennifer. "Kim told us you've also been receiving threats."

Jennifer paused, letting out a small puff of air through her nose as she pursed her lips. "First off," she said, "I need to establish that I think all of this"—she waved her hand in a small circle—"is unnecessary."

"Aunt Jen," Kim pleaded, "this is serious."

"Oh, it is. I know it is." Jennifer cocked her head, her eyebrows raised. "And you don't seem to care that whoever is sending these messages to us might get *more* upset if they find out you're trying to figure out who they are."

"The person is already threatening my job," Kim said, sounding frustrated. "What else can they do?"

Jennifer began counting on her fingers. "Break into your car, break into your home, cause you bodily harm—"

"I don't think the person is planning on physically harming Kim," Charlotte cut in. She shrank back a bit when Jennifer's gaze moved to her. Charlotte wasn't easily intimidated, but this woman had a *severe* "don't fuck with me" face.

"And how do you know that?" Jennifer said sternly.

"The letters?" Charlotte said meekly, before clearing her throat. "The letters," she repeated, more confidently. "The person clearly wants to scare Kim into quitting, so if they were planning on threatening her life, they would've just said that."

"Hm." Jennifer stared at Charlotte for a long moment, then

retrieved her purse from the floor next to the chair. She pulled out several pieces of paper, as well as three envelopes.

"I got the first text almost a month ago," she said, passing the stack of papers to Gabe, who sat closest to her. "I'd get a new one every few days. Last week, the first letter appeared in my mailbox. Typed, unsigned. Two more letters came after that, with the most recent one arriving the other night."

"Night?" Lucy asked. "It wasn't delivered with the rest of the mail?"

Charlotte took the stack from Gabe and examined one of the envelopes.

"Blank," she said, showing it to Lucy. "This wasn't mailed; it was dropped straight into the mailbox."

"Maybe there's a secret message on the envelope," Gabe suggested, taking it back from Charlotte and holding it up to the light. "You know, the kind you need a blacklight to see."

"Why would the person making threats leave an invisible message?" Charlotte asked.

Gabe lowered the envelope, returning it to her. "There are no bad ideas."

Charlotte flipped through the printed-out texts and letters. Each message was no longer than three sentences, all demanding that Jennifer not run for the Board of Education. One text just read **STOP.** Which was either another threat, or the sender trying to opt out of a promotional campaign and accidentally sending it to the wrong person.

"Do you know what they meant by, 'There's more where that came from'?" Charlotte asked Jennifer, holding up the letter she was quoting.

"Not when I first read it," Jennifer said. "I found the letter when my husband and I returned home Monday evening. The next morning, I realized the tires of my car had been slashed."

"Oh no!" Lucy exclaimed.

"Which is why," Jennifer continued, looking pointedly at

Kim, "I'm not exactly enthusiastic about potentially angering this individual more than we already have."

"Is that the only thing they've done other than send these texts and letters?" Charlotte asked, handing the papers to Lucy.

Jennifer thought for a moment. "Every time a new letter shows up," she said, "the reelection signs in my front yard are torn out of the ground or ripped in half. They aren't hard to replace. Nothing else has happened."

"When did you get your first letter?" Lucy asked Kim.

The other teacher thought for a moment. "It was two weeks before this past Monday."

"So Kim's letters started coming in *after* the texts to Jennifer started," Charlotte said, mostly to herself. "The earliest text is dated October ninth, so—"

Gabe had already pulled up the calendar on his phone. "Kim got her first letter exactly two weeks after the first text was sent," he said, scrolling with his thumb.

Charlotte read the text sent to Jennifer on October 9th.

Stop running for the board of education or else.

"The bad guys always say, 'or else,' but never specify or else *what*," Gabe said, reading over her shoulder.

"I mean, Kim's last letter did," Lucy pointed out.

"So why didn't Jennifer get a more specific threat, too?" Gabe asked. "Were they just warning about the slashed tires?"

Charlotte rested her forearms on her thighs, thinking. "Maybe Kim's threat *was* the 'or else,'" she mused.

"You think someone's using me to get to Aunt Jen?" Kim asked, her eyebrows knitting together.

Jennifer was watching Charlotte, her expression somber.

"I'm not sure," Charlotte admitted. She needed to stop thinking out loud so much. People would often take her theories as fact when she was on a case, and go jumping to conclusions without any further evidence. "But it would explain why your threats started coming in later. Once the person realized your aunt wasn't going to give in easily, they might've brought you in to try to intimidate her."

"Kim almost didn't tell me about the letters," Jennifer said, looking sideways at her niece.

"You didn't tell me about *yours*," Kim shot back accusingly. "I wouldn't have known about them if I hadn't seen the texts."

She turned to Charlotte as Jennifer fell silent. "We were having dinner together, and I saw the texts on her phone when she went to the bathroom. Once I realized she was getting threatened, too, I told her about my letters."

"When was this?"

"Last week."

Jennifer's silence was bolstering Charlotte's confidence. "What did you think when you found out Kim was also being threatened?"

Jennifer's shoulders slumped slightly. She shook her head. "I felt . . . guilty." She gripped her knees, staring at the floor. "I *did* suspect that the threats directed at her were because of me. Kim wouldn't be dealing with this if I wasn't in politics. I offered to get her transferred to another school in the district—"

"I'm not qualified to teach high school, and I don't want to teach elementary," Kim said firmly. "We only have one middle school, and I'm not leaving the district so close to being tenured." She sat back in her chair. "And I don't blame you for this. No one could've seen this coming. For god's sake, it's only the Board of Ed, even if you are the president."

Charlotte saw Jennifer's jaw tighten slightly when Kim said "only the Board of Ed."

"You're running for president?" Lucy asked quickly, clearly sensing the sudden tension.

Jennifer shook her head. "A person gets nominated to be president by their fellow board members," she said. "But I've been president for years, so . . ."

"It's in the bag," Gabe finished.

"Unless I drop out of the reelection race. Which I'm not planning on doing."

"Is there anyone else running for the board who might be interested in being president?" Charlotte asked.

Jennifer snorted. "Vincent Welles. He's also up for reelection. He'd take the presidency in a heartbeat if he thought he had the votes."

"And would he?" Charlotte pressed. "Have the votes, I mean, if you were out of the picture?"

Jennifer thought for a moment. "Yes, I guess he probably would. Vincent is the most self-important man you'll ever meet. It kills him that I have more responsibilities on the board than he does."

Charlotte thought Jennifer seemed pretty self-important herself, but added "Vincent Welles" to the top of her mental suspect list. Glancing sideways, she saw Gabe type *Vincent Welles* into a note on his phone titled SUSPECTS. She fought the urge to smile, instead chewing on the inside of her cheek as she thought.

"Would anyone else benefit from you dropping out of the election?" Lucy asked.

"What about Mrs. Parnell?" Kim said to her aunt.

Charlotte's head snapped up as Jennifer rolled her eyes. "Why? What'd she do?" she asked, a little too eagerly.

Lucy nudged her gently with her knee. Charlotte shot her an innocent look as Gabe said, "Who?"

"She's the vice principal of the middle school," Kim said. "She and Aunt Jen have a . . . contentious relationship."

"That woman is out to get me," Jennifer stated firmly. "Three years ago, we held an auction as a fundraiser for the district. I donated a signed copy of a bestselling novel. Mary Parnell had the nerve to accuse me, in front of everyone at the event, of forging the signature."

"You *did* forge the signature," Kim said pointedly.

"So what if I did?" Jennifer sat back in her chair, raising her chin.

Charlotte's eyebrows shot up.

"It was a *fundraiser*," Jennifer continued. "For the *schools*. She had no right to embarrass me like that. It was a power play to make me look bad and to make her look good."

Forging for a school fundraiser. Charlotte wasn't sure whether to be impressed, appalled, or intimidated. Settling for a mix of all three, she continued listening.

"Aunt Jen threatened to put Mrs. Parnell on paid leave," Kim explained, shifting uncomfortably in her seat. "But she didn't."

"It was right before election season, and I was up for reelection," Jennifer said, shrugging. "I didn't want it to become a whole thing. But now she has it in for me. I truly wouldn't be surprised if she sent these messages. She would *love* to see me off the Board of Ed."

Charlotte thought about that. As much as she disliked Mrs. Parnell, the vice principal didn't strike her as the anonymous-threats-and-blackmail type. Regardless, she added Mrs. Parnell to her suspects list, watching Gabe do the same on his phone.

"Anyone else?" Lucy asked.

Jennifer pursed her lips. "There are probably a few old clients who aren't my biggest fans," she said, thinking. "But I can't think of why any of them wouldn't want me to run for reelection."

Charlotte started to get a buzzing feeling in her head that she got whenever she was feeling overwhelmed with information. She had two different lines of thought she wanted to address, and wasn't sure which way to go first.

Thankfully, Lucy jumped in with another question, making Charlotte's choice for her. "Who knows you worked at a strip club in college?" she asked Kim.

Her coworker bit her lip as she thought. "I don't know. Twenty people? More? I wasn't super public about it for my own safety, but a good amount of people know." She began counting off her fingers. "Obviously, the people I worked with. Close family. My college friends . . ." She paused, her mouth falling open slightly. "Oh. Daniel."

"Oh," Lucy said, seemingly intrigued by this new information. "*That's* interesting."

Charlotte looked at her, then back at Kim. "And Daniel is . . . ?"

"My ex," Kim explained. "He works at the school. PE teacher."

"Yee-ikes," Gabe said, stretching the word into two syllables. "Teachers' lounge must be awkward."

Kim shook her head emphatically. "No, no, it was a pretty amicable breakup. We both agreed it wasn't working out. We're not, like, *friends*, but we're still friendly."

"So he wouldn't want to, say, blackmail you to get you to leave the school?" Charlotte asked.

"I don't *think* so," Kim said, her brow furrowing. "I mean, we broke up like six months ago. Part of the reason was because I felt like after five months of dating I still didn't know him very well, but it seems a bit much for him. He's a pretty chill guy."

"And has no reason to want me to drop out of the election," Jennifer added pointedly.

Charlotte scowled at the older woman's tone, which heavily implied that Charlotte was grasping at straws. "I understand that," she said carefully, trying to keep her tone even. "I'm just gathering information. We don't know anything for sure at this point, so—"

"I know who you are, Charlotte Illes," Jennifer cut in, her eyes steely. "I've lived in this town for a long time, and I remember when you were all anyone could talk about. It was impressive when you were a child, but this is serious business, and I just want to be sure you know what you're doing, and that you won't do anything that will endanger my niece or me."

Charlotte stiffened as Lucy and Gabe both started to protest, but Kim's voice rose above theirs.

"Aunt Jen!" she admonished, her expression hardening. "I can take care of myself, and I've asked Charlotte to help. We agreed that if I'm not going to quit my job, we need to figure out who's threatening us."

"*You* decided that," Jennifer replied. She sat back, holding up her hands in surrender. "But fine. If she can find the person who's threatening me, I'm not going to get in the way."

"*I just want to be sure you know what you're doing.*"

Charlotte stared at the papers in her lap as Jennifer's words echoed in her head. Did she know what she was doing?

"Are you concerned about your house?" she asked quietly, willing herself to focus.

Jennifer frowned. "What was that?"

Charlotte took a deep breath, inhaling the scent of baking brownies that had begun to waft in from the kitchen. "This person was sending you texts," she said. "And then last week began hand-delivering letters to your home." She turned to Gabe, who was much easier to look at than the scary expression on Jennifer's face. "Why is that?"

Gabe thought for a moment. "WiFi broke?" he offered.

Charlotte gave him a *yeah, could be* shrug. "Or," she continued, "they're trying to send you a message."

"They know where you live," Lucy said, following Charlotte's line of thinking.

"Election Day is in less than a week," Charlotte said to Jennifer. "They'll be getting more desperate. They've tried to scare you by showing you they know where you live, then by slashing your tires. Their next step *could* be to make that point even clearer."

Jennifer brought the tips of her fingers to her brow, closing her eyes for a moment. When they opened again, she said, somewhat begrudgingly, "What do you suggest I do about it?"

"You could get a camera for your door," Gabe suggested. "Seems like a pretty easy way to catch someone coming to your house."

"I already suggested that," Kim said, a tinge of irritation in her voice as Jennifer shook her head. "She won't get one."

"Those things get hacked into all the time," Jennifer said firmly. "I don't want one anywhere near my home. It's bad enough knowing this person is coming to my house when no one's there . . ."

Charlotte stopped chewing on the inside of her cheek. "They come when no one's home?"

"The first letter arrived on Thursday, the second on Saturday, the third on Monday," Jennifer said. "Each time during the evening, while my husband and I were out at school events."

"When is the next time you and your husband will both be out of the house?" Charlotte asked.

Jennifer let out a puff of air through her nose as she pulled out her phone to check her calendar.

Sorry for inconveniencing you, Charlotte thought, pressing her lips together to avoid accidentally speaking out loud.

"Tomorrow night," Jennifer said, referencing her phone. She placed it down on the coffee table in front of her, revealing a phone case covered in a sunflower pattern that was so cheerful and cartoonish in comparison to its owner's general disposition that Charlotte pressed her lips even tighter to prevent herself from laughing.

"There's an event at the high school," Jennifer continued. "We'll be out of the house from seven to ten." She raised an eyebrow. "You expect another letter to arrive then?"

"It makes sense, based on the arrival times of the others," Charlotte said. She pulled out her phone, unlocking it. "I can go keep an eye on your house while you're out and see if anyone shows up. Where do you live?"

"Make sure you're there as soon as I leave," Jennifer said after giving Charlotte her address. "Vincent Welles makes brief appearances at most of the same events I attend. If he's the one behind this, he must be doing it right after I leave the house."

"Or right before you get home, if he leaves the events early," Charlotte said. "But yes, I'll get there by seven."

"I'll come with," Gabe said, tapping his feet excitedly. "Baby's first stakeout!"

Jennifer frowned as Charlotte nudged him with her elbow. She didn't want them to give Kim's aunt any more reasons to doubt that they were taking this case seriously. Gabe shrugged at her as Lucy spoke up.

"Kim and I have more parent/teacher conferences tomorrow night," she said, "or else I'd come, too. You guys—"

She stopped. Charlotte knew she wanted to give them a "don't do anything dangerous" lecture, but decided to save it for later.

Sure enough, as soon as they said their goodbyes and began walking away from Kim's townhouse, Lucy said, "You're not going to confront anyone who might show up to Jennifer's house tomorrow night, right?"

Charlotte stared at the sky. "Hm . . ."

"*Right?*" Lucy asked Gabe.

"Hm . . ." Gabe echoed.

Swinging around to block their path, Lucy crossed her arms as the other two stopped short. "I'm serious. You don't know how dangerous this person is. Just get a good look at them, snap a photo, and let them leave."

"Yes, Mom," Charlotte said solemnly.

Lucy raised her eyebrows. "Do you want me to bring your actual mom into this? Who do you think she'll agree with?"

"Luce." Gabe wrapped an arm around her shoulders, steering her down the sidewalk as Charlotte followed. "As a detective, it's part of the job to take some risks for the sake of solving the case."

"You're talking like I don't have your mom's number, too," Lucy said.

Gabe dropped his arm. "We'll be careful."

Lucy looked at Charlotte, who nodded.

"Okay," she said, not sounding like she fully believed them.

They continued walking to where they'd parked their cars as

Charlotte mulled over the information they'd been given, trying to ignore the uncomfortable feeling that had been sitting in her chest ever since Jennifer said, *"I know who you are, Charlotte Illes."*

It would be one thing if she was in a city far away from Frencham, solving mysteries for people who knew nothing about who she was as a kid. It was another to have people with these already-established expectations of her—whether they be high, like her mom's or Landon's; or low, like Mrs. Parnell's or Jennifer Falcone's. She didn't know which she disliked more.

What she did know was that while Lottie was good, *she* was going to be better. Better and *different*.

"So what are you thinking?" Lucy asked as they reached their cars.

Charlotte kicked at the pavement. "I'm thinking that Jennifer kind of sucks and I don't want to do this for her," she grumbled.

"She's scary," Gabe agreed. "Intense vibes. I was torn between wanting to hide from her and asking her to do the cerulean monologue from *The Devil Wears Prada*."

"Kim told me she ran for mayor, like, fifteen years ago," Lucy said, leaning against the trunk of Gabe's car. "She lost. Kept trying to get her foot in the door of politics. Finally she ran for Board of Ed and won, and she's been there ever since."

"She doesn't like me," Charlotte said.

Lucy gave her an amused look. "Since when have you cared about *that*?"

"I *don't* care." Charlotte crossed her arms defensively. "I just don't like that she's judging me based on what she thinks she knows about me, that's all."

Lucy shrugged. "Sometimes you gotta work with people who don't like you. That's life, my love."

"Yeah," Gabe agreed. "Like Susan from my old job. She was always accusing me of leaving early and napping at my desk."

"You *were* leaving early and napping at your desk," Lucy pointed out.

Gabe pulled his shoulders up, baffled. "She didn't have to *judge me* for it, though."

"So what're you really thinking?" Lucy asked Charlotte. "About the case?"

Charlotte looked back up at the sky, which was fading to a dusty pink as the sun dropped closer to the horizon. "I'm wondering why this person is telling Kim to leave the school. If they're only trying to use her to get to Jennifer, why not just include the threats to Kim in the letters to her aunt? Or why don't they tell Kim to convince Jennifer to drop out of the race?"

"You're saying maybe the person has something specific against both of them?" Gabe brightened. "Like my blood feud theory!"

"Except," Lucy said, "none of the suspects so far seem to have anything against both of them. Parnell likes Kim. And Daniel doesn't have any reason to want Jennifer off the board."

"Right, the ex who she still works with," Gabe said, pulling out his phone. "I knew there was someone else to add to the suspects list. Messy, messy, messy . . ."

"I'll see if I can talk to Daniel at school tomorrow," Charlotte said. "And . . . ugh. Parnell."

"What's her deal?" Gabe asked as he typed.

Charlotte rolled her eyes. "Just another person who judges me for my past."

"She was always the one who busted Charlotte when she 'got creative' with school rules while working on a case," Lucy explained. "She doesn't like either of us very much."

"'Got creative' is a very nice way of putting it. Thanks, Luce," Charlotte said appreciatively.

"What about the guy from the board?" Gabe looked up from his list. "Vincent Welles?"

"I'll see how it goes with the others, first," Charlotte said. "For all we know, we might see him at Jennifer's house tomorrow night and wrap up this case right there."

"At a safe distance," Lucy added.

"Did you guys hear about that bear they saw wandering around town?" Gabe asked quickly. "We probably shouldn't be standing around out here."

"I'm hungry," Charlotte announced before Lucy could (rightfully) accuse Gabe of changing the subject. "Gabe, hungry?"

"Starving, always."

"Lucy, hungry?"

Lucy crossed her arms. "At a safe distance. *Promise.*"

Charlotte snapped a finger gun at Gabe. "Pie Street?"

"I was thinking the same thing. You and me, same wavelength."

Lucy sighed. "I could eat."

Q

Gabe began conducting social media reconnaissance of Daniel Symanski over a large buffalo chicken pizza. Unfortunately, as Lucy confirmed was the case for most teachers, his accounts were all set to *private.*

They were sitting around a table at Pie Street, a pizza spot that was the Place to Be for Frencham high school seniors who drove off campus during their lunch period. That evening, however, the patrons of Pie Street were a middle-aged couple, a small book club, and three twenty-five-year-olds cyberstalking a middle school PE teacher.

"I found an article about his high school basketball team," Gabe said after two minutes of digging. He looked up. "Does that do anything for you?"

"Do you follow him?" Charlotte asked Lucy.

"No. I don't really know him."

"Request to follow him," Gabe ordered.

Lucy made a face. "I feel like that's weird."

She huffed as the other two continued to stare at her expectantly. "*Fine.*"

Unsuspecting Daniel accepted the follow request within minutes, and Gabe commandeered Lucy's phone to scroll though the man's Instagram profile.

"Boring . . . boring . . . boring . . . *girlfriend*?" Gabe squinted at the phone, rotating it to present the photo on the screen. "Siblings or dating: What do you think?"

Charlotte and Lucy examined the photo of Daniel with a woman who did vaguely look like she could be related to him.

Before Charlotte could give her guess, Lucy gasped and said, "Is that *Ellie Flynn*?"

Gabe tapped on the photo to bring up the name on the tagged account. "Yeah. Who is that?"

"She's the librarian at the middle school." Lucy's jaw threatened to fall off her face. "I didn't know they were dating."

"I wonder if Kim knows," Charlotte said, staring at the photo.

"Probably not," Lucy answered. "She blocked him on everything after they broke up."

"Very healthy decision after a breakup, in my opinion," Gabe said. "Except you have no idea when your coworker ex starts dating someone *else* you both work with." He shook his head, pleased with the drama. "*Messy* . . ."

Without warning, Gabe dropped, sliding down his chair and disappearing under the table.

Lucy and Charlotte looked at each other in confusion, then both ducked their heads under the table. Gabe was sitting on the floor, arms wrapped around his knees, a guilty expression on his face.

"You good, bud?" Charlotte eyed a piece of bright pink gum that was stuck to the underside of the table, dangerously close to her hair.

"Keep your voice down!" Gabe hissed.

Charlotte paused. "You good, bud?" she whispered.

"Aaron and River just walked in," Gabe said in a low voice, naming two of his friends from college who lived in the area. "I told them I couldn't hang out tonight because I had a family thing."

"Why—"

"Go away!" Gabe shooed them with his hands. "You're drawing attention to me, and normally I love that, but I don't need it right now."

Charlotte and Lucy withdrew from underneath the table, twisting in their seats to see Aaron and River putting in an order at the counter.

"He's been acting weird lately," Lucy said softly to Charlotte.

"Who, the guy hiding under the table? Nooo."

"But it's more than that." Lucy leaned in. "He hardly goes out anymore. At first I thought he was just being really present to help me through the breakup, but now his behavior's verging on hermitic. For him, at least."

"Solid SAT word," Charlotte said. "He hangs out with us, though. And didn't he go to a drag brunch last weekend?"

"But he just went home afterwards. Have you ever seen Gabe just *go home* after a drag brunch?"

"No, he gets way too hyper and has to immediately go do another activity."

"Exactly."

Charlotte felt a tap on her leg.

"Are you guys talking about me?" came a whisper from below.

"No, we're talking about the *other* grown adult man under the table. Keep hiding." Charlotte extended her leg to make sure he'd retreated back to his hiding spot. "Maybe he had a fight with his friends or something."

"All of them? He has multiple groups."

"Hm. I don't know." Charlotte stared at Aaron and River, as if they might do something to explain why Gabe lied to them about being busy.

Gabe's friends (if that was still their status) had by this point received and paid for their pizza. Charlotte and Lucy looked away as they headed for the exit.

"All clear," Lucy declared as the door swung shut behind them. "Watch your—"

Thump. "Ow."

"—head."

Gabe emerged from below, rubbing his scalp. "I know you guys have questions, but can we just go back to the mystery? I don't really wanna . . . I just want to focus on the mystery right now."

Resisting the urge to pry, Charlotte said, "Okay. So Kim's ex, who she works with, has a new girlfriend, who also works with them. Even if Daniel doesn't have an issue with working in the same building as his ex-girlfriend, his *new* girlfriend might have an issue with it."

"So Ellie's a suspect," Lucy finished.

"What's her vibe?" Gabe asked.

Lucy shrugged. "I don't know her very well, either. I've only been at this school for two months!" she added defensively as Gabe groaned. "And they don't exactly throw mixers for us to meet other teachers and find out if they seem like the type to blackmail their ex."

"Or their boyfriend's ex," Charlotte added.

"Ellie Flynn," Gabe murmured to himself, adding her to his suspects list. "But it's the same thing as Daniel, right? She *might* have something against Kim, but does she have anything against Jennifer?"

Charlotte shrugged, taking a bite of her pizza. "Guess we gotta find out."

Chapter 5

Dodgeball: A Chapter

Three slices of pizza later, Charlotte drove home. She found her mother lounging on the couch, a reality show playing on the TV while she typed on her laptop.

"Hey," Charlotte said, standing in the doorway to the living room.

"Hey, bub." Evelyn finished the sentence she was typing, then looked up. "Here's something I haven't asked in a while: How was your first day of school?"

"It was fine." Charlotte shrugged. "The kids can be kind of wild sometimes, but it went well enough."

"Bet it made you appreciate what Lucy does even more, huh?"

"Yeah." Charlotte remembered what Lucy had said about Parnell not liking her because she was friends with Charlotte. "Hey, was I, like . . . I don't know. Was I a difficult child?"

Evelyn closed her laptop, apparently sensing that this was a "close the laptop" type of conversation. "Well, for starters, I don't think there's such a thing as a 'difficult child.' Every child has their own unique needs."

"But I mean—" Charlotte struggled for words. "I always had

this memory of my younger self being, like, pretty universally beloved. I didn't think that at the time, obviously, but looking back, that's what I always thought. But I know a bunch of people didn't like me. I think I made a lot of people's lives difficult. So I—"

"Whoa, okay, hold on." Evelyn took off her glasses, the conversation now seemingly leveling up to "glasses off." "You upset some people because you got them in trouble for doing bad things. And helped a lot more people by doing so."

"I'm not just talking about people I caught," Charlotte said, feeling frustrated. She didn't even know exactly what she was trying to say, much less how to express it to her mother. "I mean, I just feel like I barreled through everything, trying to solve cases and not caring about stepping on toes, or breaking rules, or what people thought of me—"

"Is that not admirable?" Evelyn asked, her expression thoughtful. "Other than the 'breaking rules' part. As your mom, I have to condemn that. Or at least pretend not to notice."

Charlotte shook her head, trying to figure out how to make her point. If she wanted to act like an adult, she knew she had to express herself like one.

"I'm going to do it differently this time," she finally said. "That's all I'm saying. I'm not gonna do it the Lottie Illes way, where you crawl through vents and break into lockers and get your friends into trouble. I'm an adult now. I'm gonna solve this case like an adult."

Evelyn's eyes widened excitedly. "You have a new case?"

"Yes." Charlotte gave her a pointed look. "So don't tell anyone else I'm available, because I'm not."

Her eyes narrowed as a guilty expression crossed her mother's face. "What?"

Evelyn gave her a bashful smile. "So I went to get my hair done today—".

"*Ma.*"

"Haley at the salon is always kvetching about losing customers," her mother continued, "and how she thinks someone's stealing them from her, so I thought maybe you could look into it." She threw her hands up defensively, sitting back into the couch. "I'll tell her you're busy, it's fine."

"Good."

"I just don't see why you can't work two cases at once," her mom added innocently, returning her glasses to her face and opening her laptop again.

"Because that's the Lottie Illes way," Charlotte reminded her, tapping on the side of the doorway for extra emphasis. "And I'm. Not. Doing. That."

🔍

Waking up for her second day of school wasn't much easier than the first. Lucy didn't call her this time, instead sending just one text to confirm that Charlotte had made it out of bed (she had).

Mrs. Parnell appeared in the main office again as Charlotte was signing in.

"Good morning, Mrs. Parnell," Charlotte said in what she hoped was a pleasant tone, accepting her room key and attendance sheet. She'd overheard some kids the previous afternoon talking about Parnell getting a couple of custodians to move the vending machine in the cafeteria away from the wall. She was tempted to tease the vice principal about it, but knew she shouldn't antagonize her right before trying to find out if she had anything to do with the threatening messages.

"Your mug is particularly smiley today," she said instead, pointing at Parnell's travel mug. "Always used to cheer me up, seeing that face. Good times."

Parnell narrowed her eyes. "What do you want?"

"No, I don't—I just . . ." Charlotte floundered. Whenever Lottie needed to get information out of Parnell (which she'd attempted many times, to varying degrees of success), she would usually just create a distraction so she could sneak into the vice principal's office. Or, she'd bribe a kid on the school newspaper to pretend to interview Parnell, asking her the questions Lottie needed answers to.

But Charlotte wasn't a kid anymore. *No reason we can't have an open, semi-honest conversation, right?*

"I'm just still adjusting to this whole substitute teacher thing," she admitted. Not a lie, she *was* still adjusting to it. "I was wondering if we could meet sometime so you could give me some pointers?"

Parnell was still squinting suspiciously at her. "Can't Ms. Ortega give you *pointers?*"

"Yeah, well . . ." Charlotte dug deep. "She . . . doesn't have the long-term experience in education that you do. I mean, you were a teacher for years, and a vice principal after that. I don't think I could get a better source of advice at this school."

She waited, holding her breath, hoping she hadn't laid it on too thick.

Apparently, even Parnell wasn't immune to flattery. The older woman let out a *hmph*, but her expression relaxed.

"Fine," she said. "Come to my office during your lunchtime."

Charlotte stiffened instinctively at the phrase "come to my office" before reminding herself that this was the result she had wanted.

"Perfect, thank you," she said, edging around Parnell to exit the office before the vice principal could say anything else, like, "We can do this over email," or, "I just remembered you still owe me two detentions. See me after school."

A couple minutes later, Charlotte knocked on Lucy's classroom door before letting herself in.

"Hey, hypothetically, could Parnell make me do detention . . ."

She trailed off as she saw Lucy swipe at her eyes as she swiveled around in her desk chair.

"What happened?" Charlotte asked.

"I'm fine," Lucy said, her voice cracking slightly on the last word. She moved around some papers on her desk. "Just . . . having my regular daily cry."

"You usually do your daily cry during your planning period," Charlotte said, lowering her chin. "Who am I fighting?"

Lucy let out a watery laugh. "Do you *want* detention?" She rubbed her eyes with the backs of her hands as Charlotte approached her desk. "I just had my monthly meeting with Mrs. Hernández," she said. "It was actually *last* month's meeting, but she's been busy, apparently. Usually we meet after school, but she moved it to this morning."

Lucy shrugged, her voice climbing higher as she spoke. "She was just saying all her usual stuff about how I'm not teaching right, and how I need to be teaching out of a textbook, and how Kim and I are putting the kids at risk of falling behind—"

"Did you say, 'Hey, see these grades? My students are doing great'?" Charlotte scowled. "'Thanks for coming in, don't let the door hit you on your way out'?"

Lucy shook her head. "Wouldn't make a difference. She's convinced that her way is the only way." Her lip started to tremble. "She said she was disappointed in me."

"Cool, what's her room number?" Charlotte headed for the door.

"No, no-no-no." Lucy waited until Charlotte reluctantly returned. "It's fine. She's not the problem. I know I . . . I just have to work on not letting things like this bother me." She sucked in a deep breath, letting it out in a slow stream of air. "I'm good. I'm good!"

Charlotte gave her a wary look. Her hand had started inching towards her phone to call Gabe, even though she knew there was no chance he was even awake yet.

"I'm *good*," Lucy said for a third time. She shot Charlotte a double thumbs-up and a weak smile.

"Alright," Charlotte said. "Seriously, though. Just say the

word. I'll fight a middle-aged woman, I don't care." She put up her fists, giving the air a couple of punches before a twinge shot through her shoulder. "Ah—ow." She winced, rubbing her back.

"It's the thought that counts," Lucy said drily.

December 10th, 2009

This was the end of Lottie Illes.

"Come on, Lottie," Mr. Burke called up to her. She didn't even know how she could hear him from so far away. He was at least a mile below her.

"It's only fifteen feet," Lucy yelled. "You can do it."

Lottie gripped the climbing rope, her feet pressed tightly together as she stood on a large knot, swaying gently. Her gaze swept the gym, trying to look anywhere except directly down.

Other students began joining in, calling for Lottie to climb down. Johnny R. started a chant, which was more nerve-racking than motivating.

"LOTTIE! LOTTIE! LOTTIE!"

Knowing that time was of the essence, she squeezed her eyes shut, reaching down with her feet to stand on the next knot. She kept her death grip on the rope, which burned her hands as she carefully slid down.

"Ow," she declared, presenting her bright red hands to her teacher once she was safely back on the ground. "Can I go to the nurse?"

Mr. Burke nodded—at this point in Lottie's detective career, he had no reason to suspect her request to be anything but genuine. "Alright. Take the bathroom pass. Come straight back."

Lottie suddenly swayed a bit. "Whoa." She put out her arms to steady herself, earning an eye roll from Lucy, who was watching from the side. "Feeling kind of dizzy. Can you get altitude sickness from climbing ropes?"

"No," Mr. Burke said. "But if you're feeling uneasy—"

"I can take her," Lucy volunteered, stepping in and putting Lottie's arm over her shoulder. "I'll make sure she gets there."

Lucy grabbed the bathroom pass as they both exited the gym, with Lottie swaying a little more for good measure.

As soon the door shut behind them, Lucy shrugged Lottie's arm off. "I can't believe you actually hurt your hands," she said as they started down the hall at a quick pace. "Did you really have to do that?"

"I needed a reason to go to the nurse's office," Lottie said, blowing on her stinging hands.

Lucy looked at her, baffled. "You could've just said you felt dizzy!"

"No, gotta give the nurse something to do while you get the inhaler list."

Someone had stolen Sabrina Ford's Nintendo DS out of her backpack during lunch the day before, and Lottie had been hired to track down the missing console and game cartridges. After overhearing a conversation about a kid selling DS games in the library after school, Lottie and Lucy had gone to catch the thief red-handed. However, the only thing red was the inhaler that had been left behind, supposedly by their culprit.

Lottie had hit a snag in her investigation when Parnell spotted her with the inhaler and confiscated it, knowing it didn't belong to the young detective. Hence why she and Lucy were en route to the nurse's office, in hopes of finding something that would reveal the inhaler owner's identity.

They rounded a corner, passing a hall monitor.

"Going to the nurse," Lucy explained as Lottie held up her injured hands. The teacher returned to the book in her lap.

"So what was the point of staying up there for so long?" Lucy asked as they neared the nurse's office.

"I freaked out. Too high."

Lucy stopped in her tracks. "You've climbed through the vents *twice* in the past *month*."

"Yeah, but I'm not dangling over the ground when I'm in there!" Lottie kept walking. "Come on, there's only twenty minutes left in the period."

They entered the nurse's office, where Lottie was escorted to a sink to clean her hands. She raised her eyebrows at Lucy over her shoulder, and watched her friend disappear into the little office off of the main room.

"Tug-of-war?" The nurse, Ms. Phan, turned on the cold water tap.

Lottie stuck her hands under the faucet, flexing her fingers as the cool water soothed her rope burns. "No, just regular rope climbing. And some rope-sliding."

"I'll get the salve." Ms. Phan began walking towards the smaller room, where Lucy was.

"Ow, ow ow ow ow," Lottie burst out, yanking her hands out from under the water.

The nurse turned. "What happened?"

"It hurts," Lottie said weakly, mentally willing Lucy to hurry up.

"Well, that's what the salve is for." Ms. Phan turned back around and headed for the little office.

Hands dripping with water, Lottie looked over at the beds that sat nearby. A kid was lying on his back with his eyes closed.

"I'll give you five dollars if you throw up right now," she whispered.

The kid didn't reply.

"You're no help." Lottie turned off the sink and flapped her hands to dry them as she followed the nurse to her office. Her shoulders tensed as she waited for Lucy to be discovered.

She tried not to act startled as Ms. Phan re-emerged from the office, holding a container of salve instead of the arm of a captured Lucy. Holding out her hands for salve application, Lottie tried to casually lean to one side to peer past the nurse into her office.

No Lucy.

"Okay, you're all set. Do you want gloves?"

Lottie straightened. "Uh, no, I'm okay. I just won't touch anything."

She hesitantly shuffled backwards towards the door, glancing around the room for any sign of Lucy.

"Did you need something else?" the nurse asked.

"Uh . . ." Movement from the hallway caught Lottie's eye. Lucy was peeking around the doorway, waving frantically.

"All good!" Lottie chirped, running to the door. "Thank you!"

She gave Lucy a questioning look as they retreated from the nurse's office. Once they were out of earshot, Lucy said, "Brendan."

"You only got one name?" Lottie stopped, feeling disappointed. "We needed the names of all the kids who have asthma so we could figure out whose inhaler that was."

"The red inhaler was on her desk," Lucy explained. "With a note that said, *Return to Brendan*. It's his inhaler."

Lottie gasped. "So it was Brendan in the library."

"With the inhaler," Lucy finished.

"Nice work," Lottie said, holding up her hand.

"Thank you," Lucy said proudly, high-fiving her.

They both quickly retracted their hands.

"Ow."

"Ew . . ."

Present Day

Fourth period was a planning period for the teacher Charlotte was covering. Having nothing to plan, she decided to take the opportunity to snoop. Locking up her classroom, she went to talk to Daniel.

She could hear the gym before she could see it. Bracing herself, she pushed open the door.

Immediately, Charlotte was hit by the sound of echoing yells, sneakered feet slapping against the floor, and a foam ball.

Not the sound of a foam ball. She was literally hit in the face by a foam ball.

"Ow," she said automatically as the ball bounced to the ground and rolled away. In all honesty, it hadn't hurt much (physically—emotionally, her ego was a bit bruised), but her instinct when hit in the face by something was to say "ow" no matter what level of pain she was in.

Scrunching up her nose to check for damages, she assessed her surroundings, finding herself on the outskirts of a large game of dodgeball. She scanned the gym, partially hiding behind the door for protection, searching for PE teacher Daniel.

Charlotte found him standing on the sidelines, refereeing the game. Daniel Symanski: early thirties, white, with a ruddy complexion. He had short auburn hair, and dark blue eyes that followed the students as they hurled dodgeballs at one another. His gray T-shirt and dark blue basketball shorts were accessorized with a metal whistle hanging from his neck and his teacher ID on a green lanyard.

She waited for the team across from her to thin out a little more before venturing into the gym, hugging the wall as she hurried out of range of the projectile-wielding tweens.

"Hi," she said, sidling up to Daniel. "I'm Charlotte. New substitute teacher. Are you Daniel?"

"I am," he replied, keeping his eyes on the game but reaching out a hand for her to shake. "Are you looking for a student?"

Charlotte tried to think of what Gabe would say in this situation. Realizing that he would probably jump straight to flirting, she opted instead for WWLD? (What Would Lucy Do?)

"I had a little free time, so I just thought I'd go around and introduce myself to some of the other teachers," she explained. *Damn, I should've brought muffins or something.* "I asked—"

"Max!" Daniel yelled, causing Charlotte to jump in surprise. "GET YOUR FEET OFF THE LINE!"

"They're OFF!" a kid yelled back, stretching over the line on the floor that split the dodgeball court as he sent a foam ball hurtling towards another student.

Charlotte paused to see if he was going to yell something else. When he didn't, she said, "I asked Kim Romano who's good to know at this school, and she mentioned your name—"

"She did?" Daniel's expression was puzzled as he glanced at her.

"Yeah!" *What would Lucy be doing with her hands right now?* Charlotte clasped them in front of her, feeling weird just having them hanging at her sides. *You wouldn't have this dilemma if you'd brought a box of muffins to hold.* "She said you're really nice, and that you're great with the kids. Some of them were giving me a little trouble, so I thought you might have some advice for how to handle them."

Daniel was back to watching the game. "DESTINY, YOU'RE OUT!"

Pouting, one of the students spiked the ball she was holding and trudged off the court. The game was down to three on one side, four on the other, with the rest of the students sitting on the sidelines. Charlotte found herself subconsciously rooting for the team to her left—mainly because they weren't the team that had hit her in the face.

"Respect," Daniel said, seemingly out of nowhere.

Charlotte tried to remember if she'd asked what his favorite Aretha Franklin song was. "Sorry?"

"If you want students to listen to you, you need to get their respect."

Remembering her cover story had been to get advice from him, she returned to watching the game. "Right. That makes sense. How—"

"Did Kim say anything else about me?" Daniel interrupted.

"Oh, um . . ." Charlotte scrambled for something to say, slightly distracted by the team on her left getting another player out.

"I'm just asking because, uh . . ." He gave an embarrassed chuckle, scratching the back of his head. "We actually used to date."

"Really?" Charlotte tried to pump surprise into her voice. "She didn't mention that. Oh, oh no. Did I make things awkward by telling you she said that?"

"No, no, don't worry about it," Daniel said quickly. "We're on good terms."

"Are you?" Charlotte questioned, more Charlotte-like than she meant to. "I mean," she continued, trying to channel Lucy again, "it's just so rare to see exes get along. It's refreshing to see, honestly. I don't talk to any of my exes." That was true.

"Well," Daniel said, "you know, we're not exactly *friends*. But it's nice that she said—"

"OVER THE LINE!" Charlotte yelled, pointing as Max from the team to her right stepped across the line to launch a ball at the team she was rooting for.

She caught herself, looking at Daniel sheepishly. "Sorry."

"No, good call. AWAY FROM THE LINE, MAX."

Max barely had time to back away from the line before a ball bounced off his shoulder, bringing his team down to two. Charlotte cheered internally before returning to the task at hand.

"So . . . you don't have any issues working in the same building as your ex?" she asked lightly, hoping that her tone was giving *pleasantly surprised* and not *digging for dirt*.

Daniel shrugged. "Nope." He took a quick breath, like he was about to say something else, but just shrugged again.

Charlotte resisted the urge to scowl as she sensed information being withheld from her. *Was he going to say something about his new girlfriend?*

The kids cheered as the last two members of the right-side team were taken out in quick succession, which lifted Charlotte's spirits a tiny bit.

"Alright, pick up the balls and put them back on the line!"

Daniel called out. He looked at Charlotte. "I've gotta go help them reset."

"Sure. Thanks for the advice," Charlotte said, her mind racing. She knew it'd be weird if she waited around for him to come back.

"Oh, hey," she said as he started to walk away, "real quick: Do you know if substitute teachers are allowed to take books out from the school library?"

Daniel stopped and half turned back around. "Uh . . . I'm not sure. You can ask the librarian; she's very nice."

Charlotte snapped her fingers. "Right, Ellie. Kim mentioned her, too. Great, I'll just tell her Kim sent me."

"Uh, well," Daniel said, fully turning back around at that, "you can just tell her I sent you. We know each other pretty well."

Bet you do. "Great, I'll do that." Charlotte waved. "Thanks!"

Daniel gave her a weak wave in return before going to reset the court for the next dodgeball game. Charlotte took her leave, knowing there was no way she wasn't getting hit again if she didn't get out of there before the next game started.

She was so deep in thought as she headed back to her classroom that she almost walked right past a small group of kids huddled by a locker. She stopped as they all quickly spun around, guilt plastered across their faces.

"Oh, hey guys," Charlotte said, recognizing Isabel, Kat, and Arjun. She added knowingly, "Breaking into a locker?"

"No," Isabel said, her tone forceful as two bobby pins disappeared into her curls.

"I saw the bobby pins."

"What bobby pins?"

"Look," Charlotte said, stifling a smile, "I really don't care, but if you're out here for much longer, a teacher who *does* care is gonna bust you. Do you have the detective kit?"

Isabel paused. She looked at Arjun, who pulled the plastic sandwich bag out of one of the pockets of his cargo pants. He handed it to Charlotte, who took a quick inventory of its contents.

"Where's the screwdriver and the flashlight?" she asked.

"Nia and Neil have them," Kat said.

"Where are they?"

"We don't know," Isabel cut in as Kat opened her mouth to reply.

Charlotte narrowed her eyes, but said, "Well, you need the screwdriver to . . . actually, my phone should work. Just try not to break it."

She handed her phone to Isabel, and directed the girl to use the side of the phone to firmly tap on the padlock while Charlotte pulled down.

"Are you sure—" Kat's sentence was cut off by the sound of the lock popping open and knocking into the locker.

"Oh, *shit!*" Isabel exclaimed, returning Charlotte's phone.

She reached for the handle of the locker, but Charlotte put her hand on the door, holding it shut.

"Remember," she said in what she hoped was a stern, authoritative voice, "this power should only be used for good."

Isabel nodded solemnly. In that moment of silence, Charlotte heard a muffled, metallic *thump* from above them, and spotted the rectangular grate in the wall above the lockers. It was a sound that she'd never heard from outside of the walls, but recognized instantly.

The three kids had also turned towards the grate, but looked away guiltily as Charlotte faced them.

"Be honest with me," she said. "Is someone in the vents?"

Isabel's face was the picture of innocence. "We have vents?"

Thump.

"Isa?" came a whisper from above.

Isabel slapped her forehead dramatically.

Charlotte saw a flicker of light flash past the grating. "Is that Nia?"

"No."

"Isa!" whispered the voice again. "It's me, Nia!"

"¡Cállate!" Isabel hissed at the grate. Her eyes went wide with feigned fright. "That was a ghost, miss."

"Nia!" Arjun called up to the grate. "Are you okay?"

"I'm okay!" Nia replied. "I figured out how to get to Mr. Weissman's class for our . . . Kat, what's it called?"

"Sting operation," Kat answered.

"Oh my god, everyone shut up!" Isabel said with exasperation, gesturing wildly at Charlotte. "Ms. I is *right here.*"

"Oh, hi," Nia called. "How do you get out of here?"

"With much difficulty," Charlotte replied. "Where'd you enter from?"

"The stairs by the main office."

Charlotte frowned. "That one's like six feet off the ground." Lottie had never been able to reach the stairwell vent, even at her peak middle school height of four-foot-eleven, and Nia was a couple inches shorter than that.

"We sent Neil to boost her up, because he's the tallest," Kat explained. "Arjun volunteered, but . . ." She trailed off as she looked over at the boy, who was barely taller than Nia.

"Isabel said I was needed here," Arjun finished, seeming satisfied with his job placement.

If only Lucy or I had been taller, Charlotte thought, a little envious that Nia got to use a vent that Lottie never could.

Shaking away the ridiculous feeling, she tried to conjure up a mental map of the vents. "If you keep going forward, take the first right, the second right, and the first right again. That should loop you back to where you came from."

"Oh, okay." There was a pause. "Which way is forward?"

"You know, probably better to just push yourself backwards and retrace your path," Charlotte instructed. "Can you do that?"

"Yeah."

"Do that. Do you have the flashlight from the kit?"

"I have my phone flashlight."

Charlotte felt a hundred years old. "Alright, get to pushing."

"Okay. Bye everyone!"

"Bye, Nia," Arjun said, the nervous expression on his face indicating that he thought this might be goodbye forever.

Isabel threw open the locker as the muffled thumps of Nia crawling through the vents faded. She stuck her head inside, then groaned.

"It's not here," she reported, pulling back.

"That eliminates Darren," Kat said. She gave Charlotte a critical look. "So you're not gonna tell anyone you saw us?"

"So long as you don't tell anyone I saw you."

Arjun pulled at Isabel's arm as she closed the locker and snapped the padlock shut again. "Can we go before a real teacher catches us?"

Charlotte couldn't bring herself to feel insulted by that statement. "Alright, go make sure Nia gets out safely."

She watched the group disappear down the hallway, then returned to her classroom and sat at the desk. Having nothing better to do, she decided to try another feelings check-in.

Charlotte Illes Feelings Check-In
—Amused

The kids were funny. After hearing horror stories about misbehaving students from Lucy, she'd expected all of them to be terrors. Granted, breaking into a locker and crawling through the vents was *technically* misbehaving, but Charlotte had no problem with that kind of rule-breaking.

—Nostalgic

Sure, she could be honest with herself about that. She missed running around the school with Lucy, avoiding capture while trying to solve a mystery. That didn't mean she wanted to *relive* those days. A little nostalgia never hurt anyone.

—???

There was that dull pang of negative emotion she had felt the other day when talking to Lucy about the kids. She still couldn't put her finger on it.

Chapter 6

Everyone Can Do Crimes

Lucy's usual crew didn't show up to her classroom for lunch, and Charlotte hoped they weren't still trying to get Nia out of the vents. After eating their lunches, she and Lucy headed for Parnell's office.

"I'm still shocked she said she'd talk with you," Lucy said.

"Mm," Charlotte murmured in agreement, starting to wonder if this was some kind of trap. Her brain began running through a list of occurrences from middle school that Mrs. Parnell might have been planning on interrogating her about.

Things Lottie (Allegedly) Did In Middle School That
Mrs. Parnell Might Be Planning On Interrogating Her About
by Charlotte Illes

1. Accidentally giving one of the computer lab computers a virus when she visited a dodgy website while researching for a case
2. Pulling the fire alarm to keep Lucy from getting caught eavesdropping

3. Telling an entire Girl Scout troop that Mrs. Parnell said she'd buy twenty boxes from whoever gave her the most compelling pitch (for distraction purposes)
4. Riding a school bus all the way back to the lot and breaking into a *different* bus upon arrival
5. 2011 Talent Show Disaster

"What're you thinking about?" Lucy asked, noting the far-away expression on Charlotte's face.

"The 2011 Talent Show Disaster."

Lucy gave her A Look. "We said we'd never speak of that again."

"Well, you asked."

They walked into the main office, where Mrs. Parnell was waiting.

"I wasn't sure you were going to show up," she said, raising her eyebrows at the clock on the wall.

"Sorry for making you wait," Charlotte said. "It's lunchtime, so . . . lunch."

"Charlotte told me about your meeting," Lucy said, quickly jumping in before Parnell could decide whether Charlotte was sassing her or not. "I hope it's okay if I join. Since it's my first year here, I thought I could benefit from some advice, too."

"Hmph," Parnell replied, turning and disappearing into her office.

Charlotte and Lucy looked at each other.

"Did that sound like a positive 'hmph' or a negative 'hmph'?" Lucy whispered.

"Everything out of her mouth sounds negative. Impossible to tell."

They followed the vice principal into her office, taking the two seats that sat in front of her desk. Parnell sat on the other side, reading something on her computer.

After a solid minute of sitting in silence, just as Charlotte was debating whether she should clear her throat to remind the vice principal of their presence, Parnell exhaled loudly.

"Alright," she said, tapping her keyboard one last time before sitting back in her chair. "What do you need help with?"

Charlotte had prepared some questions to ease Parnell into conversation. Before she could say anything, however, Lucy spoke up.

"How do you get other teachers to like you?" she asked. "And, like, respect you and stuff?"

"'And stuff'?" Parnell raised an eyebrow.

Lucy's shoulders tensed. "I mean . . . et cetera."

Parnell folded her hands in her lap. "I suggest you spend more time focusing on teaching and less on worrying about what other people think of you."

Charlotte made a face at her lap. The delivery was rude, but unfortunately, Parnell had a point.

"Right," Lucy muttered. "Thanks. I'll . . . try."

Parnell's gaze moved to Charlotte. "Anything else?"

Charlotte suddenly saw an opportunity. "Was that your strategy for dealing with Jennifer Falcone?"

She continued as Parnell's eyebrows leapt with surprise. "I heard you two butted heads a while back. I think it's really admirable how you didn't let it get to you, despite her threatening your job."

"Ha!"

Charlotte and Lucy both flinched as Parnell let out a sharp laugh. It was an unfamiliar sound to both of them—in fact, Charlotte couldn't remember ever seeing the vice principal laugh before.

"Jennifer Falcone couldn't get rid of me if she tried." Parnell leaned forward, placing her folded hands on the desk. "Here's a lesson, girls: most people are full of it. Their words mean nothing, and their opinions of you mean even less."

Oh my god, Charlotte thought. *Parnell's kind of being really cool right now.*

"So you don't want her off the Board of Ed?" Lucy asked.

Parnell tilted her head in a shrug. "Doesn't matter to me

either way. I don't throw fancy back-to-school functions at my house like she does, but the rest of the board still likes me well enough."

She paused for a moment. Charlotte almost didn't believe the small smile she thought she saw tugging at the vice principal's lips, but after that surprising laugh, she supposed anything was possible.

"There's a good chance," Parnell continued, "that they'll be approving me for the principal position that's opening up here next school year."

"Oh, congratulations!" Lucy said.

"Yeah, congrats," Charlotte managed to get out before falling into her thoughts. *If Parnell needs board approval for this new job, it's in her best interest to get rid of the person on the board who doesn't like her. But she seems pretty confident she'll get the job, despite Jennifer's feelings about her.*

"It's not a done deal," Parnell was saying, "so don't go around telling people about it. There are a couple teachers here who are also applying for the position—"

"How do you feel about Kim Romano?" Charlotte asked, impatiently throwing all strategy out the window.

Parnell's face hardened. "Why?"

Lucy shot her a worried look, and Charlotte clenched her teeth with regret. Maybe the straightforward approach wasn't the best move.

"I was just thinking," she said haltingly, trying to save herself, "that . . . Kim was saying she'd be interested in being a vice principal one day. Since the position is opening up, maybe she could be a good candidate."

Parnell's expression softened a bit, though her general resting face wasn't anywhere near "soft."

"Well, she'd have to go through the application process just like everyone else." She glanced at the clock on her computer. "Was there anything else you wanted to ask me?"

Charlotte scrambled for one of her pre-prepared questions to buy time while she gathered her thoughts.

"What should I do with students who won't focus on the work I give them?" she asked. "I had a few kids yesterday who seemed bored with the assigned work, and didn't want to do it."

Parnell stared at her for a moment, as if trying to determine whether the question was genuine or not.

Finally, she said, "If the students don't do their work, it's up to their regular teacher how to deal with that. But I've found in my years that some students just need a little more of a challenge to be engaged."

Charlotte nodded absently, still thinking about Parnell's earlier responses. "Cool." She looked at Lucy. "That's all I've got."

"We should probably head back, anyway," Lucy said, standing. "Thanks for the advice, Mrs. Parnell."

"Yeah, thank you." Charlotte also stood up. "It's a great honor to be working with you."

Parnell didn't seem like she believed that. "Mhm. I'll see you girls around."

Charlotte and Lucy exited her office, and were soon walking back to Lucy's classroom.

"Did you see her face when I mentioned Kim?" Charlotte walked backwards to face Lucy as she spoke. "I couldn't tell if she was upset about Kim, or upset because it sounded like I was interrogating her."

"It's a toss-up," Lucy agreed. "It doesn't seem like she sees Jennifer as much of a threat, though."

"Yeah." Charlotte glanced over her shoulder to make sure she didn't walk into a stray sixth grader. "Could just be a front, though. Especially if she's trying to avoid suspicion for the letters."

"You're sure you're not just letting your dislike of her affect your thinking?"

Charlotte's expression grew somber. "I'm afraid Parnell

might not be as bad as I thought," she said seriously. "If she keeps it up, I might actually start liking her."

"Why, because she told me to stop caring about what people think of me?"

Charlotte shrugged. "She made some good points."

"Yeah." Lucy fidgeted with her ID. "It's just . . . the more negative feedback I get from the other teachers, the more I'm starting to believe it."

Charlotte stopped short, forcing Lucy to stop, too. "You know you're, like, a great teacher, right?" she asked in a tight voice.

"Don't strain yourself," Lucy said, amused.

Charlotte winced. Sincerity wasn't her strong suit, but she knew Lucy would just sink deeper and deeper into despair if she didn't at least attempt to pull her out. Or, at least, keep her buoyant long enough for a better-equipped emotional lifeguard (Gabe) to deal with.

They continued walking down the hall. "But really. I mean, I don't think a bad teacher would worry as much about being a good teacher as you do."

Lucy fell silent. "That makes sense, I guess," she finally said. "I don't know. I need to learn how to care less about other people's opinions of me." She clasped her hands together, holding them towards Charlotte. "Teach me your ways," she pleaded.

"Ah, the teacher has become the student," Charlotte said. "And the substitute teacher has become the . . . full-time teacher." She grimaced. "Doesn't roll off the tongue as well."

"*Teach me*," Lucy repeated.

"Well"—Charlotte clasped her hands behind her back in a way that felt scholarly—"the key is to have a general dislike of humanity as a whole."

Lucy thought about that for a moment. "I think humanity is beautiful."

"Oy. You're in trouble."

Charlotte paused as they passed the gym.

"What is it?" Lucy asked.

"Hang on." Charlotte backtracked and peeked through the small window in the door. About thirty kids were scattered around the gym, playing basketball in small groups. She spotted Daniel with one of the groups, passing the ball to a kid who went in for a layup.

"The PE teacher offices are down that hallway, right?" Charlotte stepped away from the door.

"Yeah," Lucy said slowly. "Why?"

"I'm drawing a map of the school. Why do you think?" Charlotte began heading down the hall.

"Okay, wait—" Lucy hurried to catch up. "What do you think you'd find in Daniel's office, anyway?"

"I don't know. A desk, a chair, maybe notes threatening his ex-girlfriend?"

"You know, you're in a real sassy mood today," Lucy huffed.

Charlotte paused. "Sorry. I get snippy when I'm tired."

"I know. It's okay."

They continued down the hall.

"There are two other PE teachers, you know," Lucy said in a low voice, pointing to a door ahead of them. "They share one big office. The others might be in there."

"Let's find out." Charlotte lifted a hand to knock on the door, then paused. She dropped her hand.

"Okay, so," she whispered, "I was going to knock on the door and tell you to distract them before running away to hide until you were able to draw them out."

Lucy squeaked with indignation, shaking her head. "Typical."

"But I didn't! It's important to note that I didn't end up doing that."

Narrowing her eyes, Lucy whispered, "So why didn't you? What's the new plan?"

"Oh. That's . . . still the plan." Charlotte crossed her arms. "I just realized the mature thing to do would be to tell you about it ahead of time, instead of dumping it on you at the last second so you wouldn't have the chance to argue."

"So you're saying I can argue?" Lucy crossed her arms as well.

Charlotte hesitated. "Um . . ."

They stared at each other for a moment. Then Charlotte quickly knocked on the door and scurried away.

"Oh, you . . ." Lucy made a series of indistinguishable noises as Charlotte hid herself around the corner.

The door opened and Lucy stopped making the noises, a smile jumping onto her face. "Hi, Ms. Harding!" she said brightly. "Lucy Ortega. I teach seventh grade language arts."

"Hi, Lucy," Charlotte heard a voice say. "What can I do for you?"

"Uh . . . anyone else in there with you?"

"No," the other voice said slowly. "Mr. Symanski has a class and Mr. Carter is getting lunch."

"Ah, right. Well, I need help . . . lifting something. Um, in my classroom."

"What is it?"

Charlotte winced. Nothing worse than someone asking you to clarify the details of a last-minute fake excuse.

"It's a . . . bookshelf," Lucy said. "I need to move it because it, uh, it can't be where it is anymore."

"Why not?"

Charlotte dropped her chin to her chest, suppressing a groan. Why couldn't people just do things without asking questions?

"That is a great question," Lucy replied. "One that I also asked. But . . . apparently it's a fire hazard. Can't be where it is now because . . . the fire might get it."

There was a pause. Then:

"Mm. Yeah, those fire codes are strict. I can help you move it."

Charlotte pumped her fist close to her chest as she heard the door shut.

"There are still a lot of books on it," Lucy said, her voice fading as the two teachers walked down the hall. "So I'll just need to clear those off first . . ."

Charlotte peeked out to make sure the hallway was empty. Slipping around the corner, she hurried into the PE teachers' office. Three desks sat along three different walls of the room.

"Okay," she murmured to herself, looking around. "Daniel's desk, Daniel's desk . . ."

An open and glowing laptop sat on the desk closest to her, which she assumed belonged to the teacher Lucy had just lured away.

She spotted an insulated lunch box sitting on the desk farthest from her. Ms. Harding had told Lucy that the third PE teacher had gone to get lunch.

Charlotte headed for that desk.

A metal file sorter sat on one corner of the desk, bursting with papers. To its right sat two empty plastic water bottles, a small trophy that read WORLD'S BEST COACH, a stress ball shaped like a basketball, and a green mug displaying the words FRENCHAM MIDDLE SCHOOL in yellow letters, filled with pens and pencils.

A laptop sat, closed, in the middle of the desk. Charlotte swiftly amended that, flipping it open and frowning at the password page.

After typing in a few incorrect guesses, she shut the laptop and aimed for the two drawers on one side of the desk. More papers, as well as a stopwatch, a few bags of pretzels, two metal whistles, a stack of blue papers . . .

Charlotte reached into the drawer to pull out a stack of small blue papers that were tucked to one side of the drawer.

Upon closer inspection, she saw that the papers were star-shaped sticky notes. A little note was scribbled onto each paper, all in the same handwriting. *You look cute today*; *Can't wait for tonight*; and, *Thank you for the flowers!!* Charlotte read as she flipped through them.

Why would Daniel have notes from his girlfriend stuck in the back of his bottom drawer? she thought as she returned the notes and closed the drawer. It wasn't until she stood up again (maybe the sudden change of altitude jump-started her memory) that she recalled an image of Kim's desk, on which sat a stack of light blue stationery, shaped like stars.

Messy, messy, messy . . . Gabe's voice said in Charlotte's head.

So Daniel was keeping old notes from his ex in his desk. Very interesting.

She checked the bottom drawer, which housed a pair of sneakers in a plastic bag. A significantly less interesting note to end on, but she knew by now that people didn't always fill their desk drawers in a way that would give her an optimal snooping experience.

Not knowing how much time had passed (or how much time it would take Lucy and Ms. Harding to move a bookshelf), Charlotte decided it was time to make her escape. She slowly opened the door and peeked out into the hallway. Seeing no one, she stepped out and headed back to Lucy's classroom.

She found her friend removing the last of the books from a low bookshelf.

"Oh, Charlotte!" Lucy said as Charlotte entered. "Great." She straightened, smiling at Ms. Harding. "Thanks for your help. Charlotte can move the bookshelf with me."

The PE teacher rolled up her sleeves. "It's no problem. I moved all those books; might as well finish the job."

Lucy glared at Charlotte as Ms. Harding walked over to one end of the bookshelf.

"I've got this end," she said. "Charlotte, was it? Why don't you take that end?"

"Yeah," Lucy said pointedly. "Charlotte, why don't you take that end?"

"Happy to help," Charlotte said, walking over to the bookshelf.

"Where are we moving this?" Ms. Harding asked.

Lucy surveyed her carefully curated classroom. "Um . . ."

"I think just a couple feet this way would probably be safe," Charlotte suggested. "From being a fire hazard, I mean."

"Oh, yeah," Lucy agreed. "Just a couple feet that way."

"Not sure why having it here is a fire hazard," Ms. Harding commented as she and Charlotte lifted the bookshelf and moved it slightly to the right.

"Perfect," Lucy said as they set the bookshelf down. "Thank you so much for your help."

Her smile dropped as soon as the PE teacher left the room. "You're helping me move this back, *and* returning all the books."

"Okaaaay," Charlotte said in a sing-song voice. "But if I do that, I might be too tired to tell you what I found in Daniel's desk."

Lucy narrowed her eyes. "Are you just pretending you found something to get out of physical labor?"

Charlotte sat on a desk. "No. But I'll help you move everything back."

She told Lucy about the notes from Kim.

"Weird," Lucy said, making a face. "I mean, I get keeping some stuff from past relationships, but that feels like something he should've cleared out a while ago. Do you think he forgot they were in there?"

"It's possible," Charlotte said, "but there was a lot of other stuff in that drawer. Like, pretzels. You don't put pretzels in a drawer you never go into."

"You should give that to Gabe for one of his motivational posts," Lucy said. "Feel like there's some hidden meaning in that."

The classroom door swung open as the lunchtime crew poured into the room.

"Guess what!" Nia exclaimed, running to close the distance between them before screeching to a stop. Her eyes were bright behind her glasses. "We have a lead."

"On the bobblehead?" Lucy asked, raising her eyebrows.

Nia confirmed by doing an impression of the missing item.

"Someone made an Instagram account for it," Kat said as the rest of the group hurried over. "They've already posted three times."

She held out her phone for Lucy and Charlotte to look at. The account featured a profile picture of the plastic cartoon visage of Albert Einstein, as well as three photos of the bobble-head. One showed Einstein sitting in front of an open textbook, another showed him sitting in a shoe on a tiled floor, and the third was a closeup of him peeking out of a backpack.

"How'd you find out about this account?" Charlotte asked.

"FM Shoes posted the shoe photo and tagged this account," Isabel explained.

"The . . . what?" Charlotte looked at Lucy for an explanation, who rolled her eyes.

"The kids have all these silly school-themed Instagram accounts they send photos and messages to," she said. "They have one for rating teachers—I don't approve, but I got five fire emojis—and one where they post photos of kids who fall asleep in class—"

"But Frencham Middle Shoes isn't silly!" Neil protested.

"They post photos of kids' shoes from under the bathroom stalls," Kat said. "It's dumb."

"It is *not*," Neil said again. "We wouldn't have known about the Einstein account without it!"

Charlotte was very grateful that Instagram wasn't widespread when she was in middle school. It might've helped with sleuthing, but at least she never had to worry about kids photographing her shoes in the bathroom.

"Do you know who runs the shoe account?" she asked. "They probably know who submitted the photo."

"No, they keep their identity a secret," Nia responded. "I might be able to get some information out of the photos the Einstein account posted. I just need some time."

"I mean, the bobblehead's not gonna *die*," Kat said. "I think we're fine."

"Knowing middle school boys," Lucy said, glancing at Charlotte, "it's only a matter of time before he sets it on fire or something."

"Oh, no." Arjun's face dropped. "We have to hurry."

Isabel put a hand on her hip. "Ms. Ortega, are you saying you don't think a girl could've stolen Einstein?"

"No, no," Lucy amended, smiling. "Girls can do anything boys can do."

"And people who don't conform to the gender binary," Kat added.

"Them, too."

"Everyone can do crimes," Charlotte said sagely.

"Wait, no—"

The bell cut off Lucy's response, and she shot Charlotte A Look as the kids hurried out of the classroom.

Charlotte gave her wide, innocent eyes in return. "What?"

Chapter 7

Baby's First Stakeout

If this was how tired she got after substitute teaching for a half day of school, Charlotte wasn't sure if she'd be able to make it through a full day.

Just a short nap, she told herself as she fell onto her bed, not even bothering to pull the covers over her body. *After quick little power nap, I'll be good to—*

"RISE AND SHINE," Gabe yelled, swinging the bedroom door open.

Startled, Charlotte jerked upright, her eyelids heavy. The room had grown dark, and her mouth tasted like sundried garbage. She looked at the clock on her nightstand as Gabe hit the switch by the door, the sudden light forcing her eyes to snap shut before she could read the numbers.

"Agghhhhh," she groaned. "What time is it?"

"Stakeout time, baby!" Gabe cheered, entering the room. He was wearing his green bomber jacket over a black T-shirt and black jeans. "How was substitute teaching?"

Mumbling unintelligibly in response, Charlotte rubbed her eyes.

Gabe hopped up to sit on the bed. "Have you begun executing The Plan yet?"

"I told you, I'm not doing *School of Rock* with the students."

"Fair enough," Gabe exhaled heavily. "I couldn't find a Battle of the Bands nearby, anyway."

"Shit, it's almost seven." Charlotte threw off her blankets. "Jennifer's event starts in fifteen minutes. We need to get to her house."

"I know. That's why I texted you twenty times before coming here. Your mom let me in." He paused as Charlotte climbed off the bed. "You okay?"

"I'm fine. Just needed a nap." Feeling groggy, she grabbed a sweatshirt from a pile of clothes on her desk chair and pulled it over her head.

"I can go watch the house by myself if you're not feeling up to it," Gabe offered.

"No, no. Thanks. I'm good." Charlotte widened her eyes and raised her brows to show him how awake she was. "See? Come on."

"Is that my sweatshirt?" Gabe asked as they headed downstairs.

"No."

"I don't remember you being in the Frencham Players' production of *You're a Good Man, Charlie Brown*."

"I was in the back, easy to miss."

"It's a really nice sweatshirt."

"I know, that's why I kept it when you left it here."

"SO YOU ADMIT—"

June 6th, 2011

"Slow down!"

Lottie glanced over her shoulder, careful to keep her balance on her bicycle. Behind her, Lucy was pedaling furiously to catch up as the purple streamers that hung off of her handlebars flapped in the wind.

"Hurry up!" Lottie responded, facing front again. "There's no point in doing a stakeout if we miss the thing we're staking!"

"That's not a word," Lucy called back, her voice growing louder as she closed the distance between the two bicycles. "Not in the way you're using it."

"Stakeout? That's a word."

Lucy pulled up next to Lottie's bike as the two continued down the street. "Staking."

"So why is it called a stakeout? Aren't we staking out Sprinkles?"

Lucy thought for a moment.

"I don't know," she finally admitted.

"So I'm right."

"It doesn't mean you're right just because I don't know!"

The two coasted around the corner onto the next street.

"Didn't Micayla hire you to find out where Chris was last week?" Lucy asked, weaving around a parked car. "Why're we going to Sprinkles? Shouldn't we be staking out Chris's house?"

"I still don't get what the big deal is," Lottie said. "Her boyfriend didn't come to give her a hug when she got out of practice. It's not like he didn't go to her dance show."

"Recital," Lucy corrected. "And you'll understand one day when you have a boyfriend. *Or girlfriend*," she added quickly.

"I guess." Lottie doubted that, but also knew her friend generally had a better understanding of this kind of stuff than she did.

"I can't wait to have a boyfriend," Lucy said longingly.

"I don't understand why," Lottie countered. "Almost everyone we know with a boyfriend has hired me to find out if he's dating other girls. Doesn't sound very fun to me."

"My boyfriend will be different," Lucy said firmly. "Anyway, why are we going to Sprinkles?"

"Oh, right." Lottie carefully lifted a hand to adjust her helmet, which was a hand-me-down from Landon and tended to slide down her forehead a bit. "So, Chris told Micayla that he had to visit his sick grandma, and that's why he didn't go visit her after Micayla's practice. But Chris's sister is in Landon's grade, and I got him to ask her how her grandma's doing."

"Let me guess," Lucy said. "She's perfectly healthy."

"She's dead."

"Oh no!" Lucy gasped, swerving a bit.

"No, not, like, recently." Lottie braced herself as she rolled over a pothole. "Both their grandmas have been dead for years."

"Oh." Lucy scrunched up her nose. "So he was lying."

"Of course he was lying!" Lottie yelled dramatically. Calming, she added, "But the question is: Where was he actually?"

The two came to a busy road, and slowed their bikes to a stop as they waited for the light to change at the crosswalk. Balancing on one foot, Lottie continued:

"I found out that the debate team was having a mock trial that day," she said. "And you know who's on the debate team?"

"Yeah, they only have, like, five members," Lucy said. "Sarah T . . ."

She gasped. "Sarah T!" she repeated.

"Yup," Lottie said. "His ex-girlfriend. And she *just* broke up with her boyfriend. So today in the locker room I was eavesdropping on her talking to her friends, and she said she was going on a date at Sprinkles on Saturday after dinner."

"So we're going to see if the date is with Chris?"

"Exactly."

The light changed, and they began biking again. A few minutes later, they arrived at Sprinkles, their local ice cream parlor.

"Ice Cream Boy is working today," Lottie observed as they rested their bikes against a picnic table outside the shop.

Ice Cream Boy was their less-than-subtle code name for their shared crush, a cute high school freshman who worked at Sprinkles. They watched through the front window as Ice Cream Boy scooped the eponymous dessert onto a cone and handed it to a customer. He spotted them watching through the window and gave them a wave before returning to the next customer in line.

Lucy pretended to swoon. "I won't be able to concentrate on this stakeout."

Rolling her eyes (despite the blush she felt spreading on her face), Charlotte pulled Lucy into the shop. The two emerged a few minutes later, ice cream cones in hand, and settled down at a picnic table.

"I don't think they're coming," Lucy finally said. They had spent fifty minutes talking, laughing, and daring each other to sneak peeks at Ice Cream Boy. Their ice cream cones were long gone, the sky had gone dusky purple, and the string lights that decorated the seating area had just switched on.

"Ten more minutes," Lottie insisted. She really wanted to solve this case. Plus, she was having fun, and was also procrastinating on doing her homework. "A stakeout has to be at least an hour for it to officially be called a stakeout."

"Who made that rule?" Lucy asked.

"The people who make stakeout rules!"

"So, you."

". . . yeah."

"Fine," Lucy said, folding her arms on the table and resting her chin on them "Ten more minutes. But we need to ride home really fast. My mom told me to be back by eight thirty."

Nine minutes later, Lottie sucked in a breath and tugged at Lucy's sleeve, unable to hide her excitement.

"There they are!" she whispered.

They averted their gazes as Chris and Sarah T walked past, not seeming to care who saw them as they entered the ice cream parlor holding hands.

"You were right," Lucy said once the door closed shut behind the couple.

"I usually am," Lottie replied.

They retrieved their bikes and began riding home.

"Are you free for another stakeout on Monday?" Lottie

pushed her helmet back up her forehead. "Mrs. Hendrickson hired me to figure out who's been stealing flowers from her garden while she goes food shopping on Monday afternoons. I'm gonna go right after school so I don't miss whoever it is."

"I would," Lucy replied, sounding disappointed, "but I have yearbook club until four."

"Oh, okay." Lottie thought about sitting outside Mrs. Hendrickson's house, alone, for at least the minimum hour required to call it a stakeout.

"You know," she said as they continued riding down the street, "I can wait until four."

Present Day

Gabe drove them across town to the address Jennifer had given them. It was a three-story house with a well-groomed front lawn. A walkway cut through the grass, ending at a set of stairs that led to the front porch. On either side of the walkway, close to the sidewalk, two signs stuck into the grass encouraged pedestrians and folks in slow-moving vehicles to VOTE FALCONE FOR SCHOOL BOARD.

Charlotte exhaled, relieved. She was worried they'd miss the letter-leaver, if Jennifer's theory was correct about Welles showing up soon after Jennifer left the house. But Jennifer also said the person would always attack the signs in her front yard. Seeing the signs intact told her they were still awaiting their visitor.

Parking two houses down across the street, Gabe turned off the car.

After unbuckling his seat belt to reach into the back, he pulled a giant tote bag through the space between their seats and balanced it on the center console.

He rummaged through the bag, "You slept through my texts asking what supplies a person brings to a detective stakeout, so I had to improvise."

He removed a pair of giant binoculars and held them out to Charlotte.

"No, thanks," she said.

"Okay, so, you've already broken the first rule of improv."

Charlotte gestured through the windshield at Jennifer's house. "We can see the house clearly without them."

"Fine. *I'll* use them." Gabe held the binoculars up to his face, where they gently collided with his glasses. "Hm."

After fiddling with the dials on the binoculars for all of thirty seconds, he tossed them into the back seat. "You're right, don't need those."

Charlotte had pulled the tote bag onto her lap and was sifting through the rest of its contents.

"Oh, thank god," she said, pulling out a bag of trail mix and ripping it open. "I'm starving."

"God wasn't the one who waited in the stupid long line at CVS," Gabe said.

"Thunk yub," Charlotte said through a mouthful of almonds and raisins. She removed two granola bars and a bag of gummy worms from the tote and placed them in the cupholders between their seats.

"I also got"—Gabe took back the tote bag, pulling out items to present them one by one—"tissues. Bottles of water. Aspirin. Gauze—"

"*Gauze?*"

Gabe's body convulsed into a violent shrug. "I don't know how dangerous these things can get! You told me one time you fell off a roof while on a case."

Charlotte took the gauze from him and dropped it back into the bag. "Yeah, but it was Sammie Fitzpatrick's playhouse, so it wasn't that serious."

"Fine." Gabe tossed the bag into the back seat. "Forget it." He crossed his arms and slumped into his seat.

"Wait, I wanted to see what else you got!" Charlotte insisted.

"No, you think it's dumb."

"I don't think it's dumb. I like that you're prepared."

"Well," Gabe mumbled, "I never got to be a Boy Scout, so I'm healing my inner child."

Charlotte grabbed the tote bag again. "A crossword puzzle book." She pointed at him with the book. "Very good for passing the time."

"Shut up." Gabe covered his face.

"I'm serious!" She pulled out a roll of duct tape. "Now this is *very* good. Classic detective tool."

Gabe slowly uncovered his face. "I got the extra strong kind, too," he said, pointing at the label.

"Smart. And"—she rummaged through the bag—"you got a thermometer, which is good . . . in case someone needs to take their temperature."

"Mhm."

"And some lotion—"

"For dry hands," Gabe explained.

"Of course. And I like how you brought sunscreen even though it's dark out, because, you know, skincare is very important . . ."

She trailed off as she saw Gabe clearly trying not to laugh.

"It's a really good stakeout kit," she said seriously, a laugh bubbling out on the last word.

Gabe finally broke, with Charlotte following his lead.

"This is why you need to reply to my texts when I'm stakeout shopping," Gabe said once they finally calmed down.

"Hey, you nailed it with the trail mix." Charlotte dumped another handful into her mouth, feeling new energy return to her body as the grogginess from her nap faded away.

"Do we think this person's gonna show up?" Gabe leaned forward to look out through the windshield.

Charlotte chewed thoughtfully. She knew her original theory was a bit of a leap—that the blackmailer switched from texts to letters to show that they knew where Jennifer lived, increasing the threat. When that didn't have an effect, they slashed Jennifer's tires to further their point. But regardless of the reasoning behind the change in behavior, the facts showed that the person had come to the house the last three times Jennifer and her husband were both out of the house in the evening.

"I think there's a good chance," she answered. "We'll just have to wait and see."

If they are *escalating the threat,* she thought, *what comes after slashed tires?*

"At least I can check 'stakeout' off my detective bucket list," Gabe said.

Charlotte looked at him, amused. "What else is on your detective bucket list?"

"*Tackle someone,*" he said, counting on his fingers. "Already did that one. *Say something dramatic and immediately leave the room.* Bonus points if I'm wearing a long jacket that swishes behind me as I leave. *Have a long-legged, beautiful woman waltz into my office, asking me to figure out who killed her husband.* I probably need an office for that one . . ."

"I don't think I've ever done any of those things," Charlotte said.

"Well, you probably had a short-legged, cute little girl walk into your garage and ask you to find her doll or something."

Charlotte thought for a moment. "Okay, yeah."

Gabe grabbed the crossword puzzle book and started reading clues out loud to Charlotte while she kept her eyes on Jennifer's porch.

"Hang on," he said after a little while.

"How many letters?"

"No, it's not a clue, I was just talking." He grabbed his phone from its mount on the dashboard. "This is the perfect opportunity to do a livestream."

"No," Charlotte said flatly.

"Why *not*? A fun little mid-stakeout Q and A. Gabe's Babes will love it."

Charlotte gave him a look that was fifty percent amused and fifty percent horrified. "*Who?*"

"My followers!" He looked up from his phone. "I'm still work-shopping the name. You don't like it?"

"I hate it."

Gabe waved a hand at her. "Eh, what do you know?"

"Seriously, though." Charlotte pulled herself out of the slouch she had made herself comfortable in. "You shouldn't publicize that we're on a stakeout."

Gabe laughed. "Do you think the blackmailer follows me on Instagram?"

"You have a lot of followers."

"That I do," Gabe said proudly. "Okay, fine. Just in case the blackmailer is one of Gabe's Babes—"

Charlotte made a pinched face.

"—I won't go live right now." He swiped out of Instagram, opening his messages. "I also won't post the timelapse video I took of us doing the crossword puzzle."

"The *what*?"

"The *crossword puzzle*."

Gabe ducked as a bag of chips flew past his head.

"Delete that video," Charlotte grumbled as he laughed. She slouched back into her seat.

Gabe started watching a different video on his phone.

"Watch," he said, chuckling. He began replaying the video as he held his phone out for Charlotte to watch.

Gabe's friend River (whose last appearance had caused Gabe to retreat under a table) walked up to the end of a bowling alley lane. They dropped into a low crouch and spun the bowling ball multiple times before pushing it down the lane. The ball slowly made its way towards the pins before knocking down all but one. The speakers of Gabe's phone exploded with agonized yells from unseen spectators.

"Wow." Charlotte ripped open the bag of gummy worms. "Wild stuff."

"Aaron just sent this to me," he said, pulling his phone back.

"Your friends went bowling without you?"

"If you can call that bowling," Gabe snickered.

Charlotte stared at him.

After a moment, he looked over at her. "What?"

"Why are you here?"

"Rude."

"Did they not invite you?"

"They invited me."

"So?"

Gabe shrugged. "I said maybe, but this came up, so I told them I wasn't coming. Couldn't miss a vital course in my detective training."

He reached over to grab a gummy worm out of the bag, but Charlotte jerked the bag away, narrowing her eyes. "Why did you say 'maybe' originally? You're not a 'maybe' person."

"What kind of person am I?"

Charlotte shot finger guns at him. "I'm in!" she said enthusiastically.

"Was that me?"

"That was my impression of you, yeah."

"Terrible."

Charlotte gave him A Look. "Come on. What's going on?"

Gabe hesitated, then mirrored her slouch. "They're with a bunch of Aaron's friends from work, so . . ."

Charlotte's brow furrowed. "Weren't you *just* saying the other day that you needed more friends?"

"Was I?" Gabe asked, his gaze stuck on his phone.

"The other day when I told you for the fifth time that I wasn't gonna be in a video for your disgusting gum sponsorship."

"Shit, I need to make another one of those . . ."

"And last week you literally said, 'My total number of friends is incredibly unproportional to how charismatic and charming I am.' And then Lucy said, 'Disproportionate,' and you said, 'Solid SAT word.'"

Gabe snapped his fingers, pointing at her. "Now *that* was a good impression."

"That wasn't an impression; I was just quoting you. Stop changing the subject. You said you need more friends, but Lucy told me you're not even hanging out with the ones you have."

Gabe was quiet for a moment, which was chilling.

"All of my friends keep doing stuff with other people," he finally said. "And they invite me, but meeting new people . . . I don't know, it's exhausting."

He paused. "Like in school, you'd meet someone new, and it was like, 'Cool, see you every day in chem class, new friend,' or whatever. Trying to make new friends now is just weird."

He rested his head against the driver's door. "And that's on top of, y'know, worrying if they might be transphobic. Or queerphobic. Or racist. Or a *Glee* fan."

"Weren't you a *Glee* fan?"

"My statement stands."

Charlotte pondered that. "So you've just given up on trying to meet new people?"

Gabe shrugged.

"Hm." She tapped her fingers on the car door. "Do you think Aaron and River would be friends with people like that?"

Gabe scrunched up his nose, begrudgingly acknowledging her point. "No. I mean, not on purpose."

He had begun playing with the unbuckled seat belt, pulling it back and forth across his body.

"It's just never felt like this much work to be around people before. Like, growing up with a big Filipino family, and having friends in school, there were always people to be with. It was never hard, it just happened."

He sighed. "And now it's like I'm constantly scrambling to find people and hold on to them. It just feels too important when I'm introduced to someone new, and I put too much pressure on us becoming friends, so I panic and bail when the pressure becomes too much."

"I don't know, man," Charlotte said after a moment. "I've got you, and Lucy. Landon and Olivia. My mom. I'm good with that. But you're a people person. You love people! And people tend to love you." She grimaced as Gabe looked over at her. "Or, whatever."

He smiled.

"Just go bowling with them sometime," Charlotte finished, decapitating another gummy worm with her teeth. "Worst thing that can happen is . . . you have to bowl."

"I like bowling."

"Except for the shoes."

"I *hate* the shoes."

Charlotte held out the bag of gummy worms, and Gabe took a handful.

"Thanks," he said. "That was a nice pep talk."

"Huh," Charlotte said. "That's the second good pep talk I've given today. You think this is the effect of regular therapy?"

"Could be!" Gabe stretched his arms up before resting his hands behind his head. "How much are we getting paid for this, anyway?"

"We're not."

"Not what?"

"Getting paid."

"What?! Why am I here?"

"I literally *just* asked you that."

They returned to the crossword puzzle for another half hour.

Charlotte's eyelids had just begun to droop when she saw movement from around the far side of Jennifer's house.

"Hey, hey hey hey," she said, tapping Gabe's arm as she scrambled to sit upright.

Gabe sat up as well. "Is it the blackmailer?"

They watched the figure go over to one of the signs stuck into Jennifer's lawn and kick it over.

"I'm going to venture a guess and say yes," Charlotte replied.

The figure walked up the porch steps, a dim beam of light coming from a flashlight in their hand. The nearest street lamp to the house was a couple doors down, but Charlotte could make out a black sweatshirt with the hood pulled up, and dark sweatpants—green?—with a bright yellow stripe down the side.

The figure approached the mailbox that hung by the door, pulling something out of their pocket and dropping it inside.

"Come on." Charlotte opened the car door and climbed out.

"Oh shit, okay," Gabe said, scrambling to follow. Charlotte didn't wait, jogging down the street towards the house.

She realized she probably should've gone for a stealthier approach as she watched the figure freeze, then bolt towards the end of the porch.

Charlotte started to run. "Stop!" she yelled, knowing full well that in all her years of chasing people, no one she'd chased had ever followed that command.

There was a clatter as the figure stumbled, then recovered, vaulting over the porch railing and landing in the bushes on the side of the house.

Charlotte hit the sidewalk at the same time as Gabe caught up with her, both of them hopping the curb and running past the house and around the side.

"Ow!" Gabe yelped, stumbling for a beat before regaining his stride. He glanced over his shoulder at the ground as they continued running. "The fuck was that?"

Charlotte didn't have time for questions. The figure was racing through Jennifer's backyard, which sloped downwards, away from the house, until it met the edge of a wooded area.

They sprinted down the yard, Gabe passing Charlotte as they watched the figure dive through the trees and disappear into the dark shadows of the woods.

Gabe slowed slightly. "We lost—"

Charlotte sped past him.

"—them oh fucking hell Charlotte."

He quickly caught up with her as they broke through the tree line. Dead leaves crunched under their feet as they dashed through the woods.

"Watch your step," Charlotte warned. She narrowly avoided

tripping over a fallen branch, throwing her arms out to keep her balance.

"You're talking to the *tinikling* king of my cousin Christina's eighteenth birthday party." Gabe hurdled a fallen log that Charlotte less gracefully threw herself over. "These sticks can't trip me up."

Charlotte pumped her legs harder to keep up with Gabe. A rush of excitement joined the adrenaline that was coursing through her body, and she found herself fighting the urge to grin as they barreled deeper into the woods.

Jumping over another large tree branch, Charlotte squinted through the trees. She could just make out the figure moving through the trees, but the flashlight had gone dark as the person abandoned the porch, making them harder to follow. The distance between them was growing by the second.

"This is . . . exciting," Gabe said, pausing for breath every few words. "Chasing a culprit . . . with no plan for what to do . . . if we actually catch up with them. Did you do this . . . a lot as a kid?"

Oh no, Charlotte thought. *I did.*

Distracted, she didn't see the tree branch poking into her path until it was right in front of her. She veered out of the way, the branch painfully scraping her neck.

"Aghhh!" She slowed to a standstill.

Gabe had already flown past her, but skidded to a stop and doubled back. "Are you okay?"

Charlotte touched her neck and hissed. It stung, but she didn't feel any blood.

"Fine," she said, pulling her hand away as she took a shaky breath. "Just scraped my neck."

"We might still be able to catch up—"

"No." Charlotte grabbed the back of Gabe's jacket to stop him. "This was dumb. I'm sorry."

He turned back as she released him. "For what?"

"Running after them. That was Lottie Illes behavior."

"I thought it was brave," Gabe said. "Pretty badass detective behavior."

"It was reckless and counterproductive." Charlotte took in another deep breath as her heartbeat started to slow back down. "Don't put this on your detective bucket list." She began retracing their steps.

"It wouldn't really make sense to do that, since I've already accomplished it." Gabe fell into step next to her. "But out of curiosity: Why not?"

Charlotte stomped on a branch to clear her path. "Because chasing after someone with no plan is something a child would do. And we're not children."

"You mean, you're not Lottie Illes."

Charlotte unnecessarily stomped on another branch. "Sure, whatever." Out of the corner of her eye, something moved through the trees. She turned and squinted to see through the darkness.

"You know how you do that thing where you separate yourself from who you were as a kid?" Gabe asked hesitantly. "Is that really healthy, you think?"

"Gabe . . ."

"Okay!" he acquiesced, hearing the warning in her tone. "I'll drop it."

Charlotte put her arm in front of Gabe, bringing them both to a stop as she twisted around to cover his mouth with her other hand.

"Don't yell," she said quietly. Gabe's eyes were bewildered, and he mumbled something that was muffled by her hand.

She slowly moved out of the way so he could see past her, where the large silhouette of a creature appeared through the trees.

Gabe stiffened, and she pressed her hand harder.

"*Don't.*"

She immediately retracted her hand as something wet touched it.

"Did you just lick me?" she hissed.

"Sorry, habit."

"I take back what I said. You're a child."

They watched the creature—which was more and more un-deniably a bear the longer they stared at it—continue to move through the trees parallel to them, only a few yards away. It was about three feet tall on all fours, with dark black fur and a slow, lumbering walk. Between their talking and Charlotte's exces-sive branch-stomping, it was a miracle it hadn't already noticed them. Or maybe it had, and it simply didn't care.

"Aren't you supposed to make yourself really big when you see a bear?" Gabe whispered. He slowly began to crouch. "Quick, get on my shoulders."

"*No.*"

Charlotte bent over to pull him up just as Gabe straightened. Their heads collided, causing them both to yelp with pain.

The bear, which had been slowly making its way away from them, suddenly stopped and turned in their direction.

Gabe grabbed Charlotte's arm as she gripped the front of his jacket.

"Why isn't it hibernating?" Gabe whispered. "If I was a bear, I'd be knocked out by early October. Also, why is it *here?*"

"Because humans are forcing them out of their natural habi-tats by constantly cutting down trees to build houses that no one can afford," Charlotte whispered back.

"Should we just let it kill us as an apology?"

"I'd rather not."

In one swift, startling motion, the bear pulled itself up onto its hind legs.

"Oh *shit,*" Charlotte whispered, pushing Gabe back.

"Wait, no, it's okay." Gabe slowly lifted his arms above his head and began waving them back and forth.

"I follow this conservationist who talks about bears while making cakes that look like bears," he said, raising his voice to a normal speaking volume.

"That's so specific."

"I know, it's great." Gabe continued waving his arms. "I don't think it's being aggressive; it's just trying to figure out what we are."

Unconvinced, Charlotte kept her voice low. "And you want it to think you're one of those inflatable guys at car dealerships?"

Gabe bumped her with his shoulder. "We need it to know that we're human and not defenseless prey."

"What if I'm both?"

"*Charlotte.*"

"Okay, okay!" Cautiously, Charlotte raised her arms, mimicking his movements.

"Hello, bear," Gabe said as they both swayed. "Sorry for bothering you. If it makes things better, neither of us are personally responsible for cutting down any trees. Although of course we could always be doing more. I actually ran a fundraiser last year—start moving sideways."

It took a moment for Charlotte to realize he was talking to her. "Huh?"

"Start moving sideways; slowly." He nudged her to the right, and they began shuffling to the side as he continued talking to the bear.

After an agonizingly long minute of shuffling through dead leaves as Gabe waxed poetic about the environment, the bear dropped back down to all fours and turned away. Another agonizingly long minute later, it was out of sight.

They dropped their arms, waiting another (slightly less agonizing) minute to make sure it was really gone. Charlotte let out a breath.

"Nice," she said, weakly patting Gabe's arm. "Thank you."

Gabe shrugged bashfully. "Sometimes spending way too much time online pays off."

The two of them made their way out of the woods.

"There!" Gabe said as they walked along the side of the

house. He jogged over to a spot in the grass, where a brick sat next to a partially crushed dandelion. "That's what I kicked."

He crouched down and picked up the brick, presenting it to Charlotte. "Do you think the runner dropped it?"

"It's likely," she replied, crouching down and squinting at the ground where the brick had been sitting. "This grass would be in a lot worse shape if it'd been there for a while."

"So, what?" Gabe asked as she straightened. He pulled an arm back as if to throw the brick. "You think they were planning on smashing some windows?"

"Makes sense." They continued walking. "The person was due for another escalation after the slashed tires. Breaking windows is a believable next step." Charlotte paused as they rounded the front of the house. "I'm going to check the mailbox real quick."

She climbed the porch steps, hearing the wood squeak as Gabe followed.

"Wait!" he said urgently as Charlotte reached for the mailbox.

"What?"

Gabe nervously clutched the brick to his chest. "What if they put, like, a scorpion in there or something?"

"You've gotta stop watching old *Fear Factor* clips before bed." Charlotte flipped open the lid.

Gabe whimpered as Charlotte stuck her hand into the metal mailbox. She gasped dramatically, making her eyes go wide.

"Okay," Gabe said. "You're not a good actor."

Chuckling, Charlotte pulled two envelopes out of the mailbox.

"The blackmailer left *two* letters?" Gabe asked.

Charlotte tried to read the writing on the front of the envelopes, but the light on the porch was dim. "Do you have your phone?"

"No, I left it in the car."

"Mine too."

Gabe snapped his fingers. "Flashlight. That would've been a good item for the stakeout tote."

Charlotte walked over to the edge of the porch, pausing as her foot hit something small that slid across the floor.

Gabe's head whipped towards the sound. "What was that?"

Charlotte examined the ground around them, but couldn't see anything. "A pebble," she guessed. "It looked like the person tripped over something when they started to run; it was probably that."

"See, I didn't even notice that," Gabe shook his head. "I have so much more to learn."

Charlotte leaned over the railing to try to get more light from the distant street lamp and the much more distant moon.

The first envelope was blank. Seeing as how it was addressed to no one, she took that as permission to open it. How else could they know who it was for?

The typed letter that was folded inside was nearly identical to the previous letters sent to Jennifer:

I'll break more than that next time. Drop out of the election.
Do not make me tell you again.

"So that *was* the blackmailer," Gabe said breathlessly as he read over Charlotte's shoulder.

"Did you think we just chased a postal worker through the woods?" Charlotte asked, incredulous.

Gabe made a defensive *I don't know* sound.

"Looks like they *were* planning on breaking windows." Refolding the letter and returning it to the blank envelope, Charlotte flipped over the other one. To her surprise, it was addressed to Kim.

"That's new," Gabe commented. "Why do you think they left that here?"

"I don't know." Charlotte examined the envelope. It featured the same sloppy handwriting as the other letters Kim had received, with the school's address underneath her name. The stamp in the corner had a similar cartoon animal party theme as the most recent letter; this time, it was a monkey wearing a polka-dotted birthday hat. The only difference from the other letters was that this one hadn't been stamped by the post office.

"Maybe," Charlotte ventured slowly, "this is part of the threat."

"What do you mean?"

Charlotte rested her back against the porch railing. "We think that maybe the blackmailer started targeting Kim to try to get to Jennifer, right? But the blackmailer doesn't know if Kim even told her aunt about the letters."

"Kim said she almost didn't tell her, until she realized Jennifer was also getting threatened," Gabe said.

"Right. So the blackmailer prepares this next letter for Kim, addresses it, stamps it, then realizes that it might be more effective if they just drop it in Jennifer's mailbox with her letter."

"So if Jennifer didn't know before, she will now," Gabe finished.

"Sounds like the blackmailer is getting desperate." Charlotte gestured with the envelope holding Jennifer's letter. "'This is your last warning.'"

"Election Day is this Tuesday," Gabe reminded her. "Makes sense that they'd be desperate by this point."

"Yeah." Charlotte sifted through this new information. She felt like she was adding Jenga pieces to the top of a tower that was being flimsily supported by only one block.

"Let's get out of here," Gabe said, pulling her out of her thoughts. "Too many blackmailers and black bears running around."

Charlotte returned the unaddressed envelope to the mailbox, tucking the one addressed to Kim into the pocket of her sweatshirt. They returned to the car, Gabe tossing the brick into the back seat and grabbing the tote bag.

"Here," he said, tossing her a package of disinfectant wipes. "Clean the scrape on your neck."

"It's not that bad," Charlotte said, ripping open the package anyway.

"Band-Aids." Gabe held up the box he had just removed from the seemingly bottomless bag. "I got dinosaur ones."

"It's not even bleeding," Charlotte said, but obligingly pressed a disinfectant wipe to her neck before un-obligingly yanking it away. "OW."

Gabe grabbed the wipe from her hand. "Let me do it."

Charlotte twisted away from him. "I did it already!"

"You need to wipe it—"

"You think I won't punch you, I'll do it—"

Gabe raised his eyebrows at her. "Is this adult detective behavior, or child detective behavior?"

After a five-second staring/glaring contest, Charlotte rolled her eyes, moving her hair away from her neck. "Fine, do it," she said through clenched teeth.

Gabe gently patted the scrape with the wipe.

"Ow ow ow fuck fucking fuck."

"Aaaand done." He ripped open a Band-Aid and applied it to the scrape. "I gave you the stegosaurus, because you were very brave."

"Thanks," Charlotte grumbled, slouching in her seat.

Gabe snorted.

"Can we go to the middle school?" Charlotte sat back up. "I want to give Kim the letter so we can see what it says."

"Next stop: Frencham Middle," Gabe said, turning on the car.

They drove off, leaving the blackmailers and black bears behind.

⚲

"There it is," Gabe said, staring across the football field that separated Frencham Middle School from Frencham High School. "The old stomping grounds."

Charlotte swung the passenger door shut. "Miss it?"

"Eh, some stuff, sure. Other stuff, not so much." He kicked the driver's door shut. "I'm excited to see *your* old stomping grounds." Gabe hadn't attended Frencham Middle, having moved to Frencham the summer before their freshman year of high school.

They began walking across the parking lot towards the middle school as he continued talking.

"Do they have a hallway named after you or something?" he asked. "Or a trophy case of all the newspaper clippings about you?"

"Nope."

Gabe gave her a confused look. "Not even a photo of you hanging in the main office?"

"There used to be one when I was a student," Charlotte said as they stepped up onto the sidewalk.

"Ha! Knew it."

"It had a note underneath that said, 'Do not allow within three feet of the desk.' Parnell was convinced I was stealing keys. She didn't know the secretary was helping me out."

Gabe laughed. "Why was the secretary helping you?"

"Because I was adorable."

Charlotte remembered how the middle school would seem so different at night when she was a kid. It always felt a little off whenever she'd see that building under a night sky.

This time, she realized as they rounded the corner of the school, it wasn't the time of day that seemed the most off about the school. It was the ambulance parked at the front entrance.

Chapter 8

Go Nuts

"Oh, shit," Gabe said, both of them quickening their paces as they went up the front walk to the doors. "That can't be good."

Inside the school, a handful of adults were standing by the doors, talking amongst themselves. Charlotte slowed to catch a snippet of one of the conversations:

"—rather just donate money. You couldn't pay me to eat anything that's just been sitting out there, made by god-knows-who. That poor woman . . ."

Gabe and Charlotte headed down the hall, past parents and guardians studying their paper maps of the school and standing in lines outside of classrooms. When they reached Lucy's classroom, Charlotte peeked in through the window before opening the door.

The lights were on inside, but no Lucy.

Charlotte's stomach sank. "I don't know where she'd be," she said, frowning.

"She's probably just in the bathroom," Gabe said, sounding like he was pumping extra optimism into his voice in response to her worried expression. "Should we see if Kim—"

"Coming through!"

They turned to see two paramedics rolling a stretcher down the hall as the crowd parted to let them pass. A few people stepped in front of Charlotte and Gabe to clear the way, and Charlotte craned her neck to catch a glimpse of straight brown hair on the stretcher before the paramedics continued down the hall.

"Was that Lucy?" she asked, grabbing Gabe's arm.

Charlotte's worry was clearly cracking his optimism. "I don't know," he said, frowning. "I couldn't see."

They started to follow after the stretcher, pushing their way through the people standing in front of them.

Please, Charlotte thought, *please, please, please*—

"What're you guys doing here?"

Charlotte and Gabe whirled around to see Lucy standing behind them, her brows knit with confusion. Around them, people were returning to studying their maps and standing outside of classrooms.

Gabe threw his arms around Lucy as Charlotte sent out a silent *thank you* to whoever it was she'd been saying *please* to.

"We thought that was you getting wheeled out," Gabe said.

Lucy gave them a confused smile as Gabe released her. "That woman was, like, twenty years older than me."

"We didn't get a good look," Charlotte admitted. "And you weren't in your classroom."

"I went to the bathroom," Lucy said.

Gabe nudged Charlotte. "Told you."

"I was walking back when I saw . . ." Lucy narrowed her eyes at the Band-Aid on Charlotte's neck. "What's that?"

Charlotte touched the bandage. "Nothing. Just got scratched."

"By what?"

"Car door," Gabe offered at the same time as Charlotte answered, "Door frame."

Not convinced, Lucy's eyes darted back and forth between the two of them.

"The car door frame," Charlotte finished. "I scratched my neck getting into the car." She lifted her chin slightly, hoping it made her seem more confident about her incredibly fake story.

But instead of challenging them further, Lucy's face started to crumple. "Are you guys lying to me?" Her voice wavered. "Because a lot is going on right now, and I don't know if I can handle being lied to right now."

Gabe stepped forward. "We're lying," he said, putting out his arms to comfort her. "I'm sor—"

Lucy smacked his arms away. "I *knew it*." The wounded expression immediately vanished from her face.

"I can't believe you fell for that," Charlotte groaned. "There weren't even any tears!"

"What are you lying about?" Lucy demanded as Gabe spluttered defensively. "What happened on the stakeout?"

A smile jumped onto her face as someone walked by, glancing over at them curiously while pulling on a jacket.

"Have a great night!" she called after them, waving. "Get home safe!"

As the person walked away, Lucy gestured for the other two to follow her into her classroom. Once inside, she crossed her arms and raised an eyebrow, waiting.

Charlotte gave Gabe a look that read, *This one's on you.*

"We saw someone drop some letters into Jennifer's mailbox," Gabe said. "So we . . . chased them into the woods."

"Charlotte!" Lucy exclaimed. "You ran after them?"

"Why am I the only one getting yelled at?" Charlotte demanded, gesturing at Gabe. "He went, too!"

"Gabe would follow you halfway around the Earth," Lucy said. "This has *you* written all over it."

Charlotte turned to Gabe, faux-wounded. "Only halfway?"

"You think I can afford to circumnavigate the globe? Solid SAT word. I'm giving that one to myself."

"We couldn't see them very well," Charlotte said to Lucy. "I thought I'd try to get a better look, and they ran."

"Then we saw the bear," Gabe added.

Charlotte swiveled her head to glare at him as Lucy's eyes widened. "Why. Why did you tell her that?"

"I didn't want her to start crying again!"

"She wasn't actually crying the first time—"

"Hey, okay!" Lucy clapped her hands to get their attention. "Let's put a pin in this for now. I need to go tell Kim what happened."

"Did someone get sick from eating something from the bake sale?" Charlotte asked.

Lucy nodded as Gabe stared at Charlotte. "How the *hell* did you know that?" he demanded.

"The people we passed when we first came in," Charlotte said. "One of them was talking about money and eating and 'that poor woman.' And I knew there was a bake sale tonight, because you texted me that Lucy was baking again but that she promised it was for the bake sale and not a breakup coping mechanism. Also, Kim was baking brownies yesterday—"

She paused, realizing. "Did someone get sick from eating Kim's brownies?"

Unfazed, Lucy nodded again.

"How did you know *that?*" Gabe demanded.

Charlotte shrugged. "That one was more of a guess."

"We were told not to make anything with nuts," Lucy said, "but a woman ate one of Kim's brownies and had an allergic reaction."

She reopened the door, and the three of them began walking to Kim's classroom.

"Is the woman okay?" Gabe asked.

"Yeah, thank goodness," Lucy said. "Someone got an EpiPen from the nurse's office. The paramedics came, and now they're taking her to the hospital, just to make sure she's okay."

They stopped at Kim's classroom. Lucy peeked in through the window to make sure there wasn't anyone else inside before pushing the door open.

Kim was sitting at her desk. Her shoulders tensed as she looked up, a nervous expression on her face. Seeing who it was, her shoulders relaxed slightly.

"I heard," she said. "Is she . . ."

"She's going to be fine," Lucy assured her. "I heard she wasn't having too much trouble breathing by the time they started taking her out."

Kim rested her elbows on the desk and covered her face. "What an absolute mess." She dropped her hands. "I was framed."

Charlotte raised her eyebrows. "You think?"

"Well, I know I didn't put nuts in my brownies," Kim said, opening a drawer in her desk and pulling out her purse. She stood, grabbing her coat from where it hung on her chair. "And they seem sure it was *my* brownies that gave her the allergic reaction, so . . . yeah, I think I was framed."

Kim slung her purse over her shoulder as she rounded the desk and walked over to them. Her jaw was tight with anger. "It makes sense, right? Someone's been threatening me to leave the school. Now they're actively trying to get me fired."

"It's definitely possible," Charlotte said. "With Election Day so close, this could just be another example of them stepping up their strategy out of desperation."

"I need to go tell Mrs. Parnell," Kim said, her expression cloudy with apprehension. "I don't want to wait to get an email tomorrow morning."

"We'll go with you to talk to her," Lucy said supportively.

Kim gave her a weak smile. "Thanks."

They left the room and began walking down the hall. As Gabe talked to Kim, clearly trying to lift her spirits, Charlotte fell into step next to Lucy.

"Parnell only trusts you a smidge more than she trusts me," Charlotte said quietly. "You really think she'll take your word for it that this wasn't Kim's fault?"

"Not really," Lucy replied. "But I didn't want her to feel like she's going through this alone."

"Could she really get in trouble for this?"

"I don't know," Lucy said, her tone serious. "I really don't know."

They approached the cafeteria, where a long folding table covered in a green disposable tablecloth sat outside of the doors. Several plastic containers of baked goods were spread across the table, paper labels taped down in front of each one. A large hand-drawn sign hung on the front of the table, reading, BAKE SALE (NO NUTS).

Mrs. Parnell and a younger woman stood behind the table, peeling off labels and putting lids on containers.

"Does that sign say 'Bake Sale, Go Nuts?'" Gabe whispered as they approached the table.

Lucy looked at him sideways. "Where are your glasses?"

Gabe sighed heavily, pulling his glasses out of his pocket and putting them on. "Oh. Got it."

"You were wearing those when you drove us here, right?" Charlotte asked.

"Yeah. I think so. Probably."

"*Probably?*"

Mrs. Parnell looked up as they reached the table, giving Charlotte a suspicious once-over before turning to Kim.

"Mrs. Anderson is going to be okay," she said, her expression stern. "We're packing up now, just to be safe."

"I'm glad she's okay," Kim said. She shook her head. "But . . . I promise you, I didn't put any nuts in those brownies."

"Mistakes happen," Parnell said. "Maybe you accidentally used a nut flour—"

"I didn't!" Kim burst out. Parnell's eyebrows shot up, and Kim cleared her throat. "Sorry," she said in a calmer voice. "I didn't. Someone's trying to set me up."

Charlotte was staring at the other woman at the table, who was watching Kim just as closely. The woman was in her late twenties or early thirties, white, with dark blue eyes and long auburn hair pulled into a high ponytail that fell down her back.

Charlotte couldn't read the serious expression on the woman's face, but there was something examining about it, like the woman was trying to figure Kim out.

"Why would someone want to set you up?" Parnell asked, sounding tired.

Kim opened her mouth, and for a moment Charlotte thought she was going to tell Parnell about the threats. Then her mouth closed. "I don't know," she mumbled.

Charlotte frowned, feeling bad for Kim. She wanted to tell her that she could trust Mrs. Parnell with her worries, but even if Charlotte put aside her bias towards the vice principal, she still didn't know if that would be true.

"Well," Parnell said in a tone that indicated the conversation was coming to a close, "I think that's all there is to be said." She gave Kim one final stern look before returning to cleaning up the table.

Kim paused, as if wanting to ask if she was in trouble.

"Okay, thank you," she finally said, apparently deciding not to push her luck.

Charlotte did a small hand raise. "Where are the brownies?"

Eyes narrowing slightly, Parnell said, "I put them in my office. I didn't want anyone else to accidentally take one in all the chaos."

Charlotte didn't bother asking if she could see them; the answer was already clear in Parnell's eyes.

"Let's go," Lucy said, putting a hand on Kim's arm. "Bye, Mrs. Parnell. Bye, Ellie."

Charlotte's brain whirred as the four of them walked back down the hall. *Ellie . . .*

Gabe beat her to it. "*That's* Ellie?" he asked as soon as they were out of earshot. "The librarian? Dan—" He stopped himself, shooting Kim a worried glance.

"Daniel's girlfriend, yeah," Lucy finished. "It's okay. I told Kim this morning." She grimaced. "I also told her about the old notes Charlotte found in his desk."

"Yeah, that's a little weird," Kim said, frowning. "But if they're happy together, I'm happy for them."

"She might not be so happy about *you*, though," Charlotte said.

"Ellie's a suspect," Gabe explained to Kim, pulling up the list on his phone and showing it to her.

"And she had full access to the brownies," Charlotte added. "I talked to Daniel today, and he got kind of weird when I mentioned bringing up Kim around Ellie. Like she might get upset about it."

"So you think she stuck nuts into the brownies?" Lucy asked.

"Or switched them out with different brownies, something like that, maybe. I wonder if they're in the same container Kim brought." Charlotte slowed as they approached the main office and entrance to the building. "I reeeeaaally wanna break into Parnell's office right now," she said, flexing her fingers.

"You don't have to," Gabe replied, pointing. "The door's open."

Sure enough, while the lights in the main office were out, the door was cracked the tiniest bit, held open by the dead bolt.

"Amazing the things you notice when you wear your glasses," Charlotte commented, quickening her pace.

"Ha ha."

"Kim, you should wait for us outside," Lucy said apprehensively. "You don't need to get into any more trouble tonight."

Kim hesitated, then headed for the doors.

"Keep watch," Lucy said to Gabe. "If someone tries to come in, just do that thing where you ramb—keep them engaged in conversation."

"We all know you were going to say *ramble*," Gabe said drily. He crossed his arms and leaned against the wall. "And for future reference, I prefer the word *monologue*."

Charlotte pulled the door open, letting Lucy pass through before following behind. Leaving the door propped on the dead bolt, they used the dim light coming through the crack to navigate across the room to Parnell's office.

As Lucy pushed on the door, Charlotte suddenly had a thought that probably should have occurred to her sooner: *Why did someone leave the door to the main office propped open?*

Her question was almost immediately answered as the opening door revealed a shadowy figure standing on the other side. Before Charlotte could yell, Lucy swung her leg up and kicked the figure's shoulder, sending the person sprawling to the floor.

"Holy *shit*," Charlotte gasped, pulling Lucy away from the doorway. "That was sick."

"Kickboxing," Lucy said breathlessly. "You should come with me sometime."

"I'm good, thanks."

They both peeked into the room. The figure was still on the floor, groaning. Lucy pushed the door open a little wider to let more light into the room.

Daniel sat up, rubbing his shoulder and wincing.

"What're you doing in here?" Lucy demanded.

"Hey," came a hissed whisper from behind them. Gabe was peeking in through the door. "Everything okay?"

Charlotte shot him a thumbs-up, then waved him away. "Are you here for the brownies?" she asked Daniel.

He picked up his phone, which had fallen beside him, and slowly got to his feet. "Yeah," he said, defeated.

"Why?" Lucy asked. "Were you the one who sabotaged them?"

"No," Daniel hurriedly denied, shaking his head. "I was . . . I was worried Ellie did." He continued, speaking haltingly, "We're . . . dating, and I . . . well, she's been kind of upset about Kim lately, since she's my ex, and when I heard what happened . . . I knew she was working at the bake sale, so I thought maybe . . . I don't know."

"You wanted to get rid of the evidence," Charlotte finished for him.

Daniel shrugged. "I guess, yeah. I mean, it's messed up if she did it, but she's my girlfriend."

"Supportive," Charlotte deadpanned.

"Where are they?" Lucy asked, stepping into the room.

"I don't know. I couldn't find them in the dark. I was about to turn on my flashlight when you guys came in."

Charlotte was already switching on her own phone's flash-light, following Lucy into the room. She spotted a round, plastic container decorated with multicolored cartoon stars sitting on a corner of the desk. "This is it," she said, grabbing it. "Wasn't here earlier today." She opened the box, revealing the brownies as the scent of chocolate hit her nose.

"Here," Lucy said, grabbing a tissue from a box on the desk and handing it to Charlotte. "She won't notice one missing. Let's take it and get out of here."

Charlotte scooped a brownie and wrapped it up in the tissue, then put the lid back on the container and returned it to the desk.

"After you," she said to Daniel, gesturing grandly towards the door.

He paused, glancing at the container of brownies on the desk.

"Hey." Lucy stared at him, shifting her weight to her back foot menacingly. "Get going."

"Okay, okay . . ." Daniel hurried out the door.

Gabe pushed off the wall as the three of them emerged from the office. "God, is there a single dark corner of this planet that's free of a lurking cis man?"

He watched Daniel wordlessly walk away from them, disap-pearing around the corner. "Nowhere is safe. Are you guys okay?"

"Lucy kicked him in the head," Charlotte said proudly.

"It was his shoulder," Lucy corrected modestly as she gave Gabe a low-five. "I don't have the height yet for a head-kick."

"I don't know," Gabe said as they started for the exit. "I feel like you could head-kick a short king if you wanted."

"I would never *want* that!"

They reconvened with Kim outside, filling her and Gabe in under the floodlight that illuminated the front walk of the school.

"Wow," Kim said when they were done. "I mean, Daniel's loyalty was always nice when we were dating, but kind of sucks for me now."

"He wasn't *that* loyal," Gabe pointed out. "It only took one kick from Luce to make him throw his girlfriend under the bus."

Charlotte unwrapped the brownie, sniffing it. "Huh."

"What?" Lucy asked.

Handing her the baked good, Charlotte said, "What do you smell?"

Lucy sniffed. "Chocolate. And . . . almonds?"

"*Cyanide?*" Gabe gasped.

Charlotte gave him A Look. "No. Almonds."

"Oh. That makes more sense."

"I know I sound like a broken record by now," Kim said, "but I didn't put almonds in my brownies."

"Well, there are almonds baked into them," Lucy said, breaking the brownie apart with her fingers. She held up an almond slice. "Someone must've switched yours out with these."

"Did you bring them in a container with cartoon stars on it?" Charlotte asked Kim.

"Yeah."

"So the culprit didn't just swap containers," Charlotte mused. "They had to switch out all the brownies, which would've taken a little more time."

She retrieved the brownie from Lucy, examining the broken, crumbly mess for hidden answers to their questions. "Was that the only almond you found, Luce?"

"Yeah."

"Strange," Charlotte said, her mind racing. "If their goal was to get Kim in trouble, you'd think they'd have wanted to add as many as possible to increase the chances of the nuts being discovered. Why was there only one slice in that whole brownie?"

"Maybe they really wanted someone to get sick," Lucy suggested. "So they only put in a sprinkling of almonds to keep anyone from noticing before eating it."

"Who knew what you were bringing to the bake sale?" Gabe asked Kim.

Kim frowned. "There was a sign-up spreadsheet sent out to staff and parents. Everyone had access to it."

"Great," Charlotte said. "That narrows down the list."

"They could've killed someone," Lucy said quietly.

The group fell silent as that statement sank in. Someone wanted Kim gone. And they were willing to risk lives to make it happen.

Charlotte's brain was starting to feel fried in a way that could only be fixed with food or sleep. She was too wired to sleep. "I need a milkshake," she declared, wrapping up the brownie. "And dinner. In that order."

"I'm down to dine," Gabe said.

"Join us?" Lucy asked Kim.

The other teacher shook her head, her eyes dimming with exhaustion. "I need to go home and take a long shower."

As Charlotte slipped the brownie into her sweatshirt pocket, her hand hit paper. "Oh, shit, I forgot." She removed the envelope, handing it to Kim. "We saw someone drop two envelopes into Jennifer's mailbox. Couldn't get a good look at the person besides what they were wearing."

"There was a letter for your aunt with that one," Gabe added, pursing his lips at the envelope in Kim's hands.

Kim's brow furrowed. "Why would they leave this at my aunt's?"

"I'm thinking possibly to make sure she knows that you're also being threatened," Charlotte said. "In case you didn't tell her."

"Oh." Kim flipped the envelope over in her hands, starting

to rip it open. "That makes sense." She pulled out the letter and scanned it before handing it to Charlotte, her expression somber. Lucy and Gabe leaned in as they all read:

> *Leave the school and tell your aunt to stop running for the BOE.*
> *Do it soon, or I'll tell them it's you.*

"It's basically the same message as the last one," Gabe commented, holding the letter up to the ceiling lights as if they might reveal a secret message. He was sitting next to Lucy in a padded booth at their favorite diner. Charlotte sat across from them, arms folded on the table, her chin resting on top.

"It *is* the first time the person's actually mentioned Jennifer in a letter to Kim," she pointed out. "That's new."

"Maybe they're worried the message hasn't been getting through," Lucy suggested as Gabe lowered the letter, abandoning his quest to find a hidden message. "That Kim's being threatened because of Jennifer, I mean."

"But it can't be *just* because of Jennifer, right?" Charlotte asked. "The person is telling Kim to leave the school, whether or not Jennifer drops out of the election."

"And there still isn't a suspect who has an apparent motive against both of them," Lucy said. "So what does that mean?"

"We're missing a suspect?" Gabe suggested.

"Or a motive," Charlotte said. She took the letter from Gabe, reading it again.

"'I'll tell them it's you,'" she read. "What does that mean?"

"I assumed it meant they'll tell people about Kim's old job," Lucy said.

"But why phrase it like that?" Charlotte pressed. "Who's 'them'? Why 'it's you' and not 'that you were a sex worker' or something like that?"

"Are we doing edits on the anonymous letters now?" Gabe asked. "If so, I'd like to suggest a more threatening font. Something with 'gothic' in the name, maybe."

"It's just weird wording," Charlotte said. She dropped the letter onto the table and sat back in her seat, chewing on the inside of her cheek.

"I know that face," Maggie said, stopping by their table. Maggie was the diner's manager, and had known Charlotte since before she knew the word "blackmail."

"Is it my 'I need a milkshake' face?" Charlotte said wearily.

Maggie chuckled. "Should be coming out soon," she said. "Rest of the food, too."

They thanked her, and she shot Charlotte a look that read, *Take it easy*, before continuing past them.

As Lucy and Gabe continued talking, Charlotte took the opportunity to have another therapist-mandated emotional check-in.

Charlotte Illes Feelings Check-In
—Tired

That was pretty much a constant state for her lately.

—Confused

There was something important missing from this case; she was sure of it. She just couldn't figure out what.

—Frustrated

She hated that she couldn't figure out what.

There was a lull in Lucy and Gabe's conversation, the silence bringing Charlotte back to Earth. As her surroundings came back into focus, she noticed something strange: Lucy's phone, sitting face down on the table.

"Are you hiding something on your phone?" Charlotte asked.

Lucy's hand automatically moved to the device. "What? No. Why?"

"You never put your phone face down unless you're hiding something, because you don't like making people wait for a response if they text you." The last time Charlotte had seen Lucy put her phone face down was when her friends were trying to plan a surprise party for Charlotte's twenty-third birthday. (She pretended to be surprised. No one believed her.)

"That's not entirely true," Lucy argued. "Sometimes my cousins in Puerto Rico will start spamming our group chat with memes, and I don't want to get distracted by the notifications."

"Is that what's happening now?" Charlotte asked.

Lucy waited a beat too long before replying, ". . . Yes."

"What are you hiding?" Gabe whispered, staring at Lucy's phone.

Lucy rolled her eyes. "I'm not hiding. I'm . . . avoiding." She flipped the phone over and slid it across the table. Charlotte read the text notifications from a contact named "DON'T TEXT!!!!!"

"Jake's been texting you?" Considering how erratic Lucy's post-breakup stages had been, getting a text from her ex was definitely not ideal for her already-turbulent healing process.

Gabe gasped, spinning the phone around so he could see the screen. "What's he saying?"

"He just texted me earlier to see how I'm doing," Lucy said, resting her chin in her hand.

"Didn't you tell him you needed space?" Gabe asked. "And that Charlotte was gonna go to his place and break his phone if he didn't stop texting you?"

"Well, first off, I didn't tell him the second part," Lucy said. She ignored Charlotte's indignant gasp and added, "It's been a few months. I guess he figured it's safe to say hi."

"He wouldn't feel so safe if you had told him the second part," Charlotte grumbled.

Gabe had unlocked Lucy's phone and was scrolling through the messages. "Luce! You've been *replying?*"

Lucy snatched her phone away. "I'm not trying to get back with him!" she said, sounding annoyed. "He's just being nice. I can't not reply to him."

"You can," Gabe said. "Easily."

"But you won't," Charlotte added, "because you're too nice and would rather protect his feelings than risk upsetting him by not replying. Because *you care too much about what other people think of you.*"

"Yeah, yeah, I know," Lucy said before Charlotte had even finished her sentence. She grabbed her phone from Gabe as Charlotte frowned.

She could understand Lucy wanting the good opinion of her mentor, but wished her friend could at least bring herself to not care about what her ex thought of her. *Charlotte* certainly didn't care about what Jake thought of her, which was why she briefly contemplated following through with her phone-breaking threat, despite that message never being delivered.

"So are you gonna text him back?" Gabe asked.

Lucy paused, staring at the table. "Probably," she said.

Charlotte and Gabe both groaned.

"Okay, I don't need this right now." Lucy slid out of the booth. "I need to use the bathroom."

They watched her walk away in the direction of the restrooms.

"Did we push her too hard?" Gabe asked.

"I don't know." Charlotte drummed her fingers on the tabletop. "She can knock a full-grown man to the ground with one kick, but can't stand the idea of her ex-boyfriend being upset with her. Or her mentor saying she's disappointed in her."

"She said *what?*" Gabe wrinkled his nose. "No wonder she's on edge."

"We should probably just lay off," Charlotte said.

Gabe tapped a finger on his chin. "Or . . . I can secretly block Jake's number on her phone so she doesn't get any more of his texts."

"I feel like that might be crossing a boundary, but we can keep it in mind."

Their waiter brought over their food, and Charlotte reached over her veggie wrap to take a big sip of milkshake.

"So where are we at with the suspects?" Gabe took the small cup of coleslaw that sat by his sandwich and put it next to Lucy's burger. "What exactly happened when you talked to Daniel today? Earlier today, I mean, not when you caught him brown-handed."

Charlotte cocked her head questioningly.

"Like, red-handed, but with brownies," Gabe explained. He waved a hand. "Never mind, move past it."

Charlotte removed the half pickle from her plate and deposited it onto Gabe's. "He didn't seem to have anything against Kim. Honestly, he seemed almost happy when I told him Kim had called him a good guy."

"But you said he got weird when you mentioned Ellie."

"Yeah. I said I'd tell her Kim sent me, and he got all stammer-y and said to tell Ellie that *he* sent me. Like he didn't want me mentioning Kim to her."

"Which makes sense," Lucy said, reappearing and sliding back into the booth. "He told us in Parnell's office that Ellie's unhappy with Kim because she's Daniel's ex." She grabbed a fry from her plate and dipped it into the coleslaw.

"If he's keeping those old notes from Kim in his desk," Charlotte said, "that might mean he's still hung up on her. Maybe Ellie knows about it."

"So confirmed: Ellie doesn't like Kim." Gabe pulled out his phone and proceeded to move Ellie's name to the top of his suspect list.

"Parnell also had access to the brownies," Charlotte said as

Lucy peeled the onion slice off of her burger and dropped it onto Charlotte's plate. "And she had that weird reaction when I mentioned Kim to her earlier today."

"But remember, you went into Full Interrogation Mode when you brought up Kim." Lucy pointed a fry at Charlotte. "So she might've just been reacting to that."

"Parnell also didn't really seem to care whether Jennifer gets reelected or not," Charlotte said. "She told us she's up for a new job that would require board approval, but doesn't seem worried that Jennifer hates her guts."

"Maybe she was just putting on a brave face," Gabe said. "Or she knows she can still get the votes without Jennifer."

"She *did* say the rest of the board likes her." Charlotte took a bite of her veggie wrap, chewing thoughtfully. "But she also knows me. And she knows Lucy's close with Kim. If she suspects we're investigating this, she could've been trying to downplay her motive to throw us off the scent."

"The facts are," Lucy said, "that Ellie and Parnell were the only ones with easy access to the brownies all evening."

"And Ellie seems like the biggest suspect right now," Gabe added. "We should probably talk to her tomorrow."

"We?" Charlotte asked.

Gabe put his arms in the air, grinning. "I'm coming to school!"

"Guest speaker," Lucy reminded Charlotte, picking up the ketchup bottle and shaking it. "He promised to focus more on the dangers of online parasocial relationships and protecting your privacy than about all the free stuff you can get as an influencer."

"Five minutes," Gabe said. "I have five whole minutes to talk about the free stuff."

"Are you prepared to talk to a bunch of middle schoolers?" Charlotte asked.

"Pfft," Gabe said confidently. "I get along great with tweens. I went through puberty twice, so I can really relate to the turmoil of emotions and hormones they're dealing with."

"Oh, frick," Lucy said as ketchup sprayed across her plate. "Did you guys talk about any of the other suspects while I was in the bathroom?"

"Just Parnell and Ellie." Charlotte handed her a napkin. "Daniel seems less likely, currently."

"What about the dude from the Board of Ed?" Gabe asked.

"Vincent Welles. If we're stretching the imagination, he could've gotten his hands on the bake sale sign-up list and snuck into the school tonight. Or sent someone to plant the nuts for him. What else do we know about him?"

"Not sure the best way to figure out his deal," Charlotte said. "I looked him up earlier today and couldn't find much. Just stuff about him running for reelection and his email address."

"What if we hacked into his email?" Gabe suggested, his eyes widening with excitement. "We could see if he's talking shit about Jennifer. Maybe we'll get lucky and see that he emailed someone his entire blackmail plan."

"Unlikely." Charlotte thought for a moment. "That could be interesting, though."

"How're you going to hack into his email?" Lucy asked. "You can't even log into your old Facebook account."

"How am I supposed to remember what my answer was for 'What's your favorite song?'" Charlotte asked, frustrated. "I set those security questions when I was fourteen!"

"Honestly, you're better off without it," Gabe said, taking a bite of his sandwich.

"Anyway, *I* wouldn't be doing the hacking," Charlotte continued.

Lucy looked at her questioningly. "Then who's doing the hacking?"

Chapter 9

Phish Fear Me

"If the FBI agent in my laptop is listening," Olivia said, "I am not hacking this man's email. We're all just joking around. Ha. Ha ha."

Gabe, Charlotte, and Lucy were bunched together on Gabe and Lucy's couch in front of the laptop resting on Charlotte's thighs. On the other end of the video call was Olivia Kimura, Charlotte's brother's girlfriend.

Olivia was twenty-seven years old, Japanese American, with fair skin and thick, wavy black hair that had been pulled into a messy bun on top of her head. Her dark brown eyes were partially hidden behind the reflection in the lens of her blue-light glasses.

"Honestly," Charlotte said, "I feel like there should be a less severe word for it when you're not stealing someone's info or locking them out of their account."

"Peeking," Gabe suggested. "We're just taking a peek at his email."

"Technically, right now she's phishing," came Landon Illes's voice from off-screen. "Which, if successful, will give her unauthorized access to data in a system or computer, which is the literal definition of hacking."

"Did you just Google the definition of 'hacking'?" Gabe asked.

There was a pause, then an unconvincing, ". . . No."

"I thought you said you didn't want to be involved," Charlotte said flatly. "Go away."

Landon's face came into view over Olivia's shoulder. Charlotte's older brother was twenty-eight, three years older than her. He had the same wavy, dark brown hair that could be coaxed into curls when he wasn't constantly running his hand through it, and blue eyes he inherited from their father.

"You've already made me an accessory by telling me what you're doing," Landon said pointedly.

"I didn't tell you what we're doing. I told Olivia what we're doing, and she told you, because you guys 'tell each other everything' or whatever."

"*I* made you an accessory, sorry, darling," Olivia said, reading something on the screen before resuming her typing.

"I'm surprised you're enabling this behavior, Lucy," Landon said, resting his arms on the back of Olivia's chair.

"I'm just not stopping them," Lucy replied. "That doesn't mean I'm *enabling* them."

"We're literally using your laptop right now," Gabe pointed out.

Lucy shushed him.

Olivia had finished typing and was reading something on her screen, mumbling to herself as she read. She tapped Landon's arm. "Does that look good?"

Landon slapped a hand over his eyes. "I'm not getting involved."

"SO GO AWAY," Charlotte yelled at the laptop.

"Okay, I sent it," Olivia said. "I can't say how long it'll take for him to respond. If he even responds, which he might not."

"Is this guy your main suspect?" Landon asked, uncovering his eyes.

"Not really," Charlotte admitted. "We just don't have any information on him, so this seemed like a way to get it. He definitely has a motive."

"You said he's also running for the Board of Ed?" Olivia asked.

"Yeah, and Jennifer thinks he wants to be president, but she's confident she'll get picked for it again."

"Is it really that serious?" Olivia posed. "I mean, is a Board of Education position worth threatening someone over?"

"Not to mention how they could've killed someone with those brownies," Landon added.

"Jennifer seems to take her job pretty seriously," Charlotte said. "If this guy Welles takes it even half as seriously as she does, I think he could possibly do those things."

"Plus," Lucy said, "as someone whose job is directly impacted by the decisions made by the Board of Ed, I'd say having power over what can and can't be taught in schools is a pretty big deal."

"But we still don't know why he would also involve Kim, Jennifer's niece," Gabe finished.

Olivia sat back in her chair. "Maybe he's just petty and wants the whole family gone."

"Or maybe he has some connection to Kim," Landon suggested, sounding intrigued despite his efforts to remain uninvolved. "Some reason to want her—"

"HOLY SHIT," Gabe yelled, leaping to his feet as Charlotte and Lucy both jumped at the sudden outburst. "I just cracked this case wide open."

"Want to share with the class?" Charlotte raised her eyebrows. A little part of her feared for her ego if Gabe had indeed solved the mystery before she did.

Putting her ego aside, she turned the laptop around so Olivia and Landon could watch as Gabe began his explanation.

"Welles's motive for threatening Jennifer is clear," he began, pacing across the room. "He wants that president spot, but likely won't get it if Jennifer gets reelected."

He paused, making sure he was still in frame on the video call, before pivoting and pacing in the other direction.

"The big question is, why does he want Kim gone?" he asked. "And how does he know that she danced at a strip club in college?"

Gabe stopped to face them.

"Because *he went*—"

He paused, taking a step to his right to center himself in frame. Starting again, he declared, "Because *he went to the strip club.*"

Charlotte pursed her lips, thinking. "It's not a bad theory," she said after a moment.

"Oh, come *on!*" Gabe threw his arms out, insistent. "Give me more than that. It makes perfect sense! He probably doesn't want his wife to know he went to a strip club, and he's worried Kim will tell someone."

"But this is her fourth year teaching in Frencham," Lucy pointed out. "Why did it take him this long to freak out about it?"

Gabe snapped his fingers, pointing at her. "Maybe he just found out about her recently!"

"The board has to approve all teacher hires," Lucy countered. "He was on the board when Kim was hired. Did he not realize who she was back then?"

"I don't *know.*" Gabe slumped dramatically, trudging back to the couch. He sat down heavily next to Charlotte. "Why do I have to do all the work?" he grumbled.

Charlotte patted his knee reassuringly. "It's still a solid theory," she said. "One of the most annoying things about being a detective is trying to figure out why someone did something, knowing that sometimes people just do dumb shit for no good reason."

"So maybe"—as Landon spoke, Charlotte turned the laptop back around—"he's been worried about Kim exposing him for a while, and finally just decided to do something about it."

"Right," Charlotte said. "No good reason other than reaching the end of his rope."

"No reason, just vibes." Gabe sighed. "Well, that's my theory. If I end up being right, I want full credit. If I'm wrong, we never speak of this again."

"Holy shit, he replied," Olivia said.

Charlotte was shocked. Not that she didn't have faith in Olivia—she just knew it was best to keep expectations low, especially with wild plans like this one.

"I've got the log-in info," Olivia continued as Landon watched over her shoulder, apparently having abandoned all attempts to distance himself from the operation.

"She's gonna say the thing," Gabe whispered excitedly, grabbing onto Charlotte's arm and shaking.

"Okay," Olivia said, "I have access to his email. What're we looking for?"

"Aw, man." Gabe slumped, disappointed. "I thought she was going to say, 'I'm in.' That's what that hacker always says in the movies."

"Oh, sorry." Olivia cleared her throat. "I'm in."

Charlotte leaned closer to the laptop as Gabe laughed quietly to himself. "Can you search for any mentions of Jennifer?"

There was a pause as Olivia typed for a moment. "A ton of hits," she finally said. "Might need to narrow that search."

"Hm." Charlotte tapped her pointer finger on the laptop, thinking.

"Can you search in the Sent Mail folder?" Gabe suggested.

There was another pause, longer this time.

"Wait, go back to that one," Landon said suddenly.

"What?" Charlotte asked eagerly. "What is it?"

"*Hi, Marie,*" Olivia read out loud. "*Thank you for your kind words. Hopefully I'll be reelected to the Board of Education so we can continue doing good work. I appreciate your vote, and encourage you to reelect Dola Adesina and Jennifer Falcone as well.*" She paused. "There's more, but that's the meat of it."

Lucy looked over at them, confused. "He's encouraging people to vote for her?"

"Twist," Gabe said.

"Didn't Jennifer tell you guys he hated her?" Landon asked.

Charlotte's brow furrowed. "She seemed pretty convinced he didn't like her."

"She said it 'killed him' that she had more responsibilities than he did," Lucy added. "He doesn't sound too agonized, though."

"There's a bunch of mentions of her like this," Olivia said, her eyes darting back and forth as she skimmed what was on her screen. "No sign of him showing any dislike for her."

"Weird," Charlotte said.

"Maybe she's just paranoid," Lucy suggested. "It did seem like she takes this stuff way more seriously than anyone else would."

"Olivia," Charlotte said, "can you search for 'Kim'?"

Another pause. "A couple mentions of a woman named Kimberly Reynolds?"

"Hm. Different Kim."

"Yeah, that's all. Sorry."

"Don't apologize," Lucy said, looking over at Charlotte. "I mean, this tells us something, right? Welles is probably off the suspect list."

"Seems like it," Charlotte agreed. "Thanks, Olivia. This was really helpful."

Olivia saluted. "Anything to help." She turned to Landon. "See? That wasn't so bad."

Landon pointed at the screen. "Can you log out? The longer you're in there, the more anxious it's making me."

"Okay," Olivia said, facing the camera again, "we're gonna go. See you tomorrow for dinner!"

After saying their goodbyes and hanging up, Charlotte closed the laptop, feeling discouraged. "Crossing suspects off the list isn't as satisfying as getting more evidence against a suspect."

"Better than getting nothing," Lucy commented, standing.

"I'm going to get some sheets to make up the couch." After leaving the diner, Charlotte had stopped by her house to pack an overnight bag, not knowing how long the infiltration of Welles's email was going to take.

"Olivia just reminded me," Charlotte said, turning to Gabe, "do you want to come over for Shabbat dinner tomorrow? Lucy's busy."

"Sure!" Gabe said brightly. "Love an Illes family dinner."

"Hopefully I'll be able to stay awake for it," Charlotte said, yawning.

Gabe pulled out his phone. "So the top suspect right now is Ellie," he said, referencing his suspect list. "Then . . . Parnell?"

"Are you *ranking* the suspects?" Charlotte squinted at his phone.

"I mean . . . yeah. What else am I supposed to do, put them in a bracket?" Gabe pointed at an imaginary bracket in the air in front of them. "Ellie versus Daniel, Parnell versus Welles . . ."

"Up," Lucy said, returning with an armful of sheets. Gabe and Charlotte obediently removed themselves from the couch.

"I'm fine with just a blanket," Charlotte said, stepping in to help Lucy put a fitted sheet over the couch cushions.

"Absolutely not. You need a good night's sleep—big day of sleuthing tomorrow." Lucy began unfolding the top sheet.

Charlotte yawned again. "Right now I think I could fall asleep on a rock. I'm gonna pass out before you can say, 'Wait, don't fall asleep, you haven't brushed your teeth yet.'"

"You brushed your teeth before we called Olivia," Lucy reminded her.

Charlotte spread her hands. "See? Didn't even remember. I'm exhausted."

"So, tomorrow," Gabe said, clearly having more energy than the other two as he walked around the room. "Are we talking to Ellie?"

"Yeah." Charlotte took the sheet from Lucy and tossed it messily over the couch. "I've been subbing for the same teacher, so Lucy and I share a lunch period. We can go then."

She mentally scrolled through their list of suspects. "As much as I hate to say it, I think I need to talk to Parnell again. She also had the opportunity to sabotage Kim's brownies, and I'm still not convinced that she doesn't feel threatened by Jennifer." She sat back down on the couch. "If anything, maybe we can find conflicting details between her and Ellie's stories."

"I'm getting ready for bed," Lucy said. She raised her eyebrows at Gabe. "You're probably going to want to go to sleep soon. You're not used to waking up early."

"Ohhh." Charlotte chuckled. "You're gonna be *wrecked* tomorrow."

"Pshh," Gabe said, making a face. "I'll be fine." He rubbed his hands together. "I'll be wide-awake, keeping an eye out for blue sneakers."

Charlotte stared at him. "Why blue sneakers?"

"Because—" He stopped. "Wait. You didn't see?"

Quick to the draw despite her exhaustion, Charlotte said, "Did the person at Jennifer's house have blue sneakers?"

"Yes!" Gabe seemed shocked that she didn't know this. "I thought you said you saw what they were wearing!"

"I did, but I didn't notice their shoes! How did you see that?"

"It was when we were running after them. You were busy tripping over everything."

"You tripped too!"

"Fine," Gabe said. "Can we go back to my incredible observation?"

"Yes. Oh my god!"

"Oh my *god!*"

"Oh my god," Lucy deadpanned. "Now he's never gonna fall asleep." She gestured at Gabe. "Look at him. He's practically vibrating."

Gabe was bouncing on the balls of his feet. "I don't know what you're talking about. I'm super calm and chill." He crossed his arms, clearly pleased with himself. "And also apparently an in*credible* detective."

He leapt across the room to receive a high five from Charlotte, who made a mental note to remember the new "blue sneakers" clue as her friends left the room to get ready for bed. This was the kind of progress she liked: a capital-c Clue.

Charlotte thought more about that as she changed into a soft T-shirt and pajama pants. She hadn't solved many cases as an adult, but was already noticing how few capital-c Clues there seemed to be. Somehow, things were more clear-cut when she was a kid. There was always a telltale stain on someone's shirt, or a significant scent at the scene of the crime. No one disguised their handwriting back then! If someone wrote an anonymous note, all you had to do was get a copy of their social studies homework, and they were caught.

But mystery-solving had gotten harder. And Charlotte wasn't sure if it was because the mysteries had changed, or if she had.

I have changed, she thought, lying down on the couch. *So what if I'm not solving mysteries in a day anymore? I'm not getting in trouble nearly as much as I used to. I'm going on a lot less wild-goose chases.*

She thought about the literal chase through the woods earlier that evening.

Okay, yes. That was a lapse in judgment. But for the most part, I'm different. I'm better.

Knowing that it was probably a great time for an emotional check-in, she instead grabbed her phone from her bag. Lying back down, she opened her email and saw a new message from Mita:

Charlotte,

Wanted to update you: my client's husband has agreed to settle. Couldn't have done it without your help. I owe you dinner sometime.

Best,
Mita

"What does 'I owe you dinner sometime' mean?" Charlotte asked, standing in the bathroom doorway thirty seconds later as Gabe brushed his teeth. "Is that just one of those things people say? Like, is she asking if I want to get dinner with her, or is she just being polite? You know how when people are like, 'How are you?' but they don't expect you to actually go into detail about how you are—"

Gabe spit toothpaste into the sink. "If she didn't want to get dinner with you, she could've just said thanks. Or sent you a gift card, or an edible arrangement or something." He turned the sink on. "Also, people don't casually say, 'I owe you dinner.' It's always 'coffee' or 'drinks.'"

"So you're saying she actually wants to get dinner with me."

"Yes."

"To . . . thank me?"

"Yes, and also probably because she thinks you're hot." Gabe turned off the sink.

Charlotte wrinkled her nose. "I don't think we have enough evidence to prove that."

"This isn't a *case*, wacko. I'm telling you as an expert in this kind of stuff: she's asking you out."

"Hm." Charlotte mulled that over for a moment. "I need a second opinion."

"She's gonna say the same thing!" Gabe called after her as Charlotte headed for Lucy's room. "Lucy! Tell Charlotte people think she's hot!"

Charlotte knocked on Lucy's door. "Are you asleep already? I need a second opinion."

"Come in," came a muffled reply.

The lights were still on in the room as Charlotte entered. Lucy was lying horizontally across her bed, holding a pillow over her face as her phone glowed on the comforter next to her.

"Sorry," Charlotte said, hovering in the doorway. "Is this a new pre-sleep ritual, or . . ."

"No." Lucy released the pillow with one hand to point in the general direction of where her phone sat.

"Is it Jake again?" Charlotte crossed the room to pick up the phone, skimming the email displayed on the screen. "*Dear Miss Ortega and Miss Romano blah blah blah . . . just wanted to inform you as a professional courtesy . . . she was concerned about her youngest's progress . . . I offered to facilitate a transfer to put the student in a learning environment better suited for his needs . . . Ramona Hernández.*"

Oy vey.

She looked down at Lucy—or, more accurately, the pillow that still covered Lucy's face. "Mrs. Hernández convinced a parent to transfer their kid out of your class?"

Lucy screamed into the pillow.

"Oh, okay, wow." Charlotte locked the phone and returned it to the bed. "We should all stop checking our emails right before bed. I think that'd be better for everyone."

"What's happening?" Gabe appeared in the doorway. "I heard the scream of someone losing it."

Charlotte pointed at Lucy.

Gabe blinked. "Honestly? Thought it was you."

"That's fair."

Lucy screamed again.

This is going to be a tough one, Charlotte thought, tugging at the pillow. "Can you let go? You're gonna suffocate yourself."

Reluctantly, Lucy allowed the pillow to be pulled away from her face, her expression furious as she stared at the ceiling.

"What happened?" Gabe repeated.

"Mrs. Hernández had a conference with a parent who has another kid in one of my classes," Lucy said, voice cold. "She said they were concerned about the student's progress, so she told them to have the student transferred out of my class."

"Can she do that?" Gabe asked.

"Guess so," Lucy said sharply, sitting up and rubbing her face with her hands. "I'm just so *tired*. I can't win with her. It's like she has it in for me."

"Well, you and . . ." Charlotte trailed off.

"Me and Kim." Lucy's eyebrows raised slightly. "Do you think . . . ?"

"Wait, I left the suspect list in my room!" Gabe dashed out, his voice fading as he ran. "I thought we were done for the night!"

"I don't know," Charlotte said. "Why would she threaten Kim with the letters and not you?"

"Maybe she thought she already had access to me, as my mentor," Lucy said slowly. Her expression had morphed from angry to thoughtful. "I mean, it sure *feels* like she's trying to get me to quit."

"She probably also wouldn't have any information about you to blackmail with," Charlotte added. "But there's also the recurring issue: she only has a motive for threatening Kim, not Jennifer."

Gabe rushed back into the room, holding his phone. "Oh. Are we not adding her to the list?"

"No, add her," Lucy said, picking up her phone and rolling over to put it on her bedside table. "Might as well."

The whisper of a memory tickled the back of Charlotte's mind.

"Hang on," she said, closing her eyes as she tried to remember. "Luce. Do you remember what Parnell said about the principal job?"

"Um," she heard Lucy say, "just that she was confident she'd get it, because enough people on the board like her."

"But she told us not to talk about it." Charlotte opened her eyes. "Why?"

"Because"—Lucy furrowed her brow, also trying to remember—"it's not official yet?"

"And she said there are a couple other teachers who are also applying for the job," Charlotte said. "Could Mrs. Hernández be one of them?"

Lucy bit her lip, thinking. "It's possible. She's definitely authoritative enough to go for the position."

"Wait, but does Jennifer have anything against Mrs. Hernández?" Gabe asked. "Wasn't that the whole reason why Parnell's a suspect, because she'd want Jennifer out of the way so she can get that principal job? Why would Mrs. Hernández want Jennifer gone?"

"Hm." Charlotte pursed her lips, trying to think. After a moment, she stopped trying. "Nope, that's all I got. My brain is done for the night."

"Yeah, bedtime," Lucy agreed, falling back onto her bed.

"Nobody check their phones," Gabe said, backing out of the room as Charlotte followed him out. "We don't have time for any more late-night emotional torment."

Charlotte settled back onto the couch. Against Gabe's warning, she picked up her phone and read Mita's email one more time, then marked it as unread so she'd remember to reply the next day.

As she was about to put the phone down, a text popped up in the "hot dog dudes" group chat:

> **Gabe: good niiiight**
> **Lucy: Night my loves**
> **Gabe: THIS WAS A TEST AND YOU FAILED**
> **Gabe: PUT THE PHONE AWAY**
> **Lucy:** 😕
> **Charlotte: yeah Lucy, come on**
> **Gabe: you too Illes**
> **Charlotte:** 😕

Chapter 10

Madam Librarian

The juxtaposition of late-night Gabe and early morning Gabe was startling.

"This isn't natural," he moaned, his head resting on the kitchen table, one arm slung over his eyes. "No person should be awake this early."

He gestured weakly towards the window. "The sun's not even out. Legally, if the sun's not out, the guns can't go out."

Charlotte, who had grown slightly more accustomed to this early schedule, took a sip of the smoothie Lucy had made for her. "You'll get used to it."

"Really?"

"No."

"C'mon, perk up," Lucy said, pushing Gabe's mug of coffee towards him. "I have to do this every day, and today's not even a full day of school. You can survive five hours."

Gabe took a long gulp of coffee in response.

Charlotte stared at her phone, which was sitting on the table in front of her, displaying the unanswered email from Mita. She wanted someone to notice it and bring it up, since she never got a resolution to her dilemma the night before, but she didn't want her friends to know that she cared enough to talk about it.

She continued staring at the phone as Gabe put down his mug with a *clunk*.

"It's honestly insane that they make kids get up this early to go to school," he said, shaking his head. "*My* brain doesn't even fully wake up until eleven, and I'm a whole adult. Their brains aren't developed enough to handle a nine a.m. quiz!"

Lucy hummed in agreement, clearly not hearing anything she hadn't heard or thought of before. Charlotte began to increase the brightness on her phone as Gabe continued to talk.

"Not to mention all those sports kids who get up at, like, four a.m. to go to practice." Gabe's indignation appeared to be waking him up more. Either that, or the caffeine was starting to hit. "It's horrible!"

"I feel like 'horrible' is a strong word," Lucy said as Charlotte gently pushed her phone towards the center of the table. "But it's rough seeing kids falling asleep in the middle of class."

She looked over at Charlotte. "Okay, what are you doing?"

Charlotte glanced up from the phone, which by that point had been pushed almost an arm's length away from her. "Hm? I'm just checking my email."

Lucy raised an eyebrow. "Did you develop sudden farsightedness?"

"I don't know what you mean," Charlotte said, feigning innocence as she pulled the phone back towards her.

Lucy gave her A Look. "You know how you just said last night that I always keep my phone face up?"

"Yeah."

"You always keep your phone face down. Unless you're trying to get us to notice something on it."

Charlotte tried to sound dismayed at the accusation. "That's not tr—"

"Ohhh." Gabe peered at the screen. "It's the email from Mita."

Charlotte snatched the phone away, secretly pleased they were now talking about this. "That's my private correspondence."

"You still haven't replied to her?" Gabe turned to Lucy, who had a confused expression on her face. "Mita asked Charlotte out."

"WHAT?" Lucy shrieked. "WHEN?"

"Last night," Charlotte said, wincing at Lucy's shriek. "We got distracted by the Hernández email. And she didn't ask me out; she just said that she owes me dinner for helping with her case."

"*Dinner?*" Lucy sounded impressed. "That's real. She could've just said drinks."

"That's what I said!" Gabe exclaimed.

"Okay, so"—Charlotte tried to sound casual—"what should I reply? I mean, I'm sure she was just saying it to be nice. I'm not gonna, like, name a time and place. That's weird." She paused. "Right?"

"Definitely play it cool," Gabe advised. "Just say something like, 'Happy to help. Dinner sounds great. I love eating out. Winky face.'"

"Not helpful," Lucy said sternly as Charlotte groaned and buried her face in her arms.

Gabe cackled. "Okay, okay, sorry. Couldn't help it."

"I'm just gonna say, 'Happy to help,' and leave it there," Charlotte said, her voice muffled by her arms.

"No!" Lucy exclaimed. "She'll think you're not interested. And I know you're interested, so don't even start with me."

"Fine." Charlotte lifted her head. "What do I say?"

Lucy thought for a moment. "'Happy to help,'" she dictated. "'Dinner sounds great. Let me know when you're free.'"

"Hm." Charlotte rolled the message over in her head, searching for faults. "Okay. That's good."

"'P.S. . . .'" Gabe started, a mischievous smile on his face.

"No!" Lucy and Charlotte said in unison as the latter picked up her phone and began to type.

"Oh no," she said a moment later. "How do I sign off?"

"'I've loved you since high school'?" Gabe suggested cheerfully, preemptively ducking as Charlotte looked around for something to throw at him.

"Just do a hyphen and 'Charlotte,'" Lucy said.

"That's good, that's good," Charlotte murmured as she typed it in. She hit the send button and locked her phone, putting it face down on the table.

"You sent it?" Lucy asked, appalled. "You didn't want to read it through first?"

Charlotte shook her head. "I would've talked myself out of sending it." She looked up at Lucy, concerned. "Why? Do you think it was bad? Should I have read it through?"

She picked up her phone again. "Can you unsend an email?"

Gabe plucked the phone out of her hands. "It was a good response. Now stop thinking about it."

"What else is there to think about?" Charlotte grabbed at her phone.

"The mystery you're working on?" Gabe suggested, holding it out of her reach.

"Or your job?" Lucy added. "Speaking of which, we need to get going. Gabe, are you awake enough to drive?"

Gabe blinked, arm still extended above his head like a phone-wielding Statue of Liberty. "In all the excitement, I forgot to be tired." He slumped over onto the table. "Oh, no. There it is."

Driving herself to the middle school, Charlotte went through the facts of the case, including the new discoveries from the evening before. Having learned from experience, she tried not to let herself get overwhelmed by the details, instead focusing on what needed to be done.

Talk to Ellie. Talk to Parnell.

She grimaced. *So much talking.* Charlotte wanted to *do* something. Sneak into someone's office. Eavesdrop on a conversation. Chase a suspect—

Nope. Nope, nope, nope. This is what adults do. They talk to people to get information. Grow up and deal with it.

She was still lost in thought as she sat in her homeroom, having just taken attendance. It was probably a sign that she wasn't doing her job very well when she realized Nia had been standing quietly in front of her desk for an indeterminate amount of time.

"Hey, Nia," Charlotte said, giving her head a shake as if that would quicken her return to full awareness of her surroundings. "What's up?"

Nia placed Charlotte's detective kit on the desk in front of her. "I just wanted to give this back. Thanks for letting us use it."

Charlotte picked up the bag. "Of course. I like your bracelet."

"Oh, thanks." Nia held up her wrist to display the rainbow-beaded bracelet. "Kat made it. She said she's gonna sell them for ten dollars each, but she gave it to me for free because it's good promotion for her queer-owned business."

Charlotte felt a now-familiar pang in her chest. Shaking it off, she asked, "Did you guys solve your case?"

Nia shook her head. "We thought we figured out who took it, but Isabel talked to him and he said he didn't do it."

She fidgeted with the front of her shirt. "I was wondering, um, if you knew what we should do now. Because you're a real detective."

Charlotte shook her head. "You're just as much of a detective as I am. I'm not, like, licensed or anything."

Nia's eyes widened. "Oh. Okay."

"You probably just need to talk to more people," Charlotte said, folding her hands on the desk. *Is this what it feels like to be a teacher?* "Middle schoolers aren't known for being good secret keepers. Someone's gotta know who has it."

"Mm." Nia scrunched her nose. "I really want to solve this mystery, but I . . . I don't really like talking to people."

This girl was in Charlotte's brain. "Right, okay, relatable."

Charlotte sat back, thinking. "What about those Instagram posts? Did you learn anything from those?"

Nia shrugged glumly. "I don't know . . . I was trying to see if someone's reflection was in the background of one of them, like in this mystery book I just read, but I couldn't see anything that would tell me who took the photos."

"Y'know," Charlotte said slowly, "sometimes a person can get so focused on searching for something specific that they miss something else. And sometimes it's not even what you see, but the absence of something." She winced. "Is that helpful, maybe?"

"Maybe," Nia said, her nose scrunching slightly.

"A lot of detective work is just looking for patterns," Charlotte said, "and noticing when those patterns are broken."

"Oh, I'm good at that." Nia said excitedly. "I'm gonna examine those photos again. Thank you!"

Am I . . . an educator? Charlotte thought as Nia hurried back to her seat. *I think I understand teaching now. Maybe this* is *my calling.*

She quickly abandoned that notion two periods later.

"Guys, please," she said tiredly, trying to make herself heard over the puberty-fueled cacophony that had already drawn another teacher into the room to request they quiet down. "Just talk quietly. I literally don't care if you do the worksheet or not, just keep it down."

"We already did this worksheet," one of the students called out. He was wearing a green sweatshirt with the hood pulled up, which Charlotte knew was probably against the rules but could not bring herself to care about it. "So we shouldn't have to do it again."

A few kids who had abandoned their conversations to listen immediately voiced their agreement.

"First off," Charlotte said, resting her elbows on the desk, "I literally just said I don't care if you do the worksheet or not. Second, I know that's not true, because three minutes ago I heard you tell your friend you were going to tell the sub that you already did this worksheet. Again, you guys are *loud*."

The student who spoke up rolled his eyes. "Whatever. I'm still not gonna do it."

"Fine by me." Charlotte sat back in her chair. "Not sure if the cross-country team keeps students who don't do their school-work, but . . ."

The kid narrowed his eyes. "How'd you know I run cross country?"

"You—" Charlotte paused, seeing an opportunity to enter-tain herself. "When you walked in, you had the gait of someone used to traveling long distances on foot. And when you sit, you stretch your legs out to avoid putting unnecessary pressure on your ankles."

The kid pulled his legs in, spooked.

"Whoa," another student said. "You really saw all that?"

"Yup," Charlotte lied, nodding solemnly. "But, also . . ." She pointed at the first student's hoodie, which said, FMS CROSS COUNTRY on the front in big yellow letters.

The student followed her finger. "Oh." He started laughing. "That was pretty good."

"Tell me something about me!" another student exclaimed.

Charlotte was confused, before realizing what she meant. "Oh, no, I can't really . . ."

She paused as she noticed how quiet the class had gotten. Not silent, but definitely quiet enough to keep the neighboring teachers happy. A large chunk of the class was now watching Charlotte, having seen her clock the one student as a cross-country runner (and clearly not understanding that her first two "observations" had been made up).

"Uh . . . alright." Charlotte paused for as long as she could before it got weird. "You . . . don't like this class very much."

The girl seemed a little disappointed that Charlotte hadn't figured out something cooler about her, but said, "Yeah. How'd you know?"

Honestly, it was because when the girl walked into the class-room earlier, she had said, "Yesss," under her breath upon see-ing a substitute in place of her usual teacher.

"Your posture," Charlotte said. "I can tell by the way your shoulders are tensed that your body is accustomed to being un-happy in this room. And your left foot is stretched into the aisle, like you're ready to leave as soon as you can."

The girl self-consciously retracted her left leg, slightly more impressed. "Whoa. Cool."

"Wait, do me!"

"Me next!"

"I was gonna go next!"

What did I get myself into? Charlotte thought as the kids clam-ored for a turn to be the next subject of her deductions. But, they *were* still being significantly less unruly than before she'd begun her charlatan routine, so she pointed at a kid who she'd seen walking out of the music room with a violin case the day before.

"You . . . play the violin."

"The viola!" the student replied, still surprised despite her error.

"The what?"

"It's like a violin," the kid explained. "But . . . different."

"Riiiight," Charlotte said. "That makes sense. I was actually going to say that I can tell you play a small, stringed instrument, but 'violin' didn't really feel right."

"But how did you know?" another kid demanded.

"You know, kids," she said, kicking her feet up to rest them on the desk, "you can tell a lot about a person by how they hold a pencil."

She managed to keep it up for the rest of the period, impress-ing the students with spectacular feats of deduction that were, in reality, very boring feats of deduction.

Right before the end of class, a student yelled, "How many fingers am I holding behind my back?"

Charlotte scrunched up her nose. "I'm not a *psychic.* I . . ."

She noticed a couple of kids peeking behind the back of the kid who spoke, snickering to themselves.

Realizing she had literally nothing to lose, she said, "None. It's just a fist."

The back of the room erupted.

"NO WAYYYYY."

"HOW DID SHE KNOW THAT?"

"BROOOO—"

Charlotte sat back as the bell rang, feeling a little impressed with herself despite knowing that she could have very easily been wrong. A few students even said goodbye to her as they exited the classroom, which felt pretty good. She wondered if students still gave teachers apples, and if so, if she would start receiving any apples. Then she remembered that students didn't give teachers apples when *she* was a kid. Also, she didn't even like apples that much.

"Ms. Illes?"

Charlotte yanked her feet off the desk, almost falling out of her chair in the process. The teacher from next door was standing in the doorway.

"I don't know if you knew this, but you're supposed to stand in the hallway during passing time," the teacher said.

Charlotte scrambled out of the chair. "Right, yes, coming."

Her next period did not go nearly as well, as a gaggle of twelve-year-olds roasted her outfit for half the class time.

"Would you say I dress like my whole paycheck is going into food and rent?" Charlotte asked Gabe as they walked with Lucy towards the library.

Gabe, who was adjusting his GUEST sticker, gave her a once-over. "No, you look good. Why?"

"Middle schoolers," Lucy answered knowingly. "They're ruthless."

"I like your outfit, Ms. I," Arjun commented from behind them. Lucy had brought along the lunchtime crew as an excuse to talk to Ellie, since Charlotte's only plan had been, "I'll . . . ask her for book recommendations and go from there?"

"Thanks, Arjun," Charlotte called over her shoulder. "Appreciate that."

He grinned. A pink, purple, and blue bracelet dangled from his wrist, similar to Nia's. All the kids were wearing bracelets, proving Kat's marketing campaign was going strong.

"Your shoes are cool," Neil added. "Vintage."

Charlotte glanced down at her scuffed, faded Converse. "I'll take it."

"You should experiment with more saturated colors," Kat chimed in. "You look like you might be a winter."

"I don't know what that means, but noted."

"Ms. Ortega," Isabel said, speeding up to walk alongside Lucy, "why're we going to the library? Not that I'm mad about it. Ms. Flynn is soooo pretty."

"I'm on a case," Charlotte said. "A very top-secret case that requires us to go to the library."

"Ooooo!" Nia said, bouncing excitedly. "What do we have to do?"

"Just be cool," Charlotte said, walking backwards to address the kids. "Act like you really wanted Ms. Ortega to take you to the library."

"I *love* books," Isabel declared loudly.

Charlotte pointed at her. "Exactly. Just like that."

"I need to read a book every day or I'll *die!*" Arjun added cheerfully.

Charlotte paused. "Maybe bring it down just a notch, but good energy."

Arjun gave a sharp nod to show he understood.

The school library, as had been the case for every other part of the school Charlotte had seen since starting work, had not changed much from how she remembered it. The area closest to the entrance housed several tables scattered amongst low bookshelves. Farther back in the room sat more, taller bookshelves, perfect for hiding behind to eavesdrop on conversations.

Ellie sat at the checkout desk to their right, looking up from her laptop as they walked in.

"Hey, guys," she said, smiling at the kids. "What brings you all here?"

"I need a book!" Nia said. The other kids voiced their agreement.

"Well, you've come to the right place," Ellie said. "Do you need help finding what you need?"

Nia glanced at Charlotte. "Uh . . ."

"I think you know what you're looking for, right, Nia?" Lucy said pointedly.

"Mhm!" Nia said. "Yeah, we're good."

The kids headed off towards the bookshelves.

"Let me know if you need help!" Ellie called after them. She gave the adults a quick smile before returning to her laptop.

"Hey," Lucy said, stepping towards the desk. "How're you doing? It sounded like things got really scary last night at the bake sale."

Ellie glanced back up, surprised. "Oh! I'm fine, thanks for asking." She gave them a wry smile. "I'm not the one who had to go to the hospital."

"Horrible accident," Charlotte agreed. "I'm Charlotte, by the way. Substitute teacher."

"Gabe, hey," said Gabe, pointing at his name tag. "Guest."

Ellie smiled politely. "Hi."

"How do you think that happened?" Charlotte asked. "The allergic reaction, I mean."

The librarian gave her a curious look. "Well, they said Mrs. Anderson had a nut allergy. Seems like there were probably nuts in the brownies."

"But Kim said she didn't put nuts in the brownies," Lucy said.

Ellie shrugged uncomfortably. "Like Mrs. Parnell said: mistakes happen. But what's important is that Mrs. Anderson's going to be okay."

"Definitely," Charlotte said. "If she wasn't okay, I can't imagine how that'd feel for whoever was responsible."

"It'd be pretty bad," Ellie agreed, her tone mild. She gestured to her laptop. "Sorry, I just, I need to get back to this—"

"Did Daniel tell you he tried to get rid of the brownies?" Charlotte saw Lucy and Gabe's heads whip over in perfect unison.

Ellie's eyebrows shot up. "Ex*cuse* me?"

"We saw him in Mrs. Parnell's office last night," Lucy said, sounding like she wished Charlotte hadn't brought it up, but now had to come to her defense. "He was looking for Kim's brownies."

Ellie sat still for a moment, at a loss for words. Finally, she said, "Why were *you* in Mrs. Parnell's office?"

"She got you there," Gabe murmured.

"We wanted to see how the nuts could've gotten into the brownies," Charlotte said. "And we found Daniel in there, trying to get rid of the evidence. Because he thought you might've been responsible."

"How—*what?*" Ellie was incredulous. "How do you know that?"

"He told us."

"He told. . . ." She paused, shaking her head. "I don't believe that."

"It's the truth," Lucy said. "He said he knew you were upset about his ex working at the school, and he thought maybe you were trying to get her in trouble."

"That's—" Ellie blinked a few times in rapid succession. "I can't talk about this right now."

"Would another time be better?" Charlotte pressed.

"No," Ellie said sharply, glancing in the direction of the kids before lowering her voice. "This is a conversation I need to have with Daniel, not with you."

Charlotte turned away as Lucy apologized to Ellie for upsetting her. She spotted Nia emerging from the bookshelves, looking unsure if it was okay to approach the desk. She waved the girl over, figuring they'd gotten everything they were going to get from the librarian at this point in time.

Ellie inhaled deeply as Nia approached the desk. Her face smoothing into a calm smile, she said, "What's up, Nia?"

"Do you have the eighth grade science textbook?" Nia pushed her glasses up her nose. "I saw you have other textbooks, but I couldn't find that one."

"Aren't you in seventh grade?"

"Yes," Nia replied, "but I'm . . . trying to get a head start for next year."

Ellie smiled, turning to the computer monitor that sat next to her laptop. "Let me see."

Charlotte glanced at Lucy and Gabe, and the three of them reconvened a couple yards away by a crooked sign that said SPOOKY READS FOR HALLOWEEN.

Lucy straightened the sign. "What'd you get from that?"

"Not much," Charlotte said. "Obviously she was upset, but she didn't feel the need to defend herself to us. That reads as innocent."

"Heh," Gabe said. "Reads."

Charlotte and Lucy booed him at an appropriate volume for a library.

"So where does that leave the suspect list?" Lucy asked.

"Ellie stays on it," Charlotte replied. "But I think we can bump her down a bit."

She frowned to herself. The suspects they had were becoming less and less suspicious, with no new suspects or motives on the horizon.

Gabe pulled out his phone and began typing. "That puts Mrs. Parnell back on top," he announced. "And there's also Mrs. Hernández."

"I'll try to catch Parnell at the end of the day," Charlotte said. "I'm not sure about Mrs. Hernández, but I'll figure it out."

"I have conferences after school," Lucy said. "But let me know how it goes."

"I can hang," Gabe said. "I have some stuff for work, but I can do it from my phone."

Lucy went to gather the rest of the kids as Nia finished up with Ellie. The young girl's eyes were wide with glee as they all left the library, but she said nothing as they headed back to Lucy's classroom.

"Have we firmly ruled out the possibility that we're dealing with a kid?" Gabe asked. The students were walking several feet ahead of them, talking amongst themselves. "I'm starting to feel like we might need some new suspects."

"I just can't think of any kids who'd have it out for Kim like that," Lucy said. "Despite what Mrs. Hernández might think, most of our students do pretty well. And even the ones who struggle wouldn't go so far as to *threaten* her."

"Besides," Charlotte added, "do kids these days even know how to use the postal system?" She raised her voice a bit. "Hey, you guys? Do you know what a stamp is?"

The kids looked back at her.

"Like you get on your hand?" Neil asked, holding up a fist to demonstrate.

"No, I mean, a stamp for sending mail. Like, letters."

"A postage stamp," Kat explained to Neil. "You need to put it on your letter before you mail it."

Neil shook his head. "I didn't know that."

"I did," Arjun said proudly.

"I thought the post office did that," Isabel said. "You have to put the stamp on yourself?"

Charlotte turned back to Lucy and Gabe as the kids continued to talk. "Okay, it's pretty split."

Nia remained quiet, walking a couple steps ahead of the group like she couldn't wait to return to the classroom. Once they finally arrived, the kids settled at their table at the back of the room while Lucy, Gabe, and Charlotte sat around Lucy's desk.

"I have an announcement," Nia said, standing at the head of the table. Everyone fell silent, giving her their attention.

"I solved the mystery."

Gabe looked over at Charlotte and Lucy, startled. They both shook their heads.

"Different mystery," Charlotte murmured.

The kids had broken out into multiple exclamations of disbelief, talking over each other in excitement.

"Shut up!" Isabel said loudly, despite the fact that she had been contributing to the noise just as much as the others. "Let her talk."

Nia swallowed, shooting a quick, nervous glance towards the front of the classroom. "So, um, I was examining the photos on the bobblehead Instagram account again, and in one of the photos you can see the inside front cover of a textbook, but there's no name written in it. And we're all supposed to write our names in the textbooks. So I guessed that maybe it was a copy from the library."

"Whoa," Neil said. "That's smart."

Nia continued, clearly pleased with herself. "I asked Ms. Flynn, and she said the library only had one copy of that textbook, but it was checked out. She wasn't gonna tell me who had it, but I said I really, really needed it, so she told me."

"And?" Kat said. "Who has it?"

"Matt Fisher."

The kids erupted again.

"He said he didn't have it!" Neil exclaimed.

"I'm gonna kill him!" Isabel screeched.

"Everyone, CHILL," Lucy yelled.

The kids quickly quieted.

"That was smart thinking, Nia," Lucy continued. "I'll email Mr. Weissman right now and tell him."

"Hang on," Isabel said, holding up her hands. She turned to the other kids. "We're not snitches. Right?"

Kat frowned, but shook her head. The others followed suit.

"We'll get the bobblehead back to Mr. Weissman," Isabel said to Lucy. "We don't have to tell on Matt."

"But what if he steals it again?" Arjun asked.

Isabel cracked her knuckles. "He won't."

"Isabel," Lucy said warningly.

"I'm just joking!" The girl gasped. "Can we get famous for this? We should be in the newspaper."

Kat waved her hands excitedly. "What if we got a photo taken of us with my bracelets? That'd be *great* promotion."

Charlotte shot Nia two thumbs-up. The girl grinned back.

As the kids began talking amongst themselves again, Charlotte glanced at Gabe, who'd grown uncharacteristically quiet. He was sitting back in his chair, face impassive as he stared into the middle distance.

"Hey," Charlotte said, "you good?"

"Yeah," he said, his expression vaguely confused as he stood. "I think I should . . . I need to go send an email real quick."

He turned to leave the room, pausing as he reached the door. Facing the back of the classroom, he called out, "Hey, kids?"

After a moment, the students realized they were being addressed, and one by one looked over at him.

Gabe lifted a finger, pausing like he was still formulating what he wanted to say.

"You guys . . ." he said finally, pointing at them, "are great. Keep being . . . just keep doing what you're doing. A lot of people are gonna say things . . ."

His mouth hung open slightly as he stared at the ceiling, still seemingly trying to gather his thoughts.

"A lot of people are gonna say and do things . . ." He trailed off again, shaking his head. "But you're all doing great, so . . ." He transitioned his point into a weak thumbs-up. "Just keep doing your thing, and . . . it's great. The bracelets are cool."

He nodded to himself, then exited the room.

Isabel turned to Lucy, eyebrows knit together with concern. "Is he good?"

"He's fine," Lucy said, smiling reassuringly. "You can go back to talking now."

As the kids resumed their conversation, Lucy leaned in to Charlotte, lowering her voice. "*Is* he good?"

Charlotte stared at the door, finally realizing what that strange, unidentifiable feeling she'd been having lately was all about. She stood. "I'm gonna check on him."

"Do you want me to come?" Lucy asked.

"No, it's fine. I think I know what it's about." Seeing Lucy's concerned expression, she added, "It's okay, really. I'll explain when I get back."

Charlotte found Gabe sitting on the floor outside of the classroom, his back against a locker. She slid down to sit next to him.

"Would you feel better if I chewed some of your shit gum?" she offered tentatively.

Gabe snorted. "*Splitz* Gum. And no, it's fine." He ran a hand through his hair, letting out a self-deprecating snort. "Did any of that make sense?"

"Well . . ." Charlotte said gently, ". . . I don't think *Out Magazine* is going to cover it anytime soon, but I got what you were trying to say. I'm sure the kids also did. To some extent."

They sat in silence for a moment.

"You know," Charlotte finally said, pointing across the hallway, "in sixth grade, Julie Donovan threw up right there."

Gabe made a face. "Did anyone ever throw up where we're sitting?"

"Not when I was here, but a lot of time has passed."

"Yeah." Gabe pulled his legs up, resting his arms on his knees. "It's really different."

"You mean the kids, right?"

"They're just . . ." He trailed off, helplessly waving a hand to express his loss for words.

"Lucy told me those aren't even all the openly queer kids," Charlotte said.

"Yeah, she told me, too." The corner of his mouth twitched up. "And she told me she had students in three different classes interrupt her *Little Women* lesson to talk about how Jo March is a lesbian and Louisa May Alcott was probably a trans man."

Charlotte gave a positive *hmm* in response.

They were quiet for another moment.

"Do you feel guilty for feeling sad?" Charlotte asked softly.

"Mhm." Gabe cleared his throat,. "I mean, I am so, *so* happy to see it."

"Right."

"It's amazing. Fills me with immense levels of joy and pride."

"Yeah."

"And I know they still have so much shit coming their way, and things aren't perfect, but it's still . . . it's still so *different*, and they're so . . . and I just . . ."

He paused, then looked over at Charlotte, his lips pressed tightly together. "Why couldn't—"

His voice broke, and he stopped.

"Why couldn't it have been like that for us?" Charlotte finished.

He nodded, his eyes wet as he blinked away tears.

Charlotte shifted over to sit closer, and Gabe rested his head on her shoulder.

After a minute, Charlotte said, "Kat can make you one of those bracelets. I've been told they're ten dollars each."

Gabe jerked upright, his face filled with comic disbelief. "*Ten dollars?*" He clicked his tongue in dismay. "In my day . . ."

"Yeah," Charlotte agreed, cracking a small smile. "It's really different."

Chapter 11

Mind Blown, Fine

August 31st, 2011
From: Mary Parnell
To: Frencham Middle School Staff
Subject: Back to school reminders

Hello everyone,

With the new school year right around the corner,
I wanted to send an email with some important
reminders:

1. Our first staff meeting of the year will be next
Friday.
2. Please make sure to lock your door when you
are not in the classroom, and keep close track of
your classroom key.
3. If anyone finds any plastic sandwich bags
containing screwdrivers, please bring them to my
office.
4. Lottie Illes is not allowed out of class for longer
than five minutes. If anyone sees Lottie Illes in

the hallways, feel free to escort her to where she claims to be going. She is not allowed near any ventilation grates. She is not allowed near the door to the roof. Bus monitors, please make sure Lottie Illes is only getting on her assigned bus. If she says she has written permission to get on a different bus and waves a piece of paper at you, please confirm that the piece of paper is actually written permission and not just a blank piece of paper.

5. Please put your name on any food you leave in the teachers' lounge refrigerator.

I am looking forward to an educational and fulfilling year.

Sincerely,
Mary Parnell

Present Day

Some things never change, Charlotte thought as she sat in the main office, slumped in the chair that sat across from the front desk. She had to take a moment to remind her body that she wasn't twelve, but was in fact a twenty-five-year-old with a job and responsibilities and student debt. (For some reason, that reminder didn't alleviate her anxiety.)

The school day had ended, and the secretary had told Charlotte that Mrs. Parnell was on a call, and would speak to her when she was done. Almost twenty minutes had passed since then.

Charlotte chewed on the inside of her cheek, trying to come up with the best phrasing for her queries so that Parnell wouldn't suspect she was being questioned. *So, Jennifer Falcone's a real pill, right? Wouldn't it be great if she didn't win the election?* Or, *Hypothetically, if you wanted to get a teacher to quit, how would you do it?*

The version of Parnell in her brain didn't respond well to either of those approaches, making Charlotte suspect that the real Parnell wouldn't fall for them, either.

Maybe I should just bail. She'd already tried talking to Parnell once, with mixed results. How was she supposed to convince the vice principal to speak with her again? What questions could she ask Parnell that would either incriminate her or convince Charlotte of her innocence?

The secretary stood from her chair, circling the desk and heading for the door. "I'll be right back," the woman threw over her shoulder before walking out.

Hm. Charlotte glanced at Parnell's door, her feet tapping with sudden anticipation. Ignoring her prefrontal cortex's firm recommendation that now was *not* the time for eavesdropping, she stood and crossed the room, stopping outside of the door. She turned her head and listened.

And heard nothing.

Is she even in there? Charlotte thought, pressing her ear to the door. *Has my hearing gotten that bad? Oh my god. I'm old. I—*

The door swung open. Charlotte reached out to grab the door frame to keep herself from tumbling headfirst into Mrs. Parnell.

The vice principal stared at her over the top of her glasses, her gaze severe.

"What are you doing here?" Parnell demanded.

"I . . . was . . . ." Charlotte gestured at the chair behind her. "I was waiting to talk to you, but I wasn't sure if you knew I was here. I was about to knock on the door."

They stared at each other for a moment as Charlotte resisted the urge to swallow nervously, which she was sure would make her seem even more guilty than she already did.

Finally, Parnell sighed. "What can I help you with, Ms. Illes?"

Feeling emboldened by the vice principal's somewhat softened demeanor (which was still pretty stony by regular standards), Charlotte decided to go with semi-honesty again.

"I'm investigating the brownie incident for Kim," she said. Catching the expression on the older woman's face, she added, "Not during school hours, of course."

Parnell sniffed. "So you're still doing that . . . detective thing."

"Yes," Charlotte said. "Despite my best efforts, I'm still doing that detective thing."

The door to the main office opened as the secretary reentered.

"Oh, Mrs. Parnell, good," the woman said. "There's a flooding situation in the girls' bathroom by the sixth grade hallway, and the parents keep asking why it's locked—"

"I'll handle it, thank you," Parnell said. She passed Charlotte and walked towards the door. "If you want to talk, follow me," she called over her shoulder.

It took Charlotte a moment to realize she was being addressed. When she did, she hurried after the vice principal.

"Well?" Parnell said once Charlotte caught up with her. "What did you want to ask me?"

"Really?" Charlotte was too surprised to have any other reaction. "You're gonna let me ask you anything?"

"You can ask me anything," Parnell confirmed. "That doesn't mean I'll answer it, but you can ask."

That was more like the Parnell she remembered. "Okay," Charlotte said. "Was there any point in time during the evening that the baked goods were left unattended by both you and Ellie?"

"No."

Charlotte waited to see if she'd say anything else. After a moment of silence, she said, "Was there any point when either you or Ellie left the other at the table?"

Parnell shot her a sidelong look. "Yes," she said after a moment. "We both went to use the restroom at different times."

So they both had opportunities to switch out the brownies, Charlotte thought. Although she did wonder how one of them could have hidden a bunch of brownies from the other, both before and after they made the switch.

Or, she suddenly realized, *maybe they didn't even switch out the whole batch.* Someone could've easily added a few of the nut brownies on top. Just enough to get Kim into trouble once someone noticed. That would have taken significantly less time to pull off.

"Did all of the brownies you confiscated contain nuts?" Charlotte asked.

The vice principal snorted. "I assume so. I threw them out before leaving."

Welp. Charlotte wished everyone else was cursed with her level of curiosity. Why anyone would throw out evidence before examining it thoroughly was beyond her.

Unless Parnell was the one who did it.

"Are you done already?" Parnell asked, interrupting Charlotte's thoughts. "Solved the whole mystery just like that?"

Charlotte bristled defensively, but deflated as the other woman shot her a wry smile before stopping by a storage closet.

"You're being strangely nice to me," Charlotte commented as Parnell pulled out a ring of keys and unlocked the closet. "Why?"

"Because I'm a very nice person," Parnell said simply, entering the closet and switching the light on inside.

"Not to me," Charlotte said, hovering in the doorway. "I mean, you hated me when I was a student."

Parnell paused. "I didn't *hate* you, Charlotte." She returned to the shelf in front of her, ripping open the plastic wrapping on a stack of papers and removing a single piece.

"Well, you were mad at me, like, all the time," Charlotte said, unsure if this conversation was actually happening, or if she was having a dream she'd have to tell her therapist about.

The vice principal grabbed a marker from a box and ripped a piece of tape off a roll before turning back around. "You'd break a lot of rules when you were a student here," she said. "What was I supposed to do, just let you get away with it?"

"I mean, it'd have been nice," Charlotte grumbled as Parnell switched off the light and exited the closet. "But it wasn't just the discipline. It was like you were rooting against me."

"You were a kid who liked to help people," Parnell said, locking the door. "Very bright, though probably too clever for your own good. How could anyone root against you?"

Charlotte was too flabbergasted to follow as Parnell began walking down the hall. Her mind raced to figure out how she could have possibly misinterpreted what she'd just heard.

"Wh . . . you're saying you were rooting *for* me?" She hurried to catch up.

"Remember what I said about how I didn't have to answer your questions?" Parnell's keys jingled as she returned them to her pocket.

"No, *no*, you can't just say that and not clarify," Charlotte said. Kim's brownies had taken a back seat—she needed to get to the bottom of this. "You're telling me that the whole time, while you were glaring at me and giving me detention and saying things like, 'I've got my eye on you, Lottie Illes,' that you were actually *rooting* for me?"

"Yes," the vice principal replied, as if the answer was obvious.

Charlotte threw her hands into the air, baffled. "So why were you constantly trying to stop me?!"

"Because," Parnell said as they rounded a corner, "like I said, I had to enforce the rules. What sensible adult would let a child go crawling through air ducts?"

Charlotte looked away guiltily. *Note to self: sensible adults don't let children go crawling through air ducts.*

They stopped in front of the closed door to the girls' bathroom. Parnell took the piece of tape that she'd stuck to her thumb and affixed the paper to the door.

"Besides," she continued, uncapping the marker and pointing it at Charlotte, "did my antagonism ever discourage you from your mystery-solving?"

Charlotte's brow furrowed as Parnell began writing on the paper. "No. It just made me more determined to keep it up." She rolled her eyes. "Okay, yeah, I get it."

"Get what," Parnell said, like a teacher prompting a student to explain their answer.

"You just put obstacles in my way to motivate me and, I don't know, to keep things interesting?" Charlotte remembered what Parnell had said to Lucy the day before. "You were challenging me to keep me engaged."

Parnell finished writing, the paper now displaying the message, PLEASE USE THE RESTROOM BY THE NURSE'S OFFICE.

She capped the marker. "If that's the conclusion you've come to," she said vaguely.

"Okay," Charlotte said as they began walking back to the main office. "You were secretly rooting for me as a kid. Mind blown, fine. So why are you being so open with me now?"

An expression crossed Parnell's face that had become very familiar to Charlotte as of late. It was an affectionate look, tinged with pity and concern.

"Because you have enough of your own obstacles to deal with now," the vice principal said in the kindest tone Charlotte had ever heard her use. "You don't need me to make them for you."

Charlotte was quiet as they continued walking, mulling over that statement, until they had returned to the door of the main office.

Parnell gave Charlotte one last stern look. "And you don't need to make obstacles for yourself, either."

Charlotte nodded silently as Parnell entered the office, leaving her alone in the hallway.

Damn, Charlotte thought. *How am I supposed to accuse her of blackmail after that?*

There were a few adults scattered throughout the hallways,

standing outside of classrooms as they waited for their turn to confer with the teacher inside. Charlotte found Gabe sitting at a desk he'd dragged into the hallway outside of Lucy's classroom.

"Hey," he said, continuing to scroll on his phone as she stopped in front of him. "How'd it go?"

"Had some life-shattering revelations," Charlotte said. "Not about the case. But according to Parnell, she and Ellie both had the opportunity to mess with the brownies. I'm not sure it was her, though."

Gabe looked up. "You don't have many suspects left," he pointed out. "No one's been crossed off the list yet, but you keep soft-crossing them out."

"What's soft-crossing?"

"You know, like when you draw a line through their name, but in really light pencil so you can erase it if you get new evidence against them."

"Got it." Charlotte moved to sit on the floor next to the desk. "I don't know. We have two victims, right? Kim and Jennifer. And we'll find someone with motive for threatening one of them, and instead of discovering their motive for blackmailing the other, we just find out that their motive for the first might not be as strong as we thought." She wrapped her arms around her knees and buried her face in them. "I give up."

"No, you don't."

"I'm just gonna give up for a minute, and then I'll be back."

"Fair enough."

Thirty seconds later, Charlotte heard the door to Lucy's classroom open.

"Thanks again," she heard a voice say.

"Of course!" Lucy's voice chirped. "Feel free to email me if you think of any more questions."

"I will. Have a good night."

"You, too!"

There was a brief pause. Then:

"What happened to her?"

"She's giving up for a minute," Gabe responded. "She'll be back after these messages. First message: How many more hot parents do you have conferences with today?"

"I'm back," Charlotte said loudly, lifting her head from her arms.

"And I'm an idiot," Lucy said. "Guess who I have a conference with later?"

"Who?"

"Vincent Welles."

Charlotte shook her head with sudden shock. "*Why?*"

"He's Neil's dad," Lucy said, sounding exasperated with herself. "Neil's last name is hyphenated—Donnelly-Welles—so my idiot brain didn't make the connection."

"Hey, stop talking about my friend's brain like that," Gabe reprimanded.

"Thanks," Lucy said, patting his hair, with her eyes on Charlotte. "So should I try to, like . . . get information from him? Do you *need* information from him?"

"Even if he's not much of a suspect anymore, he might know of someone else who is," Charlotte said. "Someone else on the board who has it in for her, maybe? If you're able to casually ask him about the election, that could be good."

Lucy's brow set with determination. "I'm on it. Maybe. I'll try my best. How'd it go with Mrs. Parnell?"

"Weird," Charlotte said. "I'll tell you about it later. But I don't think she did it."

Lucy's brows raised. "Did you find out why she's not worried about Jennifer keeping her from getting the principal job?"

"Well . . . no." Charlotte crossed her arms defensively. "She distracted me with other stuff."

"Ooh." Gabe's eyes went wide. "Do you think it was on purpose? To throw you off the scent?"

Charlotte paused, considering that. Was that possible? Could Parnell have just made up all that stuff about always rooting for her just to clear herself from suspicion? The woman had always been difficult to deal with, but *manipulative* wasn't a word Charlotte would easily attribute to her.

"Okay," she finally said. "Parnell is still on the list. Tentatively."

Gabe groaned. "They're all tentative! That's the point of a suspect list!"

"What about Mrs. Hernández?" Lucy lowered her voice as someone walked past them. "Are you still considering her as a suspect?"

"Oh, right," Charlotte said, remembering their newest suspect. "She should still be here for conferences, right?"

"Mhm. Are you going to try to talk to her?"

"Yeah. I'll try to . . ." She sighed. "I'll try to talk to her."

"Don't get too excited about it," Gabe deadpanned.

"No, it's not that. I just feel talked out." She waved a hand dismissively. "It's fine, I'll get a second wind soon."

"You don't *have* to talk to her," Lucy said hesitantly. "If you don't really think she's a good suspect. I mean, if you're just doing it for me, to defend me or whatever . . ."

Charlotte shook her head. "No, no, I think she definitely has potential to be a suspect. I'll talk to her."

Seeing the doubtful expression on Lucy's face, she doubled down. "I *really* think she's a suspect. Why would I talk to her just for you? I don't even like you that much!"

Lucy snorted, smiling. "Okay, fine. Her room number is 207."

Charlotte scrambled to her feet, trying to put out the vibe of someone who knew what she was doing (and where she was going—she was pretty sure 207 was on the second floor). "Alright. Time to interrogate Mrs. Hernández. Gabe, coming?"

"Yup," Gabe said, sliding out of the desk. "I made three motivational graphics, so that's enough hard work for the day, I think." He pantomimed putting a hat on his head.

"What's that?" Charlotte asked.

"Putting my detective hat on."

"There's no detective hat. I don't have a detective hat."

Gabe pantomimed putting a hat on her head. "Now you do!"

"Okay, get out of here," Lucy said as Charlotte batted the imaginary hat off of her head. "I have to prep for my next conference."

"Is that Welles?" Charlotte asked eagerly. "Can I eavesdrop?"

Lucy shook her head. "No and no. He's coming a little later with his wife. I'm not telling you when."

She shooed them away, and Charlotte and Gabe headed off down the hallway towards room 207.

"So what's the plan?" Gabe asked. "Are you just gonna start asking her about Jennifer, or . . ."

Charlotte chewed on the inside of her cheek. "Yeah, something like that, probably," she finally said.

"I've gotta say," Gabe commented, "as good as you can be at this detective stuff, plans aren't really your strong suit."

"I don't know," Charlotte said, shrugging helplessly. "Plans used to just come to me. I'll figure something out."

She knew she sounded more certain than she felt, which was helped by the fact that Gabe had (in her opinion) an unwarranted amount of confidence in her abilities. Despite subtly racking her brain for ideas as they climbed the stairs to the second floor, she still had nothing better than "Something like that, probably," as they approached Mrs. Hernández's room.

"The lights are out inside," Gabe said, peeking through the window next to the door. "Oh, wait, this is 206." He took a few steps to his right and cautiously peeked through the window into room 207.

"Is she in there?" Charlotte tried to see over his shoulder.

"She's in a conference with someone," he reported. "Oh, wait, they're pretty young . . . I think it's a student teacher." He paused, continuing to watch whatever was happening inside the classroom. "Yeah, they're just hanging out. That's a student teacher."

He turned back to Charlotte. "Do you wanna go in?"

Unfortunately, at that moment, a plan came to Charlotte.

It was unfortunate solely due to the fact that it was without a doubt a classic Lottie Illes™ plan, and Charlotte had been working very hard not to infringe upon that brand.

"What's happening?" Gabe asked, alarmed. "You look like you just remembered something terrible. What is it? Global warming? Gerrymandering? That era when everyone was obsessed with bacon for some reason?"

Charlotte groaned.

"I know! They were putting that shit on everything!"

"No, I have a plan." Charlotte scowled. "It's dumb and bad and probably won't work."

"Has anyone ever told you you'd make an *incredible* salesperson?" Gabe asked, leaning against the wall.

Charlotte pressed a fist to her forehead and closed her eyes, trying to think. She needed to get Mrs. Hernández talking about Lucy and Kim, but she probably wouldn't admit anything damning to Charlotte. *Maybe* she'd say something to her student teacher, or at least be off guard enough to let something slip. And in order for Charlotte to hear . . .

"Fine, I'll do it," she said, opening her eyes and dropping her hand. "I'm not excited about it, but I'll do it." In all honesty, Charlotte was a *little* excited about it, but since she wasn't doing a therapist-mandated emotional check-in at that moment, she didn't need to acknowledge that.

"I still have no idea what you're talking about," Gabe said as she passed him, "but I support you."

"I need to find a custodian," Charlotte said over her shoulder. "Can you go get my bag from Lucy's room?"

Gabe pushed off the wall and saluted, jogging off in the opposite direction as Charlotte went searching for a custodian. After a couple minutes of searching, she found Gerald, who, thankfully, bought her story about accidentally leaving her phone in room 206 and locking herself out.

"I didn't realize until after I returned my key," she explained as they walked back to the room. "I'd go to the main office to get it back, but . . . well, if I'm being honest, I'm a little scared of the vice principal."

"Oh, Mrs. Parnell?" Gerald pulled out his keys as they reached room 206. "Yeah, I don't blame you."

He unlocked the door, pulling it open. "There you go."

"Thank you," Charlotte said, walking inside. "I really appreciate it."

"No problem." Gerald continued standing in the doorway as Charlotte flipped on the lights.

Uh-oh, Charlotte thought.

"Um," she said, scrambling, "actually, is it okay if I stay here a bit? My friend is doing conferences right now, and she's my ride home."

She mentally crossed her fingers, hoping the custodian wouldn't suggest she just go to the teacher's lounge.

Thankfully, Gerald said, "Sure. I'll come by later to lock up."

"Thank you," Charlotte called as he let the door close behind him. She pumped her fist close to her chest, then nervously checked to make sure Gerald couldn't see her through the window.

She'd just finished pushing a desk up against a bookcase when she heard a complicated series of short and long knocks on the door.

"We should establish a secret knock," Gabe said after being let in, Charlotte's backpack hanging off his shoulder. "Every friend group should have a secret knock and a code word for emergencies."

"Do we have a code word?" Charlotte returned to the desk and gave it a shake to test its sturdiness.

"Recollect!" Gabe said, appalled. "Our code word has been 'recollect' since high school. Are you serious?"

Charlotte shook her head. "I have no memory of this."

"Ironic, considering." He looked at the desk. "So, what's the plan?"

"Bag, please."

Gabe handed Charlotte her backpack, and she crouched down, unzipping it. After digging around for a moment, she pulled out the old detective's kit Nia had returned to her earlier.

"See the vent up there?" she asked, pulling a screwdriver out of the bag.

Gabe turned his gaze to the wall above them. "Oh my god. You're going full *Ocean's Eleven.*"

"Have you seen *Ocean's Eleven?*"

"No, but I saw *Ocean's Eight.* Obviously. Are you really going in there?"

"I'm gonna try." Charlotte gestured with the screwdriver. "Once I'm in there, I need you to go into Mrs. Hernández's room and . . . mention Lucy . . . somehow."

Gabe narrowed his eyes. "Somehow?"

"Um." Charlotte passed the screwdriver back and forth between her hands. "I thought you might be able to think of something. Oh, and maybe try to find out if she's also trying to get that principal job. And if Jennifer hates her? Any of those things you can manage to work into conversation."

She braced herself for being teased about her bad plans again, but instead, Gabe seemed honored to be included in the plan-making.

"I can come up with something," he said. "Then what?"

"You'll leave, and hopefully Mrs. Hernández will start talking shit. And I'll be in the vent, listening in." Charlotte began digging around in the detective kit. "Where is that . . . dammit, the kids lost the flashlight."

Gabe cleared his throat. "You do know your phone has a flashlight."

Charlotte paused. "Oh. Right." She returned the plastic bag to her backpack, wielding the screwdriver. "Okay. Let's do this."

Gabe helped her climb onto the desk, then step up onto the bookshelf, getting her right under the vent. Charlotte began unscrewing the grate.

"How many times have you done this?" Gabe asked as she reached down and handed him the first screw to hold on to.

"Um . . ." Charlotte twisted the screwdriver, thinking. "Let's say two or three times a month, ten months in a school year . . . oh, there was also that summer program after sixth grade . . . mm . . ."

She handed him the second screw. "Let's just make it an even one hundred."

"You went into the vents *one hundred times?*"

"That's where all the action was!" Charlotte readjusted her grip on the screwdriver. "Once my reputation got around, I couldn't always just *talk* to people. Everyone always assumed I was investigating them for a case. Kids would get defensive if I just asked them what the homework was."

"That sucks," Gabe said. "I'm sorry."

"Eh, it was fine." Charlotte handed him the third screw. "It's not like they disliked me. I mean, some of them disliked me. But for most of them it was just a . . . general caution, I guess. So, when I needed to gather information, I had to get creative."

"Hence the vents?"

"Hence the vents."

Charlotte was quiet as she finished unscrewing the grate. "I feel like I'm giving up by doing this," she said.

"Why?"

Charlotte removed the final screw and pulled the cover off the wall, gently placing it down on the bookshelf next to her. "For a while, I wasn't doing any detective stuff, because I wanted to prove to myself that I was . . . I don't know, that I could be a whole person without it. I thought it was something I had to grow out of." She handed Gabe the fourth screw. "Now that I've gotten back into it, I guess I wanted to prove to myself that I wasn't . . . regressing?"

"You think going into the vents is regressing?" Gabe asked.

"I mean . . ." Charlotte gave him A Look. "It really feels like regressing."

Gabe tucked the screws into his pocket. "I don't know, Charlotte," he said. "I don't think doing something you enjoyed as a kid means you're regressing. If it is, I think every adult could use a little regression." He smirked. "As a treat."

Charlotte didn't know what to think of that. Moreover, she didn't really have the time to think of that. Gerald had said he'd come by "later," which was a very vague and therefore concerning unit of time. She had to get moving.

"I'm going in," she said. "I'll text you when I'm in place."

"Are you sure you're not gonna get stuck?" Gabe asked apprehensively as Charlotte pulled her phone out of her pocket. "I just had a *That's So Raven*-esque vision of firefighters having to cut you out of there."

"It'll be fine," Charlotte said, pumping confidence into her voice as she switched on her phone flashlight and peered into the air duct (she knew it was actually called an air duct despite always calling it "the vents"). "I had plenty of room when I was a kid. It's honestly more spacious than I remember."

"Damn. I got excited about having a bunch of firefighters in here."

Suppressing a snort of laughter, Charlotte rolled her eyes and slid her phone into the duct. She pulled herself in, shimmying forward until completely inside.

No turning back now, she thought. Not because she was fully committed to this plan, but because she really didn't want to have to tell Gabe to pull her out by the ankles.

Taking a deep breath, Charlotte began crawling through the vents.

Chapter 12

Vent Sesh

October 30th, 2009

"This is a bad idea," Lucy said with trepidation as she watched Lottie unscrew the last corner of the grate.

It was the day before Halloween, which fell on a Saturday that year, so everyone had come to school in their costumes. Lucy was dressed as Hannah Montana, wearing a pink sequined dress, white boots, and a blond wig secured to her head by a battalion of bobby pins.

Lottie was wearing Landon's old Spider-Man costume—not necessarily because she was a fan of Spider-Man, but knowing she had some vent-crawling in her near future, she had decided it was the most optimal costume choice for the day's activities.

She gently removed the grate and placed it on the floor. "You say that about all of my ideas."

"Because they're all bad." Lucy peered into the vent, wrinkling her nose. "It's dark in there."

Lottie looked in, too. "Guess they didn't think they needed to put lights in there," she commented. "But that's why I have this!" She brandished the mini flashlight she had retrieved from her detective's kit.

Lucy narrowed her eyes at the flashlight. "Was that from Mrs. B's prize box?" she asked, referring to their fifth grade teacher.

"Yeah. I picked a flashlight every time I got a prize. I have, like, twenty more of them." She handed her screwdriver to Lucy and crouched down.

They were hiding behind some bookshelves at the very back of their middle school's library. If Lottie's geography was correct, this vent would take her right to the teachers' lounge.

"Be careful," Lucy said, clutching the screwdriver as Lottie shimmied into the small space.

The flashlight turned out to be unnecessary—just a few yards ahead she could see light streaming through another grate. After about thirty seconds of crawling, Lottie found herself looking down into the teacher's lounge.

The room was empty as Lottie peeked through the slits in the grate, but having been told that this was Mr. Hoffman's lunch period, she waited.

"What's happening?" Lucy hissed.

"Nothing," Lottie whispered back over her shoulder. "Shh."

As soon as she turned back, she saw Mr. Hoffman's infamous bald spot enter the room below her, the man she'd been waiting for attached to it. He walked over to the fridge that sat in one corner, pulling the door open. A moment later, he extracted a cup of yogurt, read the label, and shut the door.

Lottie's right forearm had started to fall asleep, and she shifted to find a more comfortable position. She froze as the flashlight in her hand hit the side of the vent, causing both the top and bottom to pop off as it spilled its tiny batteries with a loud clatter. One battery rolled up to the grate, and Lottie held her breath as it fell through, landing silently on the couch that sat in the middle of the room.

Mr. Hoffman looked up in the direction of the vent, and Lottie resisted the urge to duck out of the way, knowing that the sudden movement would catch his attention more than staying very still. She lay quiet and waited.

After a tense couple of seconds, the teacher grabbed a plastic spoon from a drawer near the fridge and left the lounge.

Lottie let out her breath, then swiftly gathered the flashlight pieces and remaining loose batteries. "Coming back," she whispered to Lucy.

Crawling backwards proved to be much more difficult than crawling forward, but eventually Lottie managed to squirm her way back out of the vent.

Lucy was nowhere to be seen, but Lottie could hear her talking somewhere else in the library. She peeked around a shelf to see her friend handing a book to the librarian, Ms. Renaldo.

"—and this one might be a little hard for some of the other sixth graders, but I read it over the summer, and I think some of the eighth graders would like it. I really like that it has multiple points of view—"

Lottie saw Lucy was holding the screwdriver behind her, half-hidden by the fake blond hair that spilled down her back. Grabbing the Spider-Man mask from where she had dropped it earlier, Lottie pulled it on and circled the shelves. She crept down the aisle Lucy was standing at the end of, staying out of Ms. Renaldo's line of sight.

"Well, like I said," the librarian was saying, "I don't create the curriculums, but I'll make sure to recommend this book to any eighth graders who come in."

Lottie tugged at the screwdriver. She felt Lucy tense for a moment before releasing the tool.

Scurrying back to the vent, Lottie hastily screwed the grate back into place. Lucy reappeared just as she finished.

"That was too close," Lucy said. "I had to distract Ms. Renaldo to keep her from finding you."

"Thanks," Lottie said, pulling off the mask.

"What happened?" Lucy asked, noticing her handful of broken plastic and batteries.

Lottie dumped the remnants of the flashlight into the Spider-Man mask. "Those flashlights are *not* good for serious detective work." She headed for the front of the library. "C'mon. Let's go tell Mrs. Johnson that Mr. Hoffman's the one who's been stealing her yogurts."

Present Day

Charlotte heard a thump behind her as Gabe climbed up onto the bookshelf.

"How is it?" he whispered, his voice echoing behind her.

Honestly, it was a tighter squeeze than she had hoped just from eyeballing it. But she could move, and that was the most important thing.

"Great," she replied, pulling herself farther in as the beam from her phone's flashlight flickered off the walls of the shaft. "I could do a cartwheel if I wanted. I haven't done my stretches, though."

"Yeah, better not then."

As she continued pulling herself into the vent, she was struck with an almost overwhelming wave of familiarity. It was that specific feeling a person gets when they smell something that reminds them of their grandparents' house, or hear a song that transports them back to their senior prom.

Of course this *is what's making me the most nostalgic*, Charlotte thought, grimacing. *Typical.*

She tried to internalize what Gabe had said. *I'm not regressing. I'm a grown adult crawling through some vents to solve an adult mystery. Just your everyday adult detective stuff. Shit. Adult investigative consultant stuff.*

Squirming her way around a corner, Charlotte heard the muffled sounds of voices ahead. A flower of excitement bloomed in her chest as she spotted light coming through a grate a few feet in front of her.

After about thirty seconds of dragging her body forward,

she made it to the opening. As she gently put her phone down, Charlotte peered through the grating into the classroom.

First thing she saw was an unfamiliar woman sitting in front of Mrs. Hernández's desk. From the angle of the vent, she could only just make out the tops of two heads on the other side of the desk, presumably belonging to Mrs. Hernández and her student teacher.

The unfamiliar woman—there for a conference, Charlotte guessed—stood up. "Thank you so much," she said. "You've definitely put my worries at ease."

"Of course, of course," Mrs. Hernández said. "No need to worry; she's doing great. Just a little more time with the spelling flashcards and her grade will be up in no time."

After exchanging farewells, the woman left the room.

"How many are left?" Charlotte heard the student teacher ask.

"Only two, I think," Mrs. Hernández responded. "Oh, wait, I think someone emailed to say they won't be able to make it. Let me see who that was . . ."

There was a pause, followed by a frustrated scoff. "This new email system keeps logging me out."

Charlotte flinched as Mrs. Hernández loudly opened a drawer in her desk with a *thunk*.

"I can never remember that password," she complained. "It had to have a bunch of numbers and symbols—how am I supposed to remember all of that?"

"You know, you can have the computer remember your password for you," the student teacher suggested.

"How?"

"After you log in, it asks if you want your password saved."

There was another *thunk* as the drawer was closed. "Oh, that. No, I don't trust that. Who knows where all those passwords go?"

"Up to you," the student teacher said.

They fell silent as Mrs. Hernández typed her password in, apparently having found her password written down somewhere in her desk.

"Angela's mother," she said after a moment. "She said she won't be coming."

"I really wish you'd clean your inbox," the student teacher said. "Every time I see it, it's even worse than before. It stresses me out."

"It's all ads and junk," Mrs. Hernández said. "I just ignore it all; it's too much to delete now."

"You can unsubscribe from some of these things, if you want. And filter the emails so they're easier to delete."

"How? Show me."

As the student teacher began walking Mrs. Hernández through cleaning up her inbox, Charlotte remembered Gabe was waiting for her signal to go. In her haste to grab her phone, she accidentally knocked her arm into the side of the vent. The loud metallic *CLANG* made her wince, then freeze.

"What was *that*?" she heard the student teacher ask.

Thirteen years earlier, that question would have instantly been followed by someone yelling, "Lottie Illes, get out of there *right now.*" Lottie would have attempted to make wind noises to convince them that it was just a draft. Then she would've been threatened with an extra detention if she didn't stop making wind noises and evacuate the vents immediately. Then she would've evacuated the vents immediately.

Thirteen years later, however, all Mrs. Hernández said was, "Probably the heating system. This building is old."

Carefully unlocking her phone, Charlotte texted Gabe that he could go. She took a deep breath, her heart still racing from the near-discovery. (Although, she realized, it probably wasn't as near as she had thought. Who was going to assume that twenty-five-year-old Charlotte Illes was crawling around in the vents?)

A moment later, she heard a knock on the classroom door. It swung open, and Gabe stuck his head in.

"Hi," he said, smiling. "Mrs. Hernández?"

"Yes," the teacher replied. "You seem a little young to be my next conference."

Gabe stepped into the room, holding a book in his hand, Charlotte's backpack slung over his shoulder.

"I'm Gabe," he said, pointing at the guest badge that was still on his shirt. "I was guest speaking for Lucy Ortega's class today."

"Oh, right," Mrs. Hernández said. "I heard some of the students talking about that. You were . . . teaching them how to be YouTubers?"

"The talk was mostly about online safety," Gabe said. "Two-factor authentication, not responding to DMs from strangers, not sharing your location online, that kind of thing."

"I think I understood some of that," Mrs. Hernández said, chuckling. "Is that really something students need to be learning in their language arts class?"

"It's pretty important stuff," Gabe said. His expression was still pleasant, but Charlotte could tell by a slight shift in his tone that he was preparing himself to go on the defensive. "And there aren't any other classes that incorporate it into their curriculums. I think it's great that Lucy's taking a day to help keep her students safe online."

"Well, I think the curriculum is there for a reason, but we can agree to disagree," Mrs. Hernández said.

"You could probably use a little lesson on how to use the Internet," her student teacher teased, sounding like she was trying to lighten the tone of the conversation. "The other day I had to stop you from clicking on a link in an email that was flagged as spam."

Mrs. Hernández huffed. "It said it was from Mrs. Parnell!"

As they spoke, Gabe's eyes darted up to the grate. Charlotte knew from experience that he wouldn't be able to see her when she was still. Careful not to bump the side of the vent again, she shifted slightly so that he could see the movement.

Clearly suppressing a grin, Gabe turned his attention back to the two women. "That's a common scam," he said. "You really need to pay attention to the email address. If you want, I can take a look at your school email account and make sure you have all the security measures on. And any other accounts you might have—"

"I only have this one, and it's fine as it is," Mrs. Hernández said dismissively. "I just won't click on any more links. How can I help you?"

Good effort, Charlotte thought, realizing Gabe had probably been trying to snoop around on Mrs. Hernández's computer.

Gabe held up the book in his hand. "Lucy wanted me to ask if you were the person she borrowed this book from," he said.

"I don't lend out my books," Mrs. Hernández said. "So, no, that is not my book."

"Not even to your mentees?" Gabe slipped the book into Charlotte's bag.

Charlotte was suddenly struck with an idea. She picked up her phone and shot off a text to Gabe, hoping he'd check his phone before leaving.

"Lucy speaks so highly of you," he continued. "She respects you a lot. She thinks you could be a principal one day, if you wanted."

Mrs. Hernández let out a *hmph*. "Well, I'll believe that when she actually starts following my guidance."

Charlotte scowled—both because of the way the teacher talked about Lucy, and because she didn't take Gabe's bait. She silently applauded him for trying to see if Mrs. Hernández was going for the principal position Parnell had mentioned.

"Ms. Ortega is a great teacher," the student teacher said, jumping in again to lighten the mood as Gabe's expression hardened slightly. "The students love her."

"It seems like her way of teaching really resonates with them," Gabe agreed. "Kim's, too. They work together a lot. But you really don't like how they teach, do you?"

"Well, Miss Romano has been here for a few years, so I know there's nothing I can really do at this point about her teaching style," Mrs. Hernández replied. "But I'm still hoping I can get through to Miss Ortega."

"So you haven't tried to 'get through' to Ms. Romano?" Gabe pressed.

"She's not my mentee."

Gabe paused for a moment, and Charlotte saw he was thinking carefully through his next words. "You know, maybe instead of trying to work *on* Lucy, you should try working *with* her. Just something to think about."

He turned and walked out of the room.

Charlotte's eyebrows shot up. *Damn*, she thought, impressed. Then she frowned, realizing Gabe hadn't seen her text before leaving.

Right on cue, Gabe reentered the room.

"Sorry, almost forgot," he said, shooting A Look in the direction of the grate. "Do you have any postage stamps?"

There was a brief pause. "May I ask why?"

"You may," Gabe replied calmly.

There was another short silence.

"Why?" the teacher finally asked, somehow managing to extend the word into two syllables.

"Well," Gabe said, clearly having used the short silence to develop his story, "I'm actually an amateur common stamp collector. You've heard of rare stamp collectors, I'm sure, but I like to collect stamps that have very little monetary value. The cheaper the better, in my opinion. It's not about the worth or the historical value. I just like the little pictures."

Could've just said you needed to mail a letter, Charlotte thought, closing her eyes in defeat.

They flew back open at the sound of a desk drawer opening. Gabe walked over and held out a hand as Mrs. Hernández silently ripped a stamp off a roll and handed it to him.

Charlotte mentally apologized to Gabe for doubting his methods.

"Thanks." Gabe stuck the stamp into his jacket pocket. "This'll be a great addition to the collection." He gave an awkward wave before exiting the classroom again.

The two women were silent for a moment as the door to the classroom eased shut.

"Goodness," Mrs. Hernández finally said. "He . . . had a lot to say."

A pause.

"You don't think you're a little hard on Lucy?" the student teacher finally said.

Another pause.

"I know you were upset by that student's Instagram post," the student teacher continued. "Maybe you could talk to her—"

The classroom door opened, and Charlotte instinctively flipped off the poor parent or guardian who walked in, ending the conversation as Mrs. Hernández greeted them. She picked up her phone, reading the new messages from Gabe:

Gabe: MIC DROPPPPPPP
Gabe: check that off the detective bucket list
Gabe: you kind of ruined the moment but it's okay
Charlotte: sorry. thanks for going back
Gabe: at first I wasn't sure if that was you in the vent
Charlotte: what else could it have been???
Gabe: ghost

Charlotte huffed a quiet laugh through her nose as she began inching back away from the grate, deciding she'd gotten enough from this eavesdropping venture (pun very truly not intended). Gabe had ended up doing most of the heavy lifting, anyway. She *was* curious what Instagram post the student teacher was talking about.

A student's Instagram post . . .

She suddenly remembered Lucy telling her about the various student-run Instagram accounts.

"They have one for rating teachers—I don't approve, but I got five fire emojis—"

Interesting.

Charlotte was so lost in her thoughts as she backed up through the vent that she gave a start when her knees hit a grating, sending a loud rattle through the shaft.

"Ah, shit," she muttered, looking down through the grate into the darkened library. She'd always tried to avoid this stretch of the vents when she was a kid. None of the other ceiling grates were as high as this one.

Her stomach swooped at seeing how far from the ground she was, and she immediately closed her eyes. The exit to room 206 was several yards ahead of her, and she realized she must have turned the wrong way at the corner. Sighing, she began crawling forward.

The events that followed occurred too quickly in rapid succession for the human brain to fully process them as they were happening. The most accurate way to describe them is through a series of bullet points:

- Knee
- *CLANG*
- Nothing
- Gravity
- Slide

A scream caught in Charlotte's throat as the grate fell out from under her, the lower half of her body close behind. She thrust out her elbows, bracing her forearms against the walls of the vent to keep her upper half from following suit.

"What was that?" she heard Gabe whisper loudly. "I can't see . . . shit, where are my glasses . . ."

Charlotte didn't reply. The edge of the . . . vent hole? Whatever it was called, the edge of it was digging into her stomach, and she was afraid that speaking would cause her to lose her grip and fall through.

Taking shallow breaths, she tried not to picture her legs dangling through the ceiling of the library—or, more importantly, about the distance between said legs and the thinly carpeted floor of the library.

Muscles trembling with effort, Charlotte pushed down on her forearms, slowly pulling her left leg up in an attempt to get it back to the safety of the vent.

Her elbows slipped a bit, and she lowered her leg again, gathering energy for another try.

"Jusko," she heard Gabe say to himself. "Are you okay? What's happening?"

"All good," Charlotte grunted in reply. "Can't really talk. Trying not to die."

"Shit, shit, shit . . ." Gabe replied.

Ready to try again, Charlotte once again pushed down on her forearms and lifted her leg. With a desperate burst of effort, she managed to get her knee up and over the edge. With the support of her reclaimed knee, she pulled her other leg up and back into the duct.

Charlotte scooched a foot away from the opening before lying down, chest heaving. Worried that Mrs. Hernández or someone else might have been able to hear them speaking, she pulled out her phone (which had miraculously remained in her pocket throughout the entire ordeal) and texted Gabe a quick **I'm okay** before closing her eyes and waiting for her breathing to slow.

She heard a door open. The duct became a little brighter as the library lights flashed on.

"Can you just listen to me for a *minute*?"

Charlotte froze as the raised voice echoed from below. Despite how the pounding in her ears greatly affected her hearing, she was almost positive the voice belonged to Ellie.

Curiosity overtaking her desire to Get the Hell Out of There, Charlotte carefully sat up and looked down into the room. She could just catch a glimpse of Daniel standing near the doors of the library. Ellie was out of her line of sight, and she didn't dare move any closer to the opening to try to get a better view.

"I'm listening," Daniel said, sounding annoyed. "I've been trying to listen."

"No," Ellie replied, "you think you're listening, and then you leave and start making up stories in your head." A pause. "Did they really catch you trying to get rid of the brownies?"

"I . . ." Daniel's shoulders lifted defensively. "You got so mad about her last week, I thought . . ."

"How do you think that makes me seem?" Ellie demanded. "You literally told them that I'm out to get her!"

"I didn't—"

"Oh, so now you're going to backtrack and tell me you didn't say that?"

"I didn't say you're out to get her. I just said that I thought, maybe . . ."

"Maybe I almost *killed* someone?"

Daniel rubbed his face with his hands. "This has gotten out of control. I was just trying to protect you. I never meant for you to find out."

"Just like you didn't mean for me to find out about you looking at Kim's Instagram?"

There was a long silence.

"Are you not going to defend yourself?" Ellie demanded.

"I thought we agreed we'd move on from that."

"Yeah, well, I guess I'm having a hard time moving on from it," Ellie said. "You know, maybe *you* put the nuts in the brownies because you're mad at Kim for dumping you."

"It was a mutual breakup," Daniel muttered.

"That's not the point, Daniel."

"I'm sorry, okay? I'm sorry." Daniel dropped his shoulders. "Are we good?"

There was a long silence.

"I have to go," Ellie finally said, walking past him and into Charlotte's line of sight.

"Wait, hang on," he said, grabbing her arm. "Are we good?"

"Let go."

Charlotte tensed as Daniel appeared to only grip harder. "I just need to know that we're good," he repeated, sounding desperate.

"You're hurting me," Ellie said, her face pinched with worry as she tried to pull away.

"Just answer me!"

Without thinking, Charlotte yelled, "Hey!" She ducked away from the opening, instinctively covering her mouth as if they could hear her breathing.

"The hell—" she heard Daniel say.

Charlotte heard a door open.

"Goddamn it," Daniel muttered.

Waiting a beat, Charlotte risked a peek back down into the library. Ellie was gone, presumably through the library door that was swinging shut. Daniel stood by himself, clearly trying to figure out what had just happened.

She stayed still as the PE teacher continued looking around for a moment. Finally, shoulders slumping, he walked out of the library.

Carefully, Charlotte began crawling forward, back to room 206 and Gabe.

"Holy shit," he said, eyes wide behind his glasses as Charlotte poked her head out of the vent opening. "I was about to go in after you."

"Sorry. Took a wrong turn. Almost fell to my death. You know how it goes."

"Are you okay?"

"I'm fine," Charlotte said breezily, as if near-death occurrences were an everyday thing for her.

Gabe scrunched up his nose. "How're you planning on getting out of there?"

Resting her forearms on the edge of the opening, Charlotte peered down at the bookshelf below. "Um . . . slowly?" She started pushing herself out.

"Okay, ju—hang on." Gabe hopped on the desk and pulled himself up onto the bookshelf. "Take my . . . yeah okay . . ."

"Ow—"

"Careful—"

With much difficulty, Charlotte allowed herself to be hauled out of the vent.

"Remind me again how you managed this as a kid?" Gabe steadied her as she wobbled a bit on the landing.

"I mostly used grates that were closer to the ground. You can let go now, thanks."

Gabe released her and returned to the ground.

"So what did you hear?" he asked, passing the screws and screwdriver up to Charlotte so she could reattach the grate. "Did she say, 'That handsome young man has a point. I'm going to start being nicer to Lucy'?"

"Not exactly," Charlotte said dryly as she crouched in front of the grate. "She said you had a lot to say."

"Valid. You know, I don't think she did it."

Charlotte looked at him curiously. "Why's that?"

"Well"—Gabe climbed back up to sit next to her as she worked—"I know I didn't get anything out of her about the principal job, or Jennifer, but she seems pretty technologically challenged. And Jennifer was getting those texts before the sender switched to letters." He passed Charlotte a screw. "Mrs. Hernández doesn't seem like the kind of person who knows how to send texts from an untraceable number. She seems like her style of blackmail would be through the mail. Or by telegram."

"A reasonable deduction," Charlotte commented. She shifted her grip on the screwdriver. "I'm still stuck on that."

"On what?"

"The switch from texts to letters. I know I originally thought that maybe it was to show Jennifer the sender knows where she lives, but Parnell said Jennifer throws back-to-school functions at her house. So it's not like her address is some big secret. Plus, hand-delivering the letters only increases the person's chances of getting caught."

"Not with you chasing them," Gabe commented.

Charlotte gave him A Look.

"Too soon?"

"And why not mail them, like with Kim's letters?" Charlotte continued, turning back to the vent. "There's something in all that; I just can't figure out what."

"Oh, speaking of mailing letters . . ." Gabe dug into his jacket pocket and pulled out the stamp he had requested. "Not the same style of stamp that was on Kim's letters. Hernández is an American flag kind of gal, apparently." He returned the stamp to his pocket. "That's why you wanted me to ask for it, right?"

"Yeah."

Gabe pumped his fist close to his chest. "I'm killing it. Wow. Okay, so what else did they say when I left?"

"Not much. Someone came in for a conference soon after."

"Oh, sorry. I took too long."

"No, no." Charlotte gestured with the screwdriver as she inserted the third screw. "You ended up getting more from her than I thought you would." She nudged him with her elbow. "Not bad, rookie."

"I can't believe I'm saying this, but stop. My ego can't take much more. I'll become unbearable."

"*Become?*"

Gabe snorted.

"Her student teacher mentioned something about Mrs. Hernández being upset by a student's Instagram post," Charlotte said, starting on the last screw. "They didn't say anything else, but it made me remember this account Lucy told me about where students rate teachers."

"Oh, yeah," Gabe said. "Some kids showed it to me during one of the classes. Lucy got five fire emojis."

"Can you show me?"

"Sure."

Gabe searched for the account as Charlotte finished screwing in the grate. She sat next to him as he pulled it up.

"What're you looking for?" he asked.

"Mrs. Hernández."

He scrolled for a moment, then tapped on one of the photos in the profile's grid. "There she is. Yikes." He pointed his thumb at the description of the photo, which featured a candid of Mrs. Hernández sitting at her desk in front of her computer. "She got two nauseous faces."

"What is this rating system?" Charlotte asked.

"Basically, the kids don't love her," Gabe explained.

"Hm . . ." Charlotte sat back on her hands. "Do you think Mrs. Hernández could be jealous of Lucy? Because the kids like her and her teaching methods?"

Gabe shrugged. "I mean, makes sense. It's like when I did that social media internship in college and my supervisor kept trying to force me to post boring-ass pixelated photos even though the meme carousels I was posting were getting us, like, twenty times more engagement."

"Sure," Charlotte said, barely following. "Just like that."

"That'd mean she's not involved with the case, though. God, none of these suspicious people are actually suspects, are they?"

"Speaking of," Charlotte said, "I also saw Daniel and Ellie while I was in there."

"Daniel and Ellie were in the vents, too?"

Charlotte gave him a flat stare. "What do *you* think?"

"Did one or both of them admit that they're behind the threatening messages?" Gabe asked hopefully.

Charlotte shook her head, telling him about the conversation she'd overheard.

"Damn," Gabe said when she finished. "I mean, I'd be mad, too. Even if he was trying to 'protect her' or whatever."

"Didn't Lucy say that Kim blocked Daniel on social media when they broke up?" Charlotte asked. "But Ellie said he was looking at Kim's Instagram. How does that work?"

"Maybe he made a burner account," Gabe suggested. "There was this guy on Instagram who kept stealing my captions and, like, copying how I posed in photos. And he had *way* more followers than me. But when I called him out on it, he blocked me. So I had to make a burner account to keep an eye on him. Then he blocked *that* account—probably because I kept commenting stuff like 'stop stealing from Gabe' and 'Gabe wore it better'— so I had to make a *second* burner account. Anyway, I have more followers than him now, so, whatever."

He looked at Charlotte. "Did that answer your question?"

"You answered it with 'Maybe he made a burner account,' but I appreciated the example."

"So what does all this mean?" Gabe asked. "They both seem to think the other one could've been behind the brownies. Daniel said Ellie was mad about Kim just last week, and she had access to the brownies. Ellie thinks Daniel isn't over the breakup, and he knows Kim worked at a strip club. Where does that leave the suspect list?"

"I don't know." Charlotte slid off the bookshelf and jumped off the desk. "C'mon. Let's go see if Lucy had her conference with Welles yet."

❦

"I'll be there in a sec," Gabe said, sliding in to sit behind the desk outside of Lucy's classroom. "My boss just emailed, asking how to make a live photo a Boomerang in a story."

Charlotte paused at the door. "Gabe?"

"Yeah?"

"I don't understand your job."

Gabe reached out and put a hand on her arm. "I know," he said gently. "And that's okay."

As Charlotte entered the room, Lucy greeted her with a bright smile that instantly dropped. "Oh. It's just you."

"What a warm welcome," Charlotte deadpanned, crossing the room.

"I thought you were a parent."

"Can't say I've heard that one before. Did Welles come in yet?"

Lucy shook her head. "Should be here any minute. How'd it go?"

Charlotte gave a brief summary of her past forty minutes.

"I can*not* believe you went into the vents," Lucy said, amazed. "Tell me Gabe took photos."

"If he did, I don't want to see them." Charlotte had taken a seat on a little footstool that sat next to Lucy's desk. "What do you think about my Hernández theory?"

"Seems like a stretch," Lucy said, doubtful.

"Oh, come on," Charlotte said. "You're just saying that because you can't believe that anyone would ever feel threatened by you. This is exactly what happened with Sydney Ippolito during cheerleading tryouts."

"She was just hard on me because my back tuck wasn't tight enough," Lucy said.

"Your back tuck was fine. She was *mean* to you because all the other girls liked you more and she knew you'd get captain if you wanted it."

Lucy thought about that for a moment. "Well. That's one theory, I guess."

Charlotte rolled her eyes. While Lucy's modesty could be endearing, it made it almost impossible for her to believe that anyone could be jealous of or threatened by her. Convincing her of such would be as easy as convincing Charlotte to get back into full-time detective work. Not worth the effort.

"Just consider it," Charlotte said. "Once you know her motive, you can work your Lucy magic and get her to like you more."

"What the heck is *Lucy magic?*"

Charlotte gestured vaguely. "You know . . ."

She stopped as the door opened and Gabe poked his head in.

"Welles is coming!" he hissed. "He's down the hall."

"Can I eavesdrop?" Charlotte asked as Gabe retreated back into the hallway.

"No."

"Please?"

"*No.*"

"I'll just sit under your desk and be really quiet." As she spoke, Charlotte pulled out her phone and called Gabe, turning her volume down as she did.

"You can sit in the hall and try to listen through the door," Lucy said, not noticing the phone call being made as she pulled up a window on her computer. "That's my final offer."

"Okay!" Charlotte said, setting her phone face down on the footstool and standing. "Have a good conference!"

"I don't like how exuberantly you agreed to that," Lucy said to Charlotte's back as she headed out of the classroom.

"Solid SAT word!" Charlotte called over her shoulder, opening the door just in time to greet the two people standing on the other side.

Charlotte took a split second to study the man, who she assumed was Welles: mid-forties, white, with brown eyes and dark brown hair that appeared to be thinning. He had a black jacket slung over one sun-tanned arm, and was wearing a dark blue polo shirt with tan khakis.

"Hello," Charlotte said, stepping back and pulling the door open wider to allow the newcomers in. "Welcome . . . to the conference."

"Thank you," said the woman hesitantly as they entered the room.

"Didn't know we started employing doormen," the man said playfully. "I don't remember seeing that in the budget!"

"Mr. Welles, Ms. Donnelly, hi," Lucy said, standing up from her desk. "Thank you for coming. *Bye*, Charlotte."

"I'll leave you to it," Charlotte said, ducking her head as she stepped out into the hallway. As she did so, a flash of blue caught her eye. Craning her neck, she managed to catch a glimpse of Welles's bright blue sneakers before the classroom door swung shut.

Chapter 13

Baby Blue Shoes, Worn

"You know you called me?" Gabe was sitting at the desk out in the hall, and held up his phone as Charlotte's brain started whirring, processing what she had just seen.

"I called . . . ?" Charlotte stared at him blankly, then remembered. "Don't hang up!"

Gabe gave a start at the sudden order. "Okay." He carefully put the phone down on the desk as if the tiniest jostle could hang up the call. "What's happening?"

"A lot. Um . . ." Charlotte covered her eyes as she got her thoughts in order. "I left my phone in there and called you so we can eavesdrop."

"Oh, *nice*," she heard him say.

"And Welles was wearing blue sneakers."

Gabe was quiet for a moment. "Interesting fashion choice. Feel like it could be hit-or-miss. Did you catch the brand?"

Uncovering her eyes, Charlotte raised her eyebrows at him. "Blue. Sneakers."

Gabe stared at her questioningly for a moment. Then, his eyes went wide.

"There it is," Charlotte said, picking up his phone and sitting on the desk.

"He . . ." Gabe pointed at the classroom in shock. His expression dropped as he quickly pressed the mute button on the phone. "Just in case."

His expression returned to shock as he pointed at the classroom again. "He was the person at Jennifer's house!" he whispered.

"Seems like it," Charlotte said.

"I saw that they had blue sneakers!"

"You did."

"Just wanted to make sure we all remembered that I was the one who noticed that."

Charlotte snorted, turning up the volume on the phone. "Let's see what Lucy can get out of him."

Unfortunately, Lucy's first priority was clearly (for some reason) conducting a parent/teacher conference, not an interrogation.

"How long are these things usually?" Charlotte asked. She had returned to sitting on the floor, and was two minutes away from bashing her head through the locker behind her out of boredom.

"None of the earlier ones went this long," Gabe said, spinning his phone on the desk to amuse himself. "It sounds like Welles is very invested in his son achieving *academic excellence.*"

"That tracks, seeing as how he's on the Board of Ed," Charlotte said. "But Neil's like you."

"Weirdly good at mini golf?"

"*Artsy.*"

"Ah. I mean, I can barely draw a stick figure, but I know what you mean." He snorted. "In middle school I told my mom that the theater teacher was the only one who wasn't completely booked for conferences."

"How'd that turn out for you?"

Gabe stopped spinning his phone. "She told me it was a good

thing I was taking the theater class, because my acting needed work." He sighed. "Then she went to conferences and found out I had a C-minus in math."

He suddenly nudged Charlotte with his foot. "Daniel, Daniel," he muttered.

In her peripheral vision, Charlotte saw Daniel walking down the hallway in their direction, shoulder bag swinging from his shoulder. His pace slowed for a moment, presumably when he caught sight of them, then sped up, passing the two without even a sideways glance.

Gabe let out a low whistle as soon as Daniel disappeared around the corner. "He is mad at youuuu."

"What?" Charlotte looked up at him. "Why me?"

"You were the one who told his girlfriend he thought she'd tried to frame someone," Gabe said. "And based on what you heard in the vents, now she might be breaking up with him." He shrugged. "I mean, I'd be mad."

Charlotte crossed her arms defensively. "Whatever." She knew she probably hadn't used the most tactful approach when talking to Ellie, but if someone close to Charlotte thought she'd committed a crime and was trying to cover it up, she'd want to know about it. (Especially if they were right—she'd want to make sure they didn't make things worse with their cover-up job.)

A couple minutes later, Charlotte spotted Kim locking the door to her room a little way down the hall. The teacher noticed them a moment later and walked over. Her face was pinched with anger, and as she spoke, tears welled up in her eyes.

"I just had a conference with a parent," she said quietly, her voice shaking, "who said that every parent on the PTA received an anonymous letter asking what they were going to do about the teacher who used to be an 'exotic dancer.'"

"Oh, shit," Gabe said. "Did they know it was you?"

Something scratched Charlotte's brain, and she narrowed her eyes, following the thought.

Kim shook her head, curls bouncing. "She was just gossiping. She *did* say she didn't think it was an issue, and that other parents agreed, which was nice to hear. But some of them were making a big deal out of it, apparently."

Do it soon, or I'll tell them it's you.

"'Or I'll tell them it's you'!" Charlotte suddenly burst out, sitting up straight and looking at Gabe. "I *told* you that wording was weird."

Turning to Kim, she said, "The letter that was left at Jennifer's last night told you to leave the school and get your aunt to drop out of the election, or they'll 'tell them it's you.' They were talking about the PTA!"

She sat back against the lockers, feeling victorious for finally figuring that out. Her excitement faded, however, as Kim's shoulders slumped.

"I don't get it," she said. "If they want me gone, why don't they just tell people? Do they want to torture me? First the brownies . . ."

". . . and now they're sending blind items to the PTA," Gabe finished drily. "Seems like a pretty roundabout way of trying to get what they want."

"They'd rather you leave than get fired," Charlotte said slowly. "It seems like they're hoping if they put you through enough stress, you'll just quit voluntarily. But I don't know why."

Kim had become aware of the phone sitting on the desk, broadcasting Lucy's conference. Sounding like she wanted a distraction, she asked, "What're you listening to?"

"Lucy's in there with Welles now," Charlotte said. "Did you have a conference with him?"

Kim wiped a stray tear from the corner of her eye, blinking the rest away. "Yeah, a little while ago. Lucy texted me—sorry, I didn't realize she didn't know Neil was his son."

"How was your conference?" Gabe asked. "Did Welles seem weird in any way?"

Kim shook her head. "Not really. We mostly just talked about Neil."

"Is Neil doing okay in your class?" Charlotte asked.

"Pretty well, considering," Kim said. "He struggles a lot more in some of his other classes. His parents seemed happy to talk about his performance in a class he actually somewhat enjoys."

"Hm." Charlotte thought that Welles might have it out for Kim if he thought she wasn't helping his son enough in her class. That didn't seem to be the case.

"Anyway, I'm heading out," Kim said, pulling her jacket on. "Let me know if there are any updates."

"We're gonna figure this out," Charlotte blurted out.

Hello? she thought, appalled. *Where did that come from? Don't tell her that. Tell her you can't promise that.*

"I promise," she said instead.

Kim gave her a half-hearted smile. "Thanks."

Gabe gave Charlotte a strange look as Kim walked away.

"That was weirdly optimistic of you," he said after a moment. "I thought you were more of a 'no promises' kind of gal."

"I was. I mean, I am." Charlotte rubbed her forehead. "She just seemed so sad, and usually Lucy would say something supportive . . ."

She trailed off. The funny thing was, in that moment, she *was* confident that she'd solve the mystery. And she hadn't thought twice about expressing it. That was Lucy behavior. And—if she was being honest—Lottie behavior.

Shaking off her thoughts, she said, "I think Lucy's going to ask him something related to the case."

"How do you know that?" Gabe asked, incredulous. "We weren't even listening."

"She switched to her 'I'm trying to get information out of you but in a casual way' tone of voice," Charlotte explained, climbing to her knees so she could hear better. "Shhh."

They both crouched closer to the phone and listened.

To Lucy's credit, she clearly tried her hardest. She brought up the Board of Education, which led to a conversation about the upcoming election. When asked about the other candidates, Welles echoed what Olivia had found in his email: he was enthusiastically supporting Jennifer's reelection as much as his own.

"You wouldn't want to be board president yourself, some day?" Lucy said in a teasing tone that Charlotte envied. In instances like this, Charlotte's attempts at "teasing" tended to incline more towards "startlingly accusatory."

"Oh, I don't have time for that," Welles responded. "I have more than enough to do without being president. And I've also got two full-time jobs: architect and dad."

"Vincent would be an excellent president, though," his wife said. "I say it all the time. Didn't you tell Jennifer at that party she threw that you would take the job if she wasn't so well suited for it?"

"Oh, that wasn't serious." Welles chuckled. "Jenny knew I was only joking around."

I don't think Jenny did, Charlotte thought. Gabe snorted, clearly having the same thought.

"I think you'd do great," Mrs. Welles repeated. "Seeing as how busy it keeps Jennifer, it might get you out from under my feet whenever you're home! She at least stays at events for longer than a couple hours."

"Well," her husband responded, his chipper tone matching hers, "I'm sure Ms. Ortega would agree that if I wasn't home as often as I am, Neil would be flunking out of school by now!"

"So *she's* saying she wants him home less often," Gabe said in a low voice, "and *he's* saying she's a bad mother." He grimaced. "Are straight people okay?"

Charlotte shrugged as Lucy stammered out a response so neutral it would've made Switzerland blush.

The conference/interrogation wrapped up soon after. Charlotte and Gabe both shifted as the door opened, doing their best attempt at casual conversation as the couple exited the classroom.

"Yeah, that's what she heard, but he denied it," Gabe said to Charlotte, as if they'd been in the middle of a conversation.

"He denied it?"

"Can you believe it?"

"I can't believe it."

"Bye, have a good night," Gabe said to the departing couple. Charlotte followed his lead, waving as Welles and his wife bade them goodnight and walked away.

The lights went out in Lucy's room, and she stepped out into the hall with her bag and jacket as Gabe gave Charlotte a critical look.

"You're a terrible scene partner," he said.

"*Why?*" Charlotte asked, faux-wounded.

"I carried that whole fake conversation on my back. You were giving me *nothing*." Gabe turned to Lucy, who finished locking her classroom door. "How'd it go?"

"Fine." She dropped Charlotte's phone into her lap. "Left this in the room."

Charlotte tried to read her expression. ". . . Thanks," she said.

"I know you left it in there on purpose."

"Damn. The whole time?"

"Yes, because I knew you were up to something. You're not as slick as you think you are."

Charlotte pouted.

"We just saw Kim," Gabe said, filling Lucy in on what Kim had told them.

"Gosh," Lucy said when he finished. "You learned more out here than I did in there. Sounded like everything we already knew: Welles seemingly has nothing against Jennifer."

"We did learn one new thing," Charlotte said. "Did you see his shoes when he left?"

"Blue sneakers," Gabe confirmed. "A lot like the ones I saw on the person at Jennifer's house last night."

Lucy blinked so hard her entire head moved. "*What?*"

"So that about wraps this up, right?" Gabe clapped his hands and rubbed them together. "We'll tell Jennifer and Kim that Welles is the one sending the threats?"

"What I still don't get," Charlotte started, causing Gabe to groan and slump back into his chair, "is why Welles wants Kim to leave." She looked up at Lucy. "I thought maybe he was mad at Kim because Neil isn't doing well in her class, but she told us he's doing okay."

"Yeah," Lucy said. "His grades aren't great across the board, but I think he's doing better in language arts than most of his other classes. Welles seems to care a lot about Neil's performance, but if he was threatening the teachers of every class Neil's struggling in, there'd be a *lot* more threats flying around."

"Hang on, what about my theory?" Gabe demanded. "That Welles went to the strip club where Kim worked, and thinks she might recognize him and tell his wife about it?"

"I mentioned that to Kim earlier today," Lucy said. "She doesn't remember ever seeing him there."

"She could've just forgotten," Gabe pressed. "Doesn't mean he couldn't have recognized her."

"It's possible," Charlotte said. "But this is the man whose wife was almost *begging* him to get out of the house more. Those two pieces don't really fit."

"I *guess.*" Gabe pouted.

"I'm not completely ruling it out," Charlotte assured him. "I mean, it's the best theory we have right now. Either way, we should tell Kim and Jennifer about the sneakers. Kim just left."

"I can call her," Lucy said. "Should I tell her to pass the info on to Jennifer?"

"Y—no." Charlotte climbed to her feet. "I can go tell Jennifer. She works from home, right?"

"Yeah," Lucy said, cocking her head with curiosity. "Why the sudden uncharacteristic desire for a face-to-face interaction?"

Charlotte crossed her arms. "Last time we talked to her, I

let her get under my skin. I want to tell her face-to-face that we were able to make real progress with this mystery, even though she doubted us."

Gabe stood from the desk. "I appreciate you giving us credit for helping, but she was really just doubting *you*."

Charlotte tugged on the padlock of the locker behind her.

"What're you doing?" Gabe asked.

"Trying to open this locker so I can shove you into it."

Gabe laughed.

"I'd come with you to Jennifer's," Lucy said as they walked to the exit, "but I have to get ready for our family dinner before Eva's game tonight."

"Speaking of family dinner," Gabe said to Charlotte. "I know I said I'd come to dinner, but, um, Aaron invited me to come hang out with them and their friends again tonight, and I was thinking . . . I mean, if it's okay—"

"That's great," Charlotte said, pleasantly surprised. "Why the sudden change of heart about meeting the friends?"

Gabe stuffed his hands into his pockets. "I just . . . seeing Luce's students being so . . . *themselves*, it made me realize how much I've been letting past bad experiences with people scare me out of putting myself out there with new people."

He shrugged. "So I decided, you know, fuck it. I'm gonna meet new people, and if the friendship doesn't last, or if they don't like me, that's their loss, because I'm kind of amazing."

"I think you're *very* amazing," Lucy said, stopping Gabe to give him a hug. Charlotte kept walking for a few more paces to avoid being pulled into the embrace.

"Yeah," she said roughly, clearing her throat. "Same."

"Join the hug, Charlotte," Lucy ordered.

"I'm good, thank you." Charlotte continued walking towards the main entrance.

"I just bared my *soul*," Gabe called after her. "I deserve a hug for that!"

"Oh no, you're so far away, I can't hear you!" Charlotte pushed open the door, making her escape. "Bye!"

🔍

> **Gabe: let the record show that Charlotte Yetta Illes owes me one (1) hug**
> **Charlotte: LUCY HUGGED YOU**
> **Charlotte: IS THAT NOT ENOUGH**
> **Gabe: no**
> **Lucy: gavel emoji**
> **Lucy: Oh no I was trying to search for a gavel emoji**
> **Lucy: And then I just said gavel emoji instead**
> **Gabe: there isn't a gavel emoji**
> **Lucy: Darn**

Chuckling, Charlotte tucked her phone into her pocket and climbed out of the car. The sun was dipping low in the sky as she slammed her door shut and crossed the street, climbing the steps to Jennifer's house.

As she stepped forward to knock on the door, she felt something crunch under her shoe. Looking down, she moved her foot to reveal two small pieces of clear plastic with rounded edges, seemingly split in half by being stepped on.

She was brought back to the night before, after she and Gabe had returned from their chase.

Charlotte walked over to the edge of the porch, pausing as her foot hit something small that slid across the floor.

Gabe's head whipped towards the sound. "What was that?"

Charlotte examined the ground around them, but couldn't see anything. "A pebble," she guessed.

She crouched down to pick up the pieces as the door swung open.

"Charlotte Illes," Jennifer said, her tone mildly surprised as Charlotte scrambled to her feet. She pushed the door open. "Come in."

"Thanks." Charlotte stepped inside, shuffling her feet over the welcome mat as she deposited the pieces into her pocket. "I have some updates on the case that I wanted to share with you."

"Really," Jennifer said, leading her into a small home office. She sat at her desk and gestured for Charlotte to take a seat in an armchair that sat on the other side. "I suppose I shouldn't be surprised—your reputation precedes you."

Big tone shift from, "I just want to be sure you know what you're doing," Charlotte thought. She kept her indignant feelings at bay as she sat down.

"So," Jennifer continued, "what have you discovered?"

Charlotte told her about the figure they had seen putting the letters in Jennifer's mailbox, how Gabe noticed the blue sneakers, and seeing Welles wearing those same shoes.

Jennifer was silent as she spoke, resting her elbows on the desk and steepling her hands in front of her mouth. When Charlotte finished, the older woman sighed.

"And this is all you've found out?" she asked.

Charlotte hesitated, trying to read her face. "I mean, there've been other suspects, but none of them seem very likely. And with the shoe thing—"

"Vincent Welles was at the same event I attended last night," Jennifer said, rubbing her temples. "If you saw this person around the time you said, it couldn't have been him. So I'm afraid your 'shoe thing' doesn't hold much water."

Charlotte hesitated, her mind racing. *Welles wasn't the person who dropped off the letters? Shit. Welles wasn't the person who dropped off the letters.*

Trying to save face, she said, "Ah. Well . . . I have some other leads. It didn't make much sense why Welles would want to threaten Kim, anyway."

"To get to me," Jennifer said, as if explaining this again was exhausting her. "Whoever's sending these letters to both of us is clearly just trying to get to me. But if you saw the person last night, it wasn't Welles."

"Okay." Charlotte's mind raced, coming up empty. "Are you sure there isn't anyone else you can think of who might be sending these?"

Realizing she might be coming off as desperate, she added, "Just, y'know, if you remembered something since we last spoke."

With a sharp exhale of breath through her nose, Jennifer flipped over her phone to glance at the screen. Apparently deciding she had enough time to continue indulging Charlotte, she said, "What about Mary Parnell? Have you *investigated* her yet?"

Charlotte didn't love the unnecessary emphasis the woman put on the word "investigated."

"I spoke to her," she said. "Respectfully . . . she didn't seem to care much about you."

Jennifer stared at her for a long moment, possibly trying to determine if Charlotte was actually being respectful.

"Well," she finally said, "she likes to act as if I can't touch her. But I have influence on the board, and she's afraid of it. I know she wants that principal job next year, and if she thinks I could get in the way of that, I believe she would stop at nothing to tear me down."

Charlotte frowned. "If you have all this influence on the board, why *haven't* you gotten rid of Parnell? Seems like you want her gone as much as you think she wants you gone."

Jennifer waved a hand, rolling her eyes. "Politics and rules. Red tape."

"And this is all because she publicly embarrassed you over a fake signed book?" Charlotte pressed. "Don't you think it might be healthier to let that go?"

Jennifer tilted her chin down, her expression hard. "I'll let it go when she stops threatening me and my niece."

"Again, I'm really not sure she—"

CRASH.

Charlotte jolted back at the sudden noise, her movement causing the armchair to tip over and spill her onto the floor.

"WHAT IN THE—" she heard Jennifer yell.

Scrambling to her feet, Charlotte surveyed the room for the source of the crash. Jennifer was standing as well, staring, horrified, at the shattered glass glittering on the floor. There was a large hole in the window on the other side of the room, and it didn't take a former kid detective to deduce that it was caused by the dirt-covered rock sitting amongst the shards.

Jennifer ran to the window as Charlotte bolted out of the room.

"Where are you going?" she heard Jennifer yell after her as she sprinted through the front hall and burst out the door.

Hearing a car engine start, she continued running to her car, getting the door open just as a dark blue car peeled away from the curb a couple houses ahead of her and sped down the street.

Charlotte threw herself into the driver's seat and turned on the car, buckling her seat belt before jetting after the retreating vehicle (which she hoped was being driven by the rock-thrower, and not an innocent neighbor who happened to be running very late for an evening appointment).

She began to regret the decision to pursue this person as they got onto the highway.

You've done it again, Illes, Charlotte thought as she hit the turn signal, trying to keep up with the blue car as it dodged and weaved down the highway. *You know what would've been smart? Getting the license plate. That would've been smart. But noooo, you just had to do a car chase. At least you remembered to buckle your seat belt. Idiot.*

Her phone lit up in the cupholder next to her seat, displaying her brother's contact photo. Glancing over at it, she hesitated as she sped through a yellow light. Then, knowing Landon would probably just call again, she answered and put it on speaker.

"What. I'm busy."

"Are you gonna be home soon? Mom said dinner's almost ready."

"Yeah, I—fucking hell." The blue car careened down an exit ramp, and Charlotte had to utilize a Jersey Slide to keep up. "Yes. I'll be home soon."

"We're supposed to do the candles before sunset."

As if on cue, the interior of the car darkened as Charlotte drove down a heavily wooded street. The blue car had slowed slightly, and she slowed as well.

Do they think they lost me? she thought.

"Lottie?"

"You can light them without me if I'm not home on time," Charlotte said, watching the car continue to slow. "I'll be there soon, I promise."

The blue car pulled over to the side of the road and stopped.

"Where are you?" Landon asked.

Stopping by the curb several yards behind the blue car, Charlotte put her car into park.

"Charloooooootte!" Olivia's voice called through the phone. "Come home, I'm starving!"

"Yup, be there soon," Charlotte repeated, knowing she should probably hang up, but suddenly feeling like she didn't want to be left alone.

There was still no sign of movement from the blue car.

Keeping an eye out the windshield, Charlotte picked up her phone. "Lan? You have my location, right?"

"Yeah. Do you need me to come pick you up?"

"No, that's okay." Charlotte unbuckled her seat belt and opened her car door. She paused, twisting around and searching for anything that could function as a weapon. The back seat was painfully sparse, but she grabbed the combination ice scraper/car brush from the floor and stepped out of the car.

"What's happening right now?" Landon's voice was tinged with worry as Charlotte stuck her phone into her pocket. "Are you okay? Should I get Mom?"

"No! God, don't get Mom. What are you, twelve?" Charlotte pushed the car door shut and began cautiously walking up to the blue car, gripping the foam handle of the ice scraper with both hands.

"Can you tell me what's going on?" Landon asked in a hushed voice.

"What's happening?" Charlotte heard Olivia say.

"I don't know."

"Should I get your mom?"

"No one get Mom!" Charlotte hissed. "I'm about to talk to someone, and I just want to make sure someone knows where I am. It's fine. Now everyone shut up, because I'm about to be there."

"What—"

"Landon? Shut up."

"But—"

"Shut. *Up.*"

Charlotte heard her brother mutter something as she approached the back of the blue car, giving it a wide berth so the driver couldn't fling their door open and grab her. She held the ice scraper up, ready to strike, as she squinted through the driver's window.

"*Daniel?*"

The man was slouched in his seat, staring hard at the steering wheel. Without looking over, he reached out and pressed the button to roll the window down. Nothing happened.

"You need to turn the car back on, probably," Charlotte called through the window, still white-knuckling the ice scraper.

Daniel's chin dropped to his chest for a moment. He turned the car on long enough to roll down the window, then turned it off again.

"What the fuck, man?" Charlotte exclaimed. "Did you just throw a rock through Jennifer Falcone's window?"

Daniel looked up at her, his expression confused. "Through Jennifer . . ." His expression smoothed with realization. "Oh. Shit."

"You thought it was my house," Charlotte said, remembering

what Gabe had said earlier. "You're mad at me for getting you in trouble with your girlfriend." She lowered the ice scraper slightly.

"How did . . . ?" Daniel paused, shaking his head as he gave up on the question. "Whatever. It doesn't matter."

"No, uh-uh." Charlotte pointed at him with the ice scraper. "You can't just throw a rock through a window, lose a car chase, and say, 'It doesn't matter.' You don't get to decide that."

"I don't think you can *lose* a car chase," Landon's voice said from her pocket.

"You definitely can," Olivia's voice replied.

"Don't need the kibitzing, thanks, team," Charlotte said, pulling her phone out of her pocket. "Be home soon, bye."

She hung up the phone and returned it to her pocket, silently berating herself. Although she was pretty confident in her theory, she knew she shouldn't have given Daniel a logical excuse to use. What if he *was* actually going after Jennifer, not her?

You just had *to be a show-off,* she thought, wielding the ice scraper once more. "Talk."

Daniel stared at her, his eyes dull with defeat. "You know that'd be a lot more threatening if you weren't pointing the brush side at me."

Charlotte hesitated, then rotated the stick so the scraper side was pointing at him. "So you just threw the rock to get back at me? You're not involved with any . . . other stuff?"

"You mean the brownies?" he asked, confused.

Charlotte shrugged. She didn't want to tell Daniel his ex was being threatened with blackmail if he wasn't the one doing the blackmailing.

"No, I didn't have anything to do with the brownies." He sighed. "I was just so mad, and I was sitting in my car in the parking lot at school, and I saw you leave, and I didn't know what I was gonna do, but I followed you. I lost you at a light and caught up just in time to see you go into the house, and I saw you through the window, and I picked up a rock—"

"Okay, yeah, got it." Charlotte's mind was racing. On one hand, Gabe had found a brick that was seemingly dropped by the person they'd seen at Jennifer's house. It was suspicious that Daniel did the same thing the culprit appeared to have been planning on doing.

On the other hand, the culprit historically only took action at night, when Jennifer was out of the house. This behavior from Daniel, while similar, was out of character for their letter writer.

On that same hand, Daniel had just grabbed a rock he found in the yard. The figure from the night before had been operating on BYOB (Bring Your Own Brick).

Back to the first hand, maybe Daniel had thought the brick would still be where he dropped it, and used the rock when he couldn't find his original projectile.

Hands full of thoughts, Charlotte lowered the ice scraper. "What about Ellie? Do you still think she's behind the lett—the brownies?"

"No," Daniel said firmly. "I thought she might've done it because she . . ." He scoffed at himself, resting his head on the steering wheel. "She found out that I was using her Instagram account to look at Kim's profile."

"Because Kim blocked you," Charlotte said, remembering. "And you thought that would make Ellie go after Kim?"

"She was *really* angry." He lifted his head. "But now I think all that anger was just at me, not at Kim."

"You *think*?" Charlotte said, incredulous. "You really need to figure your shit out, man."

Daniel rubbed his face. "I know. I'm sorry. I didn't handle the breakup well, and I'm still kind of hung up on Kim, so I just . . . you know how sometimes you make a decision, and then you're like, 'Why the fuck did I do that? What's wrong with me?'"

"No," Charlotte lied.

"Yeah, well. Good for you," Daniel said, his expression sullen. "So what now?"

"An apology would be nice, to start."

He huffed air out of his nose. After a moment, he muttered, "I'm sorry."

"Hmph." Charlotte looked up and down the street. "You're gonna have to tell Jennifer, too."

"Fine," Daniel mumbled.

Charlotte paused. She knew everything about this was suspicious, but she was compelled to believe him. For the time being. Besides, the street was getting darker, and she had a dinner to get to.

"Alright." Charlotte swung the ice scraper up to rest on her shoulder. Feeling like she needed to say something to close out the interaction, she added awkwardly, "Drive . . . safe, or, whatever."

Daniel grunted in reply. With that, Charlotte walked back to her car, returned the ice scraper to the back seat, and drove home.

Chapter 14

A Sports Metaphor Actually Works

"Charlotte already has another case," her mother said, passing a bowl of green beans to Olivia. They were all sitting around the kitchen table, the Shabbat candles bathed in a warm glow from their spot on the counter.

"I heard," Landon said knowingly. "How's that going, Lottie?"

"I just started a new real job, you know," Charlotte said peevishly. "Normal families would talk about that first."

"So, not well, then," Landon replied, spreading butter on a slice of challah bread.

"How's the job going?" Olivia asked, shaking her head at Landon.

"It's okay," Charlotte said, sending a silent "thank you" Olivia's way. "Kind of tiring, but I don't have to deal with half the stuff Lucy does, so . . . it's fine."

"When are we allowed to ask about the case?" Evelyn stage-whispered to her son.

Charlotte gave her A Look. "*Ma*."

"I'm sorry! Do you want to talk more about the job? You can

talk more about the job, go ahead." Her mother picked up her glass and took a long sip to show she was done talking.

Charlotte put down her fork. "I'm stuck," she admitted. "Every suspect just keeps showing up with proof that they're probably not the culprit. I feel like I keep doing the wrong thing. I . . . I don't know."

She rested an elbow on the table, propping up her head with her fist. "I don't really want to think about it right now. Someone else go."

Obliging, Landon began talking about the video game his company had in development, their mother oohing enthusiastically while clearly not understanding most of the terms he was using.

Charlotte half listened while poking at her food, trying to focus on her brother's story instead of spiraling into self-doubt and gloom.

As dinner ended, Evelyn pointed her fork at Landon and said, "Don't leave before going through that box of stuff I left in your room. It's been sitting on the bed for months."

Landon grimaced at the assigned chore. "I'm sure it's all good to just donate."

Their mother crossed her arms, sitting back in her chair. "I just thought you might want to check to see if there's anything you want to keep. Some of it might be sentimental."

"It's just a bunch of kid stuff that's been sitting in the garage for years." Landon began collecting everyone's plates, standing. "I think I can live without it."

"Alright," Evelyn said, putting up her hands in surrender. "Thought you might want to pass those trading cards on to your kids one day, but . . ."

Landon froze midway to the sink. "What trading cards? My Pokémon cards?"

"The ones with the strange little animals."

Landon dumped the plates into the sink and bolted out of the room.

"Finally, my plan to be a gold digger might come to fruition," Olivia joked, pushing her chair back and standing.

"Don't get your hopes up," Charlotte replied. "He basically had me on retainer to find his missing cards, and they were almost always in the wash. I'd be surprised if any of them are in good enough condition to be worth anything."

Olivia made an exaggerated sour face at her. "In that case, I guess I'll go console him."

"So," Evelyn said as Olivia left the kitchen, "are you being pouty just because you're stuck on your case?"

"I'm not being pouty," Charlotte said, pouting. "I'm just thinking."

"About what?"

Charlotte chewed on the inside of her cheek for a moment. "I'm not sure I know how to be a detective anymore," she finally said.

Evelyn tilted her head. "Are you going through that again?"

"No, it's not . . ." Charlotte trailed off, trying to figure out how to verbalize how she'd been feeling. "Like, I know I'm still good. I know I *can* be a detective. But I just don't know how. As an adult, living in this decade, I don't know how to be a detective. Everything I know is from being a kid over ten years ago. Things are different now, I . . . I have a phone that has a flashlight and a camera I'm bad at using, and people are doing stuff on social media that I barely know how to navigate, and everyone treats me like an adult because, y'know, I am an adult, and some of that stuff is good and some of it is bad and sometimes it's both and I just . . ."

Charlotte took a deep breath, partially to calm her rising anxiety, partially because of the run-on sentence that left very little room for breathing.

"I wish I had instructions," she finally said. "For how to do this as an adult. I know I can do it, in theory, but I wish I knew for sure that *how* I'm doing it is . . . right."

Evelyn exhaled heavily. After a moment, she said, "Remember when you played soccer in elementary school?"

"I remember being on a soccer team for four months when I was eight," Charlotte said, "because Argentina had gotten far in the World Cup that year and Lucy was obsessed. But I don't know if 'avoiding the ball as much as possible' counts as 'playing soccer.'"

"Your coach kept telling you to try to score a goal," her mom continued, "and I could see you getting more and more frustrated, because anytime you'd try to kick the ball, another kid would kick it away from you.

"Finally, the ball came to you, and you bent down, picked it up with your hands, ran over to the goal, and threw it over the goalie's head. You turned to your coach"—Evelyn stretched her arms up and out—"threw out your arms, and angrily yelled, 'There! I did it,' and stomped away."

Charlotte snorted.

"After the game I asked why you did that, and you just shrugged and said, 'It worked.'" Her mom sat back in her chair. "Okay, story over. What's the moral?"

"You should've signed me up for softball?" Charlotte guessed.

Evelyn gave her A Look. "Try again."

"I don't know," Charlotte sighed. "When I don't follow the rules, I ruin stuff for people?"

"You *get the job done*," Evelyn said, poking at the table for added emphasis. "There's no *right* way to be a kid-turned-adult detective. But you know you're capable of getting the ball in the goal, and you're going to get it there one way or the other."

"Hm." Charlotte thought about that for a moment. Strangely, she felt a lot better. After the past few days of trying to separate herself from Lottie Illes to prove that she was "better" than she used to be, it actually felt nice to hear her mom connect her to that angry, headstrong little girl.

"Never thought a sports metaphor would work for me," Charlotte said wryly, "but that was pretty good. Thanks."

"It *was* pretty good, huh?" Evelyn pushed back her chair and stood. "Now go make sure Landon's actually sorting through that box and not just researching how much those cards are worth."

Charlotte walked into Landon's room. Her brother was lying on the floor next to a large cardboard box, scrolling on his phone. Olivia was sitting cross-legged on the bed, sifting through a deck of Pokémon cards.

"Nope, Cubone's not worth anything, either," Landon announced from the floor. "Damn."

"But they're so cute!" Olivia held up the card to Charlotte as she entered the room. "Who wouldn't pay a million dollars for that skull-covered face?"

"Mom sent me to make sure you were being productive," Charlotte said, walking in and sitting down next to Olivia.

"He hasn't looked at anything other than the cards," Olivia said, bending over with a grunt to pick up the cardboard box and rest it on her lap. "Let's see if there's anything else in here we can sell on eBay for rent money."

"Love where your head's at," Landon called from the floor. "Lottie, tell Olivia I was popular in high school. She doesn't believe me."

"You want me to lie to your girlfriend?"

"It's not a lie!" Landon protested as Olivia cackled. He sat up, indignant. "I was very well-liked in my circle of friends."

"That's not what 'popular' means," Charlotte said. "Landon was king of the nerds. He wasn't *popular*."

"The king is, like, the most popular person!"

"Historically, that is very false." Olivia sifted through the box on her lap. "Unless you're talking about Elvis, then, sure. In the fifties. Or in Vegas."

"Landon was not Elvis," Charlotte clarified.

"Did he tell you his high school reunion is later this month?" Olivia asked Charlotte. "He RSVP'd, but now he's getting cold feet."

"Makes sense," Charlotte said. "I don't know why anyone would want to subject themself to that."

"My school didn't do one," Olivia said wistfully. "I would've *loved* it."

Charlotte scrunched up her nose. "Do you really miss the people you went to high school with that much?"

"*Hell* no!" Olivia said. "But I know they're all editing the hell out of their photos, and I need to see the truth with my own eyeballs." She leaned forward to pat Landon's head fondly. "Plus, I'd get to show off my handsome boyfriend and make everyone jealous."

Charlotte nudged Landon's shoulder with her foot. "So why the cold feet?"

Landon batted her foot away. "I don't know. I just started thinking that maybe the only people who'd be there would be people who peaked in high school. I don't want to seem like I'm clinging to the past or anything."

"No one would blame you for clinging to the past," Charlotte said drily. "You were so popular."

"I was! I know you're being sarcastic, but I was!"

"Maybe a high school reunion is obsolete in this day and age," Olivia admitted. "But I don't think there's anything wrong with revisiting the past a little. I think everyone can learn something from their past selves."

Her statement was so on the nose for Charlotte's most recent emotional turmoil that her literal nose twitched a little.

"Besides," Olivia continued, "you know what they say about learning from history."

"Yeah . . . I don't think I can be doomed to repeat high school, though," Landon pointed out.

"You *were* almost doomed to repeat history class your junior year," Charlotte reminded him.

"Can we go back to trying to pay our rent with my childhood?" Landon lay back down on the floor, returning to his phone.

Charlotte reached into the box. "I don't know if you're gonna get much for this"—she pulled out a metal trophy with a gear affixed to the top—"honorable mention robotics trophy."

"Oh no, baby," Olivia said with a pitying laugh, taking the trophy from Charlotte and reading the text on the front. "'Honorable mention'?"

"That entire team was carried by me," Landon said. "I did what I could."

Olivia waved the trophy at him. "Do you want to keep this?"

"Um . . ." Landon carefully appraised the trophy. "Yes," he finally said. "Keep. That memory fuels me to do better."

"What about this?" Charlotte pulled out a T-shirt with an anime character on the front. "Does this fuel you?"

Landon stared at the T-shirt for a long moment. "I genuinely don't remember what show that's from."

"Donate," Olivia declared, taking the T-shirt from Charlotte and tossing it onto the bed. She dug into the box. "Okay, more clothes. Sweatpants?"

Charlotte gave a start as Olivia pulled out a pair of green sweatpants with a yellow stripe down the side.

"Oh, those are *old*," Landon said. "Pre-growth spurt. Definitely donate."

"Wait," Charlotte said, taking the sweatpants from Olivia before she could toss them onto the donate pile. "Where . . . what?"

A black sweatshirt with the hood pulled up, and dark sweatpants— green?—with a bright yellow stripe down the side.

"Sweatpants," Landon explained. "They keep your legs warm."

"Fuck off." Charlotte stared at the sweatpants. "I saw the culprit in my case wearing these sweatpants."

Olivia gasped. "*Landon!*"

"It wasn't *me!*" he said defensively, sitting up. "I haven't worn those in years. They're from middle school."

Green and yellow. The Frencham Middle School colors.

"Where did you get these?" Charlotte demanded.

Landon winced as he tried to remember. "God, I don't know. It was school merch; they sold it at events and stuff. Probably got them at a basketball game or something."

"Oh my god," Charlotte said, still clutching the sweatpants. "I think it's a student. The culprit's a student."

"Or an adult who still wears their sweatpants from middle school," Olivia pointed out. "Though, less likely, I guess."

"Didn't you see the person?" Landon asked. "How did you not know it was a kid?"

"It was dark!" Charlotte thought back to the figure she saw at Jennifer's house. "I know they weren't *that* short. If it was a kid, it was a tall kid."

She chewed on the inside of her cheek, shuffling around what she knew about the mystery to see if this conclusion made sense. Lucy and Kim had seemed convinced that none of their students disliked Kim enough to want her gone. And a tween caring about Board of Education politics seemed even less likely.

"Do you want us to give you the room?" Landon asked with exaggerated seriousness, seeing his sister fall deep into thought.

"There's an Instagram account," Charlotte said, suddenly remembering. "Some kids told me about it. The person who runs the account posts photos of students' shoes. The person at Jennifer's house was wearing these sweatpants and blue sneakers. If it's a student, maybe their shoes have been posted on the account."

"A shoe Instagram account," Olivia mused as Charlotte pulled out her phone to call Lucy. "When I was in middle school, all we had was a handwritten list ranking all the girls in our grade by hotness."

"That sucks," Landon said.

"What would you have ranked me?" Olivia asked.

"I wouldn't have ranked anyone; I would never pit women against each other like that."

Olivia stood to deliver him a kiss on the forehead. "That was a test. You passed."

"Lucyyyy," Charlotte groaned as Landon did a tiny fist pump. "She didn't answer. Oh, she called back. Hey, do you—"

"HEY!" Lucy yelled through the phone. Loud brass music played in the background. "I'M AT THE HIGH SCHOOL. WHAT'S UP?"

Charlotte held the phone away from her ear. "What was the name of the account—"

"WHAT?" Lucy yelled. "THE MARCHING BAND IS SO LOUD RIGHT NOW, I CAN'T HEAR YOU."

"Is that Charlotte?" a new voice said in the background.

"Ma—"

"HI, CHARLOTTE!" Lucy's mom called through the phone.

"Hi, Karina," Charlotte replied, bouncing her knee to give her pent-up energy an outlet. "Can I—"

"GIVE ME—" she heard Lucy say.

There was a brief shuffling on the line as Lucy fought for control over her phone.

"CHARLOTTE?" she finally said, the marching band in the background somehow growing louder. "WHAT'S HAPPENING?"

"What was the name—"

"WHAT?"

"WHAT WAS THE NAME OF THE ACCOUNT—" Charlotte stopped, closing her eyes and rubbing her forehead with a fist. "NEVER MIND, I'LL JUST TEXT YOU."

"JUST TEXT ME," Lucy yelled.

"I'M GONNA—oh, for the love of . . ."

Charlotte hung up, texting Lucy as Landon and Olivia resumed going through the cardboard box. Lucy texted her while she was still typing.

> Lucy: Quick, my phone's about to die
> Charlotte: what's the name of that IG account with
> the shoes

"So many rubber bracelets," Olivia said, pulling a handful of them out of the box. "Did you actually wear these?"

"No," "Yes," Landon and Charlotte said in dissonance, respectively.

Lucy: Frencham Middle Shoes
Lucy: Here's the link:

Charlotte clicked on the link as soon as it came through, immediately scrolling through the page, searching for blue sneakers.

"You've got a lot of loose quarters at the bottom," Olivia observed, shaking the box so they could all hear the rattle of coins.

"Oh, yeah," Landon said. "That was my state coin collection. Never got the full fifty. Montana always eluded me."

Olivia started picking out quarters. "Well . . . we've got about twelve bucks for rent here."

"I knew this box was gonna make us rich."

"BLUE SNEAKERS!" Charlotte yelled, holding out her phone to show them. "Blue. Sneakers."

Olivia peered at the screen. "Who do they belong to?"

"Um . . ." Charlotte pulled back the phone, then growled with frustration. "It doesn't *say.*"

"What's the caption?" Landon asked.

Charlotte glared at him. "You think I didn't check the caption?"

"I was just *asking.*"

Letting out an aggravated sigh, Charlotte read, "Blue heart emoji, fire emoji, fire emoji, blue heart emoji."

Landon pondered over that for a moment. "Yeah, that gives you nothing."

"Thanks, I know. I'm calling Gabe." Charlotte pulled up the contact and hit the call button, putting her phone on speaker. "Maybe he can message the account and get them to tell him who submitted the photo. They might know who it is."

After a few rings, Gabe's voice came through the phone. "Hello?"

Charlotte hung up.

"What just happened?" Olivia asked, confused.

Rolling her eyes, Charlotte said, "He's had that voicemail since high school."

She deepened her voice in an impression of Gabe. "'Hello? Hang on, I can't hear you, talk louder. Whoa, why are you yelling? Just kidding, this is a voicemail.' I've learned to recognize it by the first *hello*."

"I used to have a voicemail like that," Olivia said, "except in the middle of it I pretended to get hit by a bus."

She chuckled to herself as the Illes siblings stared at her in horror.

"My mom made me change it," she added, seeing their faces. "Anyway . . . can't you just message the account?"

"I could, but I don't think they'd reply to me," Charlotte said. "I was hoping Gabe could wield his social media influence. He's a lot better at this stuff than I am."

As soon as that sentence left her mouth, a memory popped into her head.

"So much important information about a post can be found in the comments."

Remembering Gabe's lesson from the week before, Charlotte pulled up the blue sneakers post again, this time clicking on the comments.

"What does 'cem' mean?" she asked, reading the first comment.

"Use it in a sentence," Landon said.

Charlotte stared at him. "This comment just says 'cem.'"

"Hm. Okay, sentence didn't help."

"Is it on the blue sneakers post?" Olivia asked.

She looked at the phone as Charlotte held it out to her. "Oh, yeah, okay. 'Cem' is slang, meaning, like, 'this is me' or 'that's so me.' I think it's short for c'est moi, which literally means 'it's me' in French."

"So if this person is saying 'it's me,' on this post . . ." Charlotte tapped on the username, adrenaline shooting through her body from the anticipation.

As the profile slid onto the screen, her eyes jumped to the profile photo. Finding only a picture of an animated character she didn't recognize, she moved on to the bolded name underneath: Neil.

"Ohhh," Charlotte said softly, taking that information in.

Neil Welles? The sweet artist kid? Some of the pieces fit. Maybe he had the same shoes as his dad, or borrowed them sometimes. It would make sense for him to own the green sweatpants with the yellow stripe, since he was a student.

She tried to remember what else she knew about the person she and Gabe had chased the night before: black hoodie, fast runner, had a flashlight. Which didn't make sense, because kids didn't use flashlights anymore.

"My dad took away my phone last week 'cuz I'm failing math."

Neil had his phone taken away. Which is why he would use a flashlight—

Charlotte suddenly remembered the plastic pieces she'd picked up from Jennifer's porch just a couple hours before, her hand darting to her pocket as she pulled them out.

"What's that?" Landon asked.

Olivia shushed him. "She's concentrating!"

Put together, the two pieces formed a perfect circle; a small plastic disc that Charlotte recognized from multiple occasions of mini flashlights falling apart in her hands as their little batteries clattered to the ground.

That shitty flashlight with those shitty little batteries.

She remembered the clattering sound she'd heard as the figure on the porch made their escape. She had assumed they'd just switched off the flashlight. But maybe the flashlight fell apart.

"Do you have the flashlight from the kit?"

"I have my phone flashlight."

Nia hadn't used the flashlight from the detective's kit when she was in the vents the other day. But when Charlotte went through the kit before going into the vents, the flashlight was missing. And Neil had been with Nia that day.

"This cliffhanger is getting physically painful," Landon said. "Who is it?"

"Neil," Charlotte responded, opening her texts with Lucy.

"That was anticlimactic," Landon said to Olivia. "I don't know who that is."

"His dad is Vincent Welles," Charlotte explained.

Olivia jolted with excitement. "So he was trying to get Jennifer to drop out of the race on his dad's behalf?"

"Something like that, I think," Charlotte said, calling Lucy again. She groaned as she was sent straight to voicemail. "Lucy's phone's dead."

"I mean, not much you can do about it now, right?" Landon said.

"I guess," Charlotte admitted. "Yeah, okay. I can wait to tell her."

She locked her phone, absentmindedly holding it to her chest as she stared at the wall.

Out of the corner of her eye, she saw Landon and Olivia exchange A Look.

"Do you want to go tell Lucy?" Landon asked.

Charlotte hopped off the bed. "Yes. Bye."

Chapter 15

Pity Party

Gabe called Charlotte back as she climbed into her car.

"I'm making *friends*," he announced, his words slurring a bit. "They're really chill. And one of them said she's gonna teach me how to play pool in a little bit, which is the hottest thing anyone's said to me this week."

"Wow," Charlotte said, buckling her seat belt. "I knew you could do it."

"And I made *three* videos for my gum sponsorship! All with different people! Everyone hated the gum, but they loved making the videos."

"That's great. I'm really happy for you."

"What's up, why'd you call?"

Charlotte switched her phone to her other hand as she put the key in the ignition. "I needed social media help, but I figured it out myself."

"Look at us! Stepping out of our comfort zones, trying new things . . ."

"Yeah. Also, update, it's Neil. Who's sending the letters."

There was a pause as the news sank in.

"Like, little artist kid Neil?" Gabe asked.

"Yeah."

"YOU SOLVED IT?"

"I think so. Lucy's phone died, but I couldn't wait to tell her, so I'm going over to your place now."

"Oh, sick, okay. I probably won't be home for a while longer."

"I know. You have to learn how to play pool."

"I can leave sooner. If you want."

Charlotte shook her head, even though he couldn't see her. "No, you keep making friends. I'm just gonna fill Lucy in when she gets back. I promise you won't miss anything."

"I already missed you solving the whole case," Gabe grumbled. "But okay. See you later."

They said their goodbyes, and Charlotte hung up and turned the car on. She was still struggling to figure out why Neil would send threats to Kim. *Even if it was just to further intimidate Jennifer,* she thought, *would he do that to a teacher he supposedly liked? Does he have a reason not to like Kim?*

Her questions remained unanswered as she pulled into the parking lot of Gabe and Lucy's apartment building. She let herself into the building with the fob she'd been given ("in case of emergency," was how Lucy put it when giving her the fob and key, knowing full well that Charlotte would take great liberties with the definition of "emergency").

After entering the apartment, Charlotte switched on the lights and plopped down on the couch. As she mulled over the facts of the case that fit perfectly with Neil being a culprit, she felt strangely numb.

Time for a feelings check-in, she thought grudgingly, taking a deep breath through her nose as she lay down on the couch.

Charlotte Illes Feelings Check-In
—Restless
—Bothered
—Unfulfilled

Charlotte scowled. These were not the feelings she was accustomed to having after solving a mystery. Those emotions were usually more of the "excited," "proud," "feeling like she could lift a car over her head" persuasion. Definitely not "unfulfilled."

Maybe that's just how things are now, she thought. *The cases aren't going to be as satisfying as they used to be. It doesn't matter if I do things the "adult way" or the "Lottie Illes way." Maybe this is a sign that I really am outgrowing mystery-solving.*

It was strange, though. Even catching the cheating husband on the wrong bus route had her feeling more accomplished than she was feeling at that moment.

She suddenly became aware of a small dinging sound that was repeatedly coming from the direction of Lucy's room. Getting up from the couch, Charlotte went to investigate.

The sound was coming from Lucy's laptop, which sat cracked open on her desk. Charlotte pushed the laptop open, seeing a new message notification in the top right corner of the lock screen.

Jake

Charlotte rolled her eyes at the sight of Lucy's ex's name. *Why is he still texting her?*

Because Lucy kept replying to him. Because Lucy was Too Nice.

Her fingers hovered over the keyboard. She knew Lucy's password. It would be so easy to—

The laptop unlocked. Charlotte looked down at her hands, not even realizing she had been typing.

Okay, wait, no. This is bad. Lucy wouldn't want you to—

The messages box popped open on the screen.

"Fucking hell," Charlotte said, yanking her rogue hand away from the trackpad. Lucy's conversation with Jake sat open on the screen, and before she could talk herself out of it, she was reading:

5:03pm

Jake: Hey, just wanted to say it was nice talking to you yesterday. I wasn't sure if you'd reply to my texts, so it was a nice surprise. Since that went so well, I was wondering if you'd want to grab drinks sometime.

6:27pm

Lucy: It was nice talking with you, too! I'm glad you've been doing well. I don't think getting drinks is a good idea. I think it's better if we don't spend time together, at least for the near future. Have a good night!

Jake: I'm not trying to get back together. It's just drinks.

Jake: We can even just do coffee sometime.

Jake: Whatever you're most comfortable with, I'm down for that. I was just hoping to talk more in person.

Jake: Alright, I'm gonna stop now. Let me know what works for you.

Jake: Can you just reply to let me know if you're definitely not interested in seeing me in person? I feel like I kind of went out on a limb, and you instantly shut me down without any room for discussion.

Jake: To reiterate, I'm not trying to get back together. I'm actually seeing someone currently, and she's great. Just wanted to catch up, for old time's sake.

Jake: Okay, now I'm starting to get worried. You never take this long to reply. Can you just reply to let me know you're okay?

Jake: I won't text again after this, but let me know when you get home.

Jake: Wish we could just talk about this like adults.

Charlotte shut the laptop as fast as she could without cracking the screen. She didn't trust herself to not reply, "KICK ROCKS, DICKWAD," or something equally as eloquent.

She stiffened as the front door opened.

"Hey," Lucy called from the other room.

"Hi, it's me," Charlotte called back, trying not to sound guilty as she stepped away from the laptop.

"Charlotte?" Lucy appeared in the doorway. "What're you doing here?"

"I have news about the case," Charlotte said, inching farther away from the laptop. "Your phone died, but I wanted to tell you as soon as possible."

"But what are you doing *here*?" Lucy asked. "In my room?"

"I . . . needed a hair tie."

They both looked over at the ceramic seashell dish of hair ties that sat in full display on top of Lucy's dresser.

"Found them," Charlotte said, pointing.

Lucy stared at her.

"So . . . how'd the game go?" Charlotte pressed on weakly, knowing she was in trouble. "Did we win?"

Lucy crossed her arms. "Word of advice," she said, "if you're trying to act natural, don't start talking about sports. What were you doing in here?"

"Okay, your laptop kept dinging," Charlotte said, pointing at the accursed device. "I came in to see what was making the noise, and I saw Jake was texting you, and—"

"You read my texts?" Lucy's face was deadly serious.

Charlotte put up her hands, defensive. "Well, technically, it was only one text from you, and like fifty texts from Jake."

Lucy pointed out the door. "Couch. Now."

Shoulders slumped, Charlotte walked past her and sat on one end of the couch. Lucy sat on the other end, arms folded.

Idiot, idiot, idiot, Charlotte's brain began playing on a loop as she waited for her friend to speak.

But then the "idiot" refrain was underscored by a kinder internal voice. *You were just worried about Lucy and got carried away. You were trying to be a good friend. She'll understand that.*

You were trying to snoop, a crueler voice said. *You just* had *to solve The Mystery of the Dinging. You don't know how to stop. You're out of control.*

"You know why this is not okay, right?" Lucy finally asked, breaking the silence.

"Yes," Charlotte said, abashed.

Lucy sighed. "Stop giving me that sad face; it's making me feel bad for you."

"Don't feel bad for me, I did something wrong. You need to be mad at me. Yell at me."

Lucy slapped the couch, a frustrated scowl crossing her face. "No, okay? No. I'm not gonna yell at you."

"Feels like you're yelling at me," Charlotte said meekly.

"I'm not gonna yell at you," Lucy repeated, her tone calming slightly. "That doesn't mean I'm not mad at you. Just because I'm handling my emotions differently than you think I should be doesn't mean I'm wrong."

Charlotte pressed her lips together as she listened.

"I know you think I shouldn't have replied to Jake," Lucy continued, "and that I'm being a pushover by talking to him even though I don't want to talk to him, but I'm handling it *my* way. And yes, maybe my way involves a little more emotional labor on my part than I should have to do, but that's my choice to make. Okay?"

Charlotte nodded.

"I know that sometimes I need to toughen up," Lucy said, fidgeting with the edge of one of the couch pillows. "Like with Mrs. Hernández. And I don't mind the occasional reminder of that. But I don't need you to fight my battles for me. I know you want to support me, but sometimes the best way you can show support is just by having faith that I can take care of myself. Okay?"

"Okay." Charlotte hesitated, then added, "I know that now probably isn't the best time to remind you that I read your texts, but it seemed like you handled Jake pretty well. Even though now he's bombarding you with messages." She gave Lucy a tight smile. "I think that was pretty tough of you."

Lucy gave her a tight smile back. "Thanks." She groaned. "I don't even want to see what he's saying."

"Um," Charlotte said hesitantly, "I am fully aware that you are capable of handling things yourself. Just want to make that clear. But . . . do you want me to block his number for you, so you don't have to?"

Lucy thought for a moment, then pulled her phone out and passed it to Charlotte. "Thanks."

"Any time." Charlotte held up the phone. "This is dead."

"Oh, right." Lucy stood and walked to her room.

"I'm sorry again for snooping," Charlotte called after her. "I don't want to sound like I'm making excuses, but I've been having a lot of trouble . . . I don't know, drawing the line, lately."

Lucy reentered the living room, phone charger dangling from her hand as she stood next to the couch. "What do you mean?"

"Like . . ." Charlotte sighed. "I was trying really hard to be a detective without being *Lottie Illes* again. Then I started doing some Lottie Illes stuff—like chasing after people and going into the vents and showing off in front of the students—and realized that maybe doing that kind of stuff as an adult isn't too bad. It's been . . . *fun.*"

Shaking her head, she said, "But now I can't resist going into my best friend's laptop even when I *knew* it was wrong, and I blurted out to Kim that I'd solve the mystery for her, and I let the kids go into the vents—"

"You *what?*" Lucy demanded, eyebrows soaring.

Charlotte waved her hands. "Nothing, I know better now, they're fine, I'll talk to them."

Lucy rubbed her face, muttering under her breath.

"I'm worried that I can't be a detective *and* a mature adult at the same time." Charlotte gave Lucy a desperate look. "Like, what if it's just impossible?"

Lucy plugged her phone into the wall, then walked back to the couch. "You want to know what I think?"

"Yes. Please."

"Okay." Lucy sat down, picked up a pillow, and threw it at Charlotte's head.

"Hey!" Charlotte pushed the pillow away.

"Get a grip," Lucy said, grabbing another pillow and lifting it threateningly. "You've been having this pity party for longer than I've been dealing with my breakup, and I think we both need to move on."

"It's not a *pity party*," Charlotte argued, holding up her hands to defend herself against any more pillow attacks. "I just don't want to lose myself in mystery-solving. I think that's a valid concern to have, considering how much of my life it took up when I was a kid!"

"You're nothing like how you were as a kid," Lucy said, rolling her eyes. "If you think you're, like, Animorphs-style turning back into Lottie Illes, I can tell you as a leading expert on Lottie Illes that you are not."

"How?" Charlotte asked. "How do you know?"

Lucy dropped the pillow, exasperated. "I don't know, Charlotte. You're nicer. Not that you were ever *mean*, but, like, Lottie Illes would've never gone along with Gabe's whole 'junior detective' bit."

Charlotte thought about that. "I guess . . ."

"And you're less pretentious," Lucy continued. "Maybe that comes from you being so insecure now, but you don't just state every theory like it's a fact. And I like that. I think it's very mature, and *very* un-Lottielike."

"Hm." Charlotte stared at her hands. "Maybe you're right."

"A third thing!" Lucy exclaimed. "You've gotten a lot better at admitting when I'm right. Could still use some work, but . . ."

Charlotte laughed. "Okay, fine. You're right."

"Just stop comparing yourself to your younger version," Lucy said. "You don't have to be exactly like her or nothing like her. Just do what feels right to you, no matter what 'Lottie' would do."

Charlotte knew she often had trouble internalizing good advice, but she recognized this moment as important, and therefore tried her best to take what Lucy was saying to heart. *Just do what feels right.*

"And don't go through my stuff again," Lucy finished.

"I won't."

Lucy scooched down the couch and wrapped her in a hug.

"I'm sorry," Charlotte said, arms pinned to her sides as she waited out the hug. She rested her head on Lucy's shoulder in reciprocation. "Are you really going to move on from your post-breakup phases?"

Lucy released her. "Yeah, it's time. Although I just found a great cupcake recipe . . ."

She stopped as Charlotte gave her A Look. "You're right. No more baking. I'm done. However"—she stood and headed for the kitchen—"we still have way too many baked goods. Want a brownie?"

"Yes, please," Charlotte called after her. "As long as it doesn't have almonds in it."

Lucy stuck her head back into the living room. "Too soon."

"Sorry." Charlotte chuckled to herself as she sat back on the couch. Neil must've managed to add the almond brownies at some point when Parnell and Ellie weren't paying attention. *Did he bake the brownies? Did he get a parent to bake them? How did he even know Kim was baking brownies for the bake sale? Maybe she mentioned it in class.*

Lucy returned to the couch, holding two small plates with a brownie on each. "So what's the news about the case?" she asked, handing a plate to Charlotte as she sat down.

"It's Neil," Charlotte said. She gave Lucy the rundown of what she had realized earlier—the blue shoes, the green sweatpants with the yellow stripe, the flashlight and its shitty little batteries.

"I can't believe this," Lucy said, her brownie sitting abandoned on the couch next to her as she listened. "*Neil?* Why?"

"I'm thinking maybe he's heard his parents talk about how his dad would be president if Jennifer wasn't on the board," Charlotte said. "Based on what his parents said during your conference with them, it sounds like Welles is super hands-on when it comes to Neil's education, and we know he struggles with school. Maybe Neil knew that if his dad became president, he'd have less time to get on Neil's case about school."

"Hm." Lucy thought about that for a moment. "Neil was pretty upset about his dad taking away his phone because of his math grade."

Charlotte slapped her knee, suddenly realizing something. Before she could vocalize the thought, however, there was a loud rattle at the front door.

They both looked over as the door opened and Gabe, leaning on the doorknob, swung into the room.

"I'm home!" he announced loudly, attempting to close the door with his foot but only managing to kick empty air. He pushed the door shut with both hands before turning back and resting against it. "I'm home," he repeated.

"You said that already," Lucy said. "How drunk are you?"

Gabe held up three fingers.

"You had three drinks?"

Gabe shook his head violently. "On a scale of one to three, I am three drunk." He displayed his three fingers again for emphasis.

"I just talked to you, like, forty minutes ago," Charlotte said, amused. "You didn't sound 'three drunk' then."

Gabe began wrestling off his bomber jacket. "Phone calls make me act sober," he explained, tossing the jacket onto a chair. "I think it's conditioner from when my mom would call me at night in college to make sure I wasn't doing drugs."

"You mean 'conditioning'?" Lucy whisked her plate off the

couch a second before Gabe flopped down, lying diagonally between her and Charlotte.

Gabe lowered his chin to give her a quizzical look. "Wuzz the stuff called that you put in your hair in the shower?"

"Conditioner."

He paused, thinking. "What'd I say?"

"You said 'conditioner,' but you meant 'conditioning.'"

"How d'you know what I meant?" Gabe demanded.

He dropped his head and looked up at Charlotte, his expression becoming nervous. "Can Lucy read minds now?" he asked in a loud whisper.

"Yes," Charlotte replied seriously, picking up her plate. "Brownie?"

Gabe opened his mouth, and Charlotte broke off a piece and dropped it in.

"I'm going to get you some water," Lucy said, standing and heading for the kitchen. "Charlotte was just telling me how she solved the case."

"Ib wus Neil!" Gabe exclaimed through a mouthful of brownie. He swallowed. "'Cuz he wants to be president."

"No," Charlotte said.

"He doesn't want to be president!" Gabe called after Lucy, correcting himself.

Charlotte stuck the rest of the brownie in his mouth.

"I think it's because he wants his dad to be busier," she explained again, "so Welles has less time to do stuff like take his phone away when Neil's not doing well in school. Which also made me realize just now that that's probably why the threats changed from texts to letters."

She dusted brownie crumbs off of her hands onto the plate. "When Neil got his phone taken away, he had to pivot to a different mode of communication. He probably knew when no one would be at Jennifer's house, because Welles goes to the same events Jennifer goes to."

Lucy had returned with a glass of water and was coaxing Gabe to sit up and drink it.

"Thubt meks sunse," Gabe said, his words garbled by the brownie he was still chewing. He accepted the glass of water from Lucy and took a long gulp.

"I think Neil got his phone taken away about a week and a half ago," Lucy said, picking brownie crumbs off of the couch. "When did Jennifer start getting her letters?"

"Around the same time, so that'd line up," Charlotte said. "Kim started getting her letters earlier, though. But Neil wouldn't have her number—he probably got Jennifer's from his dad's phone. So he began sending letters to Kim, and when he got his phone taken away, he started doing letters for Jennifer, too."

"Okay, don't drown yourself," Lucy said to Gabe, who had already downed half the glass.

"Water's good," Gabe argued, said water splashing dangerously close to the top of the glass. "I wasn't following all that, but it sounds good."

"I'm still stuck on a few details, though," Charlotte said, slumping back into the couch. "Like, how did Neil know about Kim working at a strip club?"

"Kids are finding all kinds of shit on the Internet these days," Gabe said, gesturing wildly. Lucy rescued his glass of water before it spilled onto the couch. "They're, like, scary good at doxxing people. That's why I don't post music opinions online."

"Mm." Charlotte chewed on the inside of her cheek. "I guess."

"I should probably call Kim and let her know," Lucy said, getting to her feet as she put Gabe's glass down on a side table. "She can decide how she wants to handle this."

"Is Neil gonna get in trouble?" Gabe asked, lying down in the spot on the couch Lucy had just left. He closed his eyes, folding his hands and resting them on his chest. "I like that little guy. He said he was gonna draw a new profile picture for me."

"I'm sure Kim won't want him to get into too much trouble,"

Lucy said. "Hence why I'm letting her decide how much she tells Jennifer."

"This sucks," Gabe said as Lucy went to call Kim. "I wanted it to be more exciting than this."

"Sometimes it's nice to have a break from exciting," Charlotte said, trying to convince herself of what she was saying.

"Did you ever have mysteries end like this when you were a kid?" Gabe asked, his eyes still closed. "Just kind of . . . eh?"

"Sure, probably," Charlotte said. "You don't really remember the 'eh' ones, though."

She knew, though, that even the 'eh' mysteries hadn't left her feeling like this. Something was still bothering her, and she couldn't figure out what.

Chapter 16

What

June 19th, 2012
Dear Lottie,
I don't even need to be writing this in your yearbook because
we're going to hang out all summer!! This year was bananas.
Thanks for all the times you almost got me in trouble, grrr . . .
I'm just kidding. We've had a lot of fun times, and I can't wait
to have more fun times in HIGH SCHOOL!! I'm honestly kind
of scared, but I know we'll be fine as long as we stick together.
I can hear you gagging while you read this but I don't care
MWAHAHAHA!! But anyway. I love you + I know we will be
friends for years + years + years + years to come. HAGS!!!
Love,
Lucy

Present Day

Despite vowing to avoid the middle school gymnasium at all
costs after the Dodgeball Incident, Charlotte found herself
back there Monday after school. She hadn't subbed that day.

She didn't know if she really *deserved* a day off, but she definitely felt like she needed one.

"Thanks again for coming," Lucy said as they sat down on the bleachers. "Kim usually comes with me to our kids' basketball games, but she had a student stay after school to make up some work."

"I know I give off big 'theater kid who doesn't do sports' energy," Gabe said, resting his forearms on his thighs, "but I actually really like basketball."

Charlotte was staring across the gym, where Daniel stood on the sidelines, talking to a huddle of Frencham basketball players.

"C'mon," she muttered.

"What?" Lucy asked.

"I want Daniel to look over here so I can do the 'I'm watching you' gesture." Charlotte demonstrated, pointing two fingers at her eyes before turning them to point at the PE teacher.

"Kim said he apologized to Jennifer for the window," Lucy said. "He's going to pay to get it fixed."

"He should also pay for the gas I used chasing him down," Charlotte grumbled, giving up on trying to make eye contact as Daniel sent the kids onto the court.

Gabe clapped loudly as the players started doing warm-up drills.

"Let's go, Frencham!" he yelled. "Throw that rock!"

Arjun, who was wearing a jersey that was at least one size too big, jogged over to the bleachers.

"Hi, Ms. Ortega!" he said, waving to Charlotte and Gabe as well. "Thanks for coming."

"Of course!" Lucy said, smiling. "Can't wait to see you play."

Arjun waved to Isabel, Nia, and Kat, who were sitting with a few other kids and cheered in response.

"Arjun!" Daniel called. "Get in there!"

"Gotta go," Arjun said, starting to turn. "Also, Mr. Reyes, no one says 'rock.' It's a ball."

Gabe shot him a thumbs-up. "Good looking out, Arjun."

"Neil's not here," Charlotte observed.

Lucy sighed. "Yeah. Kim wanted to talk to him before getting his parents involved, but she told Jennifer, and Jennifer immediately went to Welles's house and told him."

"So Neil's grounded?"

"Yeah. Kim talked with him today during school. He admitted to sending the letters to Jennifer to try to get his dad the presidency. It was just like you said—he'd overheard Welles saying that being president would take up more of his time, and thought his dad would pay less attention to Neil's performance in school if he got the spot."

She gave Charlotte a sad, sympathetic smile. "I think he was embarrassed about the letters to Kim. She said he couldn't admit to it when she asked him."

"Makes sense," Gabe said, watching the drills.

"Did he tell anyone else he sent the letters to Kim?" Charlotte asked.

Lucy shrugged. "She didn't say. But they got the school counselor involved. Kim's gonna make sure that Neil gets the support he needs, and not just more punishments."

"That's nice," Charlotte murmured, only half listening. She chewed on the inside of her cheek, suddenly feeling on edge.

"And Kim told Parnell about everything," Lucy added, pulling Charlotte's attention back. "Her old job, the brownies, the letters to the PTA, all of it. Parnell was super supportive. She told Kim she didn't have anything to worry about."

"Oh, good," Charlotte said. She had been realizing more and more how skewed her perception of Mrs. Parnell had been. It seemed like the vice principal wasn't too bad, after all.

Gabe clapped again as the players began a layup drill. "Let's see some hustle, kids!"

Two of the players flipped him off as they ran past.

"Real inspiring stuff, Coach," Charlotte said drily.

"I'm pretending I didn't see that," Lucy said, eyes on the ceiling, "because I don't feel like going into Teacher Mode right now. Hey, there's a balloon up there."

They all looked up at the partially deflated balloon that was stuck in the rafters. When they looked back down, Mrs. Hernández was standing on the floor in front of them, talking with someone.

Gabe started humming.

"What's that?" Lucy asked.

He stopped. "I was trying to think of some ominous theme to hum, but I couldn't come up with a specific one fast enough, so I just started humming ominously."

"Should we pretend like we don't see her?" Charlotte angled in towards Lucy. "Pretend I'm talking to you."

"You *are* talking to me."

"But pretend I'm actually saying something important."

"You're asking a lot of my imagination right now."

"Miss Ortega, Miss Illes," Mrs. Hernández called, waving.

Charlotte turned back out as Lucy returned the wave. "Hi, Mrs. Hernández. This is our friend, Gabe."

"We've met," Mrs. Hernández said, giving Gabe a tight smile. He gave a casual salute in response.

"Ah. Right." Lucy gestured at the court. "Excited for the game?"

"Oh, I'm not staying long," Mrs. Hernández said. "I was just stopping by to support the fundraiser."

She gestured to the table set up on the other side of the gym, where Jennifer and a few parent volunteers were selling snacks and Frencham Middle School merchandise for a school fundraiser.

"You have some students on the team, don't you?" Lucy asked.

Mrs. Hernández raised her eyebrows at the players warming up, as if noticing them for the first time. "Oh, yes. There's a few of them. I didn't know Darren played basketball."

"You know," Lucy said, sounding like she was choosing her words very carefully, "I've found that the kids really appreciate it when I make an effort to come to their events. It's just a little way to show them that I care, even when it's not my job to do so."

Mrs. Hernández was still smiling, but her eyes narrowed slightly. "Are you implying that I don't care about my students?"

Charlotte bit her lip to keep herself from jumping in. On Lucy's other side, Gabe was conducting a very thorough investigation of the tops of his shoes.

"No, not at all!" Lucy said, clasping her hands together. "I just think that there are certain ways to build a relationship with your students that ultimately lead to a better learning experience for them. Like not always sticking to the textbook. And going to their basketball games sometimes."

She took a deep breath. "Don't you think that maybe we can both learn from each other?"

Mrs. Hernández stared at Lucy for a moment, then turned to survey the court, where the players were practicing shooting from the three-point line.

"I'm going to visit the fundraiser now," the older teacher finally said, turning back to smile at them. "Enjoy the game."

"Bye," Lucy said weakly, watching her walk away.

"That wasn't too horrible," Gabe commented.

"Aaaand relax," Charlotte said, pointing at Lucy's white knuckles as she squeezed her hands together.

Lucy released her grip, anxiously rubbing her hands on her thighs. "That was so scary," she said. "But I'm glad I said it. Maybe we'll never get along, but I'm not going to let her get to me anymore."

She hesitated, apparently reconsidering that statement. "She might still get to me. I'm not perfect. But I'm going to *try* to not let what she says bother me anymore."

Charlotte extended her hand for a low five. Lucy obliged.

"If she *does* keep giving you issues," Gabe said, "I'm sure we could get Olivia to put a virus in her computer. Honestly, with how bad that woman is with technology, I think we could get her to put a virus in her own computer."

Lucy laughed.

"I saw her computer screen when I was getting a stamp from her," Gabe continued, "and she didn't have any bookmarked websites on her toolbar. Not a single one! Who lives their life without any bookmarks on their toolbar?"

A memory tickled the back of Charlotte's brain.

"A postage stamp," Kat explained to Neil. "You need to put it on your letter before you mail it."

Neil shook his head. "I didn't know that."

"He didn't know about postage stamps," she murmured.

Lucy looked over at her. "What's that?"

"Neil." Charlotte gazed across the court as she recalled the memory. "He didn't know about postage stamps when I asked the kids about them. How did he send those letters to Kim if he didn't know that?"

"He was probably just joking around," Lucy said.

Charlotte frowned, feeling unsettled.

The game started soon after. Lucy kept pointing out when her students had the ball while Gabe echoed directions he heard other spectators calling out to the players.

"Arms up! Arms up!" he yelled.

"We're on offense," Lucy said gently.

"Arms down! Arms down!"

Charlotte nudged Lucy, nodding past her at the other end of the gym. "Mrs. Hernández decided to stay after all."

Lucy's mentor was standing next to the bleachers, like someone who said they weren't interested in watching a movie and then ended up watching the whole thing from the doorway.

Looking pleased, Lucy returned to the game. "Growth," she said simply.

Frencham was down by five points when the whistle blew for halftime.

"This is stressful," Gabe said, stretching out his legs. "Arjun's carrying the team."

Arjun, while not necessarily carrying the team, had scored

four baskets, all of which had the three of them and Lucy's lunchtime crew on their feet, screaming.

"C'mon," Lucy said, standing. "I want to buy a snack to support the fundraiser. And because I'm very hungry."

"What's the money going to?" Charlotte asked as they made their way down the bleachers.

"'The teachers'?" Lucy said questioningly, making air quotes with her fingers. "Not sure, honestly. I don't usually see any changes from the money they get from these fundraisers."

"But that's you," Gabe said, helping Lucy step down from the bleachers onto the court. "You're 'teachers.' The money should literally go to you."

Lucy shrugged. "If I spend too much time considering how underpaid and undersupported I am as an educator, I go into a very deep emotional spiral. I try not to think about it too much. Ooh, they have Oreos!"

Jennifer was handing a patron their change as they walked up to the table.

"Hello, hello," she said cheerfully, waving goodbye to the patron before looking at the three of them. "I'm glad to see you. Charlotte, I wanted to thank you in person for catching Vincent's kid."

"It was a team effort," Charlotte said, feeling uncomfortable. "And it seems like Neil had a lot going on—"

"I agree," Jennifer said. "Vincent denies it, but I wouldn't be surprised if he put the poor boy up to it."

"That's not what I—"

"Anyway, whatever you three want, it's on me." Jennifer gestured at the table, which featured an array of snacks. "It's my way of thanking you for helping Kim and me out."

Charlotte hesitated as her friends thanked Jennifer and began perusing the snacks on the table. "Did Neil tell his parents that he sent the letters to Kim?" she asked the woman.

"Yes," Jennifer said. "He admitted to it as soon as Vincent confronted him about them."

"But specifically *Kim's* letters," Charlotte pressed. "Did he admit to those?"

Jennifer opened her mouth to reply, then closed it, glowering over Charlotte's shoulder.

Charlotte turned to see Mrs. Parnell standing behind them.

"Ms. Illes," Parnell said.

"Hi, Mrs. Parnell." Charlotte stepped out of the way to give the vice principal access to the table. Lucy and Gabe had made their selections, and were standing off to the side, waiting for her to be finished.

"Hello, Jennifer," Parnell said politely. "I'll have a bag of pretzels, thank you."

"Of course," Jennifer replied in an equally polite tone, reaching for a bag of pretzels. "And, just so you know, these are real pretzels, so there's no need to tell the whole gym that they're fake."

Parnell's jaw twitched. "Of course," she said, handing Jennifer some bills before accepting the pretzels. "Thank you very much."

As she moved away from the table, Charlotte turned to speak to Jennifer again, but the woman was already occupied with a new customer at the front of a growing line.

Shoulders slumping, Charlotte left the table, walking over to where Mrs. Parnell was opening her bag of pretzels.

"You two still really don't get along, huh?" Charlotte commented, crossing her arms uncomfortably. She still wasn't sure how to navigate this new relationship with Parnell—were they now at the "casual conversation" level?

Parnell didn't seem to take offense to the casualness of the question.

"I have nothing against Jennifer Falcone," she said, glancing over at the table. "She's just unable to let bygones be bygones." She popped a pretzel into her mouth before holding the bag out to Charlotte.

"Oh, I'm good, thanks." Emboldened by the positive response to her casual conversation, Charlotte said, "I guess you just have to roll with it, right? If you want that principal job next year, you'll probably want to get on her good side. Assuming she's reelected tomorrow."

Parnell gave a half shrug. "It really doesn't matter to me. She doesn't have a say in anything I do."

This confused Charlotte. "If she's on the Board of Education, doesn't she have a say in everyone who's hired for jobs in the district?"

"Usually, yes," Parnell confirmed. "But there's a rule that if someone on the Board of Ed has a family member working in the district, they can't speak on matters regarding that family member or any of their supervisors. Her niece is—oh, you know Kim Romano."

"Yeah, I . . . wait, okay, hang on." Charlotte's mind was racing. "So you're saying that because you're Kim's supervisor, as long as she works at the middle school, Jennifer has no power over you?"

Parnell sniffed. "Bit of a dramatic way of putting it, but yes. At least, she won't be able to have any say in whether or not I'm hired for the principal position next year. So while her pettiness is irritating, it really has no effect on my life."

Charlotte was only partially listening, her heart rate quickening as she went over this new information in her mind.

Who knew about Kim's job at the strip club?

"Obviously, the people I worked with. Close family—"

"Oh my god," Charlotte murmured.

Parnell had wandered away, greeting a parent who stood nearby. As Charlotte emerged from her thoughts, the gymnasium had begun to feel extremely loud.

"Charlotte," Gabe said, pointing at the fundraiser table. "Are you gonna get a snack?"

Feeling like she was moving through water, Charlotte followed his finger to the table, not fully processing what he had said. She watched Jennifer smile at someone as she handed them a bag of chips.

"I . . . yeah," Charlotte said. "I'll meet you guys back at our seats. I don't want to cut the line."

"Alright," Gabe said as he and Lucy began walking away. "If Jennifer offers you more free snacks, I'll take some gummy worms."

"Mhm," Charlotte replied absently. She tapped her foot anxiously, then took a step forward as the line moved up. She didn't really have a plan in mind. She considered trying to talk rationally to the woman, or saying something sneaky to catch her in a lie. Finally, Charlotte decided she'd just see what happened, and trust that she'd be able to handle it.

She hoped she knew how to handle it.

With only one person ahead of her in line, one of the parent volunteers tapped Jennifer on the shoulder, saying something in her ear.

Jennifer ducked under the table as the volunteer took over the customer interaction. When she came back up, she said, "I'll get the second box. Where's the box cutter?"

After finding what she was searching for, she walked away from the table, exiting the gym.

Adrenaline spiking, Charlotte stepped out of line and followed Jennifer out into the hall, not deciding fast enough whether she should be stealthy or not. As she left the gym, Jennifer turned, seeing Charlotte behind her.

"Oh, Charlotte, good," she said, gesturing for her to follow. "Come give me a hand. I need to replenish the snacks for the fundraiser."

"Sure," Charlotte said, trying to keep her tone neutral. She followed the woman a little way down the hall to an empty classroom. Jennifer opened the door, kicking the doorstop to hold it ajar. Inside, a few cardboard boxes sat on the teacher's desk.

Some were already opened, while some were sealed shut with tape.

"I knew we should've gotten more water bottles," Jennifer said, walking over to one of the open boxes. "Eileen said people would just go to the water fountains if they got thirsty, but once again, I've been proven correct."

She put her phone and the box cutter down on the desk as she began pulling out bottles of water.

"Like how Kim's letters were connected to yours," Charlotte said after a moment. Her thoughts were racing at too fast a speed for her to keep track of them all. Taking a leaf out of the tortoise's book, she spoke slowly to try to make it to the finish line.

"We weren't sure why someone would send threats to both of you," she continued. "But when we first spoke last week, you were sure that the person was just threatening Kim to get at you."

"That's right," Jennifer said, finishing up with the water bottles. She grabbed the box cutter and began opening one of the closed boxes. "Welles's kid was clearly trying to scare Kim to scare me. And, honestly, I'm still not convinced that Welles didn't know about it. He offered to pay for my new tires, as if that would fix everything.

"Anyway," she continued, ripping through the last of the tape, "I'm not comfortable with Kim teaching in the same school as that boy. For god's sake, he almost killed someone with that brownie stunt."

"The funny thing is," Charlotte said as Jennifer opened the box, "the idea that Kim was being threatened to get at you was just a theory I had. *I* was the first one to say that. And it wasn't even based on much. None of the threats to you two indicated that they were connected in any way. But then the next letter Kim received was the first one that specifically told her to get you to stop running for the Board of Education."

"Well, now you know that you shouldn't doubt your instincts." Jennifer paused her task to put a hand on her hip. "I think you and I are a lot alike, actually."

Charlotte blinked, her thoughts stalling for a moment. "How's that?"

Jennifer gave her what appeared to be an attempt at a sympathetic smile. "We're both powerful women who people judge by their pasts. Me with my political career, you with your . . . childhood exploits. I've faced a lot of losses in my past, but I don't let them define who I am today. And you shouldn't either."

She continued pulling items out of the box. "I think you let your doubts get in the way of embracing the most powerful version of yourself. You solved the mystery, Charlotte Illes. Don't let the doubts hold you back. Trust your instincts."

"Okay," Charlotte said. "I think you sent those threats to Kim."

Jennifer froze, and for a tenth of a second, Charlotte thought she saw fear cross the woman's face.

Then she laughed, her brows furrowing with confusion. "I don't understand. Welles's son fully admitted to it."

"Not fully," Charlotte corrected, arms stiff at her sides as her thoughts began ramping up again. "He admitted to sending *your* threats. He never admitted to sending Kim's."

"Why does it matter?" Jennifer asked, bemused. "*You* said that the two are connected."

"It was a theory that I disliked as soon as I said it," Charlotte replied. "It didn't make sense. Why wouldn't Kim's letters have mentioned you from the start if it was always about using her to get to you?"

"But they did mention me," Jennifer argued.

"*After* I shared that theory," Charlotte repeated. "It wasn't until *after* I put the idea in your head that you made sure the letters spelled out that Kim should tell you to drop out of the election. Meanwhile, the letters being sent to you never mentioned Kim at all."

"You're not making any sense, Charlotte," Jennifer said, turning back to the box. "Why would I want Kim to try to convince me to drop out of the election?"

"You didn't," Charlotte said. "Originally, you just wanted to scare her into leaving, plain and simple. But then Kim brought me into it, and things got more complicated. You realized you needed a fall guy if I managed to figure out who was sending the texts and letters to you, or else I might've found out about the letters you were sending, too. So you leaned into the theory."

"I didn't *lean into* anything." Jennifer was still going through the box, but wasn't pulling anything out, like she was purposefully avoiding eye contact. "I didn't even want Kim to know I was being threatened. She found out by accident."

"Right, right," Charlotte said. "What was that story, again? Kim saw the threatening texts when you left your phone out?"

"That's right."

Charlotte looked over at the desk, where Jennifer's phone was displaying its cheerful sunflower case. "You know," she said, "every time I've seen you, when you're not holding your phone, you put it face down."

She tapped her own phone in her pocket as Jennifer glanced towards the desk. "I'm the same way. Guess we *are* similar. My theory is, Kim wasn't telling you that she was being threatened, so you had no way to fan the flames of concern and encourage her to leave, 'for her safety.'"

Charlotte dropped her air quotes. "You purposefully left your phone out so that she'd see the texts, realize you were also being threatened, and confide in you."

Jennifer shook her head, muttering, "Ridiculous." She was still staring into the box, not pulling anything out.

"My instincts are also telling me," Charlotte continued, picking up steam, "that Neil didn't deliver two letters to your house that night. He only left one in your mailbox; the one for you. The one for Kim was already there. Unstamped by the post office because *you* put it in your mailbox for the postal worker to take and deliver the next day." Charlotte gave her a reproving look. "Might've been smarter to just take your blackmail to the nearest mailbox. Bit risky. You also sent those letters to the PTA to put more pressure on Kim to leave."

"Are you done?" Jennifer's tone was icy.

"Almost." Charlotte held her palms face up, shaking her head like Jennifer was forgetting something important. "The brownies! You weren't at the middle school during conferences that night. You were at your event."

Jennifer finally made eye contact with her, a teaspoon of relief washing over her face. "You're right. I wasn't. I had nothing to do with Kim's brownies, because *I had no reason to do that to her.*"

"We'll get to the reason." Charlotte waved her hand like she was temporarily pushing that thought to the side. "You weren't at the school that night. But you know where you *were?*"

Jennifer just stared at her.

"In the kitchen," Charlotte said. "When we got to Kim's the day she was making the brownies, you came out of the kitchen. If you knew Kim was baking for the bake sale, which she probably told you before you went over there that day, you could have easily brought a little bag of almonds, removed the tray from the oven, and poked some nuts into the batter while Kim was letting us in."

A chill raced up the back of her neck as a new thought hit her. "*That's* why there were so few almonds. It wasn't because you wanted the nuts to go unnoticed before someone ate a brownie. You didn't want *Kim* to notice them when she was cutting the brownies to be served."

"Why would I do that?" Jennifer pulled herself up to her full height, crossing her arms, her expression growing furious. "You've thrown all these accusations at me, but why? Why would I want to do this to my niece?"

"Because you're petty," Charlotte said, willing herself not to shrink under Jennifer's glare. "You're petty, and insecure, and are holding a four-year grudge against Mary Parnell. Four years ago, Mrs. Parnell embarrassed you at a school fundraiser. You said you threatened to put her on paid leave, but didn't follow through with it because you were up for reelection at the time. But you know what else happened four years ago?"

Jennifer was silent, glaring at her.

"What else happened four years ago, Charlotte?" Charlotte prompted in a small voice, gesturing for Jennifer to participate.

Not taking the cue, the other woman continued her silent glaring.

Charlotte gave up and continued. "Four years ago, Kim started working in the Frencham school district. And I very recently learned about a rule that doesn't allow Board of Education members to be involved in matters regarding supervisors of their direct relatives. With Kim working at the middle school, you have no way of getting at Parnell."

She paused to see if Jennifer would confirm, but the woman's face was still as stone, and just as silent.

"You knew Parnell is the top pick to be the new middle school principal next year," Charlotte said. "Plus, Kim becomes tenured next year. It'd probably be a lot more difficult to get her to leave the school by that point. The clock was ticking, and once you started receiving the threats from Neil, that put the idea into your head. You knew Kim would be scared of getting fired if parents found out she used to work at a strip club—"

Charlotte held up a hand as if to pause herself. "Which, can I just say? Fucked up. You doing that, *and* the fact that it was something she had to be afraid of. Fucked up."

Jennifer turned back to the box with an expression akin to guilt on her face.

"Anyway . . . where was I? Um . . ." Charlotte thought for a moment. "Oh. I think that was it." She let out a breath. "So, that's what my instincts say. What do you think?"

For a long beat, the room was silent. Eyes still on the box, Jennifer said, "I think you should've quit while you were ahead." Charlotte pursed her lips. "Yeah. Yeah, no, I tried that. But Neil being behind all the threats wasn't sitting right with me. This sits right with me. In fact . . ." She held up a finger, straightening her shoulders as she did a quick emotional check-in:

Charlotte Illes Feelings Check-In
—Contented

That was all she had time for before Jennifer spoke again.

"I think we can both agree," she said, not waiting to hear about Charlotte's feelings, "that it would be better for everyone if you kept this . . . *theory* to yourself."

"I *don't* agree," Charlotte said. "I actually very much disagree with that. I think Kim deserves to know, and I think Neil shouldn't be blamed for something he didn't do."

"He threatened *me*," Jennifer said sharply. "He sent me threats and damaged my property; he admitted to it. What does it matter if he takes the blame for this, too? He's a child, he'll be fine. This would ruin my job, my reputation, my family—"

"Very concerning that you made 'family' number three on that list," Charlotte cut in.

Jennifer paused, staring at her. Charlotte resisted the urge to cross her arms, feeling like the woman was gazing into her soul and searching for weaknesses.

"If you tell people about this," Jennifer said in a low voice, "I will make your life very, *very* difficult."

Charlotte grimaced. "Are you sure? Because I know you have this whole 'powerful political figure' vibe, but I honestly don't think there's that much you can do to me. I'm a substitute teacher."

"What about Lucy?" Jennifer raised an eyebrow. "She seems very happy with her job here. I don't think either of us wants that to change."

Charlotte narrowed her eyes. "Yeah, obviously not. But I'm assuming once this gets out, you're not going to be welcomed back onto the Board of Education. So I think her job is safe."

"I could make her job better," Jennifer said, apparently switching tactics. "Pay raise. Ensured tenure. Whatever she wants."

"I mean," Charlotte said slowly, "I don't want to speak for her, but I don't think Lucy would be okay with that if she knew it was in exchange for you getting away with blackmail. Not to mention how you could've killed someone with that brownie stunt."

"No one was supposed to *die*," Jennifer hissed. She hesitated for a moment, but her need to defend herself apparently overwhelmed whatever inner voice was telling her to stop speaking.

"They were *almonds*," she continued. "It's not like I used peanuts. No one was supposed to get sick. I just needed someone to notice and tell Mary Parnell about the nuts. Enough to get Kim into a little trouble and scare her into leaving. That's why I sent those letters to the PTA. I didn't *want* to tell people about her old job. I didn't *want* her to get fired. I just wanted her to leave of her own accord."

"It's not exactly of her own accord if she's being blackmailed," Charlotte pointed out. "She deserves the truth."

Jennifer went very still, her eyes on Charlotte as she clearly raced for some way to get out of the situation she was facing.

Seemingly finding a solution, she reached over to the desk and picked up the box cutter, pushing the blade out with her thumb.

"Oh," Charlotte said weakly, taking a step back. "Opening more boxes? I hope?"

Jennifer stared down at the box cutter, letting out a long breath. "You're leaving me with very few options, Charlotte."

"Sure," Charlotte said cautiously, staring at the blade, "but one of them is the perfectly logical option of telling Kim what you did. The other one is . . . what, stabbing me with a box cutter?"

"I'm not going to stab you with a box cutter," Jennifer said, as if Charlotte was a child who just said something ridiculous.

"Oh. Okay. Good."

"I'm going to stab *myself* with a box cutter," Jennifer continued calmly, "and tell everyone you went crazy and attacked me."

Truly at a loss for words, all Charlotte could do was stand there, dumbstruck.

"And don't try to tell me people wouldn't believe it," Jennifer said. Her expression had grown cold and cruel. "Be realistic. Former child detective, trying to relive her glory days. Substitute teaching at her old school. She solved the mystery, but wasn't satisfied with the result. She wanted something bigger, something more dramatic. Something that would get her on the news, that would make her *famous* again."

Charlotte could feel her face growing warm. "Stop it," she said softly, swallowing hard.

"She started accusing me of all sorts of things I couldn't have possibly done," Jennifer continued, her grip tightening on the box cutter. "When she realized she wasn't going to get me to admit to something I didn't do, she lost it. Said if I wasn't going to give her a good mystery to solve, she'd make one herself. Then she grabbed the blade and stabbed me. I barely got out alive."

Indignation and fury flared up in Charlotte's chest as tears pricked her eyes. She didn't know why Jennifer's words were affecting her this way. Maybe because a part of her believed this could actually happen. That people could be convinced that she would go as far as to kill someone to try to win the world's attention again.

A voice in her head that sounded eerily like Lucy told Charlotte to stop pitying herself. *The people who know you wouldn't believe that*, the voice said. *The people who love you would never believe that.*

Charlotte took a steadying breath. "It's not going to work," she said. "Put the box cutter down. It's over."

She reactively put a hand up as the other woman raised the box cutter.

"I'll say when it's over," Jennifer said, her jaw set as she angled the tip towards her shoulder.

"Stop!" Charlotte yelled, lurching forward. The voice in her head yelled the same thing, which seemed repetitive, until she realized it was actually coming from behind her.

Turning, she saw Lucy, who had yelled the same thing, and Gabe, who was holding up his phone, surge into the room.

"Enough," Lucy said, stopping a few feet behind Charlotte. "She's right. It's over. Gabe's been filming for the past two minutes."

"Still going," Gabe said, staring intently at the screen as if he would lose all the footage if he looked away. "I'm definitely low on storage, though, so if we could wrap this up, that'd be great. I've been recording a lot of gum videos."

For a moment, Jennifer seemed like she still might go through with it. Then her shoulders dropped, and she silently turned and put the box cutter down on the desk. She walked around and slumped into the teacher's chair, covering her face with her hands.

"Are you okay?" Lucy rushed over to Charlotte, Gabe close behind. "Sorry we waited so long. Gabe tried to go in earlier, but I wanted to make sure we had enough evidence."

"Good . . . good . . ." Charlotte said weakly, still staring at Jennifer. She shook her head, willing herself to focus, and moved her gaze to her friends. "Why did you come?"

"Lucy said you had your detective face on when we left you at the fundraiser table," Gabe said, stopping his recording and pocketing the phone. His eyebrows were knit together with worry. "I saw you follow her out of the gym, and we figured something was up. You should've come get us."

"Sorry." Charlotte looked back at Jennifer. "I wasn't sure . . . I didn't know it'd turn into *that*."

"Are you okay?" Lucy repeated, studying her face. "She was saying some not great stuff about you."

"I can edit that out of the video, if you want," Gabe offered, clearly trying to lighten the mood. "Or I can just put music over it and make a Charlotte Illes fancam. Your call."

Charlotte took a deep breath, straightening her shoulders. "I'm okay," she said. "I'm not gonna throw a pity party for myself."

"I think you deserve a tiny pity party after that," Lucy said gently.

"A pity chill hang," Gabe suggested. "With pity chips and salsa."

Charlotte continued staring at Jennifer, who was still sitting slumped in the chair. She suddenly felt a rush of determination to not let the woman's words ruin the satisfaction of solving this mystery. She'd done it. No matter what anyone might think of her, or what she might think of herself, she'd done it. Not the Lottie Illes way. Not in a mature, adult way. She'd done it *her* way.

(Granted, her way almost led to someone stabbing herself, but the key word there was "almost.")

Charlotte shook her head. "I'm good. I'll take a hug, though. No longer than five seconds."

Lucy and Gabe reacted before she could change her mind.

Chapter 17

Playing Bowling

"Hey there," Lucy said sympathetically, sitting down next to Charlotte. "How're you doing?"

Charlotte shot her a sideways look as she tied her shoes. "I'm fine."

"Do you want to talk about it?"

"Talk about what."

A loud cheer erupted a few lanes down from them as a group of teens celebrated one of them getting a strike. It was "party night" at the bowling alley, and the overhead lights were dimmed as colorful spotlights moved across the walls and floors, pop music blasting from the speakers.

They were sitting near Gabe's friends, who were also putting on their bowling shoes and inputting their names into the system. Gabe was having an animated conversation with a couple of people he had just met—though, just by looking at them, one would've never guessed that.

"I just know how much you agonized over inviting Mita," Lucy said sympathetically. "So it'd be understandable if you were—"

"It's fine," Charlotte said, cutting her off as she attacked the laces of her other bowling shoe. "I'd prefer if we just all act normally and have a good time together."

"Okay . . ."

Gabe vaulted over the bench and landed on Charlotte's other side.

"Hey kiddo," he said, patting her thigh. "How're you holding up, champ?"

Charlotte finished tying her shoe, then elbowed him in the ribs.

"OW. I was just *asking.*" Gabe rubbed his side. "I figured it probably didn't feel awesome to ask a girl on a date and have her ask if she can bring her girlfriend."

"Okay, first of all, I didn't *ask her on a date.*" Charlotte gestured with her hands for emphasis. "I told her I was going bowling with some people and invited her to join. And now she's here with her girlfriend, and it's great, because now I know she has a girlfriend, and you guys know how much I love learning new information about people."

Lucy and Gabe both made sympathetic noises.

"STOP. I'm *fine.*" She stood, facing them. "What's important is that we have a good time playing bowling with everyone."

"I don't think you *play* bowling," Gabe commented.

"And also," Charlotte continued, ignoring him, "that we never mention the hypothetical possibility that I was asking Mita on a date when I invited her."

"You got it," Lucy said, her expression serious. "We'll never speak of it again."

Gabe raised a hand. "What if you guys end up getting together one day? Can I tell the story at your wedding?"

Charlotte stood, heading for the rack of bowling balls. "Hilarious that you think I'd let you speak at my wedding."

It was three weeks after the Frencham boys' basketball team won their game, thanks to an exhilarating buzzer shot made by Arjun. Also, it was three weeks after Charlotte discovered that Jennifer had been behind the letters to her niece, and Charlotte had almost gotten herself framed for assault with a box cutter.

In comparison, the past few weeks had been pretty relaxed.

Lucy had sat down with Kim and showed her the video Gabe had taken of Charlotte exposing Jennifer. Kim, naturally, was shocked and horrified. She confronted her aunt, who, after a brief and half-hearted attempt at blaming artificial intelligence for the video, admitted to everything.

Jennifer was encouraged to drop out of the election for "personal reasons." In a move that was far too compassionate in Charlotte's opinion, Kim didn't report her to anyone. However, Lucy said that Kim and her immediate family were going no contact with Jennifer for the foreseeable future.

In the meantime, Vincent Welles was reelected to the Board of Education. While he was offered a nomination for president, he turned it down, citing wanting to spend more time with his son. According to Lucy, Neil wasn't too unhappy with this choice, saying that in addition to helping Neil with his schoolwork, his father was also spending more time engaging with and encouraging his son's interests.

Kim also informed Welles that his son was only half guilty (or half innocent) of the crime he'd been accused of, and apologized to Neil for the false accusation.

Charlotte also apologized, for which she received a half shrug and a, "S'kay." The next day, she was gifted an anime-style drawing of herself crawling through an air duct, which she took to mean she'd been forgiven.

"Charlotte!"

Picking up a dark red six-pound bowling ball, Charlotte saw Mita walking over, bowling shoes dangling from her hands. Close behind her was a woman with curly brown hair pulled into a low ponytail, bowling shoes also in hand.

"Hey," Charlotte said, feeling awkward as Mita gave her a hug. "Thanks for making it. I mean, glad you could make it. Thanks for coming."

"Of course, thanks for inviting us." She gestured to the other woman. "This is my girlfriend, Anna. Anna, this is Charlotte Illes, world-class detective."

"I've heard so much about you," Anna said, smiling as she held out her hand to shake.

"Most of it's probably exaggerated," Charlotte replied, shifting the bowling ball to one arm so she could shake the woman's hand. "I'm just really good at reading bus route maps."

"She saved my ass," Mita said to Anna. "I mean, I had it in the bag, but she saved me a lot of work." She turned back to Charlotte. "Honestly, I owe you one. Do they have drinks here? I'm buying; don't try to argue."

"You're a lawyer and I'm a substitute teacher," Charlotte said. "No arguments from me."

Pointing past the two women, she said, "We're at lanes eight and nine." She put down the six-pound ball. "You'll see Lucy and Gabe. I'm just"—she picked up a purple sixteen-pounder, trying and failing to not let her muscle strain show in her voice—"picking up my bowling ball."

"Great," Mita said. She and Anna both picked up ten-pound balls. "Coming?"

Charlotte jerked her head towards the rack. "I'm just gonna see if they have one in orange. It's my favorite color."

"Cool. See you down there." Giving her girlfriend a smile that said, *Shall we?* Mita led Anna over to the rest of the group.

Charlotte waited three seconds before dumping the heavy bowling ball back onto the rack with a groan. As she stretched out her arms to try to relieve the muscle ache, Lucy walked up.

"How'd it go?" She began looking through the bowling balls.

"I was very chill and mature," Charlotte said. "Except for some reason I acted like I was gonna use a sixteen-pound bowling ball, so now I have to choose between my dignity and my arm muscles."

Lucy pointed at the ball Charlotte had just abandoned. "This one?"

"Yeah. But I told them I wanted an orange one."

Circling the rack for a moment, Lucy pulled out an orange eight-pound ball. "Here. Use this."

"What would I do without you?" Charlotte asked, taking the ball from her.

"Probably a lot more stupid stuff," Lucy replied, choosing a light blue ten-pounder for herself. "But I think you've been doing a very good job keeping the stupidity to a minimum."

"Maybe that's adulthood," Charlotte said as they walked back to their lanes. "Just being a *little* less stupid than you used to be."

Gabe was standing with Mita and Anna as they put their names into the computer to start a game. Catching Charlotte's eye, Gabe pointed at the two women behind their backs and made a comically sympathetic sad face at her.

Charlotte flipped him off.

"Oh, yay!" Lucy said, looking at her phone as she and Charlotte sat down. "Kim might come after all."

"Nice." Charlotte paused, wincing. "You didn't actually invite Ellie, did you?"

Lucy sighed. "I did. She declined."

Charlotte studied her face. "Was it a nice decline, or . . . ?"

"It was . . . a bit cold." Lucy pursed her lips. "She still seems uninterested in being friendly after the whole thing with Daniel, even though they've broken up."

"I'm sorry," Charlotte said. "I should've been more careful with how I was talking to people you work with."

"It's okay," Lucy said, shaking her head. "You know why?"

"Why?"

Lucy tossed her hair and put her shoulders back as if preparing for a performance. "Because I," she declared, "don't need everyone to like me.

"How was that?" she asked Charlotte. "Did that sound good?"

"I think it matters more if you actually believe it," Charlotte said drily. "But, baby steps."

"Are you talking about Mrs. Hernández?" Gabe sat on Lucy's other side.

"No, actually," Lucy said. "She's been surprisingly chill lately. She asks a lot of questions about how I connect with the students. And she actually gives pretty good advice when she's not critiquing everything I do.

"*But*," she added, "it doesn't matter if she likes me or not, because I don't need her to like me. Or anyone to like me, for that matter."

"Okay, don't strain yourself," Charlotte said, smiling.

A new song started playing over the speakers, and Gabe's friends began talking excitedly to one another. Two of them hopped onto a bench and started dancing.

"I like your friends, Gabe," Lucy said. "They're very cool."

"Do you like . . . Zack?" Gabe subtly pointed at one guy who was walking over to the ball rack. "Because I've been told he is also recently single."

Lucy gently shoved him. "I didn't mean like *that*—"

They watched as Zack picked up a ball, his triceps flexing as he did so.

Charlotte let out a low whistle.

"—but you can give him my number," Lucy finished.

Gabe saluted. "I'm on it. Can we take a picture?"

"I'm not touching that gum," Charlotte said, wary.

"No, no," Gabe said, pulling out his phone. "I finished that sponsorship. The person I was in contact with said the brand was really happy with the results."

"That's awesome!" Lucy said.

"And—oh my god, I can't believe I didn't tell you this." Gabe bounced excitedly. "She asked if I'd be interested in going on an influencer trip for another brand her company represents."

He stood up, throwing his arms out. "It's all happening!"

Their extended group cheered in response, despite not knowing the full context of the declaration.

"Charlotte!" Mita called. "You guys ready to start?"

"Be right there," Charlotte called back, standing.

"Wait, quick selfie!" Gabe said, remembering he wanted to take a photo.

He took about a dozen photos of the three of them, his thumb rapidly tapping the screen until he was finally satisfied with Charlotte's expression.

Charlotte peered over his shoulder as he swiped through the photos. Lucy's sweet smile was consistent throughout, until she began laughing towards the end. Gabe had cycled through a variety of expressions while saying things to try to make Charlotte laugh. Charlotte's smile went from "stiff closed mouth" to "laughing so hard she was a blur."

"Absolutely posting this," Gabe said, opening Instagram and tapping on one of the non-blurry Charlotte photos. "Caption: for all your mystery-solving needs."

"You don't have my permission to post that," Charlotte said firmly.

"Also, she's still on her post-case 'hiatus,'" Lucy said, making air quotes with her fingers.

After the events of three weeks prior, Charlotte had given herself what she felt was a well-deserved break from detective work (she'd given up on trying to get "investigative consulting" to catch on). The only way she could keep her friends and family from worrying about her was by assuring them that it was only a short hiatus.

She did, however, quietly believe there was a chance that the break would be permanent. There had to be one day, surely, when she no longer itched to have a mystery to solve. Cracking this case could have been a satisfying conclusion to her short-lived return to being a detective.

Then, the other day, she found herself on the Frencham residents' Facebook page, reading a post about porch pirates and seriously considering a stakeout. That's when she realized that maybe she was ready for her break to end. (Not just because she was eager for a new mystery, but also because she'd been bored enough to check Facebook.)

"Nuh-uh," Gabe said, pointing at Charlotte. "She told me yesterday that she's back."

Lucy looked at Charlotte, grinning. "You're back?"

Charlotte rolled her eyes good-naturedly. "I guess I'm back."

Chapter 18

What??

"Remember when we fought a bear?" Gabe asked as the three of them exited the bowling alley.

"Literally no," Charlotte said. "And it worries me that you think that's what happened."

"I thought you guys scared it away," Lucy said.

"Eh." Charlotte made a face. "We kind of just did the wave until it lost interest and left."

"I heard they caught it and took it to a forest," Lucy said as they approached their cars. "I hope it's happier there."

"I want to be taken to a forest," Charlotte said. "That sounds nice. Peaceful."

Lucy's eyes went wide with excitement. "We should go camping!"

"Mm." Charlotte considered that for a moment. "Actually, maybe I don't want to be taken to a forest."

"You know," Gabe said, unlocking his car, "you're right. We didn't fight a bear. I think maybe I was remembering a different bear encounter."

Charlotte and Lucy both stared at him, bewildered. *"What??"*

Acknowledgments

People say that writing is the loneliest profession, but I feel like there has to be someone working at a fire lookout or a research station in Antarctica who'd beg to differ. Of course, that person could also be a writer, but I'd argue that their loneliness probably stems more from their remote location than from the fact that they can't tell their friend about the plot hole they're trying to fix because it revolves around the culprit and you don't want to spoil the whole book for them before it's ready to be read!

Anyway, while the process of writing can sometimes get lonely by non-Antarctic standards, I'm thankful to have had many people supporting me along the way.

As always, the first thanks must be given to my editor, Shannon Plackis. Almost any book wouldn't exist as it is without its editor, but if you know the story of how *Charlotte Illes Is Not a Detective* came to be, you know that this book very literally would not exist if it wasn't for Shannon. We hadn't gone through the editing process when I wrote the acknowledgments for the last book, so now I can also properly thank her for her incredible insight, great sense of humor, and for asking a very simple question that elevated both books to new heights: "How is Charlotte feeling?"

That wasn't an exact quote, but Shannon, as an editor, I figured you'd understand that the paraphrasing worked better for the flow of the paragraph. My point is, thank you for everything, Shannon—I need an editor, no matter what that Aerie dressing room might say!

Thank you to my agent, Melissa Jeglinski, for being a constant source of support and advice. The terrain has become a little more familiar by this point, but it's still not something I'd ever want to navigate on my own, so I continue to appreciate having you in my corner.

Thanks to my publicist, Larissa Ackerman. Multiple booksellers and librarians have told me about how great Larissa is to work with, which is always fun to hear because I love talking to people with the same opinions as me. Thank you, Larissa, for tirelessly championing *Charlotte Illes*, for your enthusiasm and support, and for coming to find me when I got on the wrong shuttle to ALA Chicago and ended up almost a mile away from where I needed to be.

A big thanks to all the folks at Kensington, including but not limited to: Lynn Cully, Jackie Dinas, Adam Zacharius, Steve Zacharius, Alex Nicolajsen, Lauren Jernigan, Kait Johnson, Vida Engstrand, Kristen Vega, Matt Johnson, Kristine Noble, and Susanna Gruninger. Thanks also to copy editor, Tory Groshong!

Thank you to my incredible sensitivity readers: Nico, Stephanie Cohen-Perez, and Patricia Ruiz. Any mistakes remain mine, but their insight and advice helped me continue to write characters better and more authentically than I ever could have on my own. I'm so grateful for not only the time and care they put into reading this book, but also for their enthusiasm and clear determination to help give these characters the portrayals they deserve.

Fun fact about me: most of my friends are teachers. I never put much thought into making Lucy a teacher, because it just made sense. In my experience, most friends are teachers. Is that not everyone's experience?

I dedicated this book to all teachers, but I need to give special thanks to my good friends Nicole, Jamie, Stanks, and Becca, who are incredible teachers and let me pick their brains about their jobs (during August, when school was definitely the last thing they wanted to be thinking about). Thanks also to Frankie, who got a couple questions thrown his way as well!

I have to also thank Jamie and Nicole for not only answering a lot of my follow-up teacher questions, but for being early readers of this book. Thank you once again for assuring me that it's a real, cohesive story, and not just the result of me having a very vivid fever dream while key slamming in my sleep. (The dent in my laptop has yet to be explained, but that's a mystery for another day.)

Thank you also to my friend Divya for spilling the EMTea and fact-checking my emergency medicine knowledge!

I see a figure in the wings gripping a hook in a very menacing fashion, so I'll start wrapping this up.

Thank you to Mia P. Manansala, Mary Robinette Kowal, and Olivia Blacke for reading *CIINAD* and writing such lovely blurbs for it. Thanks to Ben and Doug for their hard work on the *CIINAD* audiobook, and for their kindness and enthusiasm while we recorded it. Thank you to all the librarians and booksellers who hosted me for *CIINAD* events with excitement and enthusiasm, as well as all the other librarians and booksellers and reviewers who helped share this book with so much love and enthusiasm.

I know I keep using the word "enthusiasm," but I've been so truly blown away by the pure *enthusiasm* people have shown for *Charlotte Illes*. This includes my friends and family, who have never failed to support me but still continue to amaze me as they do so. Thank you to everyone who sent me a photo whenever they saw my book in the wild. Thank you for getting multiple copies to share with your families. Thank you for the long, wonderful messages that I never know how to respond to because I get too overwhelmed with emotion to think straight.

Thank you to my parents. I love you guys. I'm proud to be your kid.

And finally, thank you to the readers, and as always, especially the queer ones. To the queer adults who didn't get to experience being a queer kid in the way they deserved to: have a little regression, as a treat. Love you.